Praise for author
David Wellington
and
CHIMERA

"Sure to score with those who like a little touch of science fiction with their action thrillers."
Kirkus Reviews

"Crisply written and exciting."
Booklist

"The constant action and novel concept will satisfy fans of the genre."
Publishers Weekly

"Highly recommended because of its diverse and credible characters, as well as its confident, skillful structure and prose throughout. All hallmarks of one of the finest authors working in today's horror genre."
Bookgasm

"This is a good and entertaining read, first page to last."
Examiner.com

"A very captivating political thriller . . . definitely a page-turner."
Military Press

By David Wellington

CHIMERA
MINOTAUR
MYRMIDON

MONSTER ISLAND
MONSTER NATION
MONSTER PLANET
13 BULLETS
99 COFFINS
VAMPIRE ZERO
23 HOURS
32 FANGS

DAVID WELLINGTON

CHIMERA

A JIM CHAPEL MISSION

HARPER

An Imprint of HarperCollinsPublishers

This book is a work of fiction. The characters, incidents, and dialogue are drawn from the author's imagination and are not to be construed as real. Any resemblance to actual events or persons, living or dead, is entirely coincidental.

HARPER

An Imprint of HarperCollins*Publishers*
10 East 53rd Street
New York, New York 10022-5299

First Harper premium printing: May 2014
First William Morrow hardcover printing: August 2013

Visit Harper paperbacks on the World Wide Web at
www.harpercollins.com

10 9 8 7 6 5 4 3 2 1

For Dad

ACKNOWLEDGMENTS

I'd like to thank Diana Gill and Will Hinton, as well as everyone at HarperCollins who worked tirelessly getting this book ready for publication.

Russell Galen, my agent, deserves special mention, as this book would not have happened without him. He inspired its immediate creation, and then for years he worked with me, refining and exploring the possibilities of this book, shaping its content, and helping me rein it in when it got out of control. Russ went above and beyond his job description on this one.

Most important, though, I'd like to thank the men and women of the U.S. armed forces. This book was written because as I watched them come home from Afghanistan and Iraq I couldn't stop thinking that these young people had been given a hellish job to do, that they had done it extraordinarily well, and that they never complained. They worked and fought not for glory but for their country, and every single one of them deserves our gratitude.

CHIMERA

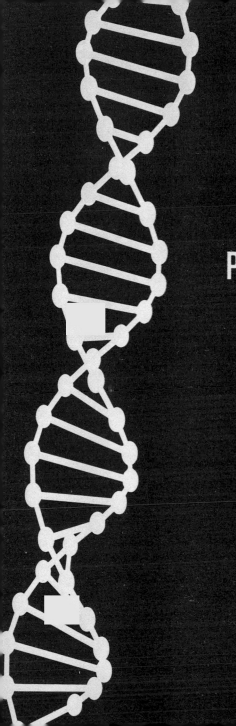

PART ONE

The forest was on fire, and the sky was full of orange smoke. Land mines kept cooking off and exploding in the distance, making Sergeant Lourdes jump every single time—and regret it every single time, since it made the barbed wire imbedded in his leg snag and tear some more.

Sweat poured down his face, chilling instantly in the cool night air. There was blood—blood everywhere—but he couldn't think about that, couldn't think about what had happened to him, about his injuries, about what was going to happen to his family without him. He couldn't think about how he probably wouldn't make it to see morning.

All he could think about was the sentry post, twenty-five yards away. The cramped little box he'd been stationed in for three years now, the box he'd come to loathe, then tolerate, then start to think of as his home away from home. There was a picture of his baby girl taped to one window. There was a flask of coffee in there and right now he was so thirsty, his mouth felt dry as a bone and—

—and he couldn't think about that. Because his uniform jacket was in there, too, hanging on the back of his wooden chair. And in the pocket of that jacket was his cell phone, his direct link to his superiors. To the people who had to know what had happened. To the people who could fix this, who could make everything okay, if he could just tell them.

Just tell them the fence was down, the perimeter defenses compromised, and the detainees were *free*.

Sergeant Brian Lourdes had a pretty good security clearance. Not enough to know why those seven men had been locked away so tight. Not enough to know why they were so dangerous they could never be set free. But enough to know what would happen if they ever did get out. Enough to know it could mean the end of America.

Of course that was never supposed to happen. When Lourdes first came to the facility in upstate New York, he'd been amazed at the level of security on Camp Putnam. The razor-wire fences stood twenty feet high, two layers with a fifty-yard stretch of minefield in between. Twenty men monitored that fence rain or shine, every day of the year. There were more than seven hundred cameras mounted on the fence posts, trained in every direction, watching every corner of that fence that surrounded over a hundred acres of forests and fields.

There was no gate in that fence, no way in or out at all. The detainees never left, and nobody ever went in to check up on them. That was how it stood when Sergeant Lourdes was assigned to this job. That was how it was supposed to be forever.

As of tonight all bets were off.

Lourdes grabbed at a tree root and hauled himself across the rocky ground. The wire in his leg felt like it was on fire, but he gritted his teeth and ignored it. He was trained for this. Trained to keep going, no matter what. Trained to know his duty. He dug his fingers down into the dirt and pulled himself another yard. The sentry box—and his phone—was getting closer.

Three years in that stupid box. Three years working the easiest and most boring job Lourdes had ever had. Every morning he had shown up at oh six hundred and logged himself in, then logged himself back out at eighteen hundred sharp. Twice a day he walked his mile-long section of the fence, checking the chain link, making sure animals hadn't burrowed underneath it, looking for signs of rust or damage. The rest of the time he just sat watching the trees beyond the inner fence, looking for any sign of movement. If he saw a bird in there, or a fox hunting for eggs, he checked a little box on a form on his computer screen and clicked the trackpad to file it. And that was it. There had never been any sign of the detainees. Wherever they were in there they kept to themselves. He'd never gotten so much as a glimpse of any of them.

Three years when nothing—*nothing* happened.

And then tonight, not an hour after his day started, before the sun even came up, everything changed. A Predator drone had come in just over the tree line, a sleek little machine that flew so low he didn't even hear its engine until it was almost on top of him. The laptop computer in the sentry box had lit up with warnings and alarms, but by then Lourdes was already jumping out of his box, running to see what was going on.

The drone was only overhead for a second. He just had time to identify it as an unmanned aircraft. *But it's one of ours*, he'd thought. *It's the good guys, just checking up on the camp.* He lifted one hand to wave at it, thinking that he would get a call on his radio at any second explaining what the drone was doing there. Instead, the Predator had attacked without warning. Rockets had streaked from pods slung under its fuselage—Hellfire missiles that slammed into the ground like giant hammers beating on the earth.

After that things got very loud and very painful. The fence exploded outward, barbed-wire shrapnel scything through the air, tearing branches off trees, making the dirt boil and jump. The drone was gone before Sergeant Lourdes even knew he'd been hit. Just before the pain started, just before he collapsed to the ground in a blubbering heap, he saw what the chopper had wrought.

A section of both fences maybe a hundred yards wide was just . . . gone. The minefield was a series of craters, entirely neutralized. On the far side of the fence a stand of trees had been knocked down, and Lourdes could see all the way in to a clearing lit only by starlight.

Lourdes had been told what to do if something like this happened, given instructions by the same LT who had promised him it never *could* happen. The satellites watching Camp Putnam, the cameras on the fence, would take care of almost everything. Automatic alarms would switch on and soldiers would be summoned; backup defenses would activate without anyone needing to push a button. But there was one thing he had to do. He had to pick up the phone and call a man in Virginia, a man who would need to know the fence was down. A man who could make everything okay, fix everything, but who needed to hear from an actual human being, needed an eyewitness account of what had happened, before he could get to work. Sergeant Lourdes just had to make that call—he just had to pick up the phone.

The phone—the satellite cell phone he was supposed to keep on him at all times—was back in the sentry box, only a few dozen yards away. Lourdes pulled himself another couple of feet. The pain didn't matter. The blood he'd lost didn't matter.

He was so close now. He felt like he could almost reach out and touch the wall of the box. Just a few more yards and—

"There," someone said, from behind him. "Another one."

"This one's mine," a second voice said.

Sergeant Lourdes closed his eyes and said a quick prayer. Then he rolled over on his back and pushed himself up on his elbows. He had to see. Three years of his life making sure these bastards didn't get out. Three years making sure they didn't end the world. He had to know what they looked like.

There were six of them, standing in a rough line near where the fence had been just a few minutes before. Big guys, young looking. Muscular, but not exactly Schwarzenegger types. Their hair was long and unkempt, and they had scraggly beards and their eyes—

Something was wrong with their eyes.

Lourdes couldn't quite make out their faces. They were silhouetted against the burning trees and the orange smoke that masked the stars. But their eyes should be glittering, reflecting some of that light. Shouldn't they?

"Freeze right where you are!" Lourdes shouted, and he grabbed for his sidearm. He lifted the heavy pistol and pointed at the closest one, the one who was already jogging toward him. He fired three times, forcing himself to aim with each shot.

The detainee ducked sideways each time, as if he were just stepping out of the way of the bullets. That was when Lourdes realized just how fast the asshole was moving. Time had slowed down, and even his racing heartbeat sounded like a dull, thudding bass line.

The detainee was on top of him so suddenly he didn't have a chance to breathe. The guy stank, but Lourdes didn't care about that so much after the detainee's thumbs sank into his windpipe and pressed down, *hard.*

Lourdes tried to raise the handgun again, but he couldn't feel his arm. Couldn't feel much of anything anymore. His vision was going black.

The last thing he saw was the detainee's eyes, staring down into his. Eyes that weren't human. They were black, solid black, like an animal's eyes.

The detainee leaned in harder with his thumbs, but it didn't matter to Lourdes. Sergeant Brian Lourdes, U.S. Army, was already dead. So he didn't see what happened next. He didn't see his killer's face split down the middle with a cruel smile.

FORT BELVOIR, VIRGINIA: APRIL 12, T+3:17

Three hundred miles away in an office cubicle, Captain Jim Chapel was trying not to fall asleep at his desk. It wasn't easy. It was too early in the year for air-conditioning, so the air in the office building at Fort Belvoir was still and lifeless, and the only sounds he could hear were the noise of fingers clacking away at keyboards and the low buzz of the compact fluorescent lightbulbs.

He sensed someone coming up from behind him and sat up straighter in his chair, trying to make it look like he was busy. It wouldn't do to have some civilian bigwig come in here and see him slouched over his desk. When the newcomer walked into his cubicle and leaned over him, though, it wasn't who he'd been expecting.

"So are you going to ever tell me what you did in Afghanistan?" Sara asked, her breath hot on Chapel's neck. She laughed. "I'll make it worth your while."

Chapel didn't move an inch. Sara—Major Sara Volks, INSCOM, to be proper about it—was leaning over his shoulder, theoretically looking at the same computer screen he'd been staring at all morning. It was displaying yet another memo about the technical details of a weapons system under development by a civilian contractor. He doubted very much she was interested in what it had to say.

Still, old habits die hard. In his head he matched up the required clearance to look at this memo with what he knew of her clearance. She was a major in

INSCOM, the army's Intelligence and Security Command. Which meant it was fine, she was more than qualified to see this, and he relaxed a bit.

Then he realized she was leaning over his shoulder, her mouth only about half an inch from his ear, and that she smelled really, really good. After that he didn't relax at all. "You know I can't talk about that," he said. "Ma'am."

Chapel moved office every few weeks as his job demanded, and every time he found himself a new cubicle he ended up having a new reporting officer—a new boss, for all intents and purposes. Major Volks was hardly the worst of the lot. She was capable and efficient enough that she didn't need to yell at her people to keep them working. She was also an audacious flirt . . . at least as far as Chapel was concerned. He hadn't seen her make eyes at any of the other men in the office, and he was pretty sure he was the only soldier in the fort who got to call her by her first name. The way she spoke to him was ridiculously unprofessional and probably enough to get both of them written up and reassigned, if he'd wanted to make a stink about it.

Not that he minded. It didn't hurt that her regulation-cut hair was platinum blond, that she had big, soulful eyes and a body sculpted by countless hours in the fort's excellent fitness center. Or that she had a mischievous grin that made Chapel's knees go a little weak.

Up to this point she'd kept her comments suggestive rather than brazen. She'd asked him a lot of questions about himself, always prodding for information she had to know he couldn't give her—like his wartime record, and what exactly his job description was now. It was the kind of flirting people in Military Intelligence did because they spent so much of their time staying secret that even the hint of disclosure was exciting.

She'd also asked him what he liked to do when he went home at night, and whether he enjoyed Italian food. There was a nice Italian restaurant not a mile outside of the fort—the implication was clear.

So far he hadn't taken the bait.

"We are silent warriors, right?" she said, a hint of a laugh in her voice. "That's the creed of the MIC." She leaned in closer, which he hadn't thought was possible before. Her shoulder touched his back. "All right. Keep your secrets. For now."

Chapel was no shrinking violet, and he was sorely tempted. And this was definitely the moment. She'd opened a door—it was up to him to walk through. He could ask her out on a date and he knew she would say yes.

Or he could say nothing and keep things casual and flirtatious and harmless between them forever.

Initiating things would put his career at risk—his career, such as it was. A series of boring desk jobs doing oversight on weapons contractors until he retired on a comfortable little pension.

Go for it, he told himself. "I will tell you one secret," he said. "I *love* Italian. And, in fact, I was thinking—"

Was it possible she could lean in even closer? She was almost rubbing his back with her shoulder. "Yes?" She reached out one hand to put it on his.

His left hand.

Damn.

He felt her flinch. Felt her whole body tense. "Oh," she said.

His left arm wasn't there anymore. He could forget that sometimes, because of the *thing* they'd given him to replace it. Some days he went whole hours without remembering what was attached to his body.

"It's . . . cold," Sara said.

"Silicone," he told her, his voice very low. "Looks pretty real, right? They did a great job making it look like the other one. There's even hair on the knuckles."

"I didn't know," she said. "You didn't say anything . . ."

"It's not a secret. Though I tend not to mention it until it comes up." He lifted the hand and flexed the fingers for her. "State of the art." His heart sank in his chest. He could pretend it was normal, pretend that there was nothing weird about his new arm. But he knew how it creeped people out. "Almost as good as the real thing."

"Afghanistan?" she asked, her eyes knowing and sympathetic. He'd learned to dread that look.

The last thing he wanted was her pity. "Yeah. It's not a big thing. Listen, as I was saying, I don't have any plans tonight and—"

"I need to think about it," she said. She stood up straight. She wasn't meeting his eyes when she spoke to him, now. "Let me get back to you. Fraternization isn't exactly permitted, after all, and—"

"I understand," Chapel told her. And he did. This wasn't what she'd been expecting. She'd been flirting with a professional soldier, a strong, vigorous man in his early forties with just a touch of gray at his temples. Not an amputee.

She turned to go, and he sighed in disappointment. This wasn't the first time things had worked out this way. He'd had years to get used to the arm—and how people reacted to it. But damn, he had really hoped that this time—

"I, uh," she said, and now she did look him in the eye. "I didn't say no. I said, let me get back to you."

"Sure," he said.

She walked away. She looked angry. Like he was the one who had brushed her off.

Well, in a couple of weeks he would be reassigned to a new office, anyway. Probably one where his reporting officer was fat and bald and smelled like cheap cigars. And it wasn't like it could have gone anywhere with Sara anyway, not with both of them hiding a relationship from their superior officers and hoping they never got caught.

He turned back to his computer and tried to make sense of the memo on his screen. He got about three sentences in before he realized he couldn't remember which weapons system this memo related to, or why any of it mattered in the slightest degree.

Grunting in frustration he pushed himself up out of his chair and logged off from the computer. There was no way he was going to get any work done, not until he got his head clear, and that meant he needed to go swim some laps.

Just as he stepped out of the cubicle he heard the chime as his BlackBerry received a new text message.

"I cannot deal with you right now," he told his phone, and walked away.

FORT BELVOIR, VIRGINIA: APRIL 12, T+4:02

When they flew him home from Afghanistan, one of the first thoughts through Chapel's mind had been that he would never swim again.

He'd grown up in Florida, swimming in the canals with turtles and manatees. He'd gotten his SCUBA certification at the age of twelve and his MSD—the highest level of nonprofessional certification—by eighteen. He'd spent more of his youth in the water than on dry land, at least according to his mother. He'd seriously considered going into the navy instead of the army, maybe even becoming a frogman. In the end, he had only decided to be a grunt because he didn't want to spend half his life swabbing decks. He had learned quickly enough that the army liked soldiers who could swim, too—it had been a big part of his being chosen for Special Forces training—and he had made a point of doing twenty laps a day in the nearest pool to keep in shape. It had become his refuge, his private time to just think and move and be free and weightless. He'd never felt as at peace anywhere else as he did while swimming.

Now that was over.

A man with one arm can only swim in circles, he'd thought. He had been lying in a specially made stretcher on board a troop transport flying into National Airport. He had spent most of the flight staring out the window, feeling sorry for himself.

His life was over. His career was over—he would never go back into the theater of operations, never do anything real or valuable again. No one would ever take him seriously for the rest of his life—he would just be a cripple, someone they should feel sorry for. He pitied himself more than anyone else ever could.

That had ended when he got to Walter Reed and started his rehabilitation. He'd been a little shocked when he met the man they sent to teach him how to live with one arm. The physical therapist had come into the room in a wheelchair because he was missing his right leg. He was also missing his right arm, and his right eye. He'd been a master gunnery sergeant with the Marines in Iraq and had thrown himself on an IED to protect what he called his boys. Not a single one of them had been injured that day. Just him. "Call me Top," he'd said, and he held out his left hand for Chapel to shake.

Chapel had reached automatically to take that hand. It had taken him a second to remember his own left hand wasn't there anymore. Eventually he'd awkwardly reached over and shook Top's hand with his right.

"See?" Top had said. "You're already getting the hang of it. You make do with what you've got. Hell, I should know it's not easy, but then, I never expected life to be easy. I know you army boys think life is one long vacation. In the Marines we have this thing called a work ethic."

"In the army we've got this thing called brains; we use that instead," Chapel had fired back. When they both stopped laughing, there were tears in

Chapel's eyes. The tears took a lot longer to stop than the laughter. Top let that go. He didn't mind if his boys—and Chapel was one of his boys now, like it or not—cried a little, or screamed in pain when they felt like it. "A soldier who can still bitch is a happy soldier," Top had told him. "When they shut up, when they stop griping, that's when I know one of my boys is in trouble."

There had been plenty of tears. And plenty of screaming. The artificial arm they gave Chapel was a miracle. It would mean living an almost entirely normal life. It functioned exactly like a real arm, and it responded to his nerve impulses so he just had to think about moving his arm and it did what he wanted. It was light-years beyond any prosthetic ever built before. But being fitted for it meant undergoing endless grueling surgeries as the nerves that should have been serving his missing arm were moved to new places, as electrodes were implanted in his chest and shoulder.

If it hadn't been for Top, Chapel was pretty sure he wouldn't have made it. He would have eaten his own sidearm, frankly. But Top had shown him that life—even a life limited by circumstance—could still mean something. "Hell, I'm one of the lucky ones," Top had told him one day while they were doing strength-training exercises.

"You've got to be kidding me," Chapel said.

"Hell, no. Everything that he took away, God made sure I had a spare handy. There's only three body parts you only get one of—your nose, your heart, and one other one, and I got to keep all those. Now, my little buttercup, shall we get back to work?"

It had taken a long time for Chapel to confess to Top what he missed the most. "I wish I could still swim," he said. "I used to love swimming. I can't get my magic arm wet, though."

"So take it off when you go swimming," Top suggested.

Chapel shook his head. "Won't work. I mean, I guess I could kick my way around a pool if I had to. If my life depended on it I could tread water just fine if I fell off a boat or something. But without two arms, I'm not going to break any speed records. I'll never swim laps again. That was the main way I got exercise before."

"I always hated swimming, myself," Top said. "Never liked going in over my head and getting water in my nose. But okay."

"Okay what?"

"Okay, starting tomorrow, you're going to teach me how to swim with one arm and one leg."

"I can't do that," Chapel said. "I don't think it can be done. And anyway, I'm not a teacher."

"So you got two things to learn with that big army brain of yours," Top said. "As usual, the marine is going to have to do the hard part. And probably drown, too. Nothing new about that, either."

Chapel had known exactly what Top was trying to do. He had wanted to shake his head and say that kind of psych-out wasn't going to work on him. But he trusted Top by then, trusted him more than he'd trusted anyone before in his life. So the next morning they had gone down to the hospital's swimming pool with a couple burly orderlies (who still had all their limbs), and Chapel had taught Top how to swim.

Top did drown, twice. Each time he was resuscitated, and each time he got back in the pool. He had to be dragged out of the water by the orderlies so many times they refused to help anymore and quit on the spot. Top put in a requisition for more orderlies, and they kept going. The results weren't ever perfect. Top swimming with one arm and one leg looked kind of like a drunk dolphin flopping back and forth in the water. He had a lot of trouble swimming in a straight line, and even one lap of the pool left him so exhausted he had to rest for an hour before he started again.

In the end, though, Top could swim. "I ever fall off an ocean liner on one of those celebrity cruises, I guess I'll be okay," Top had said when he decided they were done. When he'd successfully swum ten laps, in less than eight hours. "Now, Captain Chapel. Sir. You want to tell me why we went to all this trouble? Sir, you want to tell me why I forced you to do this demeaning task, sir?"

"Because," Chapel had said, "if I can show an enlisted man like you how to swim, sorry sack of guts that you are, I can surely figure out how to do it with my own glorious and beautiful officer's body."

"Sir, yes, sir," Top had said. "Now get in that goddamned pool or I will throw you in."

Now—years later—Chapel was up to twenty laps at a time, in less than an hour. He would never do the butterfly crawl again, but he'd mastered a kind of half stroke that used his arm mostly for steering and let his legs do all the work. Fort Belvoir had a wonderful pool in its fitness center, and he availed himself of it daily.

There was no feeling like it.

The blood-warm water streamed past him, buoying him up like gentle hands. He didn't have to think about anything else while he swam—he just focused on his body, on his movements. His muscles moved in perfect concert, his arm and his legs snapping into an old familiar rhythm. His head turned from side to side as he drew in each breath and let it out again in a long, slow exhale. There was no better feeling in the world.

Thanks, Top, he thought, as he kicked off for the start of lap seventeen.

The last time he'd seen Top had been at the master gunnery sergeant's wedding, less than a year previous. Top had walked down the aisle with two legs and two arms—the only way anyone could tell he wasn't whole was that he was wearing an eye patch. Chapel had gotten to know Top's bride a little bit and she had turned out to be the toughest, most sarcastic woman he'd ever met. She needed to be if she was going to keep up with Top.

Lap eighteen. Chapel would have stayed in the pool all day if he could have. He needed to get back to work, though. The frustration and boredom of his morning and of Major Volks's rejection were gone, or at least he'd worked off enough of that negativity to actually start drafting some memos of his own.

Still. Maybe he'd shoot for twenty-five laps today.

Across the pool. Back. He kicked off for lap nineteen.

And then stopped himself in the water before he'd gone five yards out.

"Hello?" he said.

A man in a pin-striped suit was standing at the edge of the pool, looking down at him. He had a thick white towel in his hands and something else. A BlackBerry, maybe.

"Can I help you with something? Make it quick, though," Chapel said. "I'm pretty good on the straightaways, but treading water isn't exactly my forte."

Anyone wearing that kind of suit in Fort Belvoir was a civilian, and Chapel had a bad moment where he thought the guy might be some kind of CEO from one of the corporations he was watchdogging. The buzz-cut hair said otherwise, though, as did the sheer bulk of muscle crammed into the jacket.

Chapel was trained in Military Intelligence. He'd studied all the different ways to put clues together, to draw conclusions from scant evidence. From just the look of this guy he knew right away that he had to be CIA.

The agency had tentacles everywhere, and there were plenty of them wrapped around INSCOM and Fort Belvoir. They tended to stay in other parts of the fort though, where Chapel couldn't see them, and he'd always been happy about that. Military Intelligence and civilian spies never got along.

"Listen, if you just came to watch the freak go for a swim, that's fine," Chapel said, because the guy still hadn't told him what he wanted. "But then I'll just get back to it."

The agency guy shook his head, slowly. And then he started to laugh. His whole body shook as he guffawed and chortled and chuckled.

Chapel swam over to the edge of the pool and dragged himself out. Water poured off him in torrents as he stormed around the side of the pool, headed straight for the laughing bastard. If fraternizing with Sara could cost him his career, punching out a CIA man could get him thrown in the brig, but at that moment he did not give one good goddamn. Nobody laughed at Jim Chapel like that.

Before he could land the punch, though, the CIA bastard lifted the BlackBerry he was holding and held it up at Chapel's eye level. Chapel saw that it was his own smartphone. The one he'd left at his desk when he headed for the pool.

The screen said he had twenty-seven new text messages, and three new voice mails. Chapel grabbed the phone and scrolled through the phone's logs. Every single message had come from the same number. There were e-mails, too, from a military address he didn't recognize, but he knew with a cold certainty they came from the same person who'd sent all those texts.

"When you didn't answer," the CIA man said, still burbling with mirth, "they sent me to come find you. We have to go. Now. The man who's been trying to contact you is not the kind of person you keep waiting."

Chapel stared into his eyes. They were hazel, green in the middle and gold around the edges, and they were full of laughter, still.

"Give me that," Chapel said, and grabbed the towel.

FORT BELVOIR, VIRGINIA: APRIL 12, T+4:03

Chapel read one of the e-mails for the third time, still not sure what the hell was going on. It went on for pages, but most of that was just boilerplate confidentiality statements—legalese describing what exactly would happen to anyone who forwarded or printed out the e-mail. Standard stuff for military intelligence. The only real content of the e-mail was a single line of tersely written text:

> **Report instanter DIA DX Pentagon for new orders. Reply to acknowledge.**

Chapel understood all that just fine. DIA was the Defense Intelligence Agency, the top level of the military intelligence pyramid. DX was the Directorate for Defense Counterintelligence and HUMINT— HUMINT being Human Intelligence, or good old-fashioned spycraft. DX was the group that used to give him his orders back when he was a theater operative in Afghanistan, but he hadn't worked for them for a long time—these days his work was handled directly by INSCOM, and he hadn't so much as spoken to anyone in the DIA in five years.

Technically, of course, he still had to answer all the way up that chain, and if somebody at the DIA wanted him to show up at their office and get new orders, he was required to do so. But what on earth could they want him for?

"You know anything about this, Laughing Boy?" he asked the CIA goon.

Laughing Boy shook his head. The very idea seemed to set him off on another chuckling fit. "I just do as I'm told."

Chapel stared at the man. His involvement in this—even if it just came down to fetching Chapel when he wouldn't answer his phone—added a whole new wrinkle of weirdness. On paper the DIA and the civilian CIA worked hand in glove, but everyone in the intelligence community knew there was a permanent divide and lasting hatred between the defense department and the civilian intelligence organizations. They never shared anything with each other unless they were legally required to. If the CIA and the DIA were working together, then that could only mean something really bad had happened and that rivalry had been put aside long enough to clean it up.

And somehow that meant they needed a one-armed captain from INSCOM to hold the bucket and the mop.

Chapel rubbed vigorously with the towel at the skin on the left side of his chest. Laughing Boy raised an eyebrow and Chapel grunted in frustration. "My skin has to be dry or the electrodes don't work right. Do you mind? I need to get dressed."

Laughing Boy kept giggling, but he stepped aside to let Chapel head for the locker room. Chapel sat down on a wooden bench inside and picked up the arm. It only weighed nine pounds—lighter than the original. Its silicone cover looked exactly like a real human arm up until you reached the shoulder, where it flared out into a pair of molded clamps. Putting it on was simplicity—he simply drew it over the stump of his shoulder until it fit snugly. The arm recognized automatically that it was on and the clamps squeezed down gently on Chapel's flesh until it was locked into place.

As he did every time he put it on, he ran it through a quick check to make sure everything was working all right. He lifted the arm and then swung it backward, made a fist, and then straightened his hand out like he was about to deliver a karate chop. Finally, to check the fingers he touched each of them in turn with the thumb.

Living nerves in his shoulder and chest had been rewired to replace the ones he'd lost. Sensors in his new hand sent messages to those nerves through subcutaneous electrodes. The neurosurgery had gone so smoothly that now when Chapel touched his artificial thumb to his artificial index finger, he actually felt them rubbing against each other. He could pick up a playing card with those fingers and feel the smooth coating of its lamination, or touch sandpaper and feel how rough it was.

He thought about what Top would say. *"There's guys out there with two hooks instead of hands that learn how to make omelets in the morning without getting egg all over their shirts. You, my boy, are living in science fiction tomorrowland. Is it not a glorious thing to be living in George Jetson world?"*

"Sure is, Top," Chapel said, out loud.

Jerks could laugh at him all they wanted for being a freak. Jim Chapel was whole. Top had taught him that. He was whole and vital and he could do anything he set his mind to. Whatever the DIA wanted him for, he was ready.

He dressed himself hurriedly and then tapped a

message on the BlackBerry acknowledging that he was on his way. To the Pentagon.

Coming out of the locker room he found Laughing Boy waiting for him. "All right, you delivered your message," Chapel said. "You can go now, I'm being a good boy."

Laughing Boy shook his head and chortled a little. "Nope. I'm supposed to drive you there myself. Make sure you show up."

"I know how to follow orders," Chapel insisted. Laughing Boy didn't even shrug. "Fine. We'll go in just a second. I need to let my reporting officer know where I'm going—"

Laughing Boy shook his head.

So it was one of those kinds of briefings, then. The kind where you just disappeared off the face of the earth and nobody knew where you went. This was getting weirder by the minute.

Chapel sighed. "Fine. Let's go."

POUGHKEEPSIE, NEW YORK: APRIL 12, T+4:04

Two hundred and fifty miles away, Lieutenant Barry Charles slapped the helmet of the greenest private in his squad. "We ran through this in the simulator just last month, remember? The train extraction— that's exactly how we're going to do this. Get all the nice civilians out of the car first, then we take down the target. Don't let any of the nice civilians get hurt. Don't let the target get hurt, at least not too much. We've got orders to bring him in alive. You children understand what I'm saying?"

The four men Charles commanded all saluted. In their body armor and protective masks they looked like a mean bunch of sons of bitches, Charles had to admit that. They were the best men the 308th counterintelligence battalion had ever trained, and they were ripped and ready.

"Then let's take this train. By the book, soldiers!"

The men shouted a wordless response and swarmed toward the train. Command had signaled ahead and forced the train to stop ten miles north of Poughkeepsie, out in the sticks where collateral damage would be light. The train's conductor had confirmed the presence of the target and told them which car he was in. Charles had been given only the quickest of briefings on this mission—a picture of the target and a warning that the man he wanted was potentially armed and definitely dangerous, an escapee from a DoD detention facility upstate—but he had no doubt this was going to be a cakewalk.

"Unlock the doors now," he called—he was patched in directly with the train's own radio system and the conductor was ready to do as he said.

Looking up at the train now he saw the anxious faces of commuters and tourists staring down at him. He gave them a cheery wave to put them at ease and then turned to signal to his men. There were two doors on the train car, one at either end. He had four men—one to take the door, one to provide cover. Simplicity itself. He dropped his hand and the men hit the doors running, the pneumatic locks hissing open for them. The metal side of the train pinged in the morning sun. Through the windows Charles watched his men take up stations inside the train, covering one another just like they'd been trained.

There were a couple of screams and some angry shouts, but nothing Charles wasn't expecting. Civilians started pouring out of the train car in a nearly orderly fashion. About as orderly as you could expect from citizens with no military discipline or training. Charles shouted for them to head as quickly as possible to the safety of a big box hardware store a hundred yards behind him, and they did as they were told.

"Lieutenant, sir, we have him," one of his squad called. The voice in his ear sounded pumped up and excited. "He's just sitting there, looks like he might be asleep."

Talk about your lucky breaks. "Well, whatever you do," Charles said, "don't be rude and wake him up. Are the civilians clear?"

"Sir, yes, sir," another of the squad called.

"I'm coming up. Just keep your eyes open."

Charles got one foot up on the door platform and grabbed a safety rail. He let his carbine swing across the front of his chest as he hauled himself up into the airlocklike compartment between train cars. The door that lead into the car proper was activated by a slap plate. He reached down to activate it.

Hell broke out before the door even had a chance to slide open.

"Sir, he's moving—" someone shouted.

"—does not appear to be armed, repeat, I see no weapons—"

"What the hell? What the hell did he just—"

The door in front of Charles slid open and he

looked into a scene of utter chaos. A man with a scraggly beard had picked up one of Charles's men, and as Charles watched, the target threw the soldier into one of his squad mates, sending them both sprawling over the rows of seats. A third squad member came at the target with his carbine up and ready to fire.

The target reached forward, grabbed the soldier's arm, and twisted it around like he was trying to break a green branch off a tree.

Charles heard a series of pops like muffled gunfire, but he knew what they actually were—the sounds of the soldier's bones snapping, one by one. A second later the soldier started screaming. He dropped to the floor, down for the count.

Charles started to rush forward, to come to the defense of his men, but he nearly tripped over what he thought was luggage that had fallen into the aisle.

It wasn't luggage. It was his fourth squad member. Looking down, Charles saw the man was still alive but broken like a porcelain doll. His mask was gone, and his face was obscured by blood.

Lieutenant Charles looked up at the man who had neutralized his entire squad and for a moment—a split second—he stopped and stared, because he couldn't do anything else. The man's eyes. There was something wrong with the man's eyes. They were solid black, from side to side. Charles thought for a moment he was looking into empty eye sockets. But no—no—he could see them shining—

He didn't waste any more time. He brought his carbine up and started firing in tight, controlled three-shot bursts. Just like he'd been trained. Charles had spent enough time on the firing range—and in real life, live fire operations—to know how to shoot, and how to hit what he aimed at.

Human targets, though, couldn't move as fast as the thing in front of him. It got one foot up on the armrest of a train seat, then the other was on the headrest. Charles tried to track the thing but he couldn't—it moved too fast as it crammed itself into the overhead luggage rack and wriggled toward him like a worm.

Suddenly it was above him, at head height, and its hands were reaching down for him. Charles tried to bring his weapon up, putting every ounce of speed he had into reacquiring his target.

The *thing* was faster. Its hands tore away Charles's mask, and then its thumbs went for his eyes.

IN TRANSIT: APRIL 12, T+4:41

Laughing Boy had a car waiting right outside the fitness center, a black Crown Victoria with Virginia plates. Chapel got in without a word, and the two of them headed straight for the Pentagon.

Chapel didn't ask for the man's name. CIA told you what you needed to know and they didn't like it if you asked them questions. He resolved to keep calling the guy Laughing Boy, if only in his head.

They had a long drive together during which neither of them said more than ten words. Mostly they were about whether there would be much traffic on I-95. Fort Belvoir was just south of Mount Vernon, only a few miles from the Pentagon—it wasn't a long ride—but you always hit a snarl of traffic when you approached the Beltway that surrounded the District of Columbia. Half the country seemed to be trying to get into D.C. to do some business or just see the sights. The Pentagon was still in Virginia, technically, but that didn't make things any easier. As the car slowed down to a crawl outside of Arlington, Chapel got impatient and started drumming on his side of the dashboard with his artificial fingers.

Laughing Boy seemed to find that very funny.

There wasn't a lot, it seemed, that didn't amuse Laughing Boy. He never stopped laughing the whole time they were in the car together, though as he focused on his driving it dropped to a kind of dry giggling that grated on Chapel's nerves. When they got to the Pentagon's parking entrance, he pulled the car into a reserved spot but before he got out he reached into his jacket pocket and pulled out a bottle of pills.

"Gotta show due respect, right?" Laughing Boy asked, with a hearty guffaw. He popped three pills in his mouth and dry swallowed them. The effect was almost immediate. He grimaced and rubbed at his chest and sweat broke out on his head, slicking his crew cut. Eventually he recovered and looked over at Chapel with a grim smile. "Can't take those when I'm driving."

Chapel got a quick look at the pill bottle before Laughing Boy put it away. The pills were something called clozapine—Chapel had no idea what they were for, but he did notice that Laughing Boy stopped laughing after taking them.

Thank heaven for small favors, he thought.

The two of them headed inside through the security checkpoint, where Chapel had the usual hassles that came with having part of your body replaced by metal. The soldiers who did his pat-down and search were at least respectful—he doubted he was the only amputee they'd seen that day. Chapel and the CIA man were given laminates, and a helpful guard gave them directions on how to get to the office Laughing Boy named.

Chapel was not surprised when, five minutes later, Laughing Boy ignored the directions altogether and took him deep into C Ring and to an office on the wrong side of the building. They passed quickly through, ignored by all the clerks in their cubicles, and back to an elevator in an otherwise empty hallway. When the elevator doors opened, Chapel saw two soldiers inside carrying M4 carbines. The soldiers demanded to see their laminates and then let them in. One of the soldiers punched a button marked H and they started to descend.

Chapel was a little surprised by that. The Pentagon was built in five concentric rings of office space, rings A through E. There were two sublevels underground called F and G that he knew of. He'd never heard of an H level at all.

When the elevator doors opened again, he looked out into a long hallway with unadorned concrete walls. The floor and ceiling were painted a glossy battleship gray. Unmarked green doors stood every dozen yards or so down the corridor, which seemed to stretch on forever. There were no office numbers, nor any signs distinguishing one door from another. "How do you even know which office you want?" Chapel asked Laughing Boy as they headed down the echoing hall.

"If you're down here and you don't know which one is which, you're already in trouble," Laughing Boy told him.

"This isn't where DIA DX has its offices," Chapel pointed out. "I've seen those before. This isn't—"

He stopped because Laughing Boy was staring at him. Waiting for him to ask a question. Chapel was certain there would be no answers.

"Never mind," Chapel said.

"Good dog."

The CIA man took the lead, setting off at a good clip, and Chapel followed. He did a double take when, for the first time, he saw the back of Laughing Boy's head. There was a bad scar there—more of a dent—where the flesh had turned white and no hair grew.

"Come on," Laughing Boy said. "We're already late." He stood next to a door exactly like all the others, his hand on the knob.

Chapel hurried to catch up with him. Laughing Boy turned the knob and revealed the room beyond—which was nothing like what Chapel had expected.

THE PENTAGON: APRIL 12, T+4:59

Classical music filled the air, soft and almost lost under the sound of falling water coming from a splashing fountain in the center of the space. The room beyond the unmarked door was lined with wooden shelves full of leather-bound books, and the floor was covered by a rich blue carpet. There were, of course, no windows—they had to be a couple hundred feet underground—but the fountain kept the room from feeling claustrophobic.

Armchairs upholstered in red leather were gathered around the room in small conversation areas, while to one side stood a fully stocked wet bar with comfortable-looking stools. On the other side of the room stood a massive globe in a brass stand and a giant map cabinet with dozens of drawers.

It didn't look like an underground bunker. It didn't look like an office, either. It looked like a private club, the kind of place where old diplomats would sit and discuss foreign affairs over snifters of brandy.

"Fallout shelter," someone said from behind Chapel's shoulder.

He turned and saw a man of about sixty dressed in a three-piece suit and a bow tie. The suit was tweed—elegant but not exactly stylish—and the man in it looked like a throwback to the nineteenth century, with long sideburns and a pair of tiny wire-rimmed glasses. He smiled warmly as Chapel stared at him.

"You're wondering where you are, of course," the man said. He held out a hand and Chapel shook it. "This whole level was supposed to be a private fallout shelter for the Joint Chiefs of Staff. I doubt it will surprise you to know they demanded it have a pleasant little tavern. The other rooms on this level aren't like this, sadly. Mostly they're full of metal cots and preserved food from the 1960s. This room is my favorite."

"It's . . . nice," Chapel offered. Maybe a little stuffy for his taste, but it definitely beat his cubicle back at Fort Belvoir.

"Rupert Hollingshead," the man said, and let go of Chapel's hand. "I'm the one who sent you all those pesky text messages. I am also, despite appearances, a member of the DIA directorate, though not of DX, I'm afraid."

"Captain James Chapel, sir, reporting," Chapel said, and gave Hollingshead a salute. If Hollingshead was DIA, then he had to be military, either a full bird colonel or a brigadier general. The fact that he was out of uniform didn't matter one whit.

Hollingshead returned the salute. "Oh, do be at ease, Captain. As I was saying . . . fallout shelter, yes. Never used for that purpose, of course, and abandoned for years. When I needed a quiet little place to set up shop, I figured it would do. The walls are concrete six feet thick and it's swept for listening devices every day. Can't be too careful. I do apologize, Captain, but will you allow me to show you a seat? Time is rather . . . ah. Short."

"Damn straight," someone else said.

Chapel hadn't noticed the bar's only other occupant until he stood up from his chair. This one was much more what Chapel thought of when he imagined a high-ranking intelligence official. He wore the customary black suit, power tie, and flag pin. He had heavy jowls that made him look a little like Richard Nixon, and he stood a little hunched forward as if his posture had been wrecked by years of whispering into important ears.

The two of them, Hollingshead and this man,

couldn't have been less alike. But Chapel could tell right away they had the same job. Spymasters—the kind of men who were always behind the scenes pulling strings and counting coup. The kind of men who could start wars with carefully worded position papers. The kind of men who briefed the president daily, but who never let their faces show up on the evening news.

Chapel had been in intelligence long enough to know that you never, ever questioned or messed with men like that. You saluted and you said sir, yes, sir and you did what they said and you never asked why.

You couldn't keep yourself from wondering, though.

"That's Thomas Banks," Hollingshead said. "CIA, though—shh! Don't tell anyone I told you that."

He gave that warm smile again and Chapel couldn't help but return it. He found himself liking Hollingshead already.

Banks, on the other hand, was going to be a hard man to love—that was evident from his whole manner. "We need to get this started," he growled. "We've already lost five hours. Five hours we'll never get back."

"Of course," Hollingshead said. "As for your friend here, will he be staying?"

Chapel and both officials turned to look at Laughing Boy, who had taken up a position just to one side of the door. Laughing Boy didn't so much as squirm under the scrutiny.

"He's been cleared. Your man is, too, I assume,"

Banks said. "What are his qualifications? Doesn't look like much."

"Captain Chapel's a war hero, actually," Hollingshead said. He went over to the bar and poured himself a glass of water. He raised one eyebrow at Chapel, but Chapel shook his head to say he didn't need anything. "If you were to ask him about his past, I'm sure he would be unable to tell you a thing, and quite right. His entire service record and most of what he's done since he came home is oh, quite classified. So I'll have to sing his praises myself. He was one of the first to put, ah, boots on the ground as they say, in Afghanistan, as part of Operation Anticyclone."

"What, that mess with the Taliban?" Banks asked.

Chapel had kept quiet about Afghanistan so long even hearing other people talk about it made him feel weird. He kept his peace, though—a captain didn't speak to men at this level until he was spoken to.

"Hmm, yes. He was dropped into Khost Province with a number of Army Rangers. The idea was they would make contact with some highly placed mujahideen and arrange with them to support our incursion there. This was right after September eleventh, of course, when we still thought we had friends in the Khyber Pass. Chapel and his men grew beards to honor the local customs, and, more important, they carried briefcases filled with cash. The men he was supposed to meet with were, after all, the same men the United States had once armed and paid to fight the Soviets. That all happened on your side of the aisle, Banks, I'm sure you remember—"

"That was before my time," Banks grunted.

"Of course. Of course," Hollingshead said, waving away the protest. "The point is, Captain Chapel did his job and made contact. Sadly, the men he was meeting with had already chosen their path and decided the future lay with al-Qaeda. When the negotiations, ah, collapsed, the captain found himself on the wrong end of a rocket-propelled grenade. This unfortunately killed all the Rangers with him and left Captain Chapel badly wounded. His captors refused to give him medical attention until he told them every single thing he knew about U.S. troop movements in Afghanistan. He refused. By the time our boys rescued him, his arm had gone septic and had to be removed."

"He's a cripple?" Banks demanded.

"Look for yourself, Banks. He's fine."

"This is the best man you could find me? I guess on short notice—"

"Captain Chapel has my complete confidence," Hollingshead shot back. His eyes flashed with anger. "He is exactly the man we need."

"What's he been doing since we scraped him up and brought him home?"

"Oversight on weapons system acquisitions. It should come as no surprise to anyone here gathered that the private firms we employ see defense contracts as an opportunity to rob America blind. Captain Chapel here is in charge of keeping an eye on them and bringing them to justice when they actually break the law."

"So he's a professional snitch," Banks said.

Hollingshead sighed a little. "I prefer the term

whistle-blower. The point is, simply, that you are looking at a man with Special Forces training, field experience, and a finely tuned mind for police work. Who, not least of all, knows how to keep a secret. Am I beginning to approach your idea of a satisfactory candidate?"

"Maybe," Banks said. "Considering the desperate circumstances, and the sensitivity of the matter—"

"There's certainly no time to find anyone else," Hollingshead said, with those flashing eyes again. Chapel got the sense that for all his genial nature, Hollingshead loathed Banks with a passion. Banks just seemed like he hated everyone.

Hollingshead took a sip of his water. "Captain Chapel," he said, "I'm afraid there's no room for ceremony here. We need you to come work for us and I'm sorry, but you aren't allowed to say no. As of this moment, you've been seconded to this office and I will be your new reporting officer."

"Sir, yes, sir," Chapel said.

"And God help you, I've already got a job for you. God help us all."

THE PENTAGON: APRIL 12, T+5:19

Hollingshead went behind the bar and pressed a button hidden among the whiskey bottles. On the far side of the room a shelf of books slid away to reveal a flatscreen monitor. It displayed the DIA seal, a stylized earth orbited by red ellipses and surmounted with a torch.

"This is going to be a quick briefing," Hollingshead said. He sounded apologetic. "Since most of what we have is strictly need to know. I can't stress enough how sensitive this mission is."

Chapel wanted to ask why he was privy to it, then. He was hardly the man for a top secret mission, not anymore. But he kept his mouth shut.

"A little more than five hours ago—that would be ten past six in the morning—a person or persons unknown carried out an attack on a Department of Defense facility in upstate New York. At this time we suspect domestic terrorism."

"It doesn't matter *why* it happened," Banks insisted. "Stick to the *what*."

Hollingshead took another sip of water. "Very well. The purpose of the facility is classified, but I can tell you it housed seven individuals who were not allowed to leave."

"Permission to ask for a clarification, sir?" Chapel said.

"Absolutely granted," Hollingshead told him.

"These men were prisoners?" Chapel asked.

"Need to know," Banks said. In other words, Chapel wasn't cleared to even know that the prisoners were in fact prisoners.

"The DoD refers to them as detainees," Hollingshead said.

Ah, Chapel thought. Prisoners, yes. But not criminals incarcerated in a prison. Individuals held, most likely without trial, for unspecified reasons. That suggested they were terrorists, or at least that they possessed information regarding terrorism, and had been held under extraordinary rendition.

Chapel bit his lip. He was already jumping to

conclusions and the briefing had just started. The first thing he'd learned during his military intelligence training was to never assume anything.

"Six of the individuals escaped from the facility. The seventh is presumed dead. Why we presume this is—"

"Need to know," Banks jumped in.

Hollingshead nodded. "The six who left the facility were tracked to the best of our ability, of course, and we are very good at that sort of thing. Two of them were picked up en route and . . . neutralized. The remaining four were followed by satellite reconnaissance as far as a train station in Rhinecliff, New York, where we picked them up on a closed-circuit camera." He pressed another button and the television screen flickered to life, showing grainy black-and-white footage of a train platform.

Chapel leaned forward to get a better look.

Four men were on the platform. They paced back and forth, acting agitated. It was hard to tell them apart—they all had shaggy hair and beards and their clothes were little more than rags. A train pulled up to the platform and one of them got on. The other three didn't even so much as wave good-bye.

"The four you see here each took a different train, headed to a different destination. About the same time I started texting you, I dispatched counterintelligence units to pick them up before they got off the trains. Sadly none of these units was successful."

"The detainees never showed up at the destinations? They left the trains en route?" Chapel asked.

"Ah. No. The units were—well. They are units no more."

"The detainees killed your people?" Chapel asked, amazed. The DIA didn't mess around with terrorists (assuming, of course, these were terrorists, he reminded himself). If they sent squads of soldiers to pick up the detainees, they would have gone in heavily armed and ready for anything.

"The detainees are dangerous people," Hollingshead said. "They're stronger and faster than—"

"Need to know," Banks said, nearly jumping out of his chair.

Damn it, Chapel thought. He had a bad feeling about where this was going. They were going to ask him to lead an investigation to track these men down, but they weren't going to give him enough information to do it properly. Government bureaucracy at its very worst, and he was the one who would have to take the fall.

He said nothing, of course. These men were his superiors. He didn't have to like Banks or approve of the man's obsessive need for secrecy—but he did have to treat him with respect. That was part of what being a soldier meant.

"We have to find these men, and soon," Hollingshead said. He switched off the flatscreen. "You see, they are carrying—"

"Need to know!" Banks said, nearly shouting.

Hollingshead stared at his opposite number. He didn't turn red in the face or bare his teeth or ball his fists. It was clear to Chapel, though, who had been trained to read people, that Hollingshead was about to blow his top.

"I appreciate the sensitivity of this situation," Hollingshead said. Chapel could tell he was picking his words carefully. "But you're putting my man in danger by keeping him in the dark like this."

"You know what's at stake," Banks said.

"And I'm telling you," Hollingshead replied, "that if you don't clear this particular piece of information right now, I'm pulling out of this operation."

"You wouldn't dare," Banks said, with a snort. "You know this needs to get done. You know what we stand to lose."

"Indeed. Oh, yes, indeed I do. Which is why, after ejecting you and your agent from my office, I'll take this right to the Joint Chiefs. And write it up for the president's daily briefing, where I'll suggest that we mobilize every soldier we can get our hands on until this is taken care of. Of course, the press will want to know why we're doing that."

Banks looked like he'd been hit in the face with a shovel.

"This is bigger than you or me or our little fiefdoms," Hollingshead went on. "It *should* be handled out in the open, frankly. I'm of half a mind to do this even if you relent. But I'll give you one chance to reconsider."

Banks set his mouth in a hard line. He grasped the arms of his chair hard enough that the leather creaked. Chapel expected him to jump up and walk out of the room. But he didn't.

"They're carrying a virus," Banks said, finally. "A human-engineered virus."

THE PENTAGON: APRIL 12, T+5:31

Chapel had no idea what to do with that news.

It made him want to take a shower. It made him want to shower in bleach.

He couldn't help but ask the first question that came to his mind, whether or not he was a good soldier. "A virus . . . are we talking Ebola or the common cold, here?"

"Neither, and that's the one bit of luck we've had," Hollingshead told him. "It's bloodborne, not airborne. They can only infect others by direct contact, and then only if they break the skin."

"That sounds manageable. What's the chance of them bleeding on someone? It's got to be pretty slim," Chapel said. His relief made his heart skip a beat.

Then he saw the look on Hollingshead's face—and the identical expression on Banks's features.

"Why is nobody agreeing with me?" Chapel asked.

"I mentioned the detainees were violent," Hollingshead said. "I was understating the case, honestly. They're . . ." He glanced at Banks and then at Laughing Boy, who was still standing by the door. "Mentally deranged is the nicest term I can think of. I can assure you, the chances of them breaking someone's skin—or, to be frank about it, biting them—is quite high. In fact it seems to be their chief joy in life."

"All right—that's enough," Banks said. He went over to the bar and poured himself a highball. "That is the absolute limit of need to know. Tell him what he has to do, Rupert, so he can actually get to it."

Hollingshead took off his glasses and wiped them with a handkerchief. "Easy enough to say, of course. Much easier than it will be to do. But we need you, Captain Chapel, to go into the field and recover these men."

"Sir, yes, sir," Chapel said, standing up. "You want me to lead an investigation to locate them, so we can send in appropriate squads to pick them up. I'll need to rendezvous with local police and National Guard units in New York State to—"

"No." Hollingshead held up his glasses so he could look through them, presumably so he could find any remaining smudges. Or maybe so he just didn't have to look Chapel in the eye. "No. Nothing that simple. We're asking you to go into the field and deal with these men personally."

"You mean I'm to track them down . . . on my own," Chapel said, because he was certain that was what Hollingshead had just said. Even if it made no sense whatsoever. "Four men who each took out—single-handedly—a rapid response team."

"We're saying that we need you to find them and remove them from play," Hollingshead said.

"Remove them from play?"

"If you get a clear shot on them," Banks confirmed, "you take it. Bringing them in alive is not required. They're much more valuable to us dead than they are on the loose."

"You want me to kill them," Chapel said.

"It's the damned sensitivity of the thing," Hollingshead said.

For once Banks had more to say. "The public can never find out what's happened. It can't learn where they came from, and it can't learn what they're carrying. We can't risk any more high-profile incidents. It's been hard enough covering up what happened to the original teams." The CIA director swallowed his liquor with a grimace. "It has to be just one man, to keep our involvement quiet. Secrecy is imperative here."

Jim Chapel was no stranger to the need for secrecy. He'd spent his professional life keeping secrets and not asking questions. He knew how this sort of thing worked, and he knew what Banks wasn't saying. That the blowback from a leak in this operation would be devastating. Which meant that these detainees weren't just terrorists, and the human-engineered virus they were carrying wasn't the product of some black laboratory in a rogue state.

It was something the government had made. The government of the United States. The detainees—the psychopathic, violent, homicidal detainees weren't just dangerous criminals. They were guinea pigs. Specimens that the CIA or the DoD or maybe both had experimented on. And letting that fact out of this room was unthinkable to Banks.

He noticed one other thing, too, from what Banks had said.

When Banks talked about the public—meaning the American people, the citizens of the United States—he referred to them as an "it."

He was beginning to see why Hollingshead hated this man.

THE PENTAGON: APRIL 12, T+5:35

"You'll need to leave immediately," Banks told him. "You're going to have to work damned fast if you're going to catch them. We'll do everything in our power to help you—everything that doesn't damage national security."

"I know we're asking a very great deal of you, son," Hollingshead said. "I wish I could give you opportunity to volunteer for this mission. I wish I could let you turn it down. Tell me, Captain, what are your thoughts right now?"

"Permission to speak candidly, sir?"

Hollingshead came over and put a hand on his shoulder. "Permission to swear a blue streak if you like. Permission to call us every foul name you can think of. Just be honest and tell me what you're thinking."

"I think you called in the wrong man," Chapel told them.

Banks and Hollingshead both stared at Chapel in shock.

From behind him, he heard Laughing Boy let out a little chuckle, which was cut off quite abruptly as if he were trying to suppress it.

Chapel could hardly believe he'd said it himself. For ten years he'd been slowly dying in a desk job he hated. Doing basic police work when he'd been trained to be out in the field, making a real difference. How many times had he dreamed of a moment like this, of being called back to active duty? Because it would have meant he was whole again. Not just three-quarters of a human being, but a vital man of action.

But part of what made him want that, part of why he could even hope for it, was his desire to do the *right* thing. The thing that made sense not just for him but for the country he served. And there must have been a serious miscalculation somewhere here.

He shook his head. "This isn't a matter for Military Intelligence. You have four men out there, loose in America, who sound as much like serial killers as anything else. That's the jurisdiction of the FBI, the last time I checked. If they were detainees under extraordinary rendition—even then—at most you should be working with the U.S. Marshals Service. They're the ones who track down escaped fugitives."

"I don't have time for this shit," Banks said.

"Sir, with all due respect—I'm the one running out of time," Chapel told him. "There's one other thing I have to say, though. One thing I need to make clear. You have the wrong man because *I am not a hit man*. I don't kill people for money."

"You know how to use a gun, don't you?" Banks demanded.

"The army taught me that, yes," Chapel agreed. "But I know you're a civilian, sir, and you may be operating under a common misconception about soldiers. We aren't in the business of killing random people. The mission of the armed forces is to extend U.S. policy through force only when necessary, and to use other means whenever it is humanly possible."

Hollingshead nodded slowly. He was a military man, Chapel was sure of it, so he already knew this.

"So when I find these men, I'm going to do everything in my power to bring them in alive. Or at least capture them in the safest way possible."

"Then you're a fool," Banks told him.

Hollingshead clapped his hands together in obvious excitement. "Then you will do it? You'll get them back for us?"

"Sir," Chapel said, standing at attention, "I do not remember being asked for my acceptance of this mission, sir. I remember being asked for my opinion."

"What the fuck ever," Banks said, rising from his chair and frowning in anger. "I asked for a killer and you brought me a goddamned Eagle Scout."

It was, in its way, the nicest thing Banks had said about Chapel yet. He knew he wasn't going to get anything better.

THE PENTAGON: APRIL 12, T+5:42

"I know it seems like a hard task we've given you," Hollingshead said, shrugging in apology.

"I'm just not sure how I'd even begin," Chapel admitted.

"There, at least, we can help you." Hollingshead drew a folded-up sheet of paper from his pocket. As he unfolded it and smoothed it out he said, "Now, you can't ask us how we came by this, son, or what these people have in common. But we are—let's say eighty percent—sure that our detainees will attempt to make contact with the people named on this list."

He handed the paper to Chapel. There were eight names on it, each matched with a last known address. He didn't bother reading the names yet, instead looking up at the two men facing him. "Permission to guess something, sir?"

Hollingshead chuckled. "That, I think, we can allow."

"If I were an escapee from a . . . from a DoD facility, the first thing I'd want to do was to make contact with my family. Friends, professional contacts . . . anyone I could trust. I'm assuming that's where these names come from."

"Look, Banks. Look—he's already on the case," Hollingshead said, with a warm and generous smile. "I told you he was our man."

"He's already making mistakes is what he's doing," Banks countered.

Hollingshead's smile faded. "I'm afraid that's true, son." He looked Chapel straight in the eye. "Those aren't family members or friends," he said. "The word for them is—ah, there's no good word for it, let's say—let's call them—"

"Intended victims," Banks said.

Chapel frowned. He glanced down at the list again.

"It's a kill list," Banks went on.

Chapel nearly dropped the piece of paper.

Hollingshead waved his hands in the air as if he wanted to calm everyone down. "That sounds so very dramatic! It's not wholly inaccurate, though. The one thing we are certain of is that our detainees are going to go after these names and do everything they can to murder them. Keeping these people alive—"

"—is secondary," Banks butted in. "Taking out

the targets is the only thing you need to worry about. But with this list at least you know where they're headed."

Chapel scanned the list quickly, not bothering to memorize the names. He was more interested in the addresses for the moment. In his head he put together a map of the locations. New York City, Atlanta, Vancouver in Canada—that was going to be a jurisdictional nightmare—Chicago, Denver, Seattle, Alaska. That was an awful lot of ground to cover. But it was better than just going door-to-door throughout the entire continental United States, asking if anyone had seen a shaggy-haired man with a murderous disposition.

When he had the map in his head, he glanced over the names. A couple of them were doctors, by the look of it—or Ph.D.s, at least. He only recognized one of the names. "Hayes. Franklin Hayes—he's a federal judge. He's been in the news recently."

"The president chose him to be the next justice on the Supreme Court," Hollingshead said. "He's just waiting for the Senate to confirm his appointment."

Chapel wondered if that made his job harder or easier. Harder because if someone was gunning for a high-ranking judge it would be tough to keep it out of the papers. Easier because a man like that would already have some security.

"He'll be the first one you make contact with, of course," Banks said. "He's the highest-value target."

Chapel shook his head. "With all due respect, sir, he won't." He tapped the list with his artificial index finger. "Judge Hayes is on—what? The Tenth Circuit Court? The address for him here is in Denver. If the detainees are limited to traveling by train or by bus—" He glanced up for confirmation.

"So far that's what we've seen, yes," Hollingshead confirmed. "They don't have driver's licenses or passports. They won't be able to board an airplane. And they don't know how to drive a car. That's a small bit of luck, eh?"

"—then it will still take two days for one of them to arrive in Colorado."

"That sounds right," Hollingshead confirmed.

Chapel nodded. "Meanwhile we've got two names here in New York City. An hour and a half from the Catskills by train. A detainee could already be there. Two people are already at risk. It has to be my first stop."

"Whatever!" Banks said, throwing his hands in the air. "Just do it. Hollingshead, I want constant reporting on this. Total accountability from your office."

"Of course," Hollingshead said. He was staring Chapel right in the eye while he spoke. "I'll make sure to keep you in the loop."

"As for you," Banks said, jabbing a finger in Chapel's direction, "you do what you're told, you keep your mouth shut, and you end this problem as fast you goddamned well can. You need something from CIA, we'll provide it, as long as you keep our name out of things. You have a sidearm? You're going to need one. And I want you in civvies while you're working on this. I don't want the public to see an army asshole running around in full dress uniform, shooting at our targets."

"I would need to go home and change."

"There's a rack of civilian clothing in the room back there," Hollingshead said, gesturing at a door at the back of the bar. "You can take your pick. As for a sidearm, I've already thought of that." He reached behind the bar and produced a black pistol with the squared-off lines of a SIG Sauer P228—a weapon Chapel had handled more than once, since it was common issue among the armed forces. The army, which had to have its own name for everything, called it the M11.

"Nice weapon," Chapel said. At least here he could impress his superiors with his knowledge. "9x19 mm ammunition—the favorite cartridge of police and military units everywhere. Good stopping power, but without the kick of heavier ammo so you don't have to refocus after each shot. A short slide and barrel so it's easily concealed. Normally it takes a thirteen-round magazine but you've put the fifteen-round magazine from a P226 in there—you can tell by the way the magazine sticks a little way out of the grip. Not the fanciest gun in the world but one of the most dependable."

Hollingshead glanced at Banks, looking impressed. Banks just shrugged.

Hollingshead set the pistol down on the bar and came over to shake Chapel's hand. When Chapel held out his right hand, Hollingshead grasped it— then grabbed Chapel's artificial left hand as well. He didn't flinch at all when he touched the silicone. "All right, son. Go get changed while I finish up here with our civilian friend."

"Sir," Chapel said. He headed through the indicated door and found a little room beyond, a cloak-room by the look of it. Two Z-racks of men's suits stood there, each suit wrapped in plastic like they'd just come back from the dry cleaner's. Along one wall was a dresser full of crisp white shirts still wrapped in cellophane.

He took off his cap and started to unbutton his jacket when he heard voices from the bar room beyond. He closed the door to the cloakroom but not all the way. He wanted to hear what they had to say.

"—goddamned cripple, at least tell me that robot arm of his isn't his shooting arm," Banks grumbled.

"I assure you, I didn't just pick Chapel's name out of a hat," Hollingshead replied. "He's the man we want—the man we need for this. Given some of your preconditions and your damnable sensitivity issues."

"You'd better be right. For all of our sakes." Banks grumbled something else Chapel couldn't make out. Then he raised his voice and spoke more clearly. "You've got just as much to lose here as I do, Rupert."

"A point I am firmly aware of. Now why don't you and your crop-headed monster get out of my office, so I can get back to controlling this situation?"

Chapel had to grin at that. *Crop-headed monster.* He could think of worse names for Laughing Boy—plenty of them—but that one fit just fine.

When he'd finished dressing, he stepped back out of the cloakroom to find Banks and Laughing Boy gone. They hadn't even bothered to wish him good luck. Not that he minded much.

"Look at you!" Hollingshead said. "I wouldn't recognize you. Which I suppose is the point."

Chapel ran a hand down the front of his new suit. "I haven't worn one of these in a while. I've got my dress uniforms for formal occasions, and when I'm off duty, I'm more of a polo shirt and jeans man."

"How's the fit? In the, ah, shoulders?"

Chapel had ended up taking the slacks from one suit and the jacket from a bigger one. He needed extra room in the shoulders for two reasons. One was to give the clamps that held his arm on more room. The other was to give him space to conceal his sidearm.

They taught you all kinds of fun stuff in spy school, including how to dress yourself. "It's good."

He pulled down on the cuffs of the suit jacket and stared at the dark fabric. It was the wrong color. It wasn't green or blue. It wasn't a uniform. "Sir," he said, in a small voice—because if the army had taught him one thing above all others, it was how to show respect to a superior officer. "Sir. Please. I hate to even say this out loud. But . . . I *am* a cripple. I am too old for this job, and too long out of active duty. If this mission is as important as you say—"

"Son, I'm going to mark this little moment of doubt down to pressure. The stress of a new and daunting assignment." Hollingshead stood up straight and Chapel couldn't resist coming to attention. "We're going to pretend you never said that. And if you ever call yourself that horrible name again—cripple—I'm going to start believing it, and I can't afford that. You are the right man for this job. The only man for this job. Now. I'd ask if you're ready, if you need more time," Hollingshead said, "but we don't have that luxury. I'll take you to the helipad now, and you can get started."

THE PENTAGON: APRIL 12, T+6:21

As Hollingshead led Chapel up through various layers and corridors of the Pentagon, every soldier they passed stood to attention and saluted. Clearly they knew the man—and respected him. Chapel found himself grinning, despite the screwed-up situation he'd landed in. This was a whole other world from the cubicle farm at Fort Belvoir. This was the game—the Great Game, they used to call it.

As they made their way through the lobby toward the helipad deck, a squad of soldiers at the security checkpoint stopped in the middle of searching visitors and lined up by the door like they were competing for who got to hold it open. They watched Hollingshead like he was about to perform some kind of magic trick. Hollingshead might look like a stuffy old professor from Yale or Harvard, but these men knew better.

"I have a question, sir," Chapel said.

"You're free to ask, of course." Hollingshead's mouth curled in a funny kind of smile. "I'll tell you anything I can."

"I just wanted to know—how should I be addressing you? If I'm working for you now, I'd like to know whether I should call you Colonel . . . or General."

"Are those my only options? They used to call me Commodore. Then it was Rear Admiral."

"Sir," Chapel said, his spine stiffening. "Beg your pardon. I didn't realize you were in the navy."

"Try not to hold it against me," Hollingshead said. He waved the guards away and pushed the doors open himself, letting a gust of fresh air come blasting into the security lobby.

A helicopter—a Bell 407, painted in civilian colors and with no DoD markings at all—was waiting on the Pentagon's helipad. Its rotor was already spun up by the time Chapel and Hollingshead arrived.

The noise of the chopper was enough to make it difficult for Chapel to hear what Hollingshead was saying. He'd been rambling on about what kind of support Chapel would have in his mission—an unlimited budget, the ability to requisition police and National Guard units as required—but Chapel hadn't been listening with more than half an ear. He was too busy trying to remember what he knew about New York City, a place he'd only been a handful of times in his life.

"Captain," Hollingshead said, nearly shouting over the roar of the helicopter's engine.

"Hmm?"

"Captain! I'm about to commit an act of treason! I'd appreciate it if I could have some of your attention."

That made Chapel focus, and quickly. "Admiral," he said.

"You have a number of questions, I'm sure, which haven't been answered yet. I can't tell you everything, but I can give you a little more than you've heard so far."

Chapel could barely hear Hollingshead's voice over the roar of the rotor blades, but he leaned close to catch every word. He understood how serious this was.

"What happened this morning, at the camp, was a disaster. It was supposed to be impossible. It was also, in a way, the luckiest break we're likely to get."

"Admiral?"

"The CIA—Banks, specifically—was supposed to be in charge of any escapes from that camp. He had someone in our ranks there—a mole—who was supposed to call him if such a thing happened. For reasons no one knows, the mole failed to make that telephone call. Because it is a top secret DoD facility, it was put on my desk instead. My office was given oversight on this. I mobilized the capture teams immediately. You've guessed by now what happened to them. I was quite prepared to send more men, as many as it took—this is that big a threat. But by that time, Banks had finally heard what was going on. He went straight to the president and demanded he be given this operation.

"Because time was of the essence and I was already working on this, the commander in chief decided I should remain in charge. But Banks was given veto power over every move I made. He has not been shy about using that power. It was his decision to send a single man rather than multiple teams. He is far more concerned about maintaining secrecy in this matter than in actually capturing the fugitives."

"But if they're that dangerous—"

"He feels that allowing the public to know what's going on would be an even greater threat to national security," Hollingshead said. He shook his head sadly. "He's a smart man, but I can't say I approve of his priorities. He insisted that it had to be one man for this job. He wanted to send that goon of his, but I insisted I choose the man. Any number of twenty-five-year-old Navy SEALs came to mind, but no. I wanted someone who could be discreet, somebody with some experience—no cowboys. This isn't a job for a hit man; this is far more surgical. I picked you."

"I appreciate your faith in me, sir," Chapel said. Even though he couldn't claim to understand it.

"You're going to curse my name before this over, I don't doubt it. But I need you in this role. You are the last chance to keep this thing in Military Intelligence hands. If you fail, I fail as well. Banks will gain total control over this operation. He'll send his goon in and I think you can guess what would happen then. The cretin will kill every shaggy-haired man in a five-hundred-mile radius. The collateral damage will be astonishing, and terrible. You and I both swore an oath to protect the American people. It's you who's going to have to uphold that oath, because there can be no one else, now."

"I'll—I won't let you down," Chapel promised.

"I know what we've handed you, Captain. I know how I would feel about being given a mission like this and then being told I couldn't know any of the details. We're playing a rotten joke on you, frankly, and I'm sorry. It was Banks who insisted we send you out into this with an incomplete briefing, as well."

"I understand the need for secrecy, sir," Chapel said.

"I daresay you do. What neither you *nor* I

understand—at least not completely, not yet—is just how much is going on behind the scenes. Banks is playing a very deep strategy here. He's keeping me from telling you everything I know. But he can't keep you from finding things out on your own."

"Sir?"

"Keep your eyes open, out there. Put the clues together. If you're going to actually pull this off, that's the only way. Figure out what we're not telling you—and why we *can't* tell you. Banks won't like you peeling back the lid of his box of secrets, but he can't stop you, not if you're smart about it."

Chapel nodded in understanding.

"Whatever you do," Hollingshead said, "keep yourself alive. It's imperative to me that you don't get killed out there."

"I—sir, that's—"

"Because, Captain, I don't have time to find a replacement. Now get going! I've got a little surprise for you en route. You'll get to meet your new partner."

He shook Chapel's hand and headed back into the Pentagon.

Leaving Chapel all alone—with a job to do.

BROOKLYN, NEW YORK: APRIL 12, T+6:29

In Brooklyn an old woman was just being roused from sleep. The bedside light came on with a click, and Dr. Helen Bryant's eyes flickered open. She had been in the middle of her midday nap and felt somewhat annoyed at being awoken. Then she looked up and saw a face looming over hers and fear caught flame inside her chest.

"Please," she said, clutching the sheets in her fists. "Don't hurt me. I don't keep any drugs here. They're at my clinic."

The face hovering over her was broad and cruel. Male, perhaps twenty-five years old. His hair and beard were hacked short, as if he'd cut them himself, and his eyes were hidden by large sunglasses. If she'd been a little more awake, she might have known what that meant.

"Relax," he told her, his voice a low growl that held a purr of violence ticking over like an idling engine. She tried to sit up, but a thick hand pressed down between her breasts and pushed her back. She couldn't fight that hand—it was like struggling against an industrial press. She could feel the bones of her rib cage flex as he pushed down harder. "I said relax. My name is Brody. You know what I am."

"You're not here for drugs," she said, because she was beginning to understand who Brody was. What he was.

"I said you know what I am," Brody said. "Don't mess with me." He leaned down over her, close enough she could smell the dirt on his skin. "I came a long way to find you. I had to know."

He reached up and took off his sunglasses. She had known already what she would see underneath, but still she gasped. His eyes were black from side to side. There were no irises, no whites, just featureless shiny black. Looking into them she felt like she was looking into a darkened room—anything at all could be in there. There would be no predicting Brody's behavior, she knew. He seemed calm enough now, but he could erupt in violence at the slightest provocation. He was strong enough that if that happened, one little old lady was not going to survive his wrath.

"You shouldn't be here," she said. "How did you get out?"

"I'll ask the fucking questions!" Brody shouted. He grabbed the metal bed frame underneath her and yanked hard, throwing the mattress, the box spring, and Dr. Bryant to the floor. She struggled with the sheets wrapped around her neck and arms and tried to scuttle away as he reached down with inhuman speed and grabbed her by the shoulder.

"No," she screamed, as his fingers closed around her clavicle and crushed it into powder. Pain ran screaming up and down her body as her arm twitched wildly against the floorboards. "Please—please just—tell me what you want to know! I'll tell you anything!"

Brody let her go. "That's better." He walked over to the door and shut it carefully. For a while he didn't look at her. He stared down at his hands, at the floor. "That's . . . better. Just everybody relax." Was he talking to himself, as much as to her?

He sat down in the chair by her dressing table. He dropped into it hard enough to make it creak, as if he wasn't used to fragile furniture. She supposed he wouldn't be. "You left us there. You just left us."

Dr. Bryant was in horrible pain, but she knew she had to do something. The telephone on the bed-side table was useless. There was no way help could reach her in time. There was a pen, there, however, perched on top of the crossword puzzle she'd been working on before she fell asleep. She grasped it with her weak left hand and fumbled the cap off.

"You—you didn't want us anymore," Brody said, his anger back to a low simmer. Dr. Bryant knew that the comparative calm wouldn't last. He rubbed at his hair and face with both hands. "I guess we didn't work out, huh?" A nasty grin crossed his face. "I guess we just weren't good enough."

Dr. Bryant dropped the pen. She'd managed to scrawl a message on the wall next to the bed frame. Nothing complex, but enough that the right people would understand what it meant. Assuming the right people ever saw it.

"Brody," she said, "It wasn't like that. It wasn't—"

"You said you were our mother! You stood up on the platform, and you shouted it through a loudspeaker. You were our mother, and you were going to take care of us! Make sure we were okay!"

"We did what we could," she pleaded. "It wasn't safe to—to get any closer. We sent you food, and clothes. Toys—"

"You're pretty stupid for a doctor, huh?" Brody asked. He dropped to his knees next to her and smashed her across the face with a hand like a lion's paw. "Stupid! Stupid! I know how to read, you stupid bitch! You gave us *books*. You gave us books so we could read. Did you think we wouldn't figure out what a mother was supposed to be?" He struck her again and again. "In the books, the mothers hugged their children. They loved them! You never loved us," he said, and his voice was a roar.

"It wasn't safe," she begged, in between blows.

"It wasn't safe—we couldn't—we couldn't—please stop! Please!"

Brody stopped hitting her across the face. For a moment he glared at her, his nostrils flaring. "This isn't going right."

She could only stare up at him. Blood ran down her face in streams.

"This isn't what I expected. I thought I was going to come and talk to you, just talk. That I could learn something here. But I just keep getting frustrated." He shook his head from side to side.

"Brody," she managed to squeak out, "Brody, I'm hurt. I'll . . . I'll tell you anything. I'll . . . I'll be your mother if you want, just—"

"You know what I am. You know we don't *do well* with frustration," he said. Then he grabbed her by her hurt arm and threw her across the room to smash against the vanity table on the far wall. She just had time to see her own screaming face in the mirror before she crashed into the glass with a shattering, tooth-rattling noise.

Brody hurt her more after that but thankfully she felt very little of it. She was dead long before he was finished.

IN TRANSIT: APRIL 12, T+6:46

Partner?

Chapel thought maybe Hollingshead had meant the helicopter pilot. When he climbed on board, though, he saw that the pilot was an air force kid who couldn't be more than twenty-five—and who had no idea who Chapel was, where he was going, or what his mission was.

Chapel pulled on a crash helmet and moved the integrated microphone around so the pilot could hear him. "New York City—as fast as we can get there."

The pilot confirmed, and in a moment they were airborne. The chopper cut a wide arc around the Pentagon then slewed northeast, headed straight over Washington.

Chapel sat back in his seat and let his gaze wander over the landscape. He considered taking a nap. It was going to be a long flight and there wasn't much he could do until they arrived. He was too keyed up, though. Too excited—and scared—and worried—to even think about closing his eyes.

Instead he could only let his mind race, thinking over everything he needed to accomplish, everything he could reasonably do to catch the detainees before they killed again. And about how it might already be too late for the first name on the kill list.

He was lost in his own thoughts when a voice spoke in his ear.

"Good morning, Captain," a woman said.

It was the smokiest, most sultry voice Chapel had ever heard. It was like someone was stroking his ear with a velvet glove.

He glanced over at the pilot, then back at the empty seats behind him. Whoever this woman was, she wasn't onboard.

"No," she said, with a chiding laugh. "I'm not there with you."

"Who are you?" he asked.

"Why don't you go ahead and think of me as your guardian angel?" she suggested.

"What do you mean, guardian angel?" Chapel asked.

The pilot of the helicopter glanced over at him briefly, then shrugged and went back to flying the chopper. Apparently the pilot wasn't hearing the voice in his ear.

That was probably for the best.

"Director Hollingshead asked me to keep an eye on you, cutie," the voice said. "I work directly for him, normally, but for the next few days I'm all yours."

"He mentioned something about a partner. What's your name?"

"Well, my initials are NTK."

He smiled despite himself. In other words, her very name was Need to Know. "So you're the secretive type. I can handle that," he told her. "Let's just run down the list, shall we? What is your current location? What's your rank? What's your official job description?"

"All those things are classified, and you know it. You're playing with me," she said.

"Just establishing some ground rules. All right. Let's try another one. Are you going to be waiting for me when I land in New York?" Chapel asked. "Surely you can answer that, since I'll find out one way or another in an hour."

"Captain, I'll *always* be with you. But this is as physical as I get. The sweet little voice in your ear, making helpful comments and keeping you company. I've already been briefed on your operation, and I'm looking for ways right now to help."

"I'm not sure I understand."

The voice sighed, just a little. "Let's put it this way. While you're in the field you're not going to have a lot of time to check your voice mail or look things up on Wikipedia. I'll do all that for you. If you need a map to your next target, I'll send it straight to your phone. I guess, if you really wanted to get on my bad side, you could call me your secretary. I'll keep you up to date, I'll file your reports with the DIA, and I'll make any phone calls you don't have time to make. But I can be so much more to you. I can coordinate with law enforcement and the National Guard. I can make sure people know you're coming and stay out of your way. I can get into any computer system and make it purr for you."

"Any computer? You're a hacker?"

"What an ugly little word that is. But yes. Any computer, any microchip that's hooked up to the Internet. For instance, I can do this."

She went silent for a moment and Chapel wondered what it was she thought she was doing— breaking into his bank account? Changing his e-mail password?

Then he saw his own hand come up in front of his face. His left hand. The hand rotated to face him and then the fingers wiggled. His hand was waving at him.

Sweat broke out on his forehead. He hadn't told the arm to do that—he couldn't even feel what it was doing. He grabbed the wrist of his artificial arm and forced it down into his lap. It tried to fight him, to break out of his grip, but he held on as hard as he could.

Apparently this guardian angel could take control of his arm. Any time she wanted. It had a wireless Internet connection built in, he knew that—the microcomputer built into its circuitry had to get firmware updates from time to time—but he had never considered for a moment before that that might be a security flaw.

If she could do it—anybody could.

Adrenaline surged through his body, and he fought down an urge to tear the arm off his shoulder and throw it out the helicopter's window.

Slowly he fought to regain control of himself. He glanced over at the pilot. The kid was looking at him out of the corner of his eye. He was frowning. He must have seen the whole thing.

The embarrassment helped Chapel slow his heart rate and start breathing again.

"Angel," he said, because she still hadn't told him her name.

"Ooh, I like that," she said. "From now on, that's what you'll call me."

"Angel," he said, almost growling, "don't ever do that again. Seriously."

"I know that was a little naughty of me—"

"Angel!" he interrupted. "I'm an amputee. I lost a part of myself once, do you understand? Can you understand why I would be a little sensitive about losing it again?"

She said nothing. Hopefully she was feeling terribly guilty and was too embarrassed to say anything.

"Let me show you what that was like," he told

her, because he was very close to getting furious. Nobody messed with his arm. "I'm not supposed to know anything about you. But I know you aren't military. You're a civilian."

"That's—that's strictly NTK," she gasped. "Who told you that?"

"You did."

She didn't sound so playful anymore. "Damn it, Captain. If I have a breach, I need to know about it *right now*. This is national security tech I'm working with here—if it's been compromised—"

"Relax," he told her. "Nobody's hacked your system. I just used my amazing powers of deduction. You referred to our mutual boss as Director Hollingshead. That's probably his official job title. But anyone who'd ever served in the armed forces would know better—they would call him *Admiral* Hollingshead."

That long, uneasy silence again. Maybe she was thinking that if he could figure that out he was dangerous to her. Maybe she was about to tell his arm to strangle him.

When she came back on the line, though, her voice was as sweet and sexy as it had ever been. "I think I'm going to *like* you," she said. "You're going to keep me on my toes. Well, we have just tons of work to do, don't we? Where do you want to get started?"

Chapel shook his head. This was not exactly what he'd expected when Hollingshead told him he was going to get a partner.

IN TRANSIT: APRIL 12, T+7:32

"First things first. I'll be in New York soon. The address I'm headed for is in southern Brooklyn. Is there a helipad nearby?"

"Very near by. The address you're thinking of," Angel said, "is in Brighton Beach, and there's a heliport less than a mile away, just the other side of Marine Park." Chapel's BlackBerry turned itself on and vibrated in his pocket. He took it out and looked at the map shown on the screen. Angel highlighted both the address he wanted and the location of the heliport. "You caught a break there—it's about to turn into rush hour in New York. If you had to touch down in Manhattan, you could have been looking at an hour ride on the subway."

"Considering my mission I don't think the subway would have been appropriate," Chapel pointed out.

"Sweetie, in New York, during a workday? The subway is the *only* way to get around. But seeing how close you'll be, I'll have a car waiting for you when you arrive. See how useful I can be? I'll get you a visual reference on the address as well, so you know when you get there and don't have to go hunting for house numbers."

"Good," Chapel said. "How long until I land?" He glanced out the window and saw urban sprawl beneath him, but that meant nothing—most of the land between D.C. and New York was built up to one degree or another.

"Not for another half an hour yet."

"Okay. You have my list of addresses." He didn't

want to call it a *kill list*, not when the pilot might be listening. "Can you get phone numbers for each of those names? I want to call them all now and make sure they know they're in trouble."

"That's just a piece of cake, sugar. But are you sure you want to do that?"

"Why not?" Chapel asked.

"Not to be a pill, but part of your job is making sure this doesn't get any public attention. If you tell these people that crazed lunatics are coming for them, what's to stop them from going to the media?"

Chapel frowned. "If I talk to them the right way, make sure they know that's not in their best interests, I think we can minimize that. The last thing these people want to do is advertise their locations. I just want to make sure they get somewhere safe, like a police station or an army base. Somewhere we can protect them."

"Director Banks isn't going to like that," Angel chided.

"We don't work for him. I'll handle any blowback. But I won't have these people made into sitting ducks. I'll do anything in my power to keep them alive."

Angel clucked her tongue. The sound was annoyingly loud in Chapel's headphones. "I should really run this past Director—Admiral—Hollingshead."

"Do what you have to do, Angel, but get me those phone numbers. These are human beings. They're American citizens. They have a right to protect themselves. That's not something the intelligence community gets to take away when it's convenient."

"Yeah," she said. "Yeah. Jim—"

"Call me Chapel. Everybody does."

"Okay. Chapel. I'll get those numbers. And I'll make the calls for you, that's part of my job. I'm sorry I questioned you. I don't ever get to meet the people whose lives I touch. Sometimes I forget that sort of thing."

"It's an occupational hazard. We're in the business of protecting people, but to do that, sometimes we can't tell them the whole truth. Sometimes we have to lie to them, frankly. If you do that long enough, you forget that it's not a good thing. People like Banks forget that's a regrettable necessity, not the whole of their job. I won't make that mistake, not if I can help it."

"Thanks, cutie. Okay, I'll take care of that. Anything else?"

"I need as much information on those people as you can dig up. I need to know what they do for a living, where they hang out after work, what kind of family they have."

"Want their shoe sizes? I can get those," Angel joked.

"I somehow doubt that," Chapel told her.

"Seriously? Do you know how many people buy their shoes online these days? People are lazy. They'll do anything they can online because then they don't have to get off the couch. Look at me— I'm saving the world and I can do it from my bathtub, if I feel like it."

Chapel fought down the urge to ask if she was in the bath right at that moment. He had work to do. *Focus*, he thought. "Okay. Okay. The real thing I want to know is why they're on that list. You have any idea about that, Angel?"

"I didn't get any details you haven't already heard," she told him. "Looking at this list, I don't see any immediate connections. Maybe something'll come up as I get more facts on them. Let's start with the first name on your list—the one in Brighton Beach. Name, Bryant, Dr. Helen. Lives on Neptune Avenue. Sounds like a fun place. Occupation: Genetic Counselor."

"What's a genetic counselor?" Chapel asked.

"Let me Google her . . . ooh, she's got a website! I love it when they have websites. Nice-looking lady, if your taste runs to older women. Looks like she's an ob-gyn. She sees pregnant women and helps them find out if their babies are healthy, and what they can do if it turns out the babies have genetic problems. Oh my God, that must be the saddest job in the world sometimes. Can you imagine?"

"I've never had kids. Never got the chance," Chapel said.

"A man of your age should have a wife, Chapel. A wife and lots of happy little healthy babies. I'm finding all kinds of stuff about Dr. Bryant here. Looks like she's pretty famous in certain circles—she's won all kinds of awards, gotten commendations from numerous institutes, worked for the National Institutes of Health for a long time . . . did fieldwork in Africa during the early part of the AIDS crisis. Weird, looks like there's a police bulletin about her too. Let me just take a peek . . ."

Chapel imagined Angel crouched forward looking at her computer screen, scanning through dozens of web pages at once. When she didn't come back on the line after a few seconds, he began to wonder what she'd found. "Angel? Is everything okay?"

"No, sweetie. It's not. At least, not for Dr. Bryant."

IN TRANSIT: APRIL 12, T+8:02

"Goddamn it, no!" Chapel shouted, and he punched the instrument panel of the helicopter with his good fist. The pilot started to protest, but the look on Chapel's face must have warned him off. "She can't be dead. I can't be too late."

"The police are already on the scene," Angel told him.

"Damn it," Chapel said, but more muted this time. He'd known how tight the time frame was, known that people had already died at the hands of the detainees. But this was the first civilian—the others had been military personnel. That didn't make their deaths much easier to bear. But they'd known what they were getting into, or at least known they were dealing with dangerous people. Nobody had even told Dr. Bryant she was in danger.

"Do you still want to go to Brooklyn?" Angel asked. "I can change your flight plan and take you to the next address instead."

"No," Chapel said. "No. I need to see the crime scene. There might be some evidence there that can help me track this bastard. And we know he was in the area recently—maybe I can catch him now before he moves on to the next target."

"All right, Chapel. You'll be on the ground in a few minutes."

The chopper curved in over New York Harbor and then made a straight line across Brooklyn, an endless sea of two- and three-story buildings, rows of brownstones and warehouses and churches punctuated in only a few places by taller structures. The pilot shed altitude as they came in over a rectangular slice of greenery by the ocean. It looked like a salt marsh. On the far side Chapel saw the heliport, a commercial pad with a few civilian choppers sitting dormant. Chapel slapped the pilot's shoulder in thanks, and the kid gave him a thumbs-up. Before the skids had even touched asphalt, Chapel jumped out of the side hatch. It felt good to have his feet on solid ground again, though he knew it would take a while before his head stopped thrumming with the sound of the rotor blades.

The chopper lifted off again as soon as he was clear. It would head for the nearest air base where it could refuel, in case he needed it again in a hurry. In a few seconds it was gone from view and Chapel could hear nothing but ocean waves and distant car traffic. The silence was a dramatic change.

"Did you get me that car?" Chapel asked, and when Angel didn't answer, it took him a second to realize he'd left his headphones in the chopper. He reached for his BlackBerry, wondering how he would make contact with her—she hadn't exactly given him her phone number.

Before he had a chance to call the DIA and ask to be connected to the sexiest-sounding woman working there, someone called his name and he looked up.

A courier in a FedEx uniform came jogging up and handed Chapel a package. He signed for it, and the courier left before Chapel could figure out who was sending him a parcel at a heliport he'd never heard of an hour ago.

He tore open the package and found a cell phone inside, still in its box. There was a plastic blister package in the parcel as well, holding a tiny in-ear attachment for the phone.

He managed to get all the packaging undone without too much trouble. The new phone was a touch-screen model that was all screen and no buttons. He'd always wanted one of those, frankly—the tiny keys on his BlackBerry were hard to use with his less sensitive artificial fingers. He put the earpiece in his ear and powered on the phone. It looked like its batteries had a decent charge.

"Let me guess," he said, as the screen lit up. "Is that you, Angel?"

"Hi, sweetie," she said. "I figured it was time for an upgrade."

"You know, it's DoD policy that we only use BlackBerrys," he told her. "This brand is a no-no."

"It's got sixteen times the memory and twice the screen resolution. I'm a high-definition kind of girl. It works with the 4G network and Wi-Fi and the best hands-free transceiver on the market. Namely the one in your ear right now. Keep it there—and keep the phone in your pocket—and we never have to be apart. Sound good?"

"I'm receiving you loud and clear."

"Good. And, sweetie, you don't have to shout. Just talk normally and I'll hear you. In fact, I'll hear everything you do, so I can give you advice on the fly. Your car is waiting at the entrance to the heliport. We'll get you to Dr. Bryant's place right away. In the meantime, I'll walk you through the process of migrating all your data from your old phone. I can do most of that for you from here."

What was it Top had told him about living in George Jetson land?

"Okay," Chapel said, as he jogged out of the chain-link gate of the heliport. A black car—a Crown Victoria, just like the one Laughing Boy drove—was waiting for him. He had an appointment with a dead woman.

BROOKLYN, NEW YORK: APRIL 12, T+8:12

Neptune Avenue was lined with modest houses and convenience stores, pizza parlors and medical clinics. The air smelled of the ocean and pasta sauce and was filled with the noise of cars and thumping radios. Dr. Bryant's house was a simple two-story structure with bars over its windows and a steel-core reinforced door.

"Looks like she was worried about security," Chapel said. "Not that it helped."

"That's pretty standard for New York," Angel told him. "Police records say she's had a couple break-ins before, as well. People who saw her name on the door—saw she was a doctor—and broke in looking for drugs."

"Does she keep an office here?" Chapel asked.

"No, this was just her home. Her office and her lab are a few blocks away. This is kind of a run-down area for somebody like her. I guess she wanted to live near her patients. By the looks of things, they were mostly Russian immigrants."

"You have access to her medical records?"

"Nothing privileged, though I could probably get that without too much trouble if you need it," Angel told him. "I don't see anything that stands out, right now. I don't see anything that would have made her any enemies."

"One was enough," Chapel said. He gritted his teeth and walked up to the door. A single strand of yellow police tape crossed the opening, and a uniformed police officer was standing just inside. She stared at his ID with a skeptical eye, but she let him through. Angel had already talked to the local cops and let them know he was coming.

The house was dark inside, and it took a while for his eyes to adjust. When they did, he saw the place was full of police photographers and detectives drinking coffee from Styrofoam cups. He would have preferred to visit the scene alone, but that wasn't an option.

He heard someone crying loudly in the back of the house—probably a kitchen back there; he could see the side of a refrigerator through an open door. The last thing he wanted at that moment was to be questioned by a grieving relative, so he headed up the stairs instead—that was where Angel told him Dr. Bryant had been discovered.

"I'm getting some preliminary reports now; they

were just filed by the detectives on the scene," Angel said in his ear. "Chapel, this isn't going to be pretty. It sounds like she was beaten to death in her bedroom."

"I've seen dead people before," he told her.

A detective in a cheap suit, wearing a police laminate on a lanyard around his neck, looked up and stared at Chapel. "Who the hell are you?" he demanded.

Chapel flashed his ID again, but the detective shook his head.

"How about you just tell me, instead of making me read the fine print on that thing? I figure you have a right to be here or we would have turned you away at the door. But you're no cop. I'm guessing . . . military?"

Chapel bit his lip, but said nothing.

The detective scratched at the stubble on his chin. He looked like a tough old bastard. He looked like a drill instructor Chapel had known in basic training, frankly. He looked like the kind of guy who was used to being lied to and didn't like it at all.

"I can't answer your questions," Chapel said. "I can't tell you anything. This murder is of interest to—"

"DHS," Angel whispered in his ear.

"The Department of Homeland Security," Chapel said. It was a lie, but it wasn't a ridiculous one.

The detective's eyes went wide. "Yeah, okay. I know that score." He stepped aside and let Chapel past.

"That was too easy," Chapel said under his breath.

"This is New York, sweetie. This is where 9/11

happened. They understand terrorism here—and nobody will bother a DHS agent."

"Good thinking, Angel." Chapel stepped through another doorway and walked into the crime scene proper.

He may have seen dead bodies before. He had seen the aftermath of terrorist attacks in Afghanistan. This was different, though, and his breath caught in his throat.

Dr. Helen Bryant was lying on the floor, twisted into an unnatural shape. She'd been thrown into a mirror and pieces of broken glass were everywhere, a shoal of them covering part of her face. That was a small mercy. She was an elderly woman. A little old lady. No little old lady should ever have this happen to them. It was just so . . . wrong.

One of the detainees had done this. Chapel suddenly wanted very much to kill the son of a bitch. He wanted to make the guy suffer.

Chapel forced himself to squat down and take a closer look, much as he wanted to just turn away and shake his head. He made himself look at the wounds on Dr. Bryant's body, the broken bones, the lacerations. There were no gunshot wounds, and no sign that she'd been cut with a knife.

The bastard had done this with his hands.

"Do you need us to move her?" someone asked from behind him. It wasn't the detective who had questioned him. This was a paramedic, or maybe somebody from the coroner's department. "We're almost done taking fiber and hair samples. If you need something, just ask."

Chapel looked up at the paramedic. She was

black, in her midthirties, and she looked like she was in awe of the DHS agent who had graced her crime scene with his presence.

Damn, Chapel thought. Angel's ruse had gotten him this far, but now it might cause problems. If the cops thought this case was somehow connected to terrorist activity, they might start asking questions. Well, he decided, that was for Angel or Hollingshead to take care of. He had tougher problems to solve.

He put his hands on his knees and started to straighten up. Turning his face away from the body, he caught something out of the corner of his eye. "What's that?" he asked.

The paramedic came over to stand next to him, taking care not to step on any evidence as she did so. Together they looked at the bedside table. A book of crossword puzzles and a pen lay on the floor next to the bed, and just above them, on the wall, someone had scrawled a single word.

Chapel moved closer. The letters were shaky and hard to make out, as if they'd been written by someone with a broken arm, someone in a panic, somebody who knew she was about to die. He had no doubt that Dr. Bryant had written the word.

She must have been trying to leave some kind of clue, maybe even to identify her killer. *She could have been more clear about it*, Chapel thought, and then scolded himself for thinking uncharitable thoughts about the dead. Still, he had no idea what the message meant:

CHIMERA

BROOKLYN, NEW YORK: APRIL 12, T+8:20

"Angel," Chapel said, "you ever heard of something called Chimera?"

"Sounds familiar. Give me a second." He heard the faint sound of clacking keys and knew she must be looking it up on the Internet. "Right . . . for one thing, you're saying it wrong, sweetie. It's not 'chim-ur-uh,' it's 'kai-mare-uh.' It's a monster from Greek mythology—a lion with a goat head coming out of its back and a snake for a tail."

"I'm guessing Dr. Bryant wasn't killed by some kind of weird lion creature," Chapel told her. "It's got to be something else. Was there a Project Chimera? Maybe something the CIA was involved in? Maybe that was the name of the place where the detainees were held."

"No, nothing like that is showing up. And I've got access to some pretty weird databases, so I'd expect at least a footnote somewhere."

He glanced over his shoulder to see if the paramedic was listening, but she had stepped out of the room, maybe to tell the detective about the scrawled message on the wall. Chapel stood up straight, ignoring his protesting knees.

"Maybe it's a person's name," Angel suggested. "Or at least an alias."

"Maybe," Chapel said. At the very least it was a clue. Dr. Bryant had died to give him this information. It had to mean something.

But it was going to have to wait. Dr. Bryant was dead—there was nothing more he could do for her.

There was one other name on the kill list that was located in New York City. He needed to get moving.

At the door the detective was waiting for him. "Anything you can share?" he asked.

Chapel shook his head and started to push past the man.

"Maybe you should talk to the daughter," the detective told him.

"Daughter?"

The detective nodded. "You probably heard her on your way in—she's in the kitchen, grieving pretty hard for her mom. She's the one who found the body. They were supposed to have lunch together today."

Chapel's heart went out to Dr. Bryant's daughter, but it wasn't his job to console anyone. His job was to make sure nobody else's kids had to mourn their parents today. "Did she give you anything you can use? Did she see anybody running away from the house, or tell you about any enemies Dr. Bryant might have had? Otherwise—"

The detective shrugged and pulled a notepad out of his jacket pocket. "Julia Taggart, thirty-two, lives in Bushwick. No, nothing like that. We liked her for this at first—the skinny is she and her mom had some fights, just screaming matches. But I've seen what people look like after they kill their moms and she ain't the type, she—"

"Taggart," Chapel said, his eyes going wide.

"Yeah," the detective said, "that's her name, does that mean something to you?"

Angel's voice sounded in his ear. "It definitely means something to me," she said.

"Taggart—not Bryant," Chapel said.

The detective nodded. "Sure. The deceased and her husband split up back in the late nineties, nothing weird about it, just a divorce. Dr. Bryant went back to using her maiden name, but the daughter kept her dad's."

"Number seven on the kill list is Dr. William Taggart," Angel said. "He lives in Alaska."

Chapel had already made that connection. "Yeah. I definitely want to talk to her," he told the detective.

He was led down the stairs and back into the kitchen. Afternoon sunlight streamed in through lace curtains and gave the room a yellow glow. There were cops everywhere, most of them just standing around in black uniforms or suit jackets. In the middle of this tableau, sitting at the kitchen table, was a woman in her early thirties wearing a white lab coat. Her eyes were smeared with half-melted makeup, and a teardrop had gathered on the point of her chin. She had fiery red hair that fell to her shoulders, and under the lab coat she was wearing jeans and a black sweater, with a single strand of pearls around her neck.

A cop with a notepad was trying to talk to her, but Julia Taggart just kept shaking her head. The cop wanted to clarify some details of her story, but Julia could only mutter short responses. She was clearly devastated by her mother's death.

This isn't going to be easy, Chapel thought. But he had to ask her some questions before he moved on. "Miss Taggart?" he said. The cops parted to let him through. "Julia? My name is Chapel. I'm so sorry for your loss."

She looked up at him with hopeful eyes. Like maybe he was going to come tell her that her mom wasn't really dead, that it had all been a terrible mistake.

Chapel had seen that look before. When he'd got back from Afghanistan, he had visited the family of every one of the Rangers who died the day he lost his arm. He had thought he could bring them some comfort, at least let them know their sons or brothers or husbands had died for a good cause.

Every time he'd been completely stalled—flummoxed—by that same look. That look of final, unthinking hope in the face of utter desolation.

Chapel wanted to run away. He wanted to do anything in the world except talk to this woman, now. What could he possibly tell her? *I'm so sorry, but your mother is dead and you can never know who did it, or why they did it, and even if I do catch them, I can't even tell you that.* All because the CIA didn't want its secrets getting out.

He bit his lip, hard, and sat down next to her.

"We'll get this guy," he told her. It was all he was allowed to say—the only shred of comfort he was legally allowed to give. He hated his job sometimes. "Maybe you can help me get him. I just need to know a few things."

She looked away, her eyes darting from his face. He hadn't told her what she wanted to hear. "I've already answered all your questions," she said.

Chapel didn't doubt the police had asked her a million things already, all the usual questions you asked in an investigation like this. He had a few he was pretty sure she hadn't heard before. He glanced at the cop with the notepad, though. He definitely didn't want what he was going to say written down.

"Maybe I can take you somewhere and buy you a cup of coffee," he told her. "Maybe getting away from this house will help jog your memory."

"I just . . . want to go home, now," she said, looking right into his eyes. "Can I go home? Please?"

Chapel turned to look for the detective—the man he assumed was in charge here.

"Sure," the detective said. "You want me to call a patrol unit to take her there?"

Angel spoke in his ear. "I'll have a cab out front by the time you get out the door."

"That won't be necessary," Chapel told the detective. "I'll make sure she gets home okay. Do you need to sign her out or anything?"

The detective shrugged. "We've got her information."

Chapel got up from the table and offered Julia a hand getting up. She shook him off and rose on her own, though she looked a little wobbly. She followed Chapel out of the house and down to the sidewalk where, as promised, a cab was waiting for them.

Julia stared at the cab as if she'd never seen one before. She was in shock, of course, but she pulled herself together visibly and said, "I live on—"

"Woodbine Street. Don't worry," Chapel said. Angel had already given him the address. "I've got this taken care of."

He opened her door for her and offered his arm as she started to climb in. Too late he realized he'd given her his left arm. Her hand brushed his silicone fingers and stopped there. Without getting into the cab, she stopped and lifted his artificial hand and peered at it like she was looking at a specimen through a microscope.

"Oh," she said. "This is really lifelike. I didn't even notice until just now. What is this, a DEKA Luke arm? I've read about these."

Chapel frowned. "It's the most recent version. Technically it's still just a prototype, but—"

"Typically they only give these to soldiers who have lost limbs in combat," she said. She'd had one leg inside the cab. Now she removed it and put her foot down firmly on the sidewalk. "Mr. Chapel," she said, "you're clearly not a policeman. I'm not going anywhere with you until you tell me exactly what's going on here."

BROOKLYN, NEW YORK: APRIL 12, T+8:31

"This one's sharp. Watch out, honey," Angel said.

Chapel set his jaw. "Miss Taggart—"

"It's Dr. Taggart. I'm a vet," the woman told him.

Chapel's eyes went wide. "Really?" That surprised him—she hadn't seemed the type. "Which branch of service?"

"I beg your pardon?"

"Were you in the army, the navy, the air force?"

She rolled her eyes. "I'm a veterinarian. Okay, I think we're done. I'll get my own cab, thanks." She turned and started to walk away.

"Dr. Taggart," he said, putting a little iron in his voice. The tone they'd taught him to use in officer training.

She stopped, but she didn't turn around.

"Your mother's dead, and her killer is still at large. Your father is William Taggart, right? He's in danger, too. A lot of people are in danger, and I'm trying to save them."

"My father is on the other side of the continent," she said, whirling around to glare at him. "This was just some random act of violence. Get your story straight."

"Your mother wasn't killed by some crazy drug addict looking for a fix," he told her. Even saying that much was risking his mission, but he needed to convince her of the urgency of things. "She was targeted. Singled out."

She didn't reply. She didn't walk away, either.

"If I'm going to stop what happened to your mother from happening again, I need some answers, and I need them now."

She walked toward him, coming close enough to get right up in his face. "My whole life people have kept secrets from me. I don't enjoy it. Are you going to tell me the truth, Mr. Chapel?"

"It's Captain Chapel. That's one true thing," he replied.

Her eyes took very careful measure of his face. He felt like he was being dissected in a laboratory. She shook her head—but then she got into the cab.

He climbed in beside her. The cabdriver turned and looked back at them. "You know you've been on the meter this whole time, right?"

BROOKLYN, NEW YORK: APRIL 12, T+8:37

As the cab crawled through Brooklyn traffic, Chapel watched the city go by. It seemed to take forever to pass each house, each little corner store. Time was ticking away and there was no way to get the minutes back. Chapel thought about what Angel had told him—in New York City, the subway was apparently the only way to get anywhere in a timely fashion. He should have listened to her.

"I really am sorry for your loss," he told the woman sitting beside him. "That was true, too. It's got to be . . . tough." He reached for more words of sympathy but they were hard to find. "I didn't know Dr. Bryant, but by all accounts she was a good person."

"Thanks. I guess," she said. "Yeah. She was a real saint. As long as you weren't her daughter."

"The two of you didn't get along?" The detective had said so, but he wanted to hear it from her own lips.

"We fought. I was a disappointment to her, and she never let me forget it. She wanted me to go into the family business and I didn't."

"She wanted you to become a genetic counselor?"

Julia shrugged. "Not specifically, not necessarily. But she and Dad were both scientists, *real* scientists, as she would say. They were geneticists. They met in grad school, at Oxford. He was working on a second doctorate while she got her first." She rubbed at her eyes and then stared at her hands when they came away covered in melted eye shadow. "Ugh. Do you want to know how he convinced her to marry him? He drew a Punnett square. That's a chart you make, it matches up the genes two organisms have and shows how likely their offspring are to have a certain trait. He showed Mom that if they had kids, there was a statistically significant probability they would have red hair."

"I guess it worked," Chapel said.

She grabbed a strand of her hair and pulled it around toward her eyes as if she were checking what color it was. Letting it go, she said, "Too bad he couldn't predict how they would actually get along. He left us when I was a teenager. Most of what I remember of them is the two of them shouting at each other."

"Why did they split up?"

"Like I said, people keep secrets from me. Mom would never explain—she just said it was a disagreement over ethics. Which could mean he slept around, or it could mean they differed on their views of stem cell research. Either way I'd believe it. She made him sound like the worst man on earth."

"What about you? Do you get along with him?"

"I haven't spoken to him in years," she said. "And then it was just on the phone."

Chapel tapped on the window with his real fingers. This wasn't going anywhere. He needed to get back on track. "Did your mother have an interest in mythology?" he asked.

"What on earth does that have to do with anything?" She had taken a tissue from her purse and was angrily wiping the makeup from around her eyes. When he didn't reply, she threw herself back in the cab seat and sighed. "No. I don't remember her ever talking about mythology."

Chapel nodded. "Did she know any Greek people? Maybe someone who would wish her harm?"

"Maybe the guy who runs the diner where she got breakfast."

"Cute, but not helpful, Dr. Taggart."

She sneered at him. "I have no reason to be either, so far. When are you going to start telling me what's going on?"

He could see in her eyes she was done answering questions until he gave her something. He tried to think of the best way to be evasive without sounding evasive. "The man who killed your mother had her name and address. He also had your father's."

She stared at him as if he'd told her he was an alien and he'd just come from the moon. "My mother was assassinated?" she asked.

"I know that's going to come as a shock—"

"But it's been twenty years. Why now?"

It was Chapel's turn to be surprised. "I'm not sure I follow. What happened twenty years ago that would make your mother a target for assassination?"

"I don't know," she told him. "She never told me any details. I just know that she and my father both used to work for the CIA, back when we lived up in the Catskills."

BROOKLYN, NEW YORK: APRIL 12, T+8:48

The Catskills. That was where the DoD facility was located, the one where the detainees had been held.

It couldn't be a coincidence. Chapel felt like he was looking at the pieces of a jigsaw puzzle, and two of them had just fit together for the first time.

"You have no idea what they did for the CIA?"

"None," Julia said. "They were both pretty good at keeping their secrets. By the time I was old enough to ask—to even wonder about what my parents did for a living—we had already moved to New York City and they had moved on to other jobs. I may have asked about their time as spies once in a while, but they would just tell me to mind my own business and I guess eventually I got the point."

Spies—well, that was unlikely. Dr. Bryant hardly fit the profile. But the CIA wasn't just spies; it employed thousands of civilians in all kinds of roles. All of whom were required by law never to talk about what they did. Even mentioning they had worked for the CIA, even to their own daughter, would be forbidden. "They actually said, 'we used to work for the CIA,' just like that?"

"No, of course not. Nothing like that. I only knew about it because once a year a guy from the CIA would come to our house for dinner. After we ate, they would send me to my room and tell me to play my music loud so he could debrief them."

That was standard practice for the CIA, Chapel knew. Defectors from foreign countries and anyone who worked on projects involving national security were debriefed on a yearly basis to make sure no foreign spies had contacted them and they hadn't accidentally revealed sensitive information.

"Did you ever overhear anything you weren't supposed to?" Chapel asked.

"No, never. I was still trying to be a good kid back then. I thought it would make them like me more. Mom and Dad were both cold fish, and I was always trying to find some way to get their approval. I used to look forward to the CIA guy's visits. It made me feel like my life was a little more exciting than other kids'. He was always nice to me, too. Nicer than my parents."

"Angel," Chapel said, under his breath.

"Already working on it, sugar," the voice in his ear said. "Give me a sec."

Julia stared at him. More specifically, she stared at his ear. "Oh, God," she said. "You've got a Bluetooth. What a nonsurprise."

He reached toward the hands-free set nestled in his ear, but he didn't touch it. "I need to stay connected," he told her.

"The only people in New York who wear those things are bankers and finance types," she said. "People who are rich enough that nobody dares tell them they look like douche bags. We all got pretty tired after a while of them walking around talking to invisible people all the time. It used to be you could tell if somebody was a crazy bum because he did that. Suddenly you had to take that kind of behavior seriously."

Chapel could only shrug. "Excuse me for one second," he told her.

"Whatever," she said, and turned to look out her window.

Angel eventually came back on the line. "This one took some digging. There are a lot of sealed records here . . . Helen Taggart née Bryant, William

Taggart—they were both on somebody's payroll, definitely, up until the mid-nineties. Tax records only show they worked for an unspecified government agency. That's unusual—the IRS doesn't mess around. The CIA should have been generating pay stubs and W-2 forms like anybody else."

"Sounds like they were being paid out of a black budget."

"Which is pretty much a brick wall when you're trying to follow a money trail," Angel agreed. "I did find one thing, though, that's going to make you so proud of me. William Taggart is still working as a research scientist, and that means he depends on grant money that has to be accounted for scrupulously. In 2003, he got a grant from an anonymous donor, but the check was paid by a bank in Langley, Virginia."

Which was where the CIA had its headquarters.

"That was some inspired detective work, absolutely," Chapel said. Not for the first time he uttered silent thanks that Angel was on his side. What she'd uncovered wasn't cast-iron proof that William Taggart had worked for the CIA, but it was pretty damning—and it was enough to confirm what his daughter had said.

"One other thing," Angel said, "I can definitely confirm that a William Taggart, a Helen Taggart, and a Julia Taggart all lived in Phoenicia, New York, until 1995. The elder Taggarts paid mortgage payments and property taxes there, and the woman you're sitting next to was a student at the local elementary school."

"Now you're just showing off," Chapel said, with

a chuckle. "I don't suppose there are any military bases in that area? Maybe a detention facility?"

"No likely suspects yet," Angel said, "but I'm still looking and—"

"Hey—that's my house," Julia said, rapping on the Plexiglas partition between them and the cab's driver. "Slow down. You can let me off at the corner."

"Hold on, Angel," Chapel said. Julia was reaching into her purse, but he put out a hand to stop her. "This is on me," he told her.

"Fine." She closed her purse and reached for the door handle.

"I still have some more questions," Chapel said, before she could get out of the cab. "If you'll just give me a little more of your time—"

"I don't think so," she told him. "You're definitely not coming inside, and I have to start planning my mother's funeral." Her face fell. Maybe she had been able to put aside her grief while she was talking to him, but he could see it had only been delayed. "It's bad enough she's dead. I didn't need any of this. I really didn't—"

She stopped in midsentence. She was staring through the window of the cab, looking up at her house—a modest two-story building not unlike the one where her mother had lived.

"What's wrong?" he asked. "Beyond the obvious?"

"Captain Chapel," she said. "I didn't leave the lights on when I left this morning."

He leaned across her to look up at the house. There were definitely lights on in the second-floor windows. As he watched, someone walked past the window, someone big and definitely male.

BROOKLYN, NEW YORK: APRIL 12, T+8:59

"Dr. Taggart," Chapel said, "give me your house keys, and stay in this cab no matter what happens."

Her eyes searched his face. She wasn't stupid. She knew this couldn't be a coincidence. Still, she clearly had her doubts.

"I am not kidding," he told her.

She nodded once and reached in her purse to fish out her keys. She slapped them into his outstretched right hand.

He tapped on the partition between them and the cabbie. "Wait here. Keep the meter running—it'll be worth your while."

The bearded cabdriver just shrugged.

Chapel stepped out onto the sidewalk. With his artificial left hand he brushed the front of his jacket, just to remind himself his sidearm was still there.

Approaching the house he saw right away that he wouldn't need the keys after all. The front door had been forced open. It was a heavy steel-core door with a Medeco lock, a lock that was supposed to be impossible to pick. Whoever had opened the door hadn't bothered to try. He'd simply smashed the lock mechanism, maybe with a sledgehammer. Chapel looked up and down the street but saw nobody watching him. Breaking that door must have made a lot of noise but nobody had come to investigate.

He shook his head and pushed past the swaying door. There was a second door inside, a security door with an electric buzzer. That door, too, had been smashed open and the buzzer was whining a plaintive cry.

"Up the stairs. It's the apartment on the left," Angel told him.

The building had been a single house once, from the look of it, but had been subdivided at some later point to make four apartments. Chapel headed up the stairs and found himself in a narrow corridor between two identical doors. These were simple wooden doors, child's play to kick in. It looked like both of them had been bashed open by force. Maybe the intruder didn't have an Angel to tell him which door he wanted.

Chapel drew his weapon. He reached for a safety switch before remembering there wasn't one on the P228. The handgun had an internal safety—the first pull on the trigger was a double action, cocking the hammer a moment before the handgun fired. That meant his first shot would be slightly slower than expected.

It had been a long time since he'd fired a pistol at anything but a paper target. Chapel set his jaw and pushed open Julia's apartment door with his foot.

From behind the door he heard shattering glass. Had the intruder jumped out a window? No—he could see blue glass fragments all over the floor.

The apartment might have been nice, tastefully decorated and cozy, once. He saw framed pictures of dogs on the walls and a bricked-in fireplace. Other than that the place was a shambles. The furniture had been broken into sticks of wood. Books had been torn from their shelves and thrown across the floor. Foam stuffing from ripped-up pillows and cushions floated on the air.

The place hadn't just been ransacked. It had been demolished.

A loud clattering, rattling noise broke his concentration. Stainless steel cooking implements—salad tongs, spatulas, slotted spoons—bounced and danced across the floor. The intruder must have pulled out one of Julia's kitchen drawers and just thrown it through the opening to the kitchen.

Careful not to trip on anything, Chapel advanced into the room. He was still blocking the main exit, but he stayed far enough from the kitchen entrance to not be surprised if the intruder came running out.

He cleared his throat. Summoned up his best command voice. "Stop where you are! You're under arrest!"

Silence filled the apartment. To one side of Chapel, a broken lamp rolled off a table and landed in a snowdrift of old tax forms. He managed not to jump, even as keyed up as he was.

"Step out of the kitchen. Lie down on the floor in here with your fingers locked behind your head," Chapel demanded.

The intruder took a step toward him. Chapel could hear the stamping footsteps on the wooden kitchen floor. He could hear the intruder breathing heavily, now, too. Chapel felt like his senses were coming alive, growing stronger. He remembered this focus, this clarity, from the days when he'd worked in the field.

"Step out of the kitchen," he repeated. "Lie down on the—"

The intruder didn't just emerge from the kitchen. It was like he exploded out of it, like he was a bullet fired from a gun. Chapel had never seen a human being move that fast—before this moment, he would have sworn it was impossible.

He jerked the trigger of the P228. His instincts were good, his reflexes just as sharp as they'd ever been. He was certain he'd hit his target, that the 9 mm round had caught his target in his shoulder.

The intruder didn't slow down at all. He collided with Chapel, knocking him over, sending them both rolling into the remains of a couch. Chapel saw a massive fist lift in the air, the arm behind it curling as the intruder readied a devastating blow aimed right at Chapel's head.

He managed to yank his head to one side. The fist came down with a thunderous crack. Chapel felt splinters dig into his ear and the side of his face. He glanced to the side and saw the intruder's fist buried in the shattered floorboards.

Impossible, Chapel thought. *This is impossible—*

And then strong arms grabbed him and hauled him into the air. He kicked and struggled, because he knew how hard it was to lift a human being who refused to let his center of gravity stay in one place. The hand gripping his leg squeezed. Hard. Chapel felt the muscle there, honed by years of swimming, crush and start to tear.

Then the intruder tossed Chapel into a corner of the room and made a break for the apartment door.

BROOKLYN, NEW YORK: APRIL 12, T+9:03

Chapel picked himself up off the floor and shook some dust off his jacket. His head swam for a minute, but he fought the wooziness off.

No damn time to be hurt, he told himself. Except it sounded like Top's voice inside his head. "That's right, Top," he said out loud. And then he dashed for the apartment door and down the stairs.

Chapel had gone through Special Forces training with the Army Rangers. The Rangers were famous for always being the first boots on the ground—wherever the army went, the Rangers were the first group sent in. They had a reputation for moving fast and keeping their wits about them. It had been a while since he'd used it, but conditioning like that doesn't break. He took the stairs two at a time and put his good shoulder into the door, knocking it wide open and spilling him into the street.

Just in time to see the back door of the cab slam shut, and the vehicle take off down the road at high speed. He saw two people in the backseat. One was Julia.

He was certain the other one was the intruder.

"Hell, no," he said, and lifted his weapon, aiming with both hands. The cab was already a hundred feet away and gaining speed, weaving to avoid other cars. He couldn't risk firing into its cabin in case he hit Julia by accident, so he snapped a shot at its rear right tire. The bullet dug a narrow trench through the asphalt, barely missing by a foot.

Chapel wanted to swear. He wanted to shout in frustration.

Instead he took off at a run. There was no way he could catch up with the speeding cab—his legs were strong but he was only human. He had no intention of just giving up, though.

Even if there was no hope at all.

"Chapel," Angel said. "Chapel! Tan Lexus, just ahead on your left!"

Chapel didn't waste time asking questions. He ran over to the indicated car and grabbed the driver's-side door handle. It resisted him—but then he heard a *chunk* as the door lock opened.

He had no idea what Angel was planning. He knew how to hot-wire a car, but it would take too long. This was pointless, it was just a token gesture, but—

As he slid into the driver's seat, the car rumbled to life.

"Keyless ignition," Angel said, "tied in to one of those always-on satellite services, so if you lose your keys you can just ask the nice man in India to start the car for you. Or, you know, your favorite hacker."

Chapel pulled on his seat belt and stepped on the gas.

BROOKLYN, NEW YORK: APRIL 12, T+9:04

Chapel jerked the wheel to the side to get around a slow-moving bicyclist and nearly collided with a line of cars coming the other way. He swerved back into his lane and accelerated. He could just see the cab ahead, a block away. There was a red light between them, but he took it at full speed, ignoring the horns that blared at him and the shouts of pedestrians.

He had to be careful, had to avoid accidents—it was far too easy, in the heat of the moment like this, to trade speed for safety. If he caught the intruder but ran over six pedestrians in the process, why exactly was he doing this?

The cabdriver didn't seem to have any such qualms. He sideswiped a city bus and then rocketed across his lane and half up onto the sidewalk to get around another car. The intruder must have been threatening him to make him drive like that, Chapel thought. He must be afraid for his life.

From what Chapel had seen, he had good reason to be.

"Is New York traffic always like this?" Chapel asked.

"Day in, day out," Angel told him. "There's another traffic light up ahead—I'm going to keep it green for you, but you need to watch out. Jaywalking is the official pastime in this city."

"Noted," Chapel said, palming the wheel as he gunned around a double-parked delivery van. Up ahead in the crosswalk people were standing in the street, inches from the cars that blasted past them going both ways. "You can't get these people to actually wait on the sidewalks, can you?"

"There are some things even I can't hack," Angel told him. "Sorry, sweetie."

Too much traffic. Too many people. On an open country highway Chapel could have given chase for miles. Here he was going to kill somebody if he didn't end this, and soon. The bright yellow cab was inching closer, but the cabbie was taking ever more serious risks. He blasted right through a fruit cart, sending its umbrella twirling and spattering the road and passersby with bright orange mango pulp. A woman in a business suit screamed and threw her briefcase at the cab as it nearly took her toes off.

"I need to get close and drive him off the road," Chapel said.

"Hold on," Angel told him. "Up ahead—perfect! One lane of the road up ahead is closed for construction. There's a blue wooden barrier and some orange netting making a temporary sidewalk. Do you see it?"

Chapel squinted at the road ahead. Yeah, the cab was just entering a new block where the road had been dug up. Big construction vehicles were leaning on the sidewalk and out into the street, protected from sideswipes by a blue wooden wall. Three more feet of the road had been cordoned off with traffic barrels and netting so people on foot could get around the construction.

"The intersection ahead is clear . . . now!" Angel said.

Chapel stepped on the gas and the Lexus shot through the open space, just as the traffic light overhead turned from yellow to red. The Lexus bounced and jumped on its suspension as he hit a trench dug through the asphalt, but suddenly the yellow cab was dead ahead.

Chapel pulled around the cab, trying to get level with it. He could see Julia and the intruder in the backseat. He had her in some kind of choke hold, and he was shouting at the cabbie through the partition.

There was blood on the partition. Who the hell was this guy?

He didn't look like the detainees Chapel had seen in the grainy surveillance footage Hollingshead had shown him. This guy's hair was cut short and his face was clean-shaven. Of course, that transformation would have taken only a few minutes in a train station bathroom. Chapel was certain this had to be one of the men he was looking for. It was just too unlikely that this was some random criminal who had broken into Julia's apartment the same day her mother was beaten to death.

Besides, Chapel had seen the way the man moved, the strength in his arms. That was exactly what Hollingshead and Banks had tried to warn him about. The detainees were stronger and faster than anyone Chapel had ever seen.

"Angel," Chapel said, "the owner of this Lexus—how's his insurance?"

"*She*'s got a five-hundred-dollar deductible," Angel told him.

"Send her a check," he said, and he yanked the steering wheel over to the side, slamming the nose of the Lexus right into the left rear wheel of the cab.

BROOKLYN, NEW YORK: APRIL 12, T+9:10

Metal screeched and safety glass shattered. The steering wheel jumped in Chapel's hands like a wild horse trying to break free of a rider, and the car under him skidded and floated over the asphalt, all control lost. The cab spun around and broke through the blue wooden barrier, sending broken scraps of wood flying in the air. Orange netting wrapped around the windshield of the Lexus, obscuring Chapel's view. A moment later the air bag exploded in his face and he couldn't see anything.

"The cab has stopped moving," Angel told him.

The air bag deflated almost instantly, and Chapel already had his seat belt off. He shoved the door of the Lexus open and ducked out, keeping his head low. He didn't think the detainee had a weapon but he wasn't about to find out the hard way.

Dashing around the front of car, he came at the cab with his handgun in a two-handed grip. He saw the cab was up on two wheels, its front end propped up by broken wood and a pile of gravel on the far side of the barrier. It wasn't going anywhere.

Someone tumbled out of the passenger door. He raised his weapon but lowered it again when he saw it was Julia. She looked banged up, a little, but he didn't see any blood on her. "Dr. Taggart," he called. "Are you all right?"

"He went through there," she shouted back, pointing at a building on the far side of the broken barrier.

He had to hand it to this woman. She was a civilian and she'd been through more than her share of shocks and horrors for one day, but still she kept her wits about her. She knew what was important—catching this man. She could look after herself.

Chapel clambered over the shattered barrier and ducked around the side of the gravel pile, a giant backhoe giving him cover on his other side. Dead ahead was the building she'd indicated. Its ground floor was lined in sheet glass windows, but they'd been covered over with brown craft paper held on with duct tape so he couldn't see inside. The door of the building might have been locked up tight, but now it was hanging open on one hinge. He recognized the detainee's handiwork.

"Angel," he said, "what does this building look like inside?"

"It's been gutted. Used to be a department store, but it went out of business two years ago. The current owners tore out all the copper wiring and anything else of value and have left it empty ever since."

"So you're telling me there's no power in there. No lights."

"I'm afraid so. Be safe, Chapel."

Not much chance of that.

Chapel shoved his back up against the window just to the right side of the door. The door hung open wide enough for him to get a glimpse inside. He saw a bare concrete floor, with pillars here and there holding the ceiling up. Piles of construction debris, an old wheelbarrow, and a stack of two-by-fours sat inside. The light streaming in through the broken door only illuminated a small patch of the floor.

He saw no sign of movement. For all he knew the detainee had just run through this building and out a back door. If he had, the chase was over.

Every instinct in Chapel's body told him that wasn't true. That he was standing right outside of a death trap.

He shoved the door out of its frame with one foot. The remaining hinge gave way, and it fell outward, smashing onto the sidewalk. Chapel ducked inside before the noise had stopped and got his back up against the nearest pillar.

He could hear nothing. The place stank of mildew and dust. Nothing alive but rats had been in there for a long time.

Chapel held his breath.

He waited.

Finally he heard what he'd hoped for. A footfall, the sound of someone big, human sized, crunching the dust underfoot.

"This building is surrounded," he shouted. "Your only chance is to turn yourself in. I promise we won't hurt you."

"I've been hurt before," the detainee said.

His voice came from much closer than Chapel had expected. He couldn't be more than ten feet away.

"Thanks to you, I know what it feels like to be shot."

"Yeah? How was that?"

"It woke me up pretty good. Made me not want to get shot again."

A sense of humor. Not what Chapel had expected. The detainee's voice was deep, but not gruff. It had no accent as far as Chapel could tell—which meant the detainee probably wasn't of Middle Eastern descent, nor Russian. He had considered the idea that the detainees might have been foreign combatants, al-Qaeda or Taliban who had been brought to the States for questioning, but the voice sounded altogether wrong for that.

"How are we going to play this?" Chapel asked.

"Why don't you step out where I can see you. Then we'll figure it out together."

The voice was calm. There was no fear in it. No rage, either. Chapel had seen what this man did to Julia's apartment—and to Dr. Bryant's body. That had taken real anger, blinding fury. But this man sounded about as angry as if he was trying to solve a difficult Sudoku puzzle.

"You sound like a reasonable man," Chapel said.

The voice laughed, with genuine mirth.

"You don't know anything about me," the detainee said. "Otherwise you wouldn't make that mistake."

"I know you killed Helen Bryant, and that she was just the first name on your list. I know you went to Julia Taggart's apartment, probably to kill her, too—even though she isn't on your list at all. Care to tell me why you did that?"

"Bryant had to see. She had to understand what she did to us," the detainee told him. There was an undercurrent of anger in the words, now, and Chapel knew he'd struck a chord. "As for the daughter, well. Her child—the person she made to love. To really love. I wanted to show her, show her how that hurt!"

So much for reasonable. It sounded like every word the detainee spoke now was making him angrier.

"Look, calm down; I'm actually here to help you," Chapel said.

"They have to die! They all have to die for what they did!"

Damn. Chapel had really set the guy off. He was screaming now, his words slurring with rage. Who went from calm and collected to homicidally angry that fast? "Just talk to me—explain it to me," Chapel called out. "Please! I want to understand!"

"Understand? You can't fucking understand this!"

"I want to—"

Chapel didn't get to finish the thought. The detainee hit the pillar Chapel hid behind, then, hard enough to shatter it into chips of concrete and twisted rebar. Hard enough to send Chapel sprawling forward, right into the pool of light coming in through the door.

BROOKLYN, NEW YORK: APRIL 12, T+9:14

Chapel nearly dropped his pistol as he fell forward. He barely managed to get his hands under him as broken concrete pelted his back and smacked into his head. He felt blood slicking down one side of his face, and his ears were ringing. Slowly he turned around to look behind him.

The detainee came at him roaring like an animal, arms outstretched, big fingers reaching for Chapel's flesh.

Chapel rolled out of the way, scrabbling to get his feet underneath him. He dashed into the darkness beyond the pool of light. Instantly he was blind, and he stumbled as his foot caught on a pile of two-by-fours. He went sprawling again, but this time caught himself a little better. He rolled onto his good shoulder, then onto his back. Blinking rapidly he fought to gain some kind of night vision so he could see through the murk. The daylight coming in through the broken door dazzled his eyes and kept him from seeing anything.

He heard concrete shattering again, vaguely saw pieces of acoustic ceiling tile come cascading down from above.

"I see you there," the detainee said, his voice thick with rage.

Damn—Chapel couldn't see his attacker at all. He pushed himself backward with his feet, trying at least to get a wall behind him so the detainee would have to come at him from the front. He lifted his handgun, pointed it into the darkness.

For a second the detainee was visible in the pool of light, moving so fast he was a blur. He was headed right for Chapel. Could the bastard see in the dark?

Chapel got to his feet and jumped to the side just in time. The detainee hit the wall where Chapel had been, and metal clanged as a stack of rebar went falling and clattering across the floor.

Chapel desperately tried to make out anything in the dark. There were shadows—vague shapes. He took a wild guess at where the detainee would be. He raised his weapon, aimed as carefully as he could since he didn't know what he was shooting at. It could have been a wheelbarrow or a pile of buckets.

But this shadow moved.

Chapel took the shot. The muzzle flash ruined any night vision he'd gained.

But the detainee screamed.

"Stop doing that!" the detainee bellowed. "Just give up and die already!"

Not a chance, Chapel thought. He backed away from the detainee, his artificial hand held out behind him so he wouldn't stumble over anything too big. His eyes stung with dust and darkness, so he clamped them shut.

He felt air moving over his face and his good hand. He heard broken concrete settling, heard rebar creaking as it took the weight of the building above.

The detainee was stumbling in the dark now, too. Either his night vision wasn't as good as Chapel had thought or he had lost enough blood to slow him down. Thank heaven for small favors. Chapel's artificial hand felt a pillar behind him. He pressed his back up against it. He listened.

He could hear footsteps. Coming closer.

He considered rushing for the light. In the dark like this he was clearly at a disadvantage. The light was coming from the street, though. He had to keep the detainee in the building where he controlled the situation. If the guy got out onto the sidewalk again, he might run for it, and Chapel knew he couldn't run him down on foot.

"You're tough, for a human," the detainee said.

What the hell was that supposed to mean?

Chapel had no time to think about it. A piece of concrete as big as his fist struck the pillar, just inches above Chapel's head. If it had connected, it might have fractured his skull. Chapel ducked and lifted his weapon, just as another chunk of concrete smacked into his leg.

He fired blind into the darkness, one shot, two. He had no hope of hitting the detainee.

But in the muzzle flash he saw the detainee coming toward him, saw little snapshots frozen in time as the bastard leaped into the air, arms wheeling to smash into Chapel and crush him.

Chapel jumped to the side and ran toward the windows at the front of the building. He kept well clear of the door to keep the detainee from getting any ideas.

His leg hurt. Every step was a new flash of agony. Either he'd been wounded by the chunk of concrete that hit him, or he was just now feeling the effects of when the detainee had grabbed him back in Julia's apartment.

He made it to the windows, but he could already hear the detainee running at him again, charging. Chapel reached behind him and grabbed a handful of the brown paper that covered the window. Just before the detainee reached him, he tore it free, turning his head to the side.

Bright light burst through the uncovered glass, a beam of it like a laser shining right in the detainee's face. Chapel had hoped to blind the man—if his eyes were adjusted to the darkness, the sudden light should be enough to dazzle him, at least for a moment, and let Chapel get a shot off.

The detainee laughed. He squinted his eyes shut, then opened them again.

Except—they were different now. Chapel was flummoxed by what he saw. The detainee's eyes had turned black, solid black, from side to side. No white was visible at all.

BROOKLYN, NEW YORK: APRIL 12, T+9:17

"What the hell are you?" Chapel demanded.

The detainee didn't answer. As Chapel watched, the detainee's eyes changed again. The blackness slid away from his eyes, like an eyelid drawing back. Like an extra eyelid.

Chapel thought of lizards and snakes—didn't they have an extra eyelid like that? Some kind of membrane to protect their eyes from the sun?

This made no sense. It made no sense at all.

Chapel was so surprised he failed to take the obvious shot.

The detainee grabbed up a piece of rebar from the floor. *He* wasn't surprised, and he was more than ready to end this. The length of ribbed steel bar swung through the air, slamming into the window right by the side of Chapel's good arm. Chapel managed to duck as it came around for a second strike.

Damn, the guy was fast. Weird eyes notwithstanding, his speed and strength were beyond any limit of human strength. This just kept getting harder and harder to understand.

Chapel had to jump to the side to avoid a third swing. The detainee switched his grip on the bar and jabbed at Chapel, hard enough to star the tempered glass of the window behind him.

Before Chapel could even move, another jab came, and another. One clipped the side of his head and bright lights burst behind Chapel's eyes. He lurched wildly, suddenly unable to stand up straight—which was all that saved him from being impaled as the bar came right at his chest.

If this kept up much longer, Chapel knew he would be beaten to death, his bones crushed by that length of steel. He brought up his weapon and fired—they were close enough together now he barely needed to aim.

A bright spot of blood appeared on the detainee's chest, just a little to the right of where his heart should be. It was the kind of shot that might kill a human being or might just incapacitate him—either way it would leave him down on the floor, bleeding out.

It knocked the detainee back maybe half a step. His arms went wide, the rebar whistling through the air, still clutched in one big hand.

Chapel had bought himself a split second. His head was swimming and he really wanted to lie down, but his work wasn't finished.

He raised the pistol again, this time aiming at the maniac's eye. He might have too many eyelids, but Chapel doubted they could stop a 9 mm slug.

Before he could take the shot, though, the rebar connected with Chapel's hand and sent the handgun flying. Pain lanced up Chapel's arm as far as his shoulder, like a vein of magma had opened under his flesh. He cried out—he couldn't help it—and brought his hand up close to his chest. It didn't feel broken but it was starting to go numb, which was never a good sign.

Not that it mattered, particularly.

He was face-to-face with a superstrong madman. He was unarmed. The lunatic had a length of steel bar hard enough and heavy enough to stove in a human rib cage.

Anyone else would have known that was the moment of his death.

Anyone without Chapel's training might have been forgiven for breaking down then and begging for his life.

But Chapel had trained with the Army Rangers. Some of the most elite warfighters on earth. And that training had included an intense course in hand-to-hand combatives.

"Bye, bye," the detainee said, and he brought the rebar around in a swinging arc.

Chapel shot out his good hand and grabbed the rebar in midair, not trying to stop it or even slow it down. Just getting a grip, letting his arm be carried along by its momentum. His artificial hand shot out and grabbed hold of the detainee's elbow.

The Rangers had taught Chapel that when he had a pistol in his hand, that was his best weapon. But when he didn't have a pistol, his best weapon was his enemy's own weight. Swinging the rebar forced the detainee to commit to the bar's inertia, shifting his own center of balance away from his feet. Chapel yanked him forward, adding all his own strength to the moving bar.

The detainee went somersaulting forward, carried along by his own follow-through, and went down face-first into the floor. Chapel heard the peculiar wet snap of cartilage breaking and knew the detainee's nose had shattered on impact.

The detainee moaned like an injured cow.

Maybe I got lucky and cracked his skull, too, Chapel thought. *Maybe I got really lucky and dazed him for a second.*

Chapel had never been that lucky. "Are you ready to talk?" he asked the detainee, just in case. He moved around behind the fallen maniac, his eyes scanning the floor.

"I'm ready to kill you," the detainee said, his voice distorted by his broken nose. "I'm ready to tear you a new asshole, you little—"

"Yeah. I kind of thought you'd say that," Chapel said. He found his pistol on the floor. He picked it up, took careful aim, and put two bullets in the back of the lunatic's head.

BROOKLYN, NEW YORK: APRIL 12, T+9:19

Chapel's legs felt like they were made of Jell-O. He really wanted to sit down.

He wanted to close his eyes and go to sleep.

"Uh-oh," he said. "I think I might have a concussion."

He was suddenly on the floor, looking up at the dark ceiling. He couldn't remember how he got there. His head was ringing like a bell. The detainee had smacked him in the head with the rebar, he remembered. He'd taken a blow to the head.

That didn't fill him with confidence.

"Chapel!" Angel shouted in his ear. "Chapel! You have to stay awake, honey. You have to! If you go to sleep now, you won't wake up!"

"I'll be okay," Chapel told her, not because he believed it but because he wanted to reassure her. "Don't you worry about me, sexy ghost voice."

"You're losing it," Angel said. "Your pulse is all over the place, and your blood pressure is falling. I'm calling the paramedics."

"No!" Chapel said. "This is a secret mission. No para . . . no doctors, no hospitals. They'll have too many questions. I just need to walk this off."

"Captain Chapel?" someone asked. Someone new. This voice wasn't in his head.

"Captain Chapel? Can you open your eyes?" A soft hand was on his cheek. Fingers pried his eyes open. He looked up into a beautiful face, the face of . . . well, not an angel. He didn't know what Angel looked like. He knew this face, though. It was surrounded by red hair.

Voices were clamoring near his ear, but he could barely hear them. The earpiece had fallen partially out of his ear, he realized. He tried to reach to put it back in, but his arms felt like they were made of lead.

"Captain Chapel, you need medical attention," Julia Taggart said.

"You should see the other guy."

"The man who killed my mother? He's dead. Definitely dead. Not much left of his cerebrum, it looks like. I suppose it's funny to say this, but thank you. I appreciate it."

"Sure thing," Chapel told her. "Will you help me up? I'm having trouble standing, and I need to get out of here."

"You need to go to a hospital."

"I can't do that. Just get me into a cab or something."

He saw Julia bite her lip. "Maybe I can do better than that," she said.

BROOKLYN, NEW YORK: APRIL 12, T+9:31

Arash Borhan did not need this shit. No, not at all.

Earlier that day he'd gotten a call from some sexy-sounding woman who said his cab was needed for a special fare, and that he stood to make a lot of money if he went to some address in Brighton Beach. Normally he didn't work that far south in Brooklyn, but the money the woman promised him would more than make it worth his while. So he drove down there, he picked up a man and a woman who were arguing on the sidewalk, and he drove them to Bushwick. That had all been fine. The man got out to go into a house there, while the woman stayed in his cab and the meter kept ticking away.

Then everything had gone to hell.

Some crazy mother had come rushing out of the house and jumped in the back of the cab, and when Arash demanded to know what was going on, the maniac had nearly ripped his ear off. The maniac told him to drive, to break so many laws. And then this other maniac, the man who was his original fare, had driven him right off the road.

Now his cab was wedged into a wooden construction barrier. The paint was scratched to hell, and he was missing a wing mirror. He would be lucky if the front fender could be saved at all.

He touched the side of his head. He was still bleeding, too.

"Motherf—" Arash shook his head. He would not say the swear out loud. He was a decent man. But this was just too much.

Arash had come to America in 1979 to escape the Iranian Revolution. He'd thought he was getting away from violence, that he could be safe in the States. He'd worked hard to get this cab, to become a naturalized citizen. He loved America and everything it stood for.

Except—everybody here had guns. And he had seen more violence in New York City than he'd ever witnessed in Tehran. Twice he had been robbed at gunpoint, just because he was a cabdriver and had some cash on him. This was the first time he'd actually been hurt. He found he did not like it at all.

As he stood there, wondering what to do, his fare and the woman came out of the closed-down store. He was leaning on her shoulder like he could barely walk under his own power. What was the meaning of this? "Hey! Hey, you!" he called to them. "Who's going to pay for this mess?"

The woman stared at him like he was crazy. Like *he* was crazy. "This man is hurt," she said. "He needs help." They were walking away.

"What about me? I'm wounded, too!" Arash shouted after them. They didn't so much as turn around and apologize. He would have chased them if he didn't need to stay with the cab.

He fumed for a while. He nearly swore again. But Arash Borhan had nothing if he did not have a sense of practicality. He got in his cab and worked hard at getting it free of the wooden barrier. Metal shrieked and groaned, and the front fender did, in fact, fall off. But eventually he got loose from the pile of broken wood. It felt like the cab could still drive. Well, maybe this was not the end of the world, after all.

Then someone rapped on the glass of his window, and he sighed. In New York, people saw nothing. They wouldn't care if his cab was half destroyed—they still had places to be. They would want to know if he was available for a new fare. Crazy! They were all crazy. He rolled down the window, prepared to tell some angry businessman that no, he was off duty, that he needed to get back to the garage for repairs.

The nose of a pistol came through the window and tapped Arash on his cheek.

Wonderful. This day was going to get even worse.

"I have no money," he said. "No money!"

The man holding the pistol seemed to think this was very funny, because he laughed heartily at the thought.

Arash looked at him in horror. This laughing man was wearing a black suit and had the crew cut of a soldier. But much, much worse was the dead look in his eyes. Arash knew that look. It was the look he'd fled when he left Iran. The look of a man who had no conscience. No soul.

"You've got a new fare," the man said, laughing so hard he could barely get the words out. "We're going to Bed-Stuy."

"Whatever you say," Arash told him, because you did not argue with such a man. Not when he was holding a gun.

Still it got worse, though.

It could always get worse.

"Oh no, no," Arash moaned as the laughing man loaded a dead body into the trunk of the cab. Arash recognized the dead man—it was the maniac who attacked him and forced him to drive his cab here. "No, please, no," he said, when the laughing man told him to get in the cab and drive.

It was a long way to Bedford-Stuyvesant, one of the worst neighborhoods in Brooklyn. The laughing man kept laughing the whole way. When they reached the address he indicated, Arash saw it was an abandoned warehouse. The roof was falling away, and the interior was full of rat nests and the cardboard shelters of the homeless. This was not a good place, not at all. Arash maneuvered his cab around piles of rubble to reach the very dark heart of it.

"Good. Now get out and open the trunk," the laughing man said, giggling softly to himself.

"God protect me," Arash whispered. But he did as he was told. What choice did he have? He looked down at the body curled up in the trunk. Much of the maniac's head was missing. What did this all mean? What could it mean?

The laughing man pointed at a red plastic gas can in the trunk. The dead man's hand was resting on it.

"Take that," the laughing man said, "and pour it all over him. Don't be stingy."

There was no doubt in Arash's mind what was going to happen here. The laughing man was going to make him burn up his own cab. His livelihood, the only possession Arash had that was worth anything. This was terrible.

There was nothing he could do. He opened the

gas can and poured it all over the dead man. The fumes of gasoline stung his eyes, but that was not the reason he started crying.

"You're hurt," the laughing man said, tapping Arash's bloody temple with his gun. This he seemed to find only slightly amusing. "This guy? He hurt you?"

Arash nodded. He could find no words.

"Well, that's a damned shame," the laughing man said.

Arash looked at him through a haze of tears. Was he going to find sympathy here, in the unlikeliest of places? Arash knew such men as this—soulless men—could act unpredictably at times. They could even be charitable if it suited their whim.

"Get in there with him," the laughing man said.

"I . . . what?" Arash asked.

"Get in the trunk with him. Come on. I'm in a hurry."

"This I will not do," Arash said.

"Yeah, you will. One way or another."

Arash was a practical man. He knew what danger he was in, and that he had no options left. He tried to run.

The laughing man shot him in both legs. Then he dragged him back to the cab and threw him in the trunk. The blood and gasoline from the dead man soaked into his clothes, filling his nose and mouth and making it hard to breathe. The pain in his legs was unbearable, and his brain contained nothing but clouds of pure agony.

He could barely see, could feel nothing but pain. But still he heard the laughter.

"I can put a round in your head, so you don't have to burn alive," the man said, chuckling to himself. "You want that?"

Arash Borhan was a practical man.

He squeezed his eyes shut and nodded in agreement.

BROOKLYN, NEW YORK: APRIL 12, T+10:52

"Hop up there," Julia said.

Chapel looked around the room. It was a small examination room in the back of Julia's veterinary office. A stainless steel table dominated the space, which was otherwise filled with cabinets full of medical supplies, jars of cotton swabs, dispensers for hand sanitizer, and, of course, pictures of dogs. A flatscreen monitor on one wall displayed a rotating screen saver of pictures of Portuguese water dogs.

"Do you have dogs yourself?" Chapel asked.

"I used to. Now my ex has them," she told him. "Go on. Up there," she said, pointing again at the stainless steel table. "It's clean."

"You're divorced?" he asked, still not complying.

"No. Ex-boyfriend. We were together since grad school. It got to the point where I wanted to get married and have children. He disagreed. Now he lives on a farm upstate. With my dogs." She looked at the flatscreen, which was showing at that moment a dog running across a field, its ears flapping behind it. She rubbed the corner of the screen as if she were petting the animal. "They're better off up there, of course. They need space to run, and the city air is no good for dogs. Are you going to get on that table, or should I consider this a symptom of mental deterioration?"

Chapel smiled. He did what he was told. The table had clearly been meant to hold the weight of a big dog at most. It creaked under him but it held.

"There are two kinds of head injuries," she told him, rummaging in a drawer to take out a small flashlight. "The kind that go away on their own, usually pretty quickly, and the kind that kill you. It can be hard to tell them apart. Open your eyes very wide and look straight ahead, not at me."

Chapel complied. She shone the light into his eyes, dazzling him. He tried to remember the ride over here. He recalled her dragging him out of the gutted department store where he'd left the body of the detainee. He remembered being put in a cab, and then not much more until they'd reached this place. There had been a receptionist out front, but the office was mostly deserted—Julia had canceled all her appointments for the day after finding her mother's body.

"I'm missing some time," he said. "I don't remember the ride here, really."

"Blackouts like that are common with concussion. Do you feel nauseated?"

"No," he told her. She brought out a tongue depressor and he obediently opened his mouth.

"Good. Now swallow for me."

He gulped down some air. "I appreciate this, Doc," he said.

She shrugged. "Just call me Julia. You may have saved my life, so that seems fair." She smiled. Her face was only inches away from his. She put a thumb on his left eyelid and pushed it back, staring deep into his eye. When she let go, he had to blink.

She was very close. He couldn't help but smell her faint but sweet perfume and feel the warmth of her body so near his.

"When that maniac jumped in the cab and told the cabbie to drive, I thought for sure he was going to kill me."

Chapel pulled himself back from what he'd been thinking. He put out of his mind how good she smelled, and instead he studied the woman's face. She was a lot tougher than most civilians he'd met, mentally and emotionally. She could handle this. "That was his plan. He killed your mother to make her . . . I don't know. Feel guilt for something she'd done. He thought killing you might make her see the light. The fact that she was already dead, that his plan made no sense, doesn't seem to have occurred to him."

Julia nodded. She shoved her hands in the pockets of her stained lab coat. "I gathered as much from what he said to me."

"He spoke to you? In the cab? This could be important," Chapel insisted.

"Don't get too excited. He just kept saying he was going to make my mom pay. That she owed him, and that I was how he was going to fulfill that debt. That was all he said—well, that and he kept threatening the cabbie if he didn't go faster. At one point he reached through the opening in the partition and grabbed the cabbie's ear. He nearly tore it off. I'm going to assume—because I know you won't tell me even if I'm wrong—that he was on drugs of some kind. Speed, or perhaps PCP. That's the only explanation I have for why he was so strong."

Chapel knew there was a question hidden in that statement. She was asking if he knew of another reason. He didn't, so it was easy to stay quiet. Even if he'd had an explanation, he couldn't have given it to her. *I am a silent warrior*, he thought to himself, repeating the creed of the army Military Intelligence Corps.

She reached up and touched his face again, more gently this time. Her hand was very warm.

Without warning, she leaned in and kissed him. Her lips were soft and warm, and when they pressed against his, her arms went around his neck. For a moment he couldn't think straight.

Then she let go of him and walked across the room to put her flashlight back in its drawer, as if nothing at all had happened.

"Not that I'm complaining," he said, "but what was that for?"

"Because you saved my life, and because, I guess, you avenged my mother," she said, her back turned toward him. "And maybe because I wanted to. Don't worry. I wasn't trying to start something. When you walk out my door, you're never coming back. I know that."

"Listen, Julia, I—"

"We need to make sure your brain wasn't damaged," she said, clearly intending to change the subject.

"I feel a little light-headed . . . now," he said, smiling at her.

But she was done with whatever had passed between them. She was back to her professional mien. She folded her arms and leaned against the counter behind her. "Your pupils are normal, which is very encouraging, but I'm going to ask you some questions. What city are you in?"

Chapel frowned. Seriously? She was just going to kiss him and then immediately pretend like nothing had happened? He shrugged in confusion. "New York," he told her.

"Good. What's today's date?"

"April twelfth."

She nodded. "Very good. What agency do you work for?"

Chapel reared back. He shook his head.

Julia sighed and folded her arms. "I've met enough spies in my life to recognize the type, Captain Chapel. I know you're in the intelligence community. You're tracking down assassins sent to kill former CIA employees. This has something to do with work my parents did twenty years ago, and—"

"Stop," he said. "You don't want to continue in that line."

"Oh?" she said, raising an eyebrow. "Is that a threat?"

"It's an apology, though I guess I didn't phrase it very well. I'd love to tell you what's going on," Chapel said. "Really. I think you deserve to know. The problem is, I don't really understand it myself. I was given a very minimal briefing and sent after these men. Anything I do know about them, I can't share with you."

She stared at him for a while, perhaps giving him

a chance to relent. If so, he didn't take it. Eventually she just nodded and turned away.

And that . . . was that. Whatever had happened, whatever had made her kiss him—whatever might have happened was over. She was done with him.

He had a strong urge to run away. Like he'd done something wrong. There was one thing he had to ask her, though.

"I blacked out on the way here," he said. "Some times people say things when they're blacked out that they don't mean to. Did I say anything that I wouldn't remember?" he asked.

"You kept calling out for somebody named Angel," she told him. "And you said one word a couple of times. 'Chimera.'"

Chapel nodded. "You don't know what that word means, do you?"

"I do have a postgraduate degree, Captain," she said, a nasty sneer in her voice. "A chimera is a creature with the body of a lion, a goat head on its back, and—"

"—the tail of a snake, sure," Chapel said. Enough. He should just go. There was another target in New York City he had to check on, and three more detainees out there he had to take down. There was no time for tiptoeing around this woman's feelings. "Thanks, anyway."

"Except," she said, "to a geneticist it means something completely different."

"A geneticist? Like your mother?"

"Uh-huh," she said.

BROOKLYN, NEW YORK: APRIL 12, T+11:03

"In genetics a chimera is an organism that has more than one kind of DNA in the same body," Julia told him.

"What, like a mutant?" he asked.

She shook her head. "No, a mutant is an organism that has the normal DNA for its species except a couple of genes are randomly changed from what they should be. A chimera is much weirder. Part of its normal DNA has been replaced by DNA from another source. Sometimes that happens naturally, when two eggs are fertilized in the same womb but one absorbs the other. That's one way you get people with two different color eyes, for instance— that's called chimerism. It can mean something else, though, as well. It can refer to transgenic organisms."

"Transgenic?"

"A transgenic creature is a kind of chimera where the two or more different kinds of DNA come from completely different species. I don't mean mules or ligers or that sort of thing, where you have two animals so closely related they can interbreed. Transgenics is when a human being intentionally adds unrelated DNA to an organism's genetic makeup. Say, adding firefly genes to a tobacco plant so it glows in the dark. Or growing a human ear on the back of a mouse."

Chapel's head reeled, and not from the concussion. "They can do that? And it doesn't just kill the mouse?"

"Not if it's done right. Only a small number of genes are switched, normally. And yes, we can do that now. It has been done, successfully."

"But why?" Chapel demanded. "Is this some kind of sick mad scientist thing? Like, crossing a monkey and a shark to get a monkey with big teeth?"

"It's done for slightly more noble reasons, usually. Like with spidergoats."

A vision of eight-legged goats spinning webs across mountaintops filled Chapel's head. "Now I know you're full of it."

"No, really. It's been done. They introduced some spider DNA to a goat ovum, and the result was a spidergoat. It looks just like a normal goat, but its milk contains threads of spider silk. Spider silk is much, much stronger than steel, but because of the size of spiders it's tough to harvest. Spidergoat silk is a lot bigger and longer than the stuff a spider makes. They use spidergoat silk to make body armor for soldiers. At least, they're starting to."

Chapel had good reason to appreciate body armor. Still— "That sounds ludicrous."

"It's a field that's just starting out. But the implications are incredible. They want to breed a kind of tomato chimera that contains vaccines. You could inoculate children by feeding them their vegetables. They want to make chimera animals, pigs probably, that have human organs which can be harvested for transplants."

"I am starting to feel a little nauseated, now," Chapel said. "This is messed-up stuff."

"I agree," Julia said. "But I'm willing to accept that if it means saving lives."

"Okay, okay, enough with the ethics debate."

"Why are you asking me about this?" Julia asked.

He shot a glance at her eyes and saw she was desperate to know. And for once he could answer—she would find out soon enough anyway, from the police. "Your mother wrote the word 'chimera' on her wall. Probably while she was being killed."

"Oh my God," Julia gasped.

He was sorry to have to shock her like this. But it was important. "Do you know what she was trying to tell us?"

"I have no idea," Julia said. "She never used the word 'chimera' in my presence, not that I remember. But then, she never talked about her work to me. Ever."

Chapel rubbed at his eyes with the balls of his thumbs. *Chimera* had to mean something. Helen Bryant had died to get the word to him. She must have thought he—or someone—would understand. But what could it possibly mean?

In his head he saw black eyes. The eyes of the detainee when blinding light shone on them. They had turned black because an extra eyelid had slid across the maniac's eyes.

Even at the time, Chapel had thought they looked like the eyes of a snake or something. Lots of animals had an extra eyelid, didn't they? He seemed to remember that cats and birds did, too.

No. What he was thinking was crazy. But—

"If you could do that to a goat. If you could have a pig that grows human organs—you could—you could have a human being with animal organs as well, you could make them stronger, tougher, even—"

He couldn't finish the thought out loud.

But he had another one. "Julia. What kind of research does your father do?"

She bit her lip. "He's one of the world's leading experts on gene therapy," she said. "He works with human DNA."

BROOKLYN, NEW YORK: APRIL 12, T+11:16

It was impossible. It simply couldn't be.

And yet Chapel had seen the evidence with his own eyes. The detainee in the gutted department store had been far stronger and faster than any human being had a right to be. And he'd had an extra eyelid, one that shut down automatically when he was exposed to bright light, protecting his eyes. Making them as black as eight balls in his head. He had seemed inhuman. A monster. Chapel had refused to accept that, and so he had thought of the detainee as human, completely human. He'd been of the same opinion as Julia—that the guy had to have been full of drugs to make him so inhumanly strong and resistant to damage.

But if in fact the detainee had been a chimera—a combination of human and animal genes—it made a kind of crazy sense. Chapel had seen a documentary on chimpanzees, once, that had startled him. He'd always thought chimps were just smart apes that could be trained to do circus tricks or maybe learn some basic sign language. Instead, the chimps in that documentary—wild chimps—had been incredibly strong and very dangerous. They were capable of tearing a human being to pieces, and if their territory or their dominance was threatened, they had no qualms at all about doing it.

If the detainee had possessed chimpanzee genes, or genes from some other species stronger than a human being—

"You're tough, for a human," the detainee had said to him. Because the maniac *wasn't* human. At least not entirely.

His phone was buzzing in his pocket. He pulled it out and saw the call was coming from the number (000) 000-0000. That had to mean it was an encrypted call, from Angel most likely. He hit the end button, and the phone stopped vibrating.

Before he could even put it in his pocket, it started ringing out loud. He checked and saw that he'd turned the ringer off, but apparently Angel could override that.

Probably she was just checking in to make sure he was all right. It might be something else, though. Something important.

"Oh, for Christ's sake!" Julia said, staring at him and his phone. "Either take that call or yank the battery out of that thing."

Before he could do either, the flatscreen on the wall flickered and the image there changed. It showed a line drawing of a human head with one ear highlighted. The screen animated and showed an earpiece like the one in Chapel's pocket being inserted.

Not exactly subtle.

"What the hell?" Julia asked.

"That screen must be attached to the Internet," Chapel said to her while he fished in his pocket.

He took out the earpiece and stared at it. "I have a friend who's . . . good with computers."

He put the earpiece in and was not surprised to hear Angel calling his name. "Are you alone, sugar?" she asked.

"Not quite. I—"

He turned to look at Julia, but she was already storming out of the examining room. "I've got work to do," she said, and slammed the door behind her.

"I'm alone now," he told Angel.

"That's good. I like having you all to myself," she told him. "Tell me you're okay. Your vitals look all right, though you seem tired."

"It's been a long day. Wait a minute—you can tell I'm tired from the earpiece?"

"It's got a few sneaky features. It can collect biometric data. Among other things."

"And those other things—"

"Sweetie, if you ask me about classified things, you know I have to lie. And I don't ever want to lie to you."

"Fair enough. All right, Angel. What's so important you needed to cut in on me like that?"

"I'm going to put Director Hollingshead on the line, and he can tell you all about it. Director?"

"I'm here," the admiral said. "Chapel—it sounded like you took a pretty good blow to the head, there. Are you recovered?"

"I was dazed for a minute," Chapel told him. "But I'll be all right. Dr. Taggart took care of me. She also told me a few interesting things about chim—"

"Ahem," Hollingshead broke in. "No need to tell an old dog anything about digging up bones, son."

"Ah." So Hollingshead already knew about chimeras. And what Chapel was facing. It would have been nice to have some warning, but Chapel supposed some things were meant to stay secret. Apparently so secret it couldn't even be discussed over an encrypted line. "Okay, then, sir, I'll tell you all about it some other time. Maybe in person."

"You're on the trail, son, and that's all that matters. What's the status of your, ah, investigation? What's your next step?"

"There's one more name on the list with a New York address. She shouldn't be in danger now—the other three are probably hundreds of miles from here by now. Still, it won't hurt to pay her a visit and make sure she's safe. After that, it's either Chicago or Atlanta. Any thought on where I should head first?"

"Angel's looking for clues. Maybe she'll turn something up. I know you'll make the right choice, Captain Chapel. I have utter faith in you. Director Banks on the other hand . . ."

"Oh?"

"You've got some competition, let us say. Oh, nothing you can't handle—and no one you haven't met before. Someone you've seen around the Pentagon, perhaps."

Laughing Boy. Hollingshead must be talking about Laughing Boy. "He's been activated? Maybe that's good news—two of us running down leads can cover a lot more ground than one," Chapel pointed out.

"Unfortunately he's not as proactive as you've shown yourself to be," Hollingshead said, sounding contrite. "In fact, I fear he's simply bird-dogging you. After your recent success, I sent a team to pick up what was left of the . . . fellow in question. Your new shadow got there first. What he did with the remains is currently unknown."

Chapel thought about that. If Laughing Boy had taken the body of the dead detainee, it could simply mean the CIA didn't want the local authorities claiming the remains of a man who was carrying a dangerous virus. But why not let Hollingshead's people take care of it? Banks must have had his reasons. Maybe there was something about the body he didn't want anyone else to see.

Yet another mystery to add to the already enormous pile of mysteries in this operation. Chapel shrugged it off. "At least the . . . specimen is under wraps. Do you think I need to worry about our civilian friends?"

Hollingshead didn't sound sure when he answered. "No one has declared war just yet. Chalk this one up to a shot across our bows, maybe. For now we're all pulling in the same direction," he said. "Just keep your eyes open."

"Will do, sir."

"All right, then. I'll put Angel back on, and she can help you coordinate your next move."

Chapel talked to Angel briefly, arranging to have a cab waiting when he left the veterinary clinic. Then he opened the door of the examination room and headed out to the front of the office, where Julia and her receptionist were talking quietly. Julia had a balled-up tissue in her hand, and the receptionist was rubbing her back in slow circles. Apparently

Julia had finally gotten a chance to start grieving for her mother.

"I'll be going now," Chapel told her. "If there's anything I can do—"

"You already have," Julia told him.

"I might have some more questions," he suggested. "But I'll give you some time, first. I'm . . . I'm so sorry."

She nodded. She wasn't even looking at him anymore. "You should get a CT scan at some point. Make sure your brain wasn't injured in that concussion."

"If I get a chance, I will," he told her.

"You'll want a doctor who specializes in human patients for that." She got up to unlock the front door. "I hope you'll forgive me if I say I never want our paths to cross again."

He couldn't blame her for that. "Thanks for all your help."

She shrugged. He started to walk out the door, but she stopped him by putting one hand on his artificial shoulder. He flinched, even if she didn't. He'd never gotten used to people touching him there.

"Captain," she said, "be careful. But find the rest of them, and make sure nobody else has to go through this. Grief, I mean. It sucks."

"I'll do my best," he promised her.

IN TRANSIT: APRIL 12, T+11:29

Back to work. The next name on the list was Christina Smollett. She was in New York City, too. Hopefully she was still alive.

A new cab was waiting for him in front of Julia's clinic. He climbed in, and the car rolled smoothly away before he'd even had a chance to tell the driver what address he wanted.

"All taken care of," Angel told him.

"I appreciate it." He tapped on his knee with the fingers of his artificial hand. When he'd been talking with Julia, he'd almost forgotten the time-sensitive nature of his operation. Now that he was away from her, the ticking of the clock started to bother him again. "We'll have to make this next visit quick. What can you tell me about Christina Smollett?"

Angel hummed a little tune while she worked. "Interesting," she said, after a minute.

"Anything you'd like to share?" Chapel asked.

Angel laughed. "If I understood it, I'd give you some analysis. What I'm looking at is just facts. Christina Smollett has a social security number, a date of birth—August 23, 1959—and a mailing address we already knew, 462 First Avenue, New York, where you're headed now. Beyond that? Not much. As far as I can tell she's never filed a tax form, for one thing."

"That's odd for a woman in her fifties," Chapel mused.

"Never been married, no children. No family left, either—her parents died a while back, both from natural causes and at advanced ages. No brothers or sisters. She doesn't have a bank account. She doesn't have any academic records past high school, which . . . let me check . . . she *did* graduate from, though not with particularly impressive grades. From there the list gets pretty monotonous. No driver's license. No history of service in the armed forces. No arrests, warrants for arrest, or so much as a parking ticket. Never been fingerprinted, and I can't find a single photograph of her taken after 1971. It's like she hasn't so much as touched the world in forty years."

"Sounds like she's been living off the grid," Chapel said.

"And *you* sound like you've got a theory, sweetie."

"More like a hunch," Chapel said. "I'm betting Christina Smollett works for the CIA. Probably in the National Clandestine Service. She's undercover, or at least off the books."

"They certainly don't list her on their payroll," Angel confirmed.

"Helen Bryant and William Taggart were both CIA employees. I'm pretty sure every single name on that list is or was as well. We're tracking down the people who worked on some operation in the eighties. Probably something the CIA's Directorate of Science and Technology got up to."

"Aren't they the ones who make the exploding pens and cyanide-filled false teeth?" Angel asked. "The gadget shop?"

"They do more than that. They were the ones who ran MK-ULTRA, for instance. That's exactly the shop that Drs. Bryant and Taggart would work for. And unless I'm way off, I'm willing to bet Christina Smollett worked in the directorate as well."

"Let me do some more checking, see what I turn up," Angel said.

As the cab rolled into Manhattan the traffic

picked up a little, but it wasn't long before they were on First Avenue. The cabdriver rapped on the partition and glanced over his shoulder. "You want the emergency room or the main entrance?" he asked.

"What? Emergency room?" Chapel said. "No, I'm going to a private residence. A house or an apartment building."

"Oh, sorry. With that bruise on your head I figured you were checking yourself in. You sure you have the right address?"

"Definitely. 462 First Avenue," Chapel confirmed.

"Buddy," the cabbie told him, "maybe you *should* have them take a look at your head. That's the address for Bellevue Hospital. You know—the place where they send all the crazies."

MANHATTAN, NEW YORK: APRIL 12, T+11:55

Chapel reached for his wallet to pay the cabdriver, but the man waved his hand to say no. "All prepaid, and I'm not going to take advantage of a guy like you," the cabbie said, smiling broadly.

"A guy like me?" Chapel asked.

"No offense, friend, no offense meant. I have a mother in Ohio, she's like you, okay? So I understand how hard it can be."

Chapel started to reach up to touch his artificial arm, then stopped himself.

"When you have trouble keeping track of things, right? When maybe you have memory problems. My mom's got the Alzheimer's, she's doing all right, though."

"That's . . . good," Chapel said. "I'm glad to hear it. Thanks."

Clearly the man thought he had brain damage or something. Humiliated and still a little confused by what he was doing there, Chapel climbed out of the cab and looked up at the façade of Bellevue Hospital, which looked like any other glass-fronted building in New York except it had the name "Bellevue" written up one side. Having only seen the hospital in movies before, he would have expected some huge brick monolith with tiny barred windows from which the occasional scream could be heard.

Maybe he *should* check himself in. He was definitely feeling disoriented and confused. Julia had said he was recovering nicely from his concussion, though. "Angel, do you have any thoughts about what's going on, here?"

"Just one, sugar. I'm starting to understand why Christina Smollett is so far off the radar. She's been a resident here since 1979. She's a patient in the psychiatric hospital."

Chapel frowned. "How old was she when she checked in? Wait—I can do this one in my head. She was born in 1959 so she would have been nineteen or twenty. I don't see how she could possibly have done any work for the CIA before that. And I seriously doubt the CIA has any undercover operatives in there."

"You still want to go in and talk to her?" Angel asked. "I can make the arrangements."

"Yeah, I should at least see if she can give me any new leads." Though Chapel wondered what a woman who'd been living in a psychiatric hospital for over thirty years could possibly know about genetic freaks with extra eyelids or the inner workings of secret government facilities. Still, he was here. "I won't take long. Can you have a helicopter ready to pick me up when I'm done?"

"There's a helipad on the roof. It's not open to civil aviation, but I can get you in and out before anyone knows you're there. In the meantime . . . okay, you're good. You've been added to the list of approved visitors for Christina Smollett. I've listed you as being in law enforcement."

"Thanks," Chapel said, and he hurried for the entrance. There was a metal detector inside and a couple of bored-looking uniformed security guards, one of whom was reading a newspaper. The other wrote down Chapel's name on a clipboard and then waved him through to a bank of elevators.

On the way up Angel gave him directions to the correct ward. The Psychiatric Hospital was behind a series of locked doors that security guards had to open for him. The place was clean and brightly lit, but it looked old and tired all the same, the walls painted in drab institutional colors and the endless doors all the same. Following Angel's directions, he finally reached a nurses' station where a man in purple surgical scrubs waved him over. "You're here to see Kristin, right?"

"Christina Smollett," Chapel said, glad as always that he had Angel to smooth the way for him. Without her it might have taken hours to get this far.

"Christina? We have a Kristin Smollett," the nurse told him. "Huh. Ruth? Ruth!"

An older woman in a starched white uniform

came to the window of the nurses' station and peered out with sharp eyes.

"Ruth," the male nurse asked, "Christina Smollett. Is that the same as Kristin?"

"Yes," Ruth told him, handing him a manila folder. "She'll be in her room this time of day. Dinner's in an hour; be sure to be done with your visit by then, sir."

"It shouldn't take that long," Chapel assured her.

The male nurse led him down a long corridor. He leafed through the folder while they walked. It looked like it was Christina Smollett's medical record.

"Funny," the nurse said. "I've been working here six years. I always thought her name was Kristin."

"She never corrected you?" Chapel asked.

"You haven't visited her before, have you?" the nurse inquired. He caught Chapel trying to read over his shoulder, and he snapped the manila folder closed.

"No," Chapel admitted.

The nurse gave him a shrewd look, but then he shrugged. "Somebody like Kristin, somebody who's been taking antipsychotic medication for a long time, it kind of . . . eats away at them. It keeps them from acting out, and it makes the disturbed thoughts go away. But it doesn't leave a whole lot else in there." He lowered his voice to a conspiratorial whisper. "Looking at her medication history, it's like reading a book on the history of nasty pills. The stuff we give here now is okay, it's all new wonder drugs. But back in the eighties she was mainlining Thorazine, and that stuff turns you into a zombie.

I'd be pretty surprised if *she* can even remember her name."

MANHATTAN, NEW YORK: APRIL 12, T+12:07

The nurse unlocked a door and gestured for Chapel to head into the room beyond. "I'll be out here when you're done, so I can check you back out."

Chapel thanked him and stepped inside.

The room was small but not cramped, pleasant without exactly being comfortable. There was a bed and a dresser inside, and one window that looked like it couldn't be opened. Christina Smollett was sitting on the bed. She might have been fifty or seventy. Her hair was long and gray, and it looked like it had been carefully brushed on one side and left tangled and knotted on the other. She wore a sweat suit, and she was staring at the one piece of ornamentation in the entire room, a picture taped to the wall. The picture was of Tom Selleck, a twinkle in his eye and a cocky grin half hidden behind his famous mustache.

She didn't move at all when Chapel came in. She didn't seem aware of his presence. He walked over in front of her, not wanting to block her view of the picture but needing to get her attention. "Ms. Smollett?" he asked. "Christina?"

She blinked when he said her name, but didn't move her head. Her lips were curled in a simple smile. "He always looks so nice, in his shows," she said. "Like he would be friendly if you met him."

She sighed happily.

Chapel took a deep breath. "Christina, my name is Chapel. I need to ask you some questions. I need to know if you've ever met a Dr. Helen Bryant or a Dr. William Taggart."

She stuck out her lower lip and shook her head in the negative. "I know lots of doctors, though, and they don't always tell me their names. I've known a whole bunch of doctors. Doctors like me. They say I'm a perfect patient."

"I'm sure you are," Chapel told her. "How about Franklin Hayes? He's a judge. Have you ever met a judge?"

"Oh, no. There would have been a judge at my commitment hearing. But they didn't take me to that. Mommy said they didn't want to upset me. I used to be very easy to upset." She looked back at the picture on the wall. "Do you think he would be nice, if you met him in person?"

"Tom Selleck?"

"Is that his name? I . . . I have trouble with names sometimes. I'm sorry. I'm being a terrible hostess. Can I offer you a cup of coffee? If you're hungry, I could probably make something."

Chapel glanced around the room by reflex, but of course there was no coffeemaker in the room, much less any kind of kitchen facilities.

This was going nowhere. Christina Smollett's mind was mush, to be callous about it. She wasn't there. He took the kill list from his pocket and ran down the rest of the names, but she just shook her head at the sound of each one.

What on earth did this woman have to do with chimeras and kill lists and CIA secret projects? He couldn't see any connection at all. More to the point, why would the detainees—the chimeras, as he was coming to think of them—want to kill this woman in the first place? She was no danger to them or anybody else.

If she had ever known a secret, a secret that could damage national security, it was long gone.

"You're very handsome," she said, and looked down at her hands. A blush spread across her cheeks. "I don't see a lot of white people in here. Most of the nurses are Spanish or Negroes."

". . . okay," Chapel said. "Christina, it was nice meeting you, but I think I should go now. Be . . . well." He couldn't think of anything else to say, and for once Angel was no help. "Be safe."

"You look nice. Nice and handsome. That's a very good combination in a gentleman caller. I don't get as many gentleman callers as I did when I was younger," she told him. "Will you come again, Mr. Selleck? Please tell me you'll come and see me again sometime. I'd like that very much."

Chapel stood up and walked over to the door. "Perhaps, Christina. I'm, uh, very busy with work right now, and—"

"You know what they say, a young lady with no social connections is at high risk of recidivism." It sounded like something a doctor might have said to her once. "I could backslide. I could lose all the wonderful progress I've made if I don't get to see people sometimes. If I don't get to talk to people, get social stimulation, if I—"

She stopped talking then.

Her face went white and her eyes very wide.

Chapel looked down and saw she had grabbed his arm. His left arm. Her fingers squeezed at the silicone that was wrapped around the motors there.

She grabbed the fingers of his artificial hand and brought them up to her face to look at them more closely. And then she started to scream. Piercing, hysterical cries of utter terror.

"You're not real! You're a robot! You're a robot!"

Chapel pressed up against the wall to one side of the door as Christina ran around the room, grabbing the blankets off her bed, tearing the picture of Tom Selleck off the wall. She held them close to her like armor, like they could protect her.

"He's a robot," she shrieked as the nurse came into the room. "He's not real! Don't let him touch me. Don't let him put that thing inside me! Don't let him touch me!"

The nurse stared at Chapel as he took Christina's shoulders and tried to calm her down.

"I have an artificial arm," Chapel tried to explain. "A prosthetic. She grabbed it and—and—"

"Just go. Get out—Ruth can check you out," the nurse said. He turned to Christina and tried to shush her, his hands stroking her arms.

"You're not real! You're a machine man!" she shouted.

Chapel hurried out into the hall and down toward the nurses' station, glancing over his shoulder to make sure Christina wasn't running after him. At the station the nurse named Ruth leaned out through her window. She looked at him, then down the hall toward Christina's room.

"I, uh," Chapel said. "I seem to have—"

"This is a psychiatric hospital, sir," Ruth told him. "It happens. It's best if you just leave now."

"Not a problem," Chapel said. He signed the form she put in front of him and headed for the locked doors that led off the ward.

BROOKLYN, NEW YORK: APRIL 12, T+12:16

Julia's receptionist was taking advantage of this very weird day to catch up on her filing. Portia Artiz loved her job, but she didn't know what to make of any of the things that had happened so far. The morning had been perfectly normal, a parade of dogs and cats coming through the front room, phone calls and forms to be filled out. Then Julia had said she was going to her mom's place for lunch and everything had just gone weird.

First Julia had called to tell Portia to cancel all her appointments, but she wouldn't explain why. She'd been crying on the phone and Portia begged her to say why, but Julia had a way of not letting anybody in. Portia blamed that on her mother, who everybody said was such a saint but the couple of times Portia met her she'd been a real frosty bitch.

Oh, man, she shouldn't even think things like that. Julia's mom was dead, attacked by some weirdo looking for drugs. The very thought made Portia's skin crawl. They got junkies in the office all the time, looking to score from the supply of animal tranquilizers they kept in a closet at the back of the office. Most of them were scrawny little guys, no threat to anybody but themselves. They were more annoying than dangerous—they came up with the craziest stories about why their pets needed the drugs really bad, right away, and they just didn't give up. Half of Portia's job was getting rid of them, threatening to call the police if they didn't leave. What if one of those guys was as jacked up and dangerous as the one who got Julia's mom, though? Portia shivered as she bent over the filing cabinet.

Someone rapped on the glass door behind her, and Portia jumped right into the air. She gave out a little squeak and turned to see a man standing at the door, a big guy with a smile on his face. *Probably another junkie*, she thought, until he held up a police badge and pressed it against the glass.

He started laughing and Portia realized she must look hilarious, jumping straight in the air like that. He chuckled wildly and she couldn't help herself, she had to join in. She giggled behind her hand and shook her head as she opened the door. "You scared me half to *death*," she said, still laughing. "What can I do for you? If this is about that guy who came back here earlier, the one with the concussion—" she started.

"Nope," the man said, and then he grabbed her by the throat and squeezed, hard. Portia's vision started to dim as she struggled for breath. "Not him. I'm here for your boss."

MANHATTAN, NEW YORK: APRIL 12, T+12:17

While Chapel waited on the roof of Bellevue for his helicopter he spoke to Angel, trying to figure out why someone like Christina Smollett would be a target for the chimeras.

"She's definitely not CIA," Angel said.

"Definitely. But then why is she on the list?" He crumpled the list in his hand. "Maybe this is all a snipe hunt. Maybe the list is meant to send me down the wrong path. Maybe I'm wasting my time chasing phantoms just so the CIA can have a good laugh at my expense, and—"

"No. The list is real. The names are all there for a reason," Angel said, and any trace of flirtation or sultriness was gone from her voice. "Every one of those people is marked for death, including Christina Smollett."

Chapel looked up at the sky as if he would see Angel floating there.

Interesting.

Very interesting.

"You know things you aren't telling me," he said.

"Now, sugar," she said, her voice softening again. "You already knew *that*. Don't be silly, there are all kinds of secrets that I can't—"

"In fact, you knew all about Christina Smollett before I came here on this fool's errand," he said, very carefully.

"How could I know that?"

"Because you called here, back when I asked you to let the targets know they were in danger. You knew she was a patient in Bellevue, you must have— because you talked to somebody here. Her doctors, the security guards—somebody."

"I . . . spoke to them. Yes."

"You didn't mention that before I got here. You

let it be a little surprise for me. We're not exactly on the same team, are we, Angel?" he asked. "I'm trying to save lives here. I'm trying to stop a bunch of killers. And you're not on board for that. Not fully. You have another agenda you're working here, and it's not about keeping these people alive."

He waited for her reply. For her to try to smooth things over, to explain things away. But she didn't say anything.

Eventually the helicopter came to pick him up.

IN TRANSIT: APRIL 12, T+12:22

Seen from the roof of Bellevue the sky over New York City was a deep blue-black. Up this high Chapel could even see a few stars, though most of them were lost in the haze of light that seemed to rise from the city like mist. On the western horizon a last streak of pink marked where the sun had gone down.

Out there, Chapel thought, *out past that sunset there are three more of the bastards already moving toward their targets.* Implacable killers moving fast, like sharks that had caught the scent of blood. And he had just thrown away the best weapon he had to find and fight them.

"Angel," he said, "please come in. Angel?"

There was no response.

"Angel," he said, "I'm sorry if I was rude."

She didn't reply.

"Sir?" the pilot asked, leaning across the crew seats of the chopper and shouting over the noise of the engine. "We need to get airborne."

Chapel nodded and climbed into his seat. A helmet waited for him there—he picked it up and started to pull it on when he realized he would have to take the hands-free unit out of his ear for it to fit.

His main connection to Angel. Well, she could reach him through the helicopter's radio if she felt like talking. He put the hands-free unit in his pocket and pulled the helmet on. Adjusting the microphone, he asked the pilot, "What are your orders?"

"Sir, I'm to take you to Newark Airport; that's just the other side of the Hudson River. There you will find a civilian jet waiting for you to take you wherever you want to go. I'm supposed to ask you where that is, sir. They need to file a flight plan before you arrive or you won't be able to take off."

Where indeed? The next names on the list, in geographical order, were in Atlanta and Chicago. He had to pick one and hope that he wasn't haring off after another distraction. If he chose the wrong one, if he wasted time on another red herring, he could be sentencing an innocent person to death. He pulled the crumpled list from his pocket.

He tapped his artificial fingers on his knee. The target in Chicago was named Eleanor Pechowski; the one in Atlanta was a Jeremy Funt.

Angel might have been able to help him. She might have told him which of them was a higher-value target for the chimeras. But Angel wasn't talking to him.

He remembered something he'd heard Teddy Roosevelt had said. In a crisis, the best thing you can do is the right thing. The second best was the wrong thing. The worst thing you could do was nothing.

He had to make a decision. He had to just pick one.

"Atlanta," he told the pilot. "I'm going to Atlanta next."

So he could start this whole crazy chase over from scratch.

"Might as well settle in, sir. This'll take a little while," the pilot told him.

Chapel nodded and looked out his window. They were already lifting off the hospital roof. The helicopter made a wide arc around a skyscraper and headed west, toward the sunset. At least he was making some progress.

It had been a long day and he felt like closing his eyes, maybe even getting a little sleep. The very first thing they taught him in the army was how to sleep wherever he might be, whenever he got the chance. He closed his eyes and tried to calm down his racing mind. Tried not to think about dead doctors and monsters that were part human and part something else.

Before he could nod off, though, he felt his phone jump in his pocket. He let it vibrate for a second, wondering who could be calling him. Maybe it was Angel, he thought. Or Hollingshead calling him to bitch him out for the way he'd treated Angel.

It was neither of them. The phone listed the number as having a 718 area code. He vaguely remembered that was the code for Brooklyn.

He only knew one person in Brooklyn. "Julia?" he said, answering the call. "Did you think of something that I needed to—"

"Chapel!" Julia said. She was shouting, but he could barely hear her over the noise of the helicopter. Only a few words got through. "Chapel, you—to come—man here—police—says he's police—don't know who else to—think he's—kill me!"

The phone beeped three times and the words *CALL FAILED* appeared on the screen. Chapel wasn't used to this phone—it worked differently from his old BlackBerry—but he managed to call up the recent call menu and tried to call her back. The phone beeped three times, telling him it couldn't make the connection. He tried again.

Three beeps.

Chapel could only think one thing. A second chimera was in New York—and it had decided to pick up where the first one left off. It was going to kill Julia.

"Change of plans," he told the pilot. "Take us to Brooklyn—as fast as you can!"

The pilot shook his head and looked over at Chapel. "Sir, that's not allowed. I've already put in my own flight plan, and the local authorities are very strict about civilian aircraft deviating from course over Manhattan."

"A woman's going to die if you don't turn around right now," Chapel told the man. When the pilot didn't respond instantly, Chapel grabbed the chin strap of his helmet and dragged his head to the side to make eye contact. "Turn around," he said.

The pilot was military. He knew what a direct order sounded like.

BROOKLYN, NEW YORK: APRIL 12, T+12:31

The pilot set them down on the ball field of a public park not too far from Julia's clinic. It was as close as he could get.

Chapel jumped to the ground. He took a second to get his bearings and headed for the closest exit from the park. The streets beyond were lit brightly enough, and the clinic was only two blocks away. He prayed he wasn't too late.

He'd never forgive himself if he failed to save Julia, not after he'd already failed her mother.

When he reached the clinic, he found it shut up tight for the night. An iron shutter had been pulled down over its front door and curtains obscured its windows. He was about to hammer on the door, demanding to be let in, when he heard a sudden sharp noise come from inside. A noise like a muffled gunshot.

Or one fired from a silencer.

No. Jesus no. This chimera had a gun.

Chapel looked up and saw there were no bars on the windows of the second story of the building. There was a light fixture just above the doorway that looked sturdy enough to hold his weight. He jumped up and grabbed it with his good hand, then slowly pulled himself up until he could hook one leg around it.

As a kid in Florida Chapel had climbed plenty of trees. Then in the army he'd learned to climb walls and fences. He could do this. He got a nasty twinge from his hurt leg when he put all his weight on that foot, but he managed to launch himself upward and grab the ledge of the second-story window. Desperation gave him strength as he pulled himself up so he could stand on the ledge. It was only a few inches wide, but it was enough.

He tried the window and found it opened freely. Chapel jumped through feetfirst and landed in a dark bedroom full of minimalist furniture. Thankfully there was nobody asleep in the bed. He hurried to the room's door and started to reach for the knob—then remembered his training and pressed his ear up against the door instead.

For a moment he heard nothing. Then a soft creak, as if someone had stepped on a loose stair riser. The chimera must have heard him come through the window and was coming upstairs to investigate.

The sound wasn't repeated. Chapel had no idea where the chimera was in the building. One wrong move now and he was likely to get shot. He drew his weapon and held it low, down by his thigh.

Every shred of his training told him he was in a lousy situation. There was an armed madman out there beyond the door, and Chapel had no idea of his location or if he was even alone. Opening the door would expose him to enemy fire. He glanced down at the bottom of the door and saw only darkness there—there would be no lights in the hall outside. He would be running blind, running right into what could be an ambush or a trap or who knew what. Julia could already be dead, and he might be throwing away his life for nothing—worse than that, he was jeopardizing his mission by acting like this.

He reached down and turned the doorknob.

To hell with caution, he told himself. And then he shoved the door open and threw himself into the hallway beyond, keeping low and swinging his arm up to point his pistol first one way, then the other, up and down the hall.

He saw no movement, no sign of any threat. He started to move again—

—when he heard the same creaking sound as before.

Chapel froze in place and gave his eyes a moment to adjust to the darkness. A little light came in through the windows of the bedroom behind him, enough to see that there were two other doors on the hall, and that to his left it ended in a stairwell leading down. The doors were all closed. He was certain the creaking had come from the stairs.

He strained his eyes to see anything. A silhouette. A shadow. Just a few steps from the top of the stairs, something big moved in the darkness, and he heard the creaking again.

The shape held something long and narrow— like a silenced pistol.

Chapel did what you were never supposed to do in such a situation. He improvised. Launching himself forward, he ran toward the top of the stairs and then threw himself down them, aiming right for the center of the shadow's mass.

A shot rang out, a dull roar muffled by the silencer. The muzzle flash was only a dim flicker of light, but it was enough for Chapel to see that his target was a man in a suit. In midair Chapel threw out his arms to grab the man and pull them both rolling to the floor of the stair landing. He took the fall with his shoulder and spun around, weapon up and raised and ready to fire.

The long barrel of the silencer was already pointed right at his face. He'd taken his target down, but the chimera had jumped back to his feet before Chapel could even get his bearings.

"Ah, how sweet," the chimera said. "You came back for her." The chimera seemed to find this uproariously funny. He couldn't seem to stop laughing.

That was when Chapel realized he wasn't facing a chimera at all.

BROOKLYN, NEW YORK: APRIL 12, T+12:39

"I'm just—heh—I'm going to turn on the—ha—lights," Laughing Boy said. "Okay? Nobody needs to move, I just want to. To. Heh heh heh. Get a look at you."

"Try anything and I *will* shoot," Chapel told him.

"Yeah, yeah. Ha ha ha."

Laughing Boy reached up and flicked a light switch. Chapel was ready for it, but still the sudden light dazzled him. He put his artificial hand up to shield his eyes. Laughing Boy had plenty of time to shoot him in the second or so it took his eyes to adjust, but the CIA freak didn't take the opportunity.

Once Chapel could see, he understood the situation a little better. The two of them were crammed into the narrow landing of the stairs, Chapel in a tight firing crouch, Laughing Boy hunched over just a little. Laughing Boy's silenced pistol was still pointed right at Chapel's face.

Chapel's sidearm was pointed straight at Laughing Boy's heart.

Laughing Boy couldn't stop giggling, perhaps at the absurdity of this situation. His whole body shook with mirth—except the arm that held his gun. The barrel of his pistol didn't so much as bob up and down.

"Where's Julia?" Chapel demanded. "Is she alive?"

Laughing Boy shrugged.

"Answer me!"

The CIA man smiled. He'd been laughing the whole time, but this was the first thing that made him smile. "Nobody gets to give orders around here. Not when we've both drawn down on each other."

Chapel gritted his teeth. He thought of something that had occurred to him before. "Do me a favor, then. Blink your eyes a couple of times."

Laughing Boy's smile turned into a mischievous grin. "Oh, clever. But no. I'm not one of *them*. I'm just like you."

"Bullshit," Chapel said. "We've got nothing in common."

"You'll find out."

"Enough of this. Put your weapon away or I'll shoot," Chapel demanded.

"I'm ready to die for my country," Laughing Boy said. He chuckled at the thought. "I do what I have to do."

"You're going to tell me that's why you're here? In the interest of national security?" Chapel could hardly believe it.

Laughing Boy nodded. "She was exposed to the virus. I just need to bring her in for a couple tests."

"Sure," Chapel said. "That makes sense. That's why you came with a silencer on your weapon. And why she called me to tell me you were trying to kill her."

"Oh, all right—you're cleverer than I gave you credit for, aren't you? I was going to put a bullet in her and then burn her body. But, you know, it's all details." Laughing Boy chortled so hard his concentration broke for a second.

Long enough.

Chapel shot out one leg and swept it across Laughing Boy's ankles. As he'd expected, the CIA man was fast and managed to jump back, avoiding the sweep, but that distracted him further and gave Chapel plenty of time to grab the flash suppressor on the end of the silenced pistol and shove it upward, toward the ceiling. The pistol discharged once, twice, and the stink of gunpowder filled Chapel's nose and made him want to sneeze, but he fought it back and wrestled the weapon out of Laughing Boy's hand. In a second he had his own pistol jammed up under the CIA man's chin and the silenced pistol went arcing backward, over his shoulder, to clatter on the stairs below.

"Now," Chapel said, "we start talking about who gets to give the orders."

"Told you," Laughing Boy said, his chest shaking with a case of the giggles, "I'm ready to die."

He flung himself forward before Chapel had a chance to react, pushing them both down the stairs, flying head over feet. Chapel's head spun as it struck the banister, then a riser on the way down. At the bottom he struggled to regain his feet, to spin around and find the other man. He was so disoriented it took him a second to realize he'd dropped his pistol.

Laughing Boy stood up from where he'd bent over to retrieve his own weapon. Chapel braced himself, ready to take the shots. Ready to die.

But Laughing Boy . . . laughed. Long and hard and fully, from the bottom of his chest. "Hear that?" he said. "They're never supposed to be around when you need them, right? Am I right?"

Chapel strained his ears and heard it—the sound of police sirens, coming toward them. Someone must have seen him break into the building.

"I'm going to go now," Laughing Boy said, holstering his weapon. "I hate cops, you know? So many questions, and they never believe your answers."

"It helps if you tell them the truth."

Chapel had never in his life told a joke that got such a big and heartfelt laugh.

BROOKLYN, NEW YORK: APRIL 12, T+12:46

Laughing Boy disappeared into the darkness of the building. Chapel didn't bother chasing him— he knew the man would shoot him if he tried. He grabbed his own handgun off the floor and holstered it, then searched for a door leading into the clinic. By the time he found it, red and blue lights were already stabbing through the thin curtains that covered the front windows. He heard police radios squawking, and he knew in any second they would start demanding he come out with his hands visible.

Before then, he had to know what had happened here. He had to know if Julia was still alive.

The clinic was dark, and the flashing lights made it hard to see anything. He hurried forward into the reception area and nearly slipped and fell. The floor was slick with something dark. He knew what that meant instantly.

"Oh, no," he said aloud. He crept forward until he found the receptionist's desk. Blood had splattered all the files lying there, and a woman's body lay slumped, motionless, in the chair.

Biting his lip, he used his artificial hand—it didn't have any fingerprints—to gently lift her head.

It wasn't Julia. It was the receptionist, the one he'd seen comforting Julia in her grief. There were two dark holes in her face, one in her temple, one in her cheekbone just below her eye. Blood oozed from both of them as he moved her. "I'm so sorry," he said. "You had nothing to do with this, you didn't deserve . . ."

"Chapel?" he heard someone shout, from behind him.

It was muffled, distorted, but it was definitely Julia's voice.

He made his way deeper into the clinic, past the examination rooms, past a shelf loaded down with prescription dog food. "Julia?" he called. "Where are you?"

"All the way at the back," she called out. "Is he still there?"

"He's gone," Chapel called. In the dark he stumbled forward until he found a door at the back of the clinic. A heavy, reinforced steel door with a massive lock. Bending down he saw that the paint on the lock plate had been scuffed. There were three long oval spots where the paint had been blasted away.

Laughing Boy must have tried to shoot out the lock. That almost never worked—Chapel had been taught that much when he was trained by the Rangers—but it looked like Laughing Boy had failed to find any other way to get the door open.

"I'm coming out," Julia said. The lock mechanism clicked, and the door swung open. Chapel got a look inside and realized why a veterinary clinic needed such a heavy door—the closet beyond was lined with shelves stocked with pill bottles of every type and size and description.

He only had time for a quick glance before Julia rushed out at him, a scalpel in one hand. "Tell me you don't work with him! Tell me you didn't set all this up!" she demanded.

"I swear it," he said, holding up both hands.

She stared at his left hand, and he realized it must be covered with blood.

"He killed Portia," Julia said.

"I know. But he's gone now. The police frightened him off."

Julia shook her head. Then she dropped the scalpel to clatter on the floor and rushed at him, wrapping her arms around him. "Make this stop," she pleaded. "Make it stop!"

But Chapel knew that was one thing he couldn't promise.

Laughing Boy was hunting down everyone who had come into contact with the chimeras. He was killing them and burning their bodies, just in case they'd been exposed to the virus. Just because he'd been thwarted once didn't mean he wouldn't try again. He would come back for Julia, track her down wherever she went, no matter how much police protection Chapel might arrange for her.

There was only one thing he could do.

"I have a plan to keep you safe," he told her. She pressed her face against his shoulder and sobbed noisily. "I can protect you from him, and from the chimeras. But I need you to trust me."

"Seriously? That's not going to happen, Chapel!" she wailed, pounding on his good shoulder with her fist. "After everything that happened today, you think I'm just going to put my utter faith in you?"

"I need you to—"

"I'll give you a chance," she said. "Don't blow it."

BROOKLYN, NEW YORK: APRIL 12, T+14:55

Dealing with the police took way too long. For a while they had Chapel in handcuffs and were ready to take Julia into protective custody. Eventually, though, a detective had come running over, waving his cell phone in the air. He huddled up with the cops for a while. Chapel had no idea what they said to one another, but when they were done they took the cuffs off and let him go.

As soon as he was free, his own phone chimed to tell him he had a new text message. It came from

the number (000) 000-0000 and contained only two
words:

yr welcome

Once the cops left, Chapel and Julia headed back
to the public park, where the helicopter picked them
up. It took them to the private section of Newark
Airport, where all the corporate executives stored
their G5 private jets. The plane waiting for Chapel
and Julia looked the same as all the others—sleek
and expensive.

"Does it secretly turn into a robot?" Julia asked.
"Or maybe it has hidden missile systems that flip up
when your enemies least expect it."

Chapel grinned at her. She'd been through so
much trauma that day but she was bouncing back,
delaying her grief and anger and fear because there
was still work to be done, still places to be.

There was something about this woman. Something in the way she kept surprising him. She had
been smart enough to lock herself in the drug closet
when Laughing Boy came for her. She had seen
through his necessary lies.

It didn't hurt that her delicate features were perfectly framed by her mane of fiery red hair. He followed her up the stairs of the private jet and tried
not to be too obvious about enjoying the view.

"It's just a way of getting from point A to point
B," he said. "Normally I would take military trans-
ports. There's always a transport going from one
base to another. My boss decided I needed to get to
Atlanta in a hurry, though, so he swung—this—"

He stopped because as he climbed aboard he got his first look at the interior of the jet. Instantly he knew it had to be Hollingshead's personal plane.

Most of the cabin except for the cockpit had been turned into one spacious sitting area. Four leather-covered seats faced one another in the middle of the space. They were huge and looked extraordinarily comfortable. Chapel, who was running on fumes at that point, saw at once that they could convert with a button press into reclining beds.

Clearly no expense had been spared in making the plane cozy—and elegant.

The walls of the fuselage were lined in rich, red wood, polished to a nearly mirror finish. The overhead lights were designed to look like tiny chandeliers. At the back of the cabin was a massive oak desk with built-in bookshelves. Chapel took a closer look and saw the books were real. Black elastic straps held them in so they wouldn't fall out if the plane hit any turbulence.

Hidden speakers in the ceiling played classical music at a low volume. The plane smelled not like recirculated air but like leather and sandalwood.

"This is nicer than my apartment," Julia said. "Bigger, too."

A narrow door beside the desk opened and a woman in a navy uniform came out, bearing a tray with two cocktail glasses on it. "Good evening, sir, ma'am," she nodded, and brought the tray over to a mahogany coffee table that sat in the middle of the four seats. "I'm Chief Petty Officer Andrews, and I'll be looking after you tonight. Please, have a seat and buckle yourselves in. Our flight time to Atlanta will be a little over two hours, once we're in the air. Can I get you anything while you wait for takeoff? Magazines, blankets, food?"

Chapel hadn't eaten all day, not since breakfast. It was the first chance he'd had to think of it. "I could use a sandwich," he said.

"Certainly, Captain. I have a nice roast beef with cheddar in the back. I'll just put that together for you. Ma'am?"

Julia looked up at Chapel like she wanted approval to ask for something. He shrugged.

"I guess . . . I could use a salad or something," she said, eventually.

Chief Petty Officer Andrews smiled. "I have a romaine salad with goat cheese and mandarin oranges. For dressing, I have a balsamic vinaigrette, a gorgonzola, or just oil and vinegar if you prefer your dressing on the side. Do you take croutons?"

"Um . . . yes," Julia said. Her eyes were wide, as if this were the most bizarre thing she'd seen all day.

Petty Officer Andrews smiled and disappeared through her little door again.

"I made such a mistake when I went to vet school," Julia said, when she was gone. "I should have joined the navy. Is it always like this?"

Chapel smiled. "Always," he said. "In the army we ate dirt half the time, and we used rocks for pillows. In the navy they got goat cheese and mandarin oranges."

IN TRANSIT: APRIL 12, T+15:37

The salad seemed to perk Julia up, though he could see in her eyes just how tired she was. While she ate she actually smiled at Chapel and met his eye once or twice and then turned her head away with a little laugh. "It's funny how comforting having a good meal can be," she said.

"I imagine you could use a little comfort right now," Chapel told her.

She snorted in exuberant agreement. "I need to feel normal, basically. I need to feel like I'm not about to be shot. And frankly, I need a shower and a change of clothes. And a good nap in a real bed. And a drink! Definitely a drink."

"When we get to Atlanta, sure," Chapel said. "Maybe we both need that." It had been a very long day, and it wasn't over yet. "My instinct is to keep moving, to keep working. But if I don't get a little downtime, I'm going to start getting fuzzy. Then I'll start making mistakes."

Julia met his eye directly and gave him a very warm smile. "I know you're on a tight time frame. But I want you to promise me something. The first time we get a chance, you have to let me show you how much I appreciate your saving my life."

For a moment—just a moment—Chapel thought he knew exactly what she meant by that, and the thought made him feel very hot and bothered. "You don't mean—"

Her eyes opened wide, and she put a hand over her mouth. "Jeez! No. I meant you would let me buy you dinner. Or something." She laughed and reached over and patted his wrist, defusing the sudden tension. "Wow, Chapel. You're blushing."

He turned away, because he could feel the heat in his cheeks.

"Oh, don't be embarrassed. It's cute," Julia said.

Nobody had called Chapel cute since he was seven years old. It felt very strange to hear it now.

"There's something about you, Chapel. You're a tough guy, I see that in the way you move, the lines in your face. But there's an innocence underneath it. Interesting. It's like I can see that you really believe in what you do. In who you are. You're not cynical about your job at all."

"I took an oath to protect my country," he said. "I take it pretty seriously."

Julia shook her head. "I've met spies before. They seemed to feel like having secrets made them better than everybody else."

"The opposite is usually true," Chapel said, furrowing his brow. He was distinctly uncomfortable with where this conversation was going.

Luckily Julia didn't push it any further. Though she did say, almost under her breath, "I wish I could see you in your uniform. I bet you look just adorable."

Now that was one thing no one had *ever* said about him. He pretended he hadn't heard her and went back to his sandwich.

After they finished their meal, Julia curled up in her leather seat, covered in a thick wool blanket that looked very warm, and was out like a light. Chief Petty Officer Andrews came out and touched a button on the arm of Julia's chair. It reclined smoothly and without noise, so gently Julia didn't even wake up. The chief petty officer expertly slipped a pillow under Julia's head. She smiled at Chapel, then disappeared as silently as she'd come.

Chapel watched Julia's body rise and fall with her breathing for a while. He thought about how she'd held him when he rescued her from Laughing Boy. About how good it had felt to have her body pressed up against his. He'd felt like a hero, then.

He watched her brow wrinkle and knew she must be dreaming.

She was beautiful. Beyond that, there was something more to her. Real substance. She was strong and smart and kind. He hadn't met anyone like her in a long time. He'd brought her with him to keep her safe. That was all. She had kissed him, but she'd said she wasn't trying to start anything. Whatever he was feeling now she probably didn't return it. How could she? He was a man with one arm. That was enough to put anybody off. Maybe she'd just kissed him out of pity. She'd called him cute and adorable, but those were words women used to describe babies and kittens, not men they wanted to get to know better in a romantic way. Weren't they?

Damn. He needed to stop thinking like that. He needed to stop thinking about Julia as anything but an asset that needed to be protected.

He turned his seat to face the window and watched lights blinking on the tarmac. He had to get his mind off Julia. He grabbed his phone and his hands-free set out of his pocket. He put the hands-free set in his ear and forced himself to close his eyes. "Angel," he said, "I don't know if you're listening. I wanted to say I'm sorry."

"Magic words," Angel told him. "Do you have any more of them?"

"I was letting this case get to me," he told her, "when I accused you of having your own agenda. That was wrong of me. You've done nothing but help me. You've been an utter godsend. I'm starting to see that I could never do this without you."

"That's a start," she said.

"This case—this operation—is like nothing I've ever had to do before," Chapel told her. "I'm starting to get worried. There are three more chimeras out there. There's no way I can catch them all before they kill someone."

"It's looking pretty grim, I'll admit," Angel told him.

"And now I have Laughing Boy to worry about. He's killing people, Angel. He's killing anyone who comes in contact with a chimera, just in case they're infected. He was going to kill Julia."

"I know."

"I couldn't let that happen," he said.

"I know. Director Hollingshead wasn't very happy when he heard you'd brought a civilian along for the ride, of course. But I explained everything to him and made him see it was necessary to prevent another death."

"You did that for me? Even after what I said?"

"I care, Chapel. I care about people, just like you do."

Chapel nodded to himself. He was very glad to hear it. "So he's . . . okay with this?" He glanced over his shoulder and saw Julia's sleeping face half covered by her blanket. She was beautiful like that, in repose. When she wasn't angry or grief-stricken. He wondered what it would have been like to meet her before all this. In just ordinary circumstances. But then again, how could that have ever happened? A veterinarian in New York and a defense intelligence analyst in Virginia would have very little to talk about. Almost nothing in common. "He won't demand I turn her over to the CDC?"

Angel was silent for a moment. After recent events, Chapel worried she might not come back on the line. "She could be infected, Chapel."

"I know," Chapel sighed. He'd known it from the moment he'd found Laughing Boy inside her clinic. She had, in fact, been exposed to the chimera, and if it so much as scratched her while they were in the back of the hijacked cab together, she could have the virus already. "If Hollingshead orders it, I'll bring her in. Turn her over to his doctors so they can screen her for the virus. Treat her if necessary. But I can't just send her off to face Laughing Boy on her own."

"He won't order that. Even if she does have the virus, she's probably better off with you where you can watch her and make sure she doesn't spread it. Still—it's just going to make your job harder if you have to babysit her at the same time."

"I'm not so sure about that. She's proved herself to be pretty resourceful, and she might have information I need. Answers to questions I haven't even figured out how to ask, yet."

"Fair enough. Hollingshead says it's okay, she can

travel with you. Just make sure she doesn't learn anything *too* sensitive, and it should be all right."

"That's good," Chapel said. "About Laughing Boy—what can we do about him? If he's running around killing people, then he must have gone rogue, right? Please tell me that Banks didn't order him to kill Julia. Please tell me we can have him arrested and remove him from the field."

"I wish I could," Angel said.

Chapel tapped at the armrest of his seat with his good fingers. "The CIA doesn't just kill American citizens. I mean, it has, and I suppose things happen that I don't get to hear about. But—"

"Chapel, he was authorized to do this. And the authorization came from higher up than Banks."

Chapel grabbed the armrest hard enough to make the leather creak. "So he's got a license to kill? That's something from the movies. Only the president can authorize the execution of American citizens without a trial."

"Higher up, I said," Angel told him.

Chapel shivered at the thought. "Is the threat of this virus really that high? That they would just kill people on suspicion they might have it?"

"I don't have a lot of information on it. But clearly someone thinks so," Angel told him. "This is way beyond top secret stuff. What we do know, and this from confidential sources, is that the disease caused by the virus is incurable and almost impossible to detect until it's way too late to do anything."

"Jesus." Chapel glanced at Julia again. She could be a ticking time bomb right now. She could be incubating the virus while she slept. And there was no way to know for sure. "That doesn't excuse his behavior. We need to find a way to stop Laughing Boy now. Before he can kill anyone else."

"Chapel," Angel said, "I want to tell you something. You were right."

"What?" It had been a while since somebody had said that to him.

"I do have my own agenda," she told him. "Or rather, my agenda is the same as Director Hollingshead's, and it may not match up with yours. We're not like Director Banks and his operative. We don't want to just kill people to keep this thing under control. But we do intend to control it, regardless of what that takes. Director Hollingshead can't stop Laughing Boy. He doesn't intend to try. He may not like Laughing Boy's methods—but he agrees with Banks, at least in principle, about what needs to be done. If Julia does have the virus, we won't kill her. But we will lock her up for the rest of her life in a facility like the one the chimeras escaped from. Because we have no other choice."

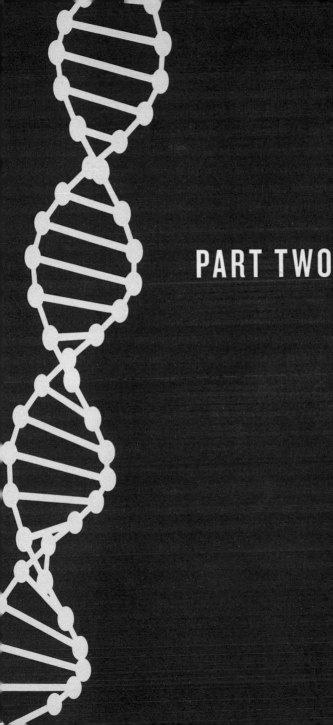

PART TWO

When Chapel was convinced Julia wasn't going to wake up at any moment, he took care of one task he'd neglected all day. Removing his jacket and unbuttoning his shirt, he plugged his artificial arm into a power outlet near his seat, using a retractable cord built into the shoulder. While he waited for it to recharge he called Angel again and asked her about the next two names on the list. "Start with the one in Chicago, first," he said.

"Eleanor Pechowski," Angel replied, and he heard her clacking at her keyboard. "Eleanor, who are you? Let's see. She's a retired schoolteacher."

"That doesn't sound like someone a genetic freak would want to kill," Chapel pointed out. "Maybe a disgruntled former student . . ."

"She worked for the UN, for a while," Angel went on. "In UNESCO. Let's see . . . she lived in New York City at the time, on Roosevelt Island. Looks like she taught English, math, and American history to the children of UN delegates. Maybe she fell in with the black helicopter crowd."

Chapel rolled his eyes. "Please tell me you're not a conspiracy nut, Angel," he said.

Angel laughed. "No, I was just kidding. But just to work at the UN schools, Eleanor Pechowski had to have a security clearance. So the intelligence community would have been aware of her."

"It's a pretty tenuous connection. Just because somebody did a background check on her doesn't mean she ended up working for the CIA. And the last time I checked, the agency didn't hire a lot of English teachers. Okay, what about Jeremy Funt, the one in Atlanta? What's his story?"

"That one's easy. He was a government employee, and all his records are right here. Nothing hidden at all."

"Tell me he worked for the CIA," Chapel said, leaning forward and nearly pulling the plug on his arm.

"Not exactly," Angel said. "He worked for the FBI."

"Huh," Chapel said. That didn't make much sense. The CIA and the FBI had little to do with each other, other than both being government agencies. They weren't even overseen by the same cabinet department. "Is it possible that's a cover?"

"Not unless it's an extremely good one. His service record is an open book, here—and it shows him working a steady load of cases from 1981 to 1996, all pretty standard stuff, missing persons, kidnappings, wire fraud. The one question mark is that he left the bureau in 1996 at the age of forty-five, long before mandatory retirement. With a file like that, normally you'd expect that he left the bureau in disgrace, that he messed up somehow and was forced to retire, but there's no indication here he was anything less than a solid asset to the bureau."

"So Funt just dropped off the bureau payroll with

no explanation, huh? That's interesting. And at least he sounds like a more likely target." He had no idea why the chimeras would want to kill Funt, but if he had to prioritize targets, an FBI agent sounded higher in value than a retired schoolteacher. It sounded like Atlanta might have been the right choice after all. "Angel, what else can you tell me about this guy? What does he do for money? Does he have any family in Atlanta?"

"I'm looking at that right now. It looks like—hold on. Chapel, give me a second here, there's something wrong with one of my laptops. Looks like somebody got a keystroke logger in my system, but that's—hey!"

"Angel?" Chapel asked.

"Somebody's piggybacking on my signal," she said, sounding indignant. "Just who the hell do they think they are? Hacking me, why, I ought to—"

Static filled Chapel's ear and then the signal went dead.

"Angel?" he called. "Angel, come in. What just happened? Angel?"

A new voice spoke to him.

"Captain Chapel, I presume," the voice said. "You and I need to have a little talk."

IN TRANSIT: APRIL 12, T+16:02

"Listen, I don't know who the hell you are, but this is an encrypted line," Chapel said, pulling his phone out of his pocket. The screen showed he was still connected to the number (000) 000-0000. There was no indication anything had changed. "Intruding on this channel is a violation of any number of laws, and—"

"Law?" The voice in his ear chuckled. It was a male voice, a little gravelly as if its owner was a habitual cigarette smoker. There was iron in that voice, but also a little silver—it was the voice of someone used to speaking for a living, like a salesman or a voice-over actor. "I know all about the law," the voice said. "I apologize for cutting in, but they weren't going to let me speak to you, otherwise."

Chapel bit his lip. This was very, very bad. If someone could compromise his line to Angel, then they could find out everything he'd said to her. They could know all his plans and everything he'd learned.

He couldn't imagine that the chimeras could be doing this. They weren't stupid, but they had shown no sign of having the kind of organization it would require to pull off this kind of stunt. He hadn't forgotten, though, that someone had to be helping them. Somebody had broken them out of the facility in the Catskills. Maybe, for the first time, he was running up against that shadowy organization.

"Tell me your name, right now, and who you work for," Chapel insisted. "That's not a request. I can have you up on charges for impeding a federal investigation—and maybe treason, too. You've made a very bad mistake contacting me like this."

"Captain, do me a favor and look at your phone. All will be explained."

Chapel frowned, but he looked down at the screen of his phone. The screen went blank and then lit up to show a grainy video feed. He saw what looked like an image of someone's office, a desk with a green blotter and behind it a window looking out onto a night-shrouded cityscape. After a moment, someone stepped into the frame and sat down behind the desk so the camera could focus on his face.

Chapel recognized the man right away. It was Franklin Hayes.

"Your Honor," he said, despite himself.

Hayes was the Denver-based federal judge whose name was on the kill list. This was one of the people Chapel was trying so desperately to protect.

So what the hell was he doing breaking into Chapel's encrypted line?

"I know this is surprising, Captain," Hayes said. He was an older man, maybe seventy, with silver hair but sharp, intelligent eyes. He wore an immaculate suit with a handkerchief perfectly folded in the breast pocket. "I know it's unorthodox. But I assure you I mean no harm."

"Your Honor, I apologize if I was abrupt, but I was serious about the breach of security. This line—"

Hayes waved one hand in dismissal. "Director Hollingshead wouldn't even tell me your name," the judge said. "Director Banks proved a little more tractable. He owed me a favor, from long ago, so I've called it in. My friends in Langley were able to tap into your line."

So Hayes had connections with the CIA? That was interesting. Chapel made a mental note to look into it. It seemed everyone on the kill list—with the exception of Christina Smollett—was related to the CIA somehow.

"I've been trying to contact you all day," Hayes said, "ever since I was informed my life was in danger."

"Yes, sir," Chapel said. "I had one of my people call you about that. I wanted to make sure you knew to get to a safe place, somewhere you could be protected."

"And I've done just that," Hayes told him. "I'm in my courthouse. I keep a cot here in case I work too late and can't go home, so I'm relatively comfortable. I have state police crawling all over this building."

"Then you should be fine. They can protect you until I arrive."

"Captain. Please don't insult my intelligence. I know what happened to Helen Bryant. And I have some notion of what kind of man is coming here to kill me. Oh, I don't know all your secrets. But Director Banks filled me in on a few pertinent details."

Chapel wanted to strangle Banks, and not for the first time. This case was so secret even the people working on it weren't allowed to know any details. Yet Banks had clearly spilled some of the unknowns to a civilian, just because he'd asked nicely.

"I know," Hayes went on, "that the man in question is more than a match for a few state police. They're little more than highway patrolmen. I need better protection than this. I think I might rate a personal visit from the one man we know is capable of taking out one of these killers."

"I'm sorry?" Chapel asked.

"I'm saying, Captain, that I want you to come here, to Denver, and protect me personally. Director Banks tells me I'm the highest-value target on your list. That I deserve the best protection. It's clear that you're it."

"With all due respect, Your Honor, that's not possible right now," Chapel said. "I'm in the middle of an investigation, and I can't break it off now."

"I understand you're on your way to Atlanta," Hayes said, as if Chapel had said nothing. "That's good, you're headed in the right direction. It will only take a few more hours in the air for you to get here, to Denver. I'll have a car waiting for you at the airport and it will bring you straight to me. I'll let you know when I have the name of the liaison you'll be working with—"

"Your Honor," Chapel cut in, "I'm sorry, but the answer is no."

Hayes waved his hand in dismissal again. "I'll give you complete autonomy on how you want to set up your defenses. You'll be in charge of my escort and you can requisition any more units you need from the local police department, should—"

"I said no," Chapel said, more forcefully.

If anything, that just made Hayes look confused.

Judges had a lot of power. In their courtrooms, they were like gods, able to hand down judgments and throw anyone in jail on contempt charges. Chapel could only imagine how godlike a federal judge must feel most of the time.

Chapel had met enough generals to know that people like that, people who thought of themselves as omnipotent, stopped understanding the word *no*. It didn't just make them angry—they fell out of practice with knowing what it meant. People did what they said, all the time, and nobody ever questioned them.

So it took a few seconds for the negation to sink into Hayes's head.

Eventually he pursed his lips and said, "I can make a lot of trouble for you."

"Is that a threat, Your Honor?" Chapel asked.

"I'm a federal judge, Captain. I don't make threats."

The implication was clear. Hayes didn't need to make threats—when he could make promises instead. Chapel forced a smile onto his face. He was making a bad enemy here, and he knew it. He was about to inherit all kinds of problems. But for this one brief moment it felt pretty good to tell the judge where to stick it. "I'm in the middle of my investigation. More lives than just yours are at stake. The person of interest won't reach Colorado—can't reach Colorado—in less than twenty-four hours from now. If I can't stop him before that, I'll see you in Denver before he arrives. But in the meantime I have other work to do. So no, I won't be coming directly to you."

"Now listen here," Hayes said. "I don't remember requesting your opinion, and I won't put up with—"

A hand fell on Chapel's shoulder.

He jumped in his seat. Swiveling around, he saw Julia standing behind him. She was looking down at his phone.

On the screen, Hayes had gone silent. His face was a mask of utter surprise.

"Why are you talking to Agent Hayes?" Julia asked.

"*Agent?*" Chapel asked.

The screen of his phone went black, instantly.

IN TRANSIT: APRIL 12, T+16:14

"I'm so sorry," Julia said. "I didn't mean to see anything I wasn't supposed to, or . . . or whatever. I just woke up because I heard you shouting at that man, and I came over . . . I guess I shouldn't have. I'll go back to my seat now."

"No, Julia, it's fine," Chapel said, grabbing her hand before she could walk back to her seat. "I'm sorry, I was a little worked up there. But what did you mean when you called him Agent Hayes? He's a judge."

"He is?"

"You didn't recognize him? He's been in the news recently. He's about to become a Supreme Court justice."

Julia shrugged. "I get my news from the *New York Times*, not the TV, so I don't know what a lot of people look like. I mean, I've heard about Franklin Hayes, but . . . wow. I guess I never put two and two together. It can't be the same guy, can it?"

Chapel squeezed her hand. "Care to let me in on what you're thinking?"

Julia inhaled deeply. "This is getting weird."

"This case? Yeah, it has its peculiarities," Chapel said.

"No," Julia said. "I mean the way you're holding my hand."

Chapel glanced down and saw he was still holding on to her. He let go. "Sorry. Like I said, I'm a little worked up."

"Just . . . never mind," she said. "Look, I told you a while back about how I knew my parents were in the CIA. Because an agent came to dinner once a year to debrief them. His name was Agent Hayes, and I'm pretty sure it was the same man you were just talking to. He looks a little older, obviously, but yeah, that was him."

"That's actually really important," Chapel told her. "It helps me fill in a couple of blanks."

"You're welcome, I guess," she said.

"I need to talk to somebody about this. I might have some more questions, but first—"

"I'll be right over here," Julia said, walking over and patting the headrest of her seat. "In the meantime, though, I think I'll go back to sleep."

"Uh, okay," Chapel said.

Their eyes met and something passed between them. Chapel wasn't sure exactly what, and he didn't have time to think about it. Maybe she was starting to think she'd made the wrong decision, coming along with him. Or maybe . . .

He put that thought out of his head right away. That couldn't possibly be right.

"Angel," he said, to clear his mind. "Angel, are you there?"

"I'm back," Angel told him. "What happened there?"

"Franklin Hayes broke into your signal. *The* Franklin Hayes. He had some help from Banks, by the sound of it."

"Banks hijacked my line?" Angel sounded mortified. "That son of a . . . I can't believe it. Well, I mean, I believe he would do such a thing. I just can't believe he actually pulled it off."

"I think we need to assume from now on that he can hear everything we say," Chapel told her. "I don't like that much, but—"

"I'll do what I can to change that," Angel told him. "It means switching to a new system, cutting myself completely out of the network for a while, rebuilding my public and private keys, getting a whole new block of IP addresses. I'll be offline while that's going on—I won't be able to contact you at all. And it'll take some time."

"We don't have a lot of that," Chapel told her.

"I know. It'll take about four hours, and even then I can't guarantee he won't pull that stunt again. But it's something we need to do. Director Hollingshead will freak out when he hears about this. Oh my God, I have so much work to do here. I thought I was secure! I mean, I've got firewalls in here, I've got 256-bit encryption, I've got defenses nobody's supposed to know about. All of it military spec. I'm supposed to be invisible here. I feel like somebody broke into my house and went snooping through my underwear drawer, Chapel."

"I can imagine," he told her. "Angel, before you go offline, I just need to know a couple of things. I need you to look at Franklin Hayes. Apparently he worked for the CIA at some point. Can you confirm that?"

"Should be no harm in looking. Wow. That was easy. It's on his public website. Yep, before he became a judge he worked for the CIA, back in the eighties and early nineties."

"As an asset?"

"No, as a lawyer. Nothing clandestine," Angel said. "The CIA has its own cadre of lawyers. Just like the Mafia does and for the same reason—because so much of what it does is illegal. It looks like his time there was pretty mundane. His records aren't even classified. Let's see what I can pull up."

Chapel waited while she tapped at her keyboard.

"Huh," she said, finally. "Interesting. Franklin Hayes was lead counsel on a couple of high-profile cases. Civil liberties lawsuits, mostly—American citizens claiming the CIA had trampled on their rights. Ninety percent of his cases were settled out of court, but that isn't unusual. Corporate lawyers have the same ratio, typically. I'm running through the list of his cases . . . huh. Oh, boy. Chapel, you're going to like this."

"Go ahead."

"One of the cases was brought by the family of a young woman who had been committed to a mental hospital for schizophrenia. She claimed the CIA had sent one of their spies to sneak in her window every night and . . . ah . . . take advantage of her in her bed. The case was thrown out for lack of evidence. The judge who heard it chastised the family for wasting the court's time. Franklin Hayes was counsel for the agency on that case."

"Why is that relevant?" Chapel asked.

"Because the name of the girl was Christina Smollett."

IN TRANSIT: APRIL 12, T+16:23

"Holy shit," Chapel said. He wasn't a big fan of pointless vulgarity, but this situation seemed to warrant it. "That's no coincidence."

"Definitely not," Angel said. "I'll forgive you for sullying my ears with such language," she went on. "Because right now I feel like fucking swearing myself. I have no way of knowing what the connection actually amounts to. I'm being honest with you here, Chapel. I don't have any information on what the CIA might have actually done to Christina Smollett. But there has to be some relevance. The CIA did *something* to her, and she associated it in some way with being sexually assaulted."

"And Franklin Hayes smoothed it over," Chapel said. "Covered it up."

"Worse than that. He tried to countersue the family for besmirching the name of the CIA," Angel went on. "The judge dismissed the countersuit but agreed to seal all testimony heard in the case. The whole thing was spun as some crazy girl making impossible accusations, and the CIA just didn't want the public to make something out of nothing. But if there wasn't something there, we wouldn't be talking about it right now."

"I'm not a big fan of the CIA right now," Chapel said, which was putting it mildly. "But even I don't believe they're in the business of raping schizophrenics." The words felt ugly in his mouth, but that was what they were talking about. He sighed. "If the records are sealed, I guess there's no way for you to find out what the testimony said."

"This was back in the late eighties, before anything was digitized," Angel told him. "Assuming it wasn't actually destroyed, all that testimony is locked away in a filing cabinet somewhere. Short of breaking into a courthouse and stealing the physical papers, no one is ever going to see it—and that's more your area than mine."

"I'm no thief," Chapel told her. "I'm not about to do that. So we'll have to find some other way of getting the information. Someone has to know what happened. Franklin Hayes, for instance. I bet he knows all about it."

"Too bad you just turned him into an enemy," Angel pointed out.

"Did you hear our conversation?"

"All of it. In fact, so did Director Hollingshead. I woke him up and let him listen in. He's very interested in what Banks did to my computers. And so am I. Chapel, I need to get started on sweeping my gear and moving to new servers. We can't let them just eavesdrop whenever they want. In fact, if they know what we've just been talking about . . . well. They're not going to like the fact we made this connection."

"True enough. All right, Angel. Do what you need to do. We're still a ways from Atlanta, and after we land, I'll be doing some legwork anyway. I'll need to check in with—"

"Chapel, until we're secure again, it's better if I don't know the details."

"Got it. Thank you, Angel. Thanks for everything."

She didn't respond. The hands-free unit in his ear had already switched off.

ATLANTA, GEORGIA: APRIL 12, T+17:53

The jet set down at Hartsfield-Jackson airport in the middle of the night. Chief Petty Officer Andrews brought them cups of hot coffee and croissants while they taxied to the gate and waited for clearance to debark. Chapel had to admit that if he had to fly, this was the way to go. Hollingshead was a lucky man. Before he knew it, he and Julia were whisked through the terminal and out to where a car was waiting for them.

The driver seemed surprised when they said they had no luggage. "Not even an overnight bag?" he asked.

Chapel just shrugged. Fatigue was starting to get to him. He needed to sleep, but that wasn't in the cards. He gave the driver Jeremy Funt's last known address.

"Seriously? That's down in Capitol View. Not the best neighborhood," the driver told him.

"It's where we're going," Chapel said.

"You're the boss." The driver got the car moving and thankfully had little to say after that. Chapel tried watching through the windows as they rolled along, trying to get a feel for this new city. It all blurred together into lights and pools of darkness. He focused on the street signs instead.

After about twenty minutes he leaned forward, a little alarmed. "You're driving in circles," he told the driver.

Had Banks set him up? Was this some kind of ploy to delay him? Or was there something more sinister going on? Was he going to be taken somewhere quiet and quietly shot?

He started to reach for his weapon.

"What are you talking about? I know this city like the back of my hand," the driver said.

"We just passed Peachtree Street," Chapel said. "Except we passed Peachtree Street ten minutes ago."

The driver laughed. "Buddy, you never been to Atlanta before, have you? Half the streets here are called that. It's the state tree. You never heard of Georgia peaches?"

"Oh," Chapel said.

He sank back into his seat.

Damn it, he was getting paranoid. Which only made sense given his circumstances, but still—he was losing it. He'd been going too long too fast, never getting a chance to rest. He needed sleep. If he didn't get it, he would probably start shooting at shadows.

He told himself he just needed to find Jeremy Funt. Once he had the man located and under protection, he could rest.

Just a little while longer.

Within thirty seconds his head fell back against the seat and he was asleep.

ATLANTA, GEORGIA: APRIL 13, T+19:01

"Hey. Hey, buddy! We're here!"

Chapel's eyes snapped open. They felt gritty and raw. All of him felt gritty and raw. Where was he? What was . . .

Right. It all came flooding back. He stirred himself, sat up. Adjusted his jacket. He touched Julia's shoulder, and she slapped his hand away.

"Take your time," the driver told him.

Chapel nodded and rubbed at his face with his hands. His silicone left hand dragged in his stubble, but the irritation helped wake him up a little. He rubbed Julia's shoulder with his good hand. "It's time to wake up," he told her.

She shifted in her seat, making little sounds of annoyance. Then she leaned forward and laid her head on his chest, one of her arms snaking around his waist. "Let me sleep in today," she said. "The little Chihuahuas can wait."

She was so warm against his body in the chilly air-conditioned cab. Chapel felt his body stirring. He put his good hand on her hair and stroked it gently.

Whoa, he told himself. Not appropriate.

He thought of when she'd been examining him in her clinic, and she'd kissed him. That had just been a reward for saving her, though. Except—she had said that it was also maybe because she'd *wanted* to kiss him.

Her hair was soft and slightly curly. It felt good in his fingers. This was totally wrong, he thought.

He had a mission to complete; there was no time for this. But he wanted so desperately to just lean in and kiss her awake.

"Oh, no," she said, and sat bolt upright. "Oh my God."

"It's not what—"

"Oh my God," she said again. "Oh God. Chapel. I—I am so sorry."

"You are?" he asked.

"I thought you were somebody else. My ex-boyfriend. Wow," she said. "That was not appropriate, huh? I'm really sorry."

Chapel reached for the handle of his door. "It's fine. Really," he said. He opened his door and stepped out onto the sidewalk. Harsh sodium lamps burned down from above, pushing away shadows that refused to be completely contained. The buildings on either side of him were mostly one- and two-story houses with peaked roofs. Each had a patch of green lawn out front, and most had a tree or two. It looked nothing whatsoever like New York City.

"Do we need to pay the driver?" Julia asked, coming up beside him.

"No—no—it's all taken care of," he said, a little too quickly.

She gave him a weak smile. He turned toward the car, intending to ask the driver to wait while they went inside, but the cabbie was already pulling away. He waved furiously to call the man back, but it was no use.

Oh, well. He could always call for another car. Even without Angel's help he supposed he could manage that.

"So what's the plan, here?" Julia asked.

"The man who lives here, Jeremy Funt, is like your father—at least in that the chimeras want to kill them both." She winced and he immediately felt like an ass. She knew her father's life—just as her own—was in danger, and she didn't need to be reminded of the fact. "I'm going to get him, and you, out of here. And then I'm going to sit here all night waiting for a chimera to show up. If I can, I'll take it into custody."

"How do you know the chimera will come here?" she asked, rubbing at her eyes.

"I don't, really. But I'm operating under the assumption the chimera has the same list I do, which is how I got this address. Huh. No lights on in the house."

Julia shrugged. "It's late. Maybe he's asleep, like a sane person."

"Maybe," Chapel agreed. If it was him, if *he* knew a psychopath was coming to kill him, Chapel would keep a light on. It would at least make it easier to see the maniac when he arrived. "Come on." He went up a narrow gravel driveway to the front door of the house and knocked loudly. He glanced around at the surrounding houses. Plenty of them still showed lights. He could see the blue glow of a television set through one window across the street and hear people laughing somewhere nearby. A dog was barking a few streets away. It wasn't *that* late.

When there was no answer to his knock he looked around until he found a doorbell and tried that. Still no response.

"Maybe he was really sane, and he went somewhere else. Since he knew the chimera was coming. You did let everyone know they were in danger, right?" Julia asked.

"It was the first thing I did."

Something here just wasn't right. He knocked again, knowing there would be no reply. "Okay. I need to get inside, whether he's here or not, so I can lay my ambush for the chimera. Stand back and watch the street. If you see anyone looking at us and wondering what we're doing, let me know. If you see a police car, let me know."

"I'm guessing, in this neighborhood that's a pretty rare sight," Julia told him.

"Keep an eye out anyway." Chapel flexed his shoulder. It had been a long time since he had knocked a door down with brute force. He had little choice, though. He grabbed the doorknob, intending to lift the door in its hinges and then ram it with his shoulder.

Except the knob turned freely in his hand.

The door swung open. It wasn't locked.

Something here was *definitely* not right.

ATLANTA, GEORGIA: APRIL 13, T+19:12

Chapel drew his weapon and stepped inside the dark house. He motioned for Julia to follow him, then pulled the door shut behind him. "Look for a light switch," he told Julia. Then he turned to face the darkness and called out, "Mr. Funt? I'm a federal agent. I'm here to protect you."

He didn't expect a response, and he didn't get one.

Behind him he heard a click, and then the lights came on.

The house was tastefully, if plainly, furnished. The front door opened on a living room with a large television set, a comfortable-looking sofa, and a beaten-up coffee table that might have been an antique, once. Bookshelves lined the far wall, but they were half empty.

Two archways led off the main room, one to what looked like a kitchen—he could see a refrigerator and a stove through the arch—and one to what presumably was a bedroom. A curtain of beads hung down from that arch. Chapel pointed his weapon toward each arch and called out Funt's name again.

It was possible this was a colossal waste of time. Maybe no chimera had come to Atlanta at all. Maybe all three of them were in Chicago already and were beating Eleanor Pechowski to death while he stood here, wondering what to do next.

That kind of thinking didn't help at all. "Stay close to me," he told Julia, but she was already walking over to the coffee table.

"Does this guy look like a slob to you?" she asked.

Chapel wondered what she was getting at, but he glanced around the room. There were coasters on the coffee table, and no empty cans or glasses lying around. "Not at all," he said. "The opposite, in fact."

Julia ran one index finger along the top of the coffee table. She held it up where he could see it—it was covered in dust. "He hasn't been here in a while."

Chapel frowned. That had to mean something important, but—what? Even if Funt had vacated the house as soon as he got the call from Angel, that was still less than twenty-four hours ago. Dust didn't accumulate that quickly.

"You have a list of addresses for the people the chimeras want to kill," Julia said. When he started to protest, she held up both hands. "I'm not asking any questions, don't worry. You can keep your secrets. I just wanted to point out that maybe your list isn't up to date. Funt might have moved out of here a while ago."

"Maybe," Chapel agreed. "I'm going to check the kitchen. Stay here."

Julia looked annoyed at being ordered around, but there wasn't much he could do about that. He didn't have time to ask her permission every time he needed her to do something. Civilians were fine in principle, he thought, until you needed them to follow orders.

He went into the kitchen and found another light switch. The kitchen was as Spartan as the living room, with a small table pushed up against one wall and only one chair. There was thick dust on the table, but when he checked the stove and the countertops they were clean. No dust on them at all. Funt might have moved out weeks ago—but he had come back at least once.

"I'm going to check the bedroom," Julia called.

"No! Wait for me," he shouted back, but he knew she wouldn't listen. He turned to leave the kitchen when he caught another look at the table—and the dust on top of it.

Someone had written a message in it, presumably using his finger. Chapel bent low to get a look at it in better light.

IF YOU WANT TO FIND ME
I'VE GONE UNDER
THE UNDERGROUND

"Oh shit!" Julia called.

Chapel ignored the message in the dust and raced back into the living room. He saw Julia standing in the beaded curtain, holding it back with one hand.

"I think we're too late," she said. "I think he's dead."

ATLANTA, GEORGIA: APRIL 13, T+19:46

Chapel raced over to her side. He put an arm out to stop her from going any farther, then peered into the darkened bedroom. Like the rest of the house it was only semifurnished. There was a single bed up against the far wall, and a dresser standing next to the window.

The sheets of the bed had been pulled up over a human-sized form. It looked very much like someone had died in their sleep and had the sheets drawn over his face.

Chapel noticed a strange, acrid smell in the air. At first he thought it had to be the stench of decay, that the body had been left there long enough for it to start rotting. But he knew the smell of death, and this wasn't it. This smelled more like benzene or maybe diesel fuel.

"Just like my mom," Julia breathed. She sounded like she was close to going into shock—or maybe like she would start screaming.

Chapel stepped toward the bed, intending to throw the sheet back and see if it was really Funt lying there. Something about the position of the body seemed wrong. The body had been lain out carefully, its legs together and its arms at its sides. The way bodies looked when they were lain in their coffins.

The chimera he'd fought in New York wouldn't have bothered to do something like that. He'd made no attempt to pose Helen Bryant—he'd just killed her and then left her in a heap.

That smell. It was very strong over by the bed. Chapel reached down and touched the sheet near the body's head. He grasped the edge of the sheet and started to pull it down.

Behind him he heard a click as Julia switched on the bedroom light.

Two things occurred to him in that moment. One was that the form under the sheet was too lumpy. Up close it didn't look so much like a human being anymore.

The other thing was that he distinctly heard some kind of fizzing sound. It had started the same moment Julia switched on the lights.

He yanked the sheet back and saw what was really there.

Red plastic canisters, the kind used to store gasoline. Or diesel fuel. There were eight of them in the bed, grouped together to resemble a human body. They had yellow plastic screw lids. Chapel unscrewed one and the smell nearly overpowered him. It wasn't just diesel fuel in there—the diesel had been mixed with fertilizer.

He was looking at a homemade bomb.

That fizzing sound . . .

It had to be the noise of a burning fuse, which was lit when Julia flipped the light switch.

"Get out! Front door! Now!" Chapel shouted, turning around and pushing Julia ahead of him, through the beaded curtain. He caught her wrong and she nearly went sprawling, nearly fell right onto the coffee table. Chapel grabbed her around the waist with his artificial arm and bull-rushed the front door, slamming up against it because he'd forgotten it opened inward.

Behind him he heard a *fwoosh* as the fuse burned down and set the first canister alight.

The bedroom window exploded outward in a gout of flame and smoke, glass and wood bursting outward in a cone that shredded the hedges and set fire to a tree ten feet away. A billowing wave of smoke came rushing out the front door, and with it a shock wave that smashed Chapel's face to the side as pieces of burning and broken furniture stormed past him. He slammed his eyes shut to protect them even as the heat hit him, making him feel like he was being roasted alive.

In a moment it was over except for the smoke and the car alarms and the ringing in his ears. He looked down and saw he was lying on top of Julia, his artificial arm wrapped around her head, presumably to protect her from the blast.

"Are you okay?" he asked her.

She nodded. Her eyes were very wide. Clearly no one had ever tried to blow her up before.

Chapel wished he could say the same.

He looked up and saw every light on the street was on now, every house awake and alert. People had come out onto their porches to see what was going on. Some of them were standing in the street, watching Funt's house as it went up in flames.

He looked down and saw he was still lying on Julia. He released her head from his cradling arm, and she pulled herself out from beneath him. Carefully he got to his feet, then helped her up as well.

"I get the feeling Jeremy Funt was expecting us," Julia said.

Chapel shook his head. He felt a little dizzy from the blast, still. *If you want to find me I've gone under the underground. . .*

Who the hell was this guy, and what game was he playing?

LANGLEY, VIRGINIA: APRIL 13, T+21:02

Policemen in fireproof suits climbed over the remains of the charred house like ants on a discarded candy bar. Fire engines were parked three deep in front, their engines idling noisily while water leaked from their hose connectors. Up and down the street the locals were leaning off their porches, trying to get a better look.

Tom Banks watched it all on a fifty-inch screen. The image was grainy, especially blown up that big. It was coming through the lens of a cameraphone and the resolution just couldn't keep up. Every time Laughing Boy moved, the view distorted and broke down into pixels as big as Banks's thumb.

"Fertilizer bomb," Laughing Boy confirmed. He'd been on the scene just minutes after the explosion and he'd been liaising with the local cops the whole time. "You know what that looks like. Heh. Domestic terrorism."

"I thought you took your medication," Banks said, annoyed as always by his underling's constant giggling.

"Oh, I did," the operative confirmed. "Just thought that was funny."

Banks poured himself a scotch and soda. It looked like he would be up all night. "I don't suppose we got lucky and they pulled any bodies out of there? Say, a one-armed gimp and a redhead with a nice ass?"

"They made it out. Cops are looking for 'em right now," Laughing Boy replied. "Jeremy Funt, too. They want to know why he would blow up his own house."

"Figures. Hollingshead will make that heat go away," Banks said. He sighed deeply.

"You want me to help the cops out? Or maybe make this problem go away by myself?" Laughing Boy asked.

"Not yet," Banks told him. "There'll be time for that after Chapel leads us to Funt. The chimera might do it for us, too. Chapel's gotten lucky so far, but luck runs out."

"And if it doesn't—"

Banks frowned. "When I give the word, you can kill Chapel. Not before."

"Yes, sir," Laughing Boy said.

ATLANTA, GEORGIA: APRIL 13, T+24:43

Orange light touched Chapel's eyes. He opened them and looked around, uncertain for a moment where he was. He was lying in a bed, covered by a thick blanket. He was wearing nothing but his pants.

Motel room, he thought. That was right. He and Julia had checked in last night. He had said he would lie down for a little while, expecting his racing thoughts to keep him awake. Then . . .

His mouth tasted awful. Slowly he sat up and looked around. He heard water running, and decided that Julia must be taking a shower in the bathroom. Her clothes were draped over the back of a chair. His were folded neatly on top of a dresser.

He must have been so tired he just passed out. He couldn't remember undressing. He reached up with both hands to rub at his face. His right hand touched his cheek. He felt his left hand moving, but it never made contact. He tried to lift it to his face again, and it felt like it went right through him. He had the unnerving sensation that it was passing right through his flesh.

With a start he looked down and saw that his arm was gone.

Chapel was no stranger to the phantom limb effect. Before he'd been fitted with his prosthesis, he'd constantly felt like his arm was still there and he just couldn't see it. He'd been able, in his mind, to move his left hand, to make a fist. For the first few months after the amputation, he'd experienced severe pain in that hand. That was normal, they told him. The body's image of itself wasn't based on present reality but on muscle memory, and his brain was just having trouble remembering that part of his body was missing. He often woke up in the morning thinking his arm was still there. Each day brought a fresh shock when he recalled what he had become.

He had a brief moment of panic until he saw the arm, sitting on a coffee table near the room's door. It was plugged in and charging. So were his and Julia's phones, and his hands-free set.

He didn't remember doing any of that. He didn't remember taking off his arm. He couldn't imagine doing it in front of Julia.

And yet here he was.

Another moment of panic came when he looked at the clock. It was nearly seven in the morning—he must have slept until the dawn light came and found him. He stared at the curtains over the room's single window and saw the light coming through was strong and clear. He had been asleep for more than four hours.

Plenty of time for the chimeras to find their targets. Plenty of time for people to die.

He jumped out of the bed and grabbed his hands-free set. Shoving it in his ear, he called, "Angel? Can you hear me?"

"I'm here, sunshine," she said. She sounded almost as tired as he felt. Had she spent the entire night reconfiguring her servers?

"Thank God you're back," Chapel said. "I've missed you. Are you okay? You sound like you didn't sleep at all."

"Aren't you sweet?" she said, with a little laugh. "I didn't, but I popped a few energy drinks and now I'm fine. This wasn't my first all-nighter. You'll be glad to know I'm back up to full speed. Rebuilding my system took a little longer than expected, but we should be safe now—no CIA sneaks listening in. Are you ready to get back to work?"

"Yeah. Listen, the first thing we need to talk about—the police here might be looking for me. I managed to blow up Funt's house last night."

"I've been keeping an eye on you," Angel said. "You do know how to have fun, sugar. As for the police, they were looking for you, yes. I took care of that."

"Thanks." Chapel wondered what she had told them to keep them off his tail, but he supposed it didn't matter. There were far more important things to discuss. "Angel, I need you to check in on Eleanor Pechowski for me. I need to know she's still alive."

"Then I've got some good news. I spoke with her about twenty minutes ago. After I told her she was in danger, she went to stay at a friend's house. I have a police detail watching the place twenty-four seven. She's as safe as she can be."

That was one stroke of luck. "I'm beginning to think I made the wrong choice," Chapel told her. "It seems Jeremy Funt might be able to take care of himself." He briefly filled her in on what they'd found in his house. "The funny thing is, there was at least a week's worth of dust there. Like he'd been expecting this. He had plenty of time to plan and set his booby traps. Did you contact him yesterday?"

"I did. He thanked me for the information and said he would be careful. Tell you the truth, he didn't seem particularly surprised."

"Hmm." Chapel wondered how Funt could have known what was coming. The chimeras had only broken out of their detention facility a little more than—he checked the clock again—twenty-four hours ago. "He must know something we don't."

"Then I'd say you made the right choice, coming to Atlanta," Angel told him. "Presuming he's willing to share."

"That's a big presumption. From what I've seen so far he's a sneaky bastard. He nearly killed me and Julia last night. If I didn't think he could explain a few things, I'd be tempted to just leave him to his own devices. Anyway, we don't even know if a chimera is coming here, much less—"

"Ah," Angel said.

"What is it?"

"I guess you haven't had a chance to watch the local news," she said. "Last night a man was killed at the Atlanta train station. The suspect is described as large and athletically built, with haphazardly cut hair."

"Sounds familiar," Chapel said. It sounded like the chimera he'd killed in New York. Well, there it was. He at least hadn't wasted all this time on a wild goose chase. "Do the police have any idea where he is?"

"None whatsoever. I'm keeping my ears open, though—I can hear all their chatter. If they catch sight of him, you'll know about it."

"Thanks. Okay, next up—"

He stopped because the shower had turned off in the bathroom and the door was opening. Julia stepped out, wearing only a towel. Her wet red hair was draped forward over one shoulder, its curly ends touching the top of her breasts.

"Angel, stand by," Chapel said. He took the hands-free set out of his ear.

"Good morning," Julia said. She stood framed in the doorway, not moving.

"Hi. I guess I fell asleep," he said, because his brain wasn't bothering to engage very well with his mouth.

"Yeah. You conked out. I had to undress you—I hope you don't mind. I just wanted to make you comfortable. I slept in the chair, there," she said, pointing to where she'd left her clothes. "I woke up a little while ago. Figured I'd take this chance to get clean."

"Sure," he said.

"Chapel, you're staring," she said, and a blush appeared on her cheeks.

"So are you," he said.

She couldn't seem to take her eyes off his left shoulder.

"I'm sorry," Julia said. "I just—I'd kind of stopped thinking of you as only having one arm. The prosthesis is so realistic."

"It fools a lot of people. But not forever." Chapel gave her a wan smile. He supposed this moment had been bound to come. He'd started thinking of Julia as more than just an informant. More than just someone he was trying to protect.

He'd known he found her attractive. Seeing her

standing there in just a towel, he felt it more than ever. But he'd also seen something else in her, in her resourcefulness, in her toughness. Something he found rarely in anyone of either gender. Something he'd come to admire. He'd honestly begun to think that maybe they could share something more than just . . . whatever they were to each other now.

But he'd been fooling himself, of course.

He was still a freak. Still three-quarters of a man. He could forget that himself, sometimes. This recent adventure had made him feel more whole than he had in a long time. But it was still true.

"You must have seen this last night," he said, gesturing at his shoulder with his chin. "You took the arm off."

"It was dark," she said, "and I was so exhausted I barely knew what I was doing. I just hope I didn't hurt you."

"I'm fine. Do you want me to put a shirt on? I'm sorry, this has to be unpleasant for you. You don't need to see me like this." He reached for his T-shirt.

"No," she said, and he saw her swallow. She was steeling herself for something.

He figured he knew what it would be. When people found out about his disability, they typically had one of two reactions. They either pretended it didn't exist and looked away—and made a point of never looking at his arm again, even when he had the prosthetic on. Or they pretended like it didn't bother them, like it was perfectly normal that Chapel only had one arm.

Both reactions used to disgust him. Eventually he'd come to respect that people just didn't know how to process him. He didn't fit into their view of normalcy and so they would always be awkward around him.

Julia came over to the bed and sat down next to him. Close enough he could smell her freshly shampooed hair, feel the warmth of her body. A sweet kind of torture. She reached up with her right hand and touched his stump with one finger. "Is this okay?" she asked.

"Sure," he said. "It doesn't hurt."

She smiled. "This is excellent work," she told him. She ran her finger along the scar there. Stroked the skin with the back of her hand. "I—oh, God. Just tell me to shut up if I say something offensive. But I've done some amputations myself. On dogs and cats, of course. It can be tricky, depending on what you've got to work with."

"Did you ever fit a prosthesis for a dog?" he asked. "Or maybe a peg leg for a parrot?"

She laughed. "You think you're being funny. But people go crazy over their pets. There's nothing they won't pay for if they think it'll make their pets happy. Dogs with three legs are pretty common and they get along just fine. They learn to hop, and in six months they forget they ever had four legs. But yeah, I've seen prosthetic legs on dogs. Nothing as useful as what they gave you."

She was stroking his shoulder and his chest by that point. Her fingers wove into his chest hair.

He couldn't help himself. He leaned in to kiss her.

Her lips were soft and warm, and they parted slightly. He touched her tongue with his. Her eyes were closed and she sank against him, nothing between them but a towel, and he started to reach for her with his hand, his real hand.

"Last night in the car," she said, "when I fell asleep. I curled up with you. I said I thought you were my ex. That wasn't true. It just felt good to have . . . someone that close. A little comfort."

"After the day you had, I'm pretty sure you're allowed to want that," he told her. He stroked her wet hair.

She leaned forward and buried her face in the crook of his neck. Her lips brushed his skin. "Chapel, is this okay?" she asked. "Us? Now? Do we have time? I could really use some more comforting."

"Me too," he said. "The bad guys can wait."

ATLANTA, GEORGIA: APRIL 13, T+25:07

Her towel had already fallen to her waist, exposing her breasts. He cupped one with his hand, and she sighed and pressed close to him. She reached down and unbuttoned his pants, and together they pushed them down and off the bed. Her towel went away and they were naked together. He kissed her throat, her chest, her lips. She pushed him back onto the bed and straddled him. She was ready for him, and he was definitely ready for her.

He started to speak her name, but she put a finger to his lips. Her eyes were closed as she rode him, her hips rocking back and forth slowly, her body shuddering just a little. Her red hair was slicked back and curly tips of it brushed her shoulders, stuck to her chin. She gasped a little, and he put his hand on the small of her back, guiding her, pulling her toward him.

It had been a long time. He didn't want it to end too soon, so he sat up and kissed her deeply, then flipped her over on her back. She laughed, her legs flailing in the air. Her eyes were watching his face, trying to figure out what he was going to do next. He knelt between her legs, then slid down and buried his face in the red hair between her thighs, breathing in the smell of her, tasting her wetness. Her whole body jerked as his tongue touched her, as it flashed between their bodies.

Her fingers grabbed at his hair and his ears as she squirmed and shook. Squeaks of pleasure broke free from her mouth as he matched the rhythm of her hips, as he slid one finger inside her and found just the right spot. She tasted amazing, fresh and clean and just a little musky, and his excitement only grew as she got closer and closer. In a moment she came, smearing his face and chin with her wetness.

She put her hands over her face as if she was embarrassed. He climbed back up toward her and pulled her hands away and saw her mouth was open, her eyes barely focusing on him. He dug his arm under her back and pulled her to his chest. She was so wet he had no trouble sliding inside her and he thrust against her, making her gasp again, this time finding his own rhythm. She wrapped her arms around him and pulled him still closer, pulled him down on top of her. Her hands grabbed the muscles of his back and squeezed as he thrust deeper.

She let out a little cry and kissed his neck, his ear. "It's okay," she whispered. "I'm protected."

It only took a few more strokes. He thrust deep inside her and went rigid as his body exploded, as every muscle in his back and legs tensed and then released and he came, his eyes tightly shut, his skin on fire as she kissed him again and again, everywhere she could reach.

ATLANTA, GEORGIA: APRIL 13, T+25:52

Julia went to the bathroom to clean up and dress. At the bathroom door she turned to look back at him. She laughed a little, her eyes studying his face.

Chapel smiled back at her.

"I can't believe we just did that," she said, her eyes watching his face very carefully.

"Having second thoughts?" he asked.

"Hell, no. I needed it." She looked at him for a moment longer, then shook her head and stepped inside the bathroom.

When the door closed, he just fell back against the sheets and breathed for a while. That had burned off a lot of tension.

When she came back out, she announced she was going to go out and find them some breakfast and a few toiletries—things they hadn't had time to acquire in the mad rush since they'd left New York City. Chapel could tell she just wanted to be alone with her thoughts for a while and he just told her to be safe.

He just lay there for a while when she was gone, reveling. Amazed at what had happened between them. The few women he'd been with since he lost his arm had all wanted him to wear the arm while he made love to them, though none of them had wanted it to touch them. They'd found ways to ignore it.

Julia hadn't asked for that. She'd seen what he looked like with no arm, with his shirt off. It hadn't stopped her.

It had been all about the moment, of course. The adrenaline of the last twenty-four hours. The constant threat of danger and death. It made people do things they wouldn't ordinarily do. Chapel knew all about that. He knew it couldn't last.

But. But—wow. Damn. It had felt so right. And Julia hadn't been creeped out. She hadn't been thinking of him as less than whole, as part of a man. She'd simply wanted him, wanted to be with him, as he was.

It was more than he'd hoped for in a very long time.

Eventually the afterglow started to wear off. Chapel started to think about chimeras and CIA killers and the desperate situation he was in once again. He knew he had to get back to work.

Still, he let himself just be happy, just for a moment.

When he'd luxuriated in that enough, he found the hands-free unit and put it back in his ear. "Sorry about cutting you off like that, Angel."

"No worries, sugar," she said.

"Angel," Chapel said carefully, because he'd just

thought of something, "you weren't—listening to any of that. Were you?"

"Of course not, Chapel. I understand when people need a little privacy."

"Uh-huh," he said.

"I didn't hear a word. Though, if you want some romantic advice—"

"At the moment I'd prefer to know where Jeremy Funt is," Chapel said, to change the subject.

"I'm ahead of you there, except I don't have any answers," Angel told him. "I've been trying to call him every five minutes, but I can't get through. All my calls go straight to voice mail. I've left a bunch of messages, but there's been no response. I thought if he knew who you were, he might be willing to come out of hiding."

"He's scared. He's gone to ground. He knew, somehow, that a chimera was coming here. He knew long before the chimeras even left the Catskills." Chapel scratched his head. "The booby trap in his house was meant to catch a chimera. But he also left a cryptic message behind, telling anyone where to find him. Does that make sense to you?"

"No, but then I'm not a paranoid FBI agent being hunted by a genetic freak," Angel pointed out.

"Right. Me neither." Chapel sighed. He went to the bathroom and splashed water on his face and scrubbed himself with a soapy washcloth. "I need to think like him. I need to figure out what he would do, if I'm ever going to find him. If he left that message, he wanted somebody to follow it. Maybe you have to be the right person to know what it means. Maybe it's some kind of private joke."

"Chapel," Angel said, "I need to point something out to you."

"Hmm?" Chapel asked, lost in thought.

"Despite appearances, I'm not actually omniscient," she said.

"I'm sorry, Angel. I'm not following."

She sighed deeply. Even her sighs sounded sexy. "You never actually told me what the message said. I am a trained intelligence analyst. I might be able to help you, if you'd like to share."

Chapel laughed. "Angel, I sometimes forget you're not sitting on my shoulder watching everything I do. I'm so sorry. Yeah, the message. It said 'If you want to find me, I've gone under the underground.' Does that mean anything to you, just off the top of your head?"

"No, but that's why God invented the Internet. Let's see." He heard her clacking keys. "It seems like he meant for you to find him, so the answer should be obvious, right? Except what I'm turning up, it's all really confusing. Under the underground, that sounds like a riddle. Let me search some riddle databases."

Obvious, Chapel thought. *The answer should be obvious.* She was right—Funt wouldn't make the puzzle impossible. He would make it as simple as he could. In fact, it might not be a puzzle at all.

In a flash of inspiration, he went and fetched his phone. He'd never actually bothered using it to surf the web—Angel had handled all that for him up to now. He opened up the mobile browser and pecked in a few characters with his index finger.

"Oh," he said, because before he could even finish

typing in his search, Google was already suggesting what he wanted to look up. He touched the screen and it filled up with links. "Ah," he said.

"What's going on?" Angel asked. "Chapel, you're making noises like you've figured something out."

"You were overthinking it," he told her.

"What?"

"You expected it to be a riddle. So you figured it had to be a puzzle to be solved. That's the kind of thing you're good at. But it occurred to me, if Funt wanted to be found—and it looks like he definitely does—he wouldn't bother making us solve a word game to know his location."

"Now I'm really confused," Angel admitted. "It's not like he left you a street address to go to."

"He kind of did," Chapel said. "Just now, on my phone, I googled 'Underground Atlanta.' And now I know where Funt is."

ATLANTA, GEORGIA: APRIL 13, T+26:15

"This is not what I expected, not at all," Chapel said, when he and Julia climbed out of a cab downtown. Before them a massive sign read simply UNDER-GROUND. A dark entrance below it led into a cavern-like space.

Just after the Civil War, after Sherman burned the city to the ground, Atlanta had put itself back together, growing and flourishing in the Recon-struction. This whole section of the city had grown faster than the rest as bigger buildings were built and viaducts were raised to carry railroads and then vehicular traffic. The area under the viaducts, which had been at street level in the nineteenth century, had eventually been buried in new construction until the city streets were a whole story higher than they used to be.

Entire city blocks lay down there, covered over and buried as the city grew up around them. Once, Chapel knew from what he'd read about the place, it had been a zone of speakeasies during Prohibition. Then it had been taken over by squatters and the homeless. Now Underground Atlanta was a giant shopping mall.

And, apparently, a bolt hole for an ex-FBI agent named Jeremy Funt.

Chapel and Julia headed inside, joining the flow of early morning shoppers and tourists. Inside, the Underground was paved with brick and lit only sporadically by overhead fluorescents and the occasional light well. It was full of brightly lit shops and souvenir stands, carts selling T-shirts advertising HOTLANTA or THE A, places to get your hair braided or your ears pierced, displays of antique cars and jazz legends and old railroad history. Someone was singing nearby, though Chapel couldn't see where. The place's weird acoustics distorted the singer's voice and made the plateglass windows of the shops around him shake. The Underground smelled of pretzels and old beer and even older mildew.

"Let's find our man fast and get him out of here," Chapel said, frowning. He definitely did not like how public this place was. If a chimera came here, looking for Funt, the collateral damage could be devastating.

"Why is he here in the first place?" Julia asked.

Chapel shrugged. "Based on what we saw last night—the way he rigged his house—Funt's crazy. A paranoid. I expected him to have some underground bunker hidden away on some compound out in the country, a place full of guns and bottled water and a copy of *The Turner Diaries*." He glanced around. "Not this."

Up ahead there was an indoor waterfall where children were playing, splashing one another and passersby. There was a tourist information stand there, a little booth with no one in it. There were brochures available, though, and Chapel grabbed one. "He said he was under the Underground, whatever that means." He glanced through the brochure, looking for any clue that might tell him where to go next.

Julia grabbed one for herself and started reading it. "Apparently there used to be a wax museum down here. That's kind of creepy. I can imagine Funt hiding in an abandoned wax museum. The chimera might be confused by all the statues and not know who to beat on first."

"It's a thought," Chapel said. He shook his head and folded his brochure up again. Jammed it in his pocket. "Maybe we can ask someone." He turned around, looking for anyone who might meet his eye.

The first person he saw was an old guy with a straggly beard wearing a green army jacket. He had a cardboard sign around his neck that read HUNGRY VET PLEASE HELP. When he saw Chapel looking at him, he came over straightaway.

"I'm not going to BS you," the man said. "Just

give me a moment of your time, and I'll be on my way. I am an alcoholic, it's true."

Chapel nodded. He could smell the gin on the man's breath. At least he was being honest about it.

"Any money you give me I'll take straight to the bar," the vet went on, clearly winding up to deliver a well-practiced pitch.

"What branch of the service were you in?" Chapel asked him, beginning to think maybe the army coat was just for show.

"Wait," Julia said. "Wait—maybe you can help us. Do you know this place well?"

"Like the back of my hand," the drunk said, staring down at his hands as if he'd never seen them before.

"Oh, come on," Chapel said.

"We need to find some place here. The place underneath the Underground. Does that make sense?"

"Well," the drunk said, stretching it out to multiple syllables. "Well, this is about as low as you can get in Hotlanta. About as far down as we go. Except the utility basement, there's that."

"A basement?" Chapel asked. "Where's the entrance?"

The drunk stared at him shrewdly.

"It's extremely important," Julia said. "Can you please show us where it is?"

"I'll do it," the drunk told her, "on one condition only, from which I will not budge. Should you require my services, on this I must insist—"

"What is it?" Chapel asked.

"That the beautiful lady will consent to give me a kiss." He batted his eyelashes at Julia.

"That's definitely not going to happen," she told him. "How about this?" she held up a twenty-dollar bill, folded neatly and tucked between two of her fingers.

"Right this way," the drunk said, and started off into the darkened paths between the shops of the Underground. The twenty was already gone, presumably hidden somewhere on his person.

He moved fast, zigzagging through the crowd. Most people drew back when he got too close. Others just ignored him. He weaved and bobbed back and forth, somehow never touching anybody. Chapel had to constantly apologize to the people he bumped into while trying to keep up. He glanced back over his shoulder and saw Julia just pushing her way through. Apparently growing up in New York City had taught her how not to get lost in a crowd.

They passed by plenty of closed stores and little stages where jazz bands vied for attention. Shoppers milled around a few of the businesses, but mostly people just seemed to want to get in Chapel's way. Just as he was starting to get seriously annoyed, the drunk stopped abruptly and turned to face him.

"And here we are, at our destination," the drunk announced, raising his arms like a tour guide.

"Where?" Chapel demanded. He looked around and couldn't see any doors leading to hidden basements. Just a lot of thuggish-looking teenagers standing around being bored. There was a big Coca-Cola mural on one rough brick wall, and what looked like a very uncomfortable bench or maybe a utility box.

"Oh ye of little faith," the drunk said. He tapped the utility box with his foot.

Chapel went around the side of the thing and saw that it was fronted by a pair of low wooden doors, no higher than his waist. It was a hatch to a utility area.

"Okay. Fine. You can go now," Chapel said to the drunk. He was already trying to figure out how he would get through those doors. They looked like they'd been permanently sealed shut.

The drunk started to fume in protest.

"Thanks," Julia said, "you've been very helpful."

"How about a hug?" the drunk asked.

"How about not?"

She could clearly take care of herself. Chapel was too busy to pay attention. He was feeling around the edges of the doors. Funt wanted to be found, Chapel was sure of that. So he wouldn't be hiding behind a sealed door.

Chapel's fingers found a concealed latch on one side of the doors. He slipped it open and the doors parted. Beyond them he could see a dark stairway leading down.

Jackpot.

He looked around and saw that no one was watching him. He would have much preferred to come back later, after everyone had gone, but he just didn't have the time. He looked up and saw that Julia had gotten rid of the drunk by giving him more money. Well, as long as he left, that was fine.

"That's where we're going?" she asked.

"That's where I'm going," Chapel told her. "You're staying right here."

ATLANTA, GEORGIA: APRIL 13, T+26:36

"You can't be serious," Julia said. "I've come all this way, and now—"

"The last time we tried to find Funt, we were both nearly killed by an improvised bomb," Chapel pointed out. "There's no telling what's down there, waiting for me."

"And you think you're safer on your own?" Julia asked. Her eyes were bright with anger. "I'm not some kid you're being paid to babysit, Chapel."

"No. You're a civilian who doesn't need to know all the facts of this case."

Even as the words came out of his mouth he knew he'd made a bad mistake with her. He could see in her eyes that he'd picked exactly the wrong thing to say.

Her mouth compressed in a hard line, and she folded her arms across her chest. "And that's all that I am. Right?"

He racked his brain for some way to explain what he'd meant better, to smooth things over. But there was no time for that. "I have to go, now. Lives are at stake," he said, which even to his own ears just sounded *bad*. "Listen, I need you to stay up here and watch for cops. If they come down after me, it'll spook Funt and he'll run away."

She shook her head and looked away from him.

At least she wasn't arguing the point.

He ducked through the short doors of the hatch and headed down the stairs.

Angel's voice sounded in his ear. "That's not the fastest way to a woman's heart, sugar," she said.

Chapel looked up and saw Julia's legs framed by the open hatch above him. He whispered his reply so she wouldn't hear it. "I'm still a professional, Angel. I have questions for Funt. He has information I need. Information a civilian shouldn't hear."

"I'm torn here," Angel said. "The part of me that works for Hollingshead thinks that's absolutely right, and that you're acting exactly as you should."

"And the other part?" Chapel asked.

"The part of me that's a woman thinks you're being a jerk."

"I'll settle for being half right," Chapel told her.

The stairs before him led down into a dark cavernous space filled with looming shapes. A storage area full of crates. He could see very little while his eyes were adjusting, but eventually he made out a line of pale light ahead in the darkness. It was coming from underneath a door. He reached for the knob and found it wasn't locked. Beyond lay a corridor painted glaring white, lit by fluorescent bulbs that buzzed angrily as if annoyed at his intrusion.

"—having trouble—" Angel said in his ear. "—losing your telemetry and—"

"Angel?" Chapel asked. "Angel, you're breaking up."

"—signal. You're pretty far beneath the—"

"Angel?" Chapel called. "Angel, repeat. Please come in."

A burst of static sounded in his ear, but it cut in and out.

Apparently there were some places even Angel

couldn't tread. The vast amount of concrete and steel over Chapel's head must be blocking her satellite signal. Damn. He hated proceeding without her watching over his shoulder.

ATLANTA, GEORGIA: APRIL 13, T+26:47

Chapel stepped into the white hallway. Three doors, also painted white, led off the corridor in a number of directions. One of them was a heavy reinforced steel door with a sliding plate set into its face. Its latch was protected by a massive combination lock. Chapel lifted the lock and found it had rusted shut—it might have been hanging there for twenty years, for all he knew. The sliding panel looked like it was painted shut.

He could hear music. Faint music that sounded tinny like it was coming from a transistor radio. He banged on the door for a while, but there was no response. He tried the second door, but that was locked, too.

He headed down the corridor to the final door. The music seemed louder there. He rested his ear against the door and through it he could almost make out what song was playing. The sound had to be coming from behind that door.

His instinct was to draw his weapon. It was possible the chimera had beaten him here.

But he'd seen no sign of a struggle. "Mr. Funt!" he shouted. "Turn off your music and listen to me! I'm here to help!"

There was, of course, no reply.

Chapel grunted in frustration and grabbed the knob of the door before him. It turned easily and the door opened on well-oiled hinges.

Beyond lay a linen closet with a number of shelves. On one shelf sat the radio, playing some light jazz.

On another shelf sat a squarish box made of green metal, slightly convex, propped up on a pair of scissor-shaped legs. In raised lettering on the front of the box was the legend FRONT TOWARD ENEMY.

Chapel knew instantly that it was a claymore antipersonnel mine.

ATLANTA, GEORGIA: APRIL 13, T+26:51

Julia considered just leaving. After what Chapel had said to her, she was righteously angry—after everything she'd been through, for him to talk to her like she was an unruly child . . . it was sorely tempting to just walk away, to get a cab to the airport and go . . . somewhere else.

She was smart enough to know that would be a terrible idea, though. Laughing Boy was still out there somewhere, looking for her. He would eventually find her. And if she didn't have Chapel around to protect her when that happened, she would die.

But damn Chapel! She'd thought, after what had happened that morning, that maybe there was something between them beyond just his business. She'd begun to think . . . well, she had no idea what she'd begun to think. But that was over now. Right out of the question. He'd gotten what he wanted. He was the big strong knight in shining armor and she had fallen straight into his arms—arm—like she'd been following some cheesy Hollywood script, and she hated herself for that a little. Now that he'd fucked her he had lost all interest in her as a human being, clearly. Just like every other man she'd ever met before. If he thought she was going to share his bed again tonight, he was sorely mistaken. She was her own woman and she could make her own choices.

She couldn't just walk away from him, obviously. She was stuck with him. But while he was off gal-livanting around, at least, she considered herself on her own recognizance.

There were shops around her, places she could go find some fresh clothes. Places to get something to eat. She *was* hungry.

And maybe if she left, the homeless guy would leave her alone.

"Do you like jazz?" he asked her, for the third time. He had a hopeful twinkle in his eye. Still.

"Not particularly," she said.

Chapel had been down there for what felt like fifteen minutes. What was taking him so long? He just had to grab Funt and come back up. That shouldn't have taken more than a few minutes. She wondered if maybe he'd stumbled on some booby trap down there and gotten himself blown up.

It would serve him right, she thought. Leaving her here with this wino so she could watch for the police.

From what she could tell, Underground Atlanta wasn't exactly high on the list of places cops went to hang out. It was clogged with homeless people and drug dealers.

"You're not a tourist, I can tell," the drunk said, as if he'd just proved he was Sherlock freaking Holmes. "That guy you're with, he's some kind of—what? Urban explorer? Thrill-seeking spelunker?"

"He's a building inspector," Julia said, thinking on her feet. "I'm his assistant. We had reports that radon gas was leaking from this place, so he went down to check out just how deadly it is. Just standing here is probably giving you cancer."

The drunk's eyes went wide, but then he laughed. It was not a sound she particularly cared for. Not after the previous day, when she'd had to lock herself in her own drugs closet while a laughing man claiming to be a cop tried to shoot her.

"You're just foolin' an old fool," the drunk said. "Tell you what. Let's play a game. The game's called Truth or Dare. You can pick which one—"

"I've played Truth or Dare before," Julia said.

"I'll just bet you have," he said, with a leer.

Julia just sighed.

"Okay, I pick Dare," the drunk said, and he moved around her until she couldn't help but look in his face.

"I dare you to go brush your teeth," Julia said. She turned away from him, not even wanting to look at him anymore.

But then she saw something that made her blood run cold. A man in a charcoal gray suit. A man with a crew cut and a pair of thick black sunglasses, despite the gloom of the Underground. She knew his face.

It was Laughing Boy.

And he was walking right toward her.

ATLANTA, GEORGIA: APRIL 13, T+27:56

Chapel knew all about claymore mines.

They were designed to shred people. Nestled inside that green box were approximately seven hundred steel balls embedded in C-4 plastic explosive. When the mine went off, it would send all of them screaming forward, right through his body. The force of the explosion would deform them into the shape of bullets. Anyone standing as much as fifty meters away from the explosion would be cut to ribbons by the blast. As close as Chapel was, there would be little left of him afterward but red goo.

He threw his artificial arm up to protect his face. It would do no good at all, but it was a reflex action. So was screaming. He managed not to do that.

Instead he shouted, "Funt, I'm DIA!"

He knew something else about claymore mines, too. They weren't actually mines at all. They weren't designed to go off when you stepped on them or crossed a tripwire. They were designed to be remotely detonated by someone with a triggering device, someone nearby.

The claymore didn't explode. At least not for the moment.

Instead, Chapel heard a shrieking sound just behind him. He braced himself for instant death coming from some other quarter. When he didn't die, he slowly turned around and looked at what had made that noise.

The sliding panel in the reinforced steel door to his side was drawing back, tearing the paint around it as it moved. When it was retracted all the way, he saw a face behind it—the face of a man maybe sixty years old, wearing a pair of thick-lensed glasses. The eyes behind those lenses were hugely magnified. Chapel saw them narrow as they peered toward him.

"DIA?" the man asked. "They sent somebody from Military Intelligence this time?"

This time? Chapel shook his head. No time to unravel that, not with a claymore mine right behind him. "My name's Chapel. Captain Jim Chapel. I was sent to protect you from the chimeras," Chapel told him. His arm was still up across his face. Slowly he lowered it. "Please, please, do not detonate this thing. Are you still holding the clacker?"

Jeremy Funt—it could be no one else—held up the green metal detonator for the claymore. His thumb was resting on the trigger. "I am. I'm going to keep hold of it, for now. You have some kind of ID I can look at?"

"It's in my jacket pocket," Chapel told him. "I'm going to reach for it now." The man was a paranoid nut. There was nothing to be gained whatsoever by spooking him. If he thought Chapel was reaching for a gun, he might detonate the claymore on instinct. "Is that all right?"

"Sure. Just do it slow."

Chapel nodded and carefully removed his laminate from his pocket. He held it up before Funt's eyes and let the man read it.

"I hope you'll forgive me," Funt said, "if I'm a little careful."

"I understand," Chapel said. "There's one of

them in Atlanta right now. We have to assume he's coming for you."

Funt shrugged. "So what else is new? That's an old, old story."

Chapel frowned in confusion. "I'm sorry? You're used to being hunted down by dangerous lunatics?"

"If by 'dangerous lunatics' you mean 'CIA hit men,' then . . . yes," Funt replied.

ATLANTA, GEORGIA: APRIL 13, T+27:03

"Come on, come on," Julia whispered, pressing the redial button on her phone. "Chapel, pick up already!"

But there was no answer. This was the third time she'd tried to call Chapel's number and he still wasn't picking up.

When she saw Laughing Boy coming toward her, she'd panicked. She just ran, not knowing where she was headed, not knowing what she should do. She'd gotten around a corner and found a women's restroom and ducked inside and started dialing.

She had no illusions that Laughing Boy wouldn't follow her inside. She just hadn't known where else to go.

"Shit," she said under her breath.

And then she nearly screamed, because her phone started to buzz in her hand.

She stared at the screen and saw she was being called by someone whose phone number was listed as (000) 000-0000. What the hell?

The phone kept buzzing. She swiped the screen

to answer. "Hello?" she asked, keeping her voice as low as she could.

"Dr. Taggart," a woman's voice said, "you've been trying to call Captain Chapel for a while now. He's outside of cellular coverage and can't take your call, so I thought I'd make sure you were all right."

"Who are you?" Julia demanded. For all she knew this was somebody who worked with Laughing Boy trying to track her down.

"You can call me Angel," the woman on the other end of the line said. "I'm sure you've seen Captain Chapel talking into his hands-free unit. I believe you said it made him look like a douche bag. I was the person he was talking to."

Julia shut her eyes and tried to breathe. "Thank God. I'm in real trouble here. I need you to send help or something. There's this guy—this, I don't know, he claimed he was a policeman before, but that was in New York, this guy who tried to kill me, and—"

"You're talking about Laughing Boy," Angel said.

"Yes," Julia told her. "He just showed up here, in Atlanta. We're in some kind of underground mall and—"

"I have your location. Dr. Taggart, I need to ask you a personal question. From everything I've seen so far, you're a pretty strong woman. Would you say that's a correct assumption?"

Instantly Julia calmed down. She opened her eyes and changed her grip on the phone. "I like to think of myself as a competent person."

"Right now I need you to be one tough bitch," Angel told her.

ATLANTA, GEORGIA: APRIL 13, T+27:05

"I don't understand," Chapel said. "The CIA is trying to kill you? You know that sounds crazy, right?"

"Captain," Funt said, "I have a clacker in my hand ready to detonate the claymore mine behind you. I'm well protected behind this door. You might be smart about this and not insult me."

"That's a fair point," Chapel said.

"The CIA has been trying to kill me for nearly fifteen years. I know too much to be left free and alive. I've survived this long by being quick on my feet and not taking chances. You claim to be a DIA agent, but it would be relatively easy for a CIA assassin to fake those credentials. So I'm assuming that you're just the latest in a long line of hit men."

Chapel shook his head. "You have to believe me. You have to trust me."

"I do?" Funt asked.

"Yes! There's a man coming for you right now, someone who isn't a CIA agent but who definitely wants to kill you. I don't know what kind of threats you think you've survived all this time, but—"

"In 1998, they sent a team of men in commando gear, carrying M4 rifles, to my home. I happened to be coming back from the grocery store at the time and so I nearly walked in on them ransacking my place. I turned around and drove away and never went back. Since then I've been moving every few months, staying light on my feet. In 2001, they caught up with me in Montana. You ever been to Montana, Chapel? It's big sky country. Lots of open space, not a lot of good places to hide. They only sent one man that time, maybe because they figured I would be expecting a team, maybe because they thought they had me cornered. This guy was pretty slick. Claimed to be FBI, like I used to be. Said he wanted to discuss some old cases with me. I had him inside my house and pointing a gun at my face, ready to shoot. The only reason I survived was because I'd already poisoned his coffee."

"Jesus," Chapel said. This guy was crazy. Dangerously crazy.

"He lived. I didn't want to kill anybody, not back then. I just fed him enough rat poison to give me time to get out of there. To escape. I went to New Orleans. Now there's a place a man can lose himself. Or at least I thought so—until 2003, when the same man, the one I'd poisoned, came for me again. I couldn't take any chances that time. I set fire to my own apartment on the way out. Maybe he got out in time, maybe he didn't. I didn't go back to check. In 2006, a new guy started coming for me."

I'm going to die here, Chapel thought. *I'm going to die because this man is insane and he thinks anyone who comes looking for him is an assassin.*

"This one figured he'd play it real simple. No false ID, no tricky attempts to convince me he was an old friend. He just walked up to me in the parking lot of a Starbucks and started shooting. I got out of there by the skin of my teeth."

"So the bomb in your house—"

"Just in case," Funt explained.

The story was nuts, but it explained one thing. There had been dust all over Funt's house, far more dust than could be easily explained. At least, it couldn't be explained if Funt had set the bomb only after Angel called him.

No. This guy had been expecting an assassin for years. He had no idea that this time the assassin was real—but not human.

"Weird thing about this latest guy. He couldn't stop laughing, the whole time he was plugging away at me. He came back in 2009—it must have taken him that long to track down my newest identity. I saw him coming in time. Then in 2010—"

"Wait," Chapel said. "Hold on. Laughing? He was laughing the whole time?"

"It was creepy as hell. I don't know who you really are, Captain Chapel, but at least you *look* normal."

"I know that guy," Chapel said. "The laughing guy. He is CIA, that's true. And he's definitely a killer."

"Mm-hmm. Do you still think I'm crazy, then?"

Absolutely, Chapel thought. *But maybe not delusional*. It was possible that the CIA really was trying to assassinate Funt. The fact they'd failed so many times was a little hard to accept—but then again, how many times had they tried to kill Fidel Castro and never got him? "You said you knew too much," Chapel said. "That's why they're after you. I think I have an idea what it is you know, and why it's so sensitive."

"Figures. They would've briefed you on me when they sent you down here to kill me." Funt raised the clacker so Chapel could see it again.

"Wait! It's what I wanted to talk to you about. It's why I was sent here, yes, but to protect you!"

"Choose your next words carefully," Funt told him.

"It's about the chimeras, isn't it? That's what you know about. The chimeras they were holding in some prison camp up in the Catskills. You need to know something, Special Agent Funt. You need to know they escaped. They escaped, and one of them is in Atlanta right now, coming for you."

Funt looked like an electric shock had run through him. Chapel thought he could see the hair standing up on the man's knuckles.

"Malcolm got loose?" Funt asked. "Oh crap."

ATLANTA, GEORGIA: APRIL 13, T+27:15

"That's right," Chapel bluffed. "Malcolm. Malcolm the chimera. He had your name and address and I came here to make sure he didn't kill you."

Funt stared at Chapel. "No offense, guy, but you're not up to this. I don't know what kind of training you've had, but Malcolm—he'll be all grown up now. He'll be more than a match for anything you bring to the table."

"I can handle him," Chapel promised.

"They must not have told you anything about the chimeras. They're tougher than you can imagine, faster than anything human. They're also meaner and more—"

"I killed one in New York, yesterday," Chapel said, because he needed Funt to trust him.

"If that's true—and I doubt it," Funt said, "then you got extremely lucky. When I first saw Malcolm, he was ten years old. Even then he left me in the hospital for months. No, if he's coming here . . . I'm as good as dead. Damn, damn, damn. I've got to think. I've got to think about this."

"I can help," Chapel pleaded.

"I'll need to lay some more traps. I'll need to get a gun . . . damn. Damn! Malcolm, after all this time—he won't stop. The CIA goons, they lose their nerve after a while, but Malcolm . . . he's got good reason to kill me. And they never even need a reason. Damn!"

"Funt," Chapel said, softly, "you must realize you stand a better chance if you work with me. If you want to live through this, you can't afford to turn down any help."

Funt stared at him through the sliding hatch in the steel door. He reached up with his free hand and scratched at his eyebrows. He looked like he was about to start screaming in panic. "Not here," he said.

"Special Agent Funt—"

"I didn't live this long by being dumb! I need to think. I need to make some plans. Damn!"

"Just come with me, I'll take you someplace safe," Chapel promised.

"No," Funt said. "No. I'll give you the benefit of the doubt. I'll assume you are who you say you are. And I'll meet with you so we can figure some things out together. But not here, not now. Oh my God— what if he's already on his way? What if he's coming here right now?"

"Funt—"

"Stone Mountain. The top of Stone Mountain, eight hours from now. Just be there, and I'll find you. We'll talk."

"Please," Chapel begged.

"Not now! Not here!"

Funt slid the panel in his door shut with a clang. Chapel grabbed at it and tried to force it back open, tried pushing it with his fingers. Eventually it slid back a fraction of an inch. He pried it open the rest of the way and peered through, even though he knew what he would find.

The room beyond was empty. Funt was gone.

ATLANTA, GEORGIA: APRIL 13, T+27:21

There were a dozen stores in Underground Atlanta that sold the same ugly T-shirts and schlocky merchandise. Julia picked the nearest one and ducked inside, bending low as she flicked through a rack of cheap clothing.

"Souvenir for your trip?" the clerk asked.

Julia gave her the best smile she could manage. "I like this hoodie," she said, holding up a bright pink sweatshirt with a graphic of jazz musicians printed on the back. The musicians were picked out with glitter and sequins. "And these hats," she said, picking up an Atlanta Braves baseball cap.

"That's official Braves merchandise. See the hologram?" the clerk asked, not moving from where she leaned against her counter. "It's not a knockoff or anything."

"Perfect. Just ring these up, okay?" Julia stared through the windows of the shop, looking for any sign of Laughing Boy.

Julia had never been so frightened in her life.

Even when the chimera had jumped in the cab with her, she'd been too shocked to be scared like this.

"Wait," she said, as the clerk started bagging up her purchases. "I'm going to wear these out."

"You got it," the clerk said.

Julia pulled on the cap first. It hid most of her red hair. The hood of the sweatshirt covered the rest and zipped up easily over her black sweater. The jeans she was wearing were common enough they shouldn't make a difference. When she was finished putting on her new purchases, she looked in the mirror and barely recognized herself.

"Wow," the clerk said, and clicked her tongue. "You look like a genuine hoodrat." She laughed. "When you came in here, I made you out for some kind of lawyer or doctor or something. This makes you look ten years younger."

Julia gave her another smile. "Perfect."

She stepped out of the store trying her best to keep her head down so the brim of the cap shaded her eyes. She desperately wanted to scan the crowd and look for any sign of Laughing Boy, but Angel had been very clear—if she was going to live through this, she needed to keep a low profile.

There was an exit from the Underground straight ahead. Julia could see sunlight filtering down from the streets above. It wasn't more than a hundred yards away. She moved in that direction, forcing herself not to run. Forcing herself to act natural. It was so hard not to panic and just make a break for it.

On her left a group of boys whistled at her, but she didn't look up. On her right was a store that looked like it had been closed for years, judging by the dust that had collected in the display windows. She caught her reflection in the grease-smeared glass and saw that she was fidgeting with her hands. She forced herself to shove them into the pockets of her new hoodie.

Fifty yards to the exit. She let herself walk a little faster.

Twenty yards.

Fifteen.

"Nice try," Laughing Boy said, stepping out from behind a cart that sold cell-phone accessories.

She squeaked a little in panic and turned around, intending to run back the way she'd come as fast as her legs would carry her. Before she'd taken a step Laughing Boy grabbed her arm. He squeezed hard enough on her bicep to make her squeal again.

"Maybe you think I won't do anything out here in public," he told her, his voice little more than a whisper. He giggled every time he stopped for breath, a raspy sound like his constant laughing had dried out his mouth. "So help me God, I will shoot you in front of a hundred witnesses if you try to fight me or run."

"Just don't hurt me, please," she begged.

"Really? Are you that stupid? I have no idea what Chapel sees in you. Come on. Walk at a normal pace. You were doing a pretty good job for a while there. The clothes might have thrown me off if I didn't watch you buy them."

"You saw me the whole time?"

"Sweetheart, I've got eyes in the back of my head. You'd do well to remember that. Now come on. We're headed over there." He pointed her toward the closed-up store. "I've got a nice little place in the back all ready for you."

"Who the hell are you?" she asked.

"Exactly what you think. The guy who's going to kill you." He chuckled at the thought.

"But the laughing—what's that about?" she asked.

"It's a medical condition, and I'll thank you not to be rude about it," he told her. "I'd expect better from the likes of you. It's called hebephrenia."

"That's a kind of schizophrenia, isn't it?" she asked.

"That's right, I forgot you were a doctor of some kind. No, this is different. It's neurological, not psychological. I took a metal fragment in the head a while back, in Iraq. Messed up the wiring. I've been laughing ever since and I can't stop. I have drugs to stop the laughing, but when I take them I can't drive or shoot straight. And today I need to shoot."

Julia bit her lip and tried not to scream. "I-Iraq," she forced herself to say, instead. "So you're a veteran, like Chapel?"

"Chapel was in the army. I was a civilian consultant. This is the place."

They had reached the closed store. The teenaged boys lounging across the way watched her as she was marched up to the doors. What would happen if she screamed for them to help? Would Laughing Boy shoot them? Could he shoot them all before they overpowered him?

Or would they just run off as soon as he drew his gun?

"Go on," Laughing Boy said. "It's not locked."

Julia's body was very close to freezing in fear. She

could barely move her arms. "You want me to go in there," she said, as if clarifying an order.

"Yep," Laughing Boy said, giggling.

"Why are you doing this?" she demanded. "I don't know anything!"

"Chapel didn't tell you about the virus? Come on. I don't have all day. I've got lots of other people to round up."

Julia reached out and touched the handle of the door. It opened outward. She pulled it toward her and looked inside to see the interior of the shop, which was dark and stank of mildew. What a horrible place to die.

"Walk inside and turn around to face me. Then put your hands behind your neck and lace your fingers together." He laughed. "Seriously, I just want to get this over with. I don't get any thrill from killing people. It's just my job." He chuckled again.

She felt like her legs were made of wood. She couldn't feel her toes.

She did what he said. To the letter.

"Good," he told her, taking a step inside the store. He let the door swing shut behind him. "Now—"

"Now!" Julia shouted.

The drunk vet who'd been waiting for her inside the store did exactly as she'd told him to. He had a length of iron rebar in his hands, and he swung it at Laughing Boy's head with all his strength.

ATLANTA, GEORGIA: APRIL 13, T+27:23

Julia wasn't there when Chapel came back up through the hatch. He panicked for a second and then he called for Angel, hoping she might know where Julia might have gone.

"Hold it together, sugar," she told him. "Just head to your left. Now, up ahead—see that abandoned store?"

"Just tell me if she's all right, Angel," Chapel pleaded.

"Just fine. Door's open."

Chapel shoved open the door and pushed through into the store beyond.

He could not have expected what he saw.

Laughing Boy was sprawled out on the floor, his arms above his head and his wrists tied together around a support pillar. He was chuckling softly to himself, though he wasn't smiling. There was a nasty-looking bruise on the side of his head.

Julia had been hiding behind the pillar. She came out into the open, and Chapel saw she was holding a silenced pistol. It had to be Laughing Boy's.

Perhaps strangest of all, the drunk guy in the army coat was standing up against one wall, holding a length of rebar like a club.

"You—" Chapel started.

"Name's Rudy, not that you asked," the drunk told him. "You did ask about my service record. First Battalion, Third Marines."

Chapel nodded slowly. "Army Rangers," he said.

"A grunt, huh? I guess I can forgive you for being an asshole, then. Since it comes with the branch."

Chapel found himself smiling. "You rescued Julia?" he asked.

"Not exactly." Rudy nodded at her. "Just came in for the assist, really, right at the end of the whole thing."

Julia was watching Laughing Boy. She wouldn't take her eyes off him. "Angel and I worked together on this. Rudy was a big part of it. You were too busy playing James Bond to get involved."

Chapel's smile died on his face. "I'm just glad you're okay."

Laughing Boy's whole body shook with mirth. "Okay? Okay. Yeah, we're all okay in here. Too bad it can't last."

Julia kicked him in the ribs. "It won't last for you, that's for sure," she said.

Chapel put the scene together in his mind. Laughing Boy must have been following them this whole time, waiting for a time when Chapel and Julia weren't in the same place. He'd moved in when he got his chance, but Julia, working with Angel and Rudy, had somehow lured Laughing Boy in here and gotten the better of him. His first thought was one of immense relief that it had worked out like that—that Julia was still alive.

His second thought was that they were all in deep shit.

"Go ahead, Chapel," Julia said.

"Go ahead and do what?" Chapel asked.

"Interrogate him! Find out why he's chasing us."

"Julia—" he began.

It was Laughing Boy who answered that, though. "He knows that already. It's because of the virus, of course. Why don't you ask Captain Jimmy here about that? About the virus?"

Julia's eyes flicked toward Chapel, but she was smart enough not to lower the gun or look away from Laughing Boy for long. "Chapel?" she said.

"I'll tell you about it later," he told her. "I don't want to say anything in front of him."

"Then—then ask him about the chimeras. He must know more than we do," Julia pointed out.

"I'm sure of it. I'm also sure he's not going to tell us what we need to know."

"He will if you torture him," Julia suggested. "I don't like it, Lord knows I'm not comfortable with any Guantanamo Bay shit. But if anybody ever deserved it—"

"Won't work," Laughing Boy said, chuckling.

"He's right," Chapel told her.

"You don't know how to waterboard somebody? They didn't train you in that?" Julia demanded.

"They taught me all about interrogation techniques," Chapel confirmed. "And why they're no good."

"Let me guess," she said. "Anything you can do to him, he knows some way to resist it. Damn it!"

"No. The problem is, torture works too well. Ten minutes in he'd tell us everything we wanted to hear. He'd tell us anything at all, to make us stop. He'd tell us ten different stories. One of them might even be true, but we'd have no way to know which one. There's also the fact that it's illegal."

"I don't care! This isn't just about your case, Chapel. This man is a murderer. He needs to pay!"

She was right—there was no question about that. She was also fooling herself. Chapel wondered if there had ever been a time in human history when the people who needed to pay actually ended up doing it. The sad fact was that men like Laughing Boy were above the law.

Chapel wasn't in the business of righting wrongs. He was in the business of protecting people. Right then, that meant getting Julia away from that place.

"Just put the gun down," he said. "We need to get out of here. Somebody might have seen you and him coming in here. They might have called the cops. If they come and find us like this—"

"No! No way! We are not going to just let him go!"

"We'll leave him here, like this. He can explain to the cops how he wound up in this position. He won't name us—he doesn't dare."

"This asshole kills people! He killed Portia, my receptionist! And who knows how many other people?"

Chapel walked over toward her and held out his hand so she could give him the silenced pistol. She didn't move an inch.

"It's all right," he said. "Just give me the gun."

"No," she told him, and he saw in her eyes that she didn't trust him. No more than she trusted Laughing Boy. "No. I don't think so."

"How does this end?" he asked her.

"You know what he's capable of. He's worse than the chimeras!"

"Tell me how it ends," he asked her, quietly.

On the ground Laughing Boy started to guffaw.

"Does it end with you shooting him in the head? I don't think it does. You're not a killer, Julia." He held out his hand again. "You're better than him."

"You could kill him," Julia pointed out. "You have a gun, too."

Laughing Boy crowed at the thought. "He doesn't have the balls!"

Chapel shook his head. "I guess that's the difference between you and me. You seem to think it's an act of courage to shoot a defenseless man tied up on the ground. I don't."

"Nah," Laughing Boy said. "Nah. The difference is that you're one of those military types who takes the whole *defense* thing too seriously. The difference between you and me is that you think your job is to protect America."

"That *is* my job," Chapel said. "What's yours?"

"I'm here to make sure America *wins*. No matter what it takes."

"Shut up!" Julia shouted at him. "Shut up and stop laughing!"

Laughing Boy chuckled to himself.

Julia lifted the pistol and sighted down its barrel.

"Julia, if we kill him, it won't even *matter*," Chapel told her. "They'll just send somebody else. There is absolutely nothing to be gained from this."

"We have to do something," she said.

"And we will. But not now. We're done here," Chapel said. "Julia, give me the—"

Julia squeezed the trigger of the pistol.

ATLANTA, GEORGIA: APRIL 13, T+27:29

She jumped as it went off, perhaps not expecting it to make so much noise. Silencers could cut down the decibels of a gunshot but only so much—the pistol still roared like a lion when it fired.

Blood spurted out of Laughing Boy's shoe. She'd shot him in the foot.

"Jesus fuck!" Laughing Boy shouted, and his leg flopped around like a landed fish. For a second nobody moved. Finally Chapel recovered and moved closer to Julia.

She looked like she'd seen a ghost.

"That," Chapel said slowly, "will definitely slow him down."

"I was aiming for his head," she told him.

Chapel had no idea what to make of that.

He took the pistol from Julia—she didn't fight him this time—and wiped the grip with the tail of his shirt. When he was sure it was clean, he slid it into the darkness at the back of the abandoned store. "Now we really have to go. Rudy—you too."

The ex-marine nodded. He didn't look particularly shocked by what he'd seen. Less so than Julia, for sure. He went to the door and held it open for Julia, who marched out with her head down. She looked like she was near tears.

Chapel took one last look at Laughing Boy. He was still bleeding, though not too badly. His face was screwed up with pain, but he was still chuckling.

"I'll tell you one thing," the CIA man said. "You

don't even need to torture me. She's going nowhere. She might have the bug."

"She might not," Chapel said, and he turned to go.

"Maybe," Laughing Boy said. "Maybe you've got it, too."

Chapel's blood froze.

He'd considered that before, of course. Anyone who came into contact with the chimeras was at risk of contracting the virus. And he had been in very close contact with the one in New York.

He hadn't let himself think about it consciously, not before that. He'd put it away in the box of things he had to worry about later.

It would have to stay there, for now. He closed the door behind him and faced Rudy and Julia. Nodding, he led them deeper into the mall. There was no sign anyone had heard the gunshot or wanted to investigate it if they did. When he was sure they were in the clear, Chapel turned to Rudy and offered his hand.

"I'd rather have a kiss from her," the vet said.

Julia had been lost in her own thoughts. She came to long enough to look him in the face. "How about a hundred dollars?" she asked.

"That works, too," Rudy told her.

She handed over the money and then turned away, clearly not wanting to look at either of them for a while.

"Maybe we can do better than that," Chapel said. "Rudy—I misjudged you, and I'm sorry. I thought you were just a drunk."

"Probably because I told you I was, when we first met," Rudy said. He had a sunny smile on his face.

The hundred-dollar bill was already tucked away in one of his pockets. "I got no illusions. I'm an alcoholic, through and through."

"You ever thought about changing that?" Chapel asked.

"Sometimes," Rudy admitted. "The tough part's getting started, though."

Chapel nodded. He didn't have time to help Rudy get to an AA meeting or a rehab facility. But he knew somebody who might. "I've got a friend. You'd like him—he's a jarhead like you. Dumb as a box of rocks, but he's got the heart of a bear." He reached into his pocket and took out a scrap of paper and a pen. He wrote down Top's name and phone number and handed it to the ex-marine. "Tell him a one-armed grunt gave you his name."

Rudy stared at the slip of paper.

"No obligations," Chapel said. "Just—if you want to talk to someone. Someone who gets it. Top's your man."

Rudy nodded and took the number. "Thank you kindly. But who's this one-armed fellow I'm supposed to know?"

Chapel smiled. "Just say what I told you, and he'll know who it is. Now, listen. I hate to be rude. Again. But—"

"But it's best for all of us if I just walk away now and pretend I never saw you. That's one thing us marines can actually figure out. When to keep our damned mouths shut," Rudy agreed. He gave Chapel a mock salute, turned on his heel, and walked away.

Chapel sighed in relief. That could have gone

much worse. He reached for Julia's arm, but she pulled away from him. He could only imagine what she was going through. She'd probably never fired a pistol before. She'd certainly never tried to kill anybody before.

"Just talk to me," he said. "Just tell me—"

"No," she said, turning to face him. She drew herself up to her full height. Visibly composed herself. "You tell me. Tell me about this virus."

ATLANTA, GEORGIA: APRIL 13, T+28:44

Back at the motel he told her everything.

He had struggled with it in the cab ride back. He was duty bound not to reveal any of the limited information he had about the chimeras.

But she had a right to know.

He took the hands-free unit from his ear and buried it inside his jacket, along with his phone. Then he turned on the cold water tap in the bathroom. He didn't want Angel to hear him talking about this. Not if he was going to be blunt about it. "The chimeras I'm chasing are escapees from a facility in the Catskills," he told Julia, when he was sure he'd taken enough precautions. "They were held there a long time. Maybe all their lives. They were locked up not just because they're so obviously dangerous, but because they are carriers for some kind of virus."

"Like Typhoid Mary," Julia suggested.

"Who?" Chapel asked.

Julia shook her head in disbelief. "You've never

heard of her? She was a woman who lived in New York a hundred years ago. She was a carrier for typhoid fever—she never actually got the disease herself, but she worked as a cook for a number of families and everywhere she worked she ended up giving the disease to whoever ate her food. She refused to believe that she had the disease, since she didn't show any symptoms."

"What happened to her?" Chapel asked.

"Eventually she had to be quarantined. She spent the rest of her life—thirty years—on an island in the East River, all alone."

Thirty years, Chapel thought. If Julia was locked up somewhere like that, she might live another fifty years. How long would the chimeras have lived if nobody let them out of their cage?

"This virus the chimeras are carrying—" Julia began.

"It's why I'm so desperate to catch them. It's why this is so important that some people are willing to kill over it."

"Yes. I grasped that part already," Julia said. She sat up very straight on the end of the bed, her hands folded in her lap. "Is it airborne?"

"No. It can only be passed on through exchange of body fluids."

"That's not as comforting as it sounds," she said, and the look on her face must have been the one while explaining to her clients how distemper or kennel cough worked. "Diseases vary in how difficult they are to pass on—HIV, for instance, is actually very difficult to transmit, that's why it mostly spreads through sex and blood transfusions. Other bloodborne illnesses are much more robust. For some of them a chimera could sneeze on someone, or spit on them, and transmit it. What disease are we talking about? Some kind of flu? A retrovirus? Ebola?"

"I don't know. It's classified."

Julia frowned. "Classified. They didn't even tell you that much?"

"Just that it's hard to detect, and that there is no cure or vaccine."

"Fuck," Julia said.

"But you don't have it," Chapel told her.

"I don't? How do you know that? You haven't taken any blood or tissue samples that I'm aware of. Maybe while I was sleeping, but I imagine I would have noticed that."

"I wouldn't do that to you without your knowledge."

She sighed. "Then how can you possibly know I'm not infected, Chapel?"

"I just do. Your contact with the chimera was minimal. He didn't bite or scratch you when you were in that cab, and—"

"He manhandled me. Something could have happened. Why did you keep this from me? I thought Laughing Boy was just a homicidal lunatic. There seemed to be a lot of that going around! I had no idea this was a public health issue. Chapel—what if I kissed Rudy, like he wanted? I could have given it to him. Shit—I *did* kiss you, and more."

"I had contact with the chimera as well. And I know I don't have it," Chapel told her.

"Good God, Chapel! Either of us could have given

254 / David Wellington

it to the other. Oh, God—why didn't I wait at least until we had some condoms? I was so caught up in the moment. I didn't even think about STDs, much less this! Chapel, what if I had it, and you didn't, but I gave it to you this morning? Huh? What if it was the other way around? *What if you gave it to me when you made love to me?*"

Chapel's mouth fell open. That was—that was a horrible thought. That was beyond thinking about. "But we don't have it," he insisted.

"How can you know that for sure?"

"Because I would feel it. I would know somehow!"

She stared at him. "You do know I have some medical training, right? I mean, I've patched you up a couple of times now. They call me Doctor Taggart. I went to school for this. I know exactly how easy these things spread. I'm going to go out on a limb here. The chimeras didn't just pick this up naturally, did they?"

"No. The virus is human engineered," Chapel confirmed.

"You mean weaponized," she said.

The word hung in the air like the first drops of rain before a hurricane hits.

"I don't know," Chapel said. "It's—"

"Classified. Which might as well be a yes." Julia got up and walked into the bathroom. She started washing her hands vigorously. It looked like a reflexive action, something she'd learned to do whenever people started talking about viruses around her.

He *had* forgotten she was a doctor. He'd forgotten she probably knew a lot more about viruses than he did. He should have been honest with her.

When she came back to the door of the bathroom and looked out at him, her eyes were haunted.
"I need to be quarantined," she said.

"No," Chapel told her. "No, we can't—"

"You do, as well. Anybody who's had contact with
a chimera."

"No! That was what Laughing Boy was after.
I refuse to accept his actions were appropriate,"
Chapel demanded.

"Call up Angel. Call her right now. Tell her we're
volunteering to go into quarantine. We shouldn't be
out in public."

Her legs quaked visibly beneath her. She dropped
to the floor, her hands rushing up to cover her face.

"Oh my God," she said. "Chapel, we could be
dying right now, and not know it. That fucking chimera might have killed me just by breathing in my
face. We could already be dead. What the hell have
you done to my life?"

Chapel might have said something, but just then
his phone began to ring. He dug it out of his jacket
and stared at it. The number on the screen read
(000) 000-0000.

ATLANTA, GEORGIA: APRIL 13, T+28:55

Chapel set the phone down on the bed. It continued
to ring.

"Just answer it," Julia told him.

Without a word he touched the screen to answer
the call. He placed the phone against his ear.

"Chapel," Angel told him, "please put me on

speaker. You both need to hear what I'm going to say."

Chapel did as he was told. He set the phone down on the comforter on top of the bed. He sat down in a chair and tried not to look at Julia.

"Doctor Taggart," Angel said, "I know what you just heard must come as quite a shock."

"You . . . heard all that?" Chapel asked.

"Give me some credit, Chapel. I'm a spy. I eavesdrop for a living. You muffled one of my microphones, but you forgot there's a normal wired telephone in the room."

Chapel looked over at the bedside table and saw it, an old beige model with a big red light that lit up if you had messages. It was such an antique piece of technology now that he hadn't even registered it. That had been a dumb mistake. Chapel knew about infinity mikes, bugs that allowed any telephone to be used as a listening device—even if the handset was resting on its cradle. He should have thought of that.

"Doctor Taggart," Angel said, "you've already shown your strength. So I won't lie to you now. Chapel's correct. You may have the virus. You may be infected already, or you could be a carrier. If you are, then you may need to be quarantined. And most likely that quarantine will be lifelong, or at least as long as it takes us to come up with some cure for the virus."

Julia wasn't looking at the phone. She had wrapped her arms around her knees and was gently rocking back and forth.

"I can give you a little comfort, though," Angel

went on. "Information on the virus is strictly need to know. But if anybody needs to know, it's you. The virus is about as fragile as the HIV virus. Once you have it, there's no way for your immune system to conquer it. But it is difficult to get from casual contact. When you were with the chimera, did he bite or scratch you? I know you'll tell me the truth."

"No," Julia said, rubbing at her nose with the palm of her hand. "He grabbed my wrists and held me down. He screamed in my face. He may have abraded my skin, and he may have gotten some saliva on me."

Angel sighed in relief. "That's good. That's pretty low on the risk scale. We can't totally rule out an infection, but . . . your chances are good. I promise."

"Yeah?" Julia said, looking up.

"Beyond that, the virus has a pretty long incubation period. Several months, in fact. And you're not contagious, even if you do have it. You won't be for a long time."

"Okay," Julia said, letting out a deep breath.

"Director Hollingshead feels the best place for you now is with Chapel. He can make sure you stay safe. We don't want you to come in just yet. At the moment, we can't even detect the virus if it's in your system. When that changes, we'll make sure you're tested—so you'll know. You'll know for sure. Only then do we need to start talking about what to do next."

"Thank you," Julia said.

"We will take care of you. No matter what, we'll make sure of that."

"I appreciate it," Julia said. A teardrop fell from her left eye.

"It's the very least we can do. Now, I'm going to have to talk to Chapel in private for a while. And I imagine you could use some time to be alone with your thoughts, after everything you've learned."

"That would be nice," Julia confirmed.

"Chapel, please put in your earpiece. Maybe you could go outside and let Julia be alone while we talk."

"I don't want to let her out of my sight, not after the last time, when Laughing Boy—"

"Laughing Boy is in a hospital about twenty miles from you, waiting to see if he's going to keep his toes," Angel said. "By the way, Doctor Taggart—nice shooting."

Julia laughed, though there were tears in her eyes. "You know I was trying to kill him, don't you?"

"He deserved nothing less. I'm just glad you made him pay. Now. Chapel?"

"Okay, okay," Chapel said, and grabbed the phone and the hands-free unit. "You going to be okay?" he asked Julia.

She glared at him.

Crap. It looked like Angel had relieved a little of her fear—but just enough to let her get angry at him again.

Maybe stepping outside for a while was an excellent idea.

ATLANTA, GEORGIA: APRIL 13, T+29:02

A long balcony ran outside the motel room, allow-ing access to all the rooms on that floor. Chapel felt exposed walking up and down, past all the curtains of the other rooms, but there was nothing for it. "Was all that true, what you told her?" he asked.

"Absolutely. I imagine it's going to be some com-fort to you, too, sweetie," Angel said. There was a distinct note of sadness in her voice. "After all, you had a lot more physical contact with the chimera than she did."

"And there are three more of them out there," Chapel said. "I'm going to probably have contact with them as well."

"You'd be in your rights to be concerned about that," Angel told him.

"I know what my job is. I didn't join the army because I thought it was going to be safe."

"I'm sure Director Hollingshead will be glad to hear that."

Chapel didn't want to think about it. He didn't want to think about the fact that he might spend the rest of his life locked up in a camp in the Catskills. "We need to get back to work," he said. That was the best way to take his mind off it, he knew.

He filled her in briefly on what Funt had told him. About CIA hit squads and Laughing Boy—and that Funt definitely knew something about the chi-meras. He even knew the name of the one coming for him.

"I guess that explains why he's on the kill list," Angel pointed out.

"Absolutely. Christina Smollett is still a mystery, but it's starting to look like this is definitely a CIA hit list. I want to take a look at the rest of the names. My feeling is that William Taggart and Franklin Hayes are the next two targets after Funt. But maybe I'm wrong. Who else do we have?"

Angel tapped away at her keyboard for a while.

"Marcia Kennedy and Olivia Nguyen," Angel said. "Kennedy is in Vancouver and Nguyen lives in Seattle."

Chapel nodded to himself. They would both be safe for the moment—it would take longer for the chimeras to get to either of those cities than it would take them to get to Denver. "What do they do for a living?" Chapel asked.

"Huh. Kennedy works at a flower shop. She's filed some tax forms, but not regularly—only for about ten years in the last twenty. She's a Canadian citizen, but she wasn't born there. Looks like her parents moved to Canada in the nineties and she went with them. She was naturalized in 1998, the same year as her parents."

"So it's a close family—do they live together?"

"No . . . but," Angel said, and clucked her tongue for a second as if she was thinking, "the parents have a house in the suburbs. She lives a little closer in to the downtown area in a studio apartment. Okay, here. The lease is cosigned by her father, Arthur Kennedy. Looks like she was the one who signed the lease in the first place, but the building owners sued her for failure to pay her rent in 2002. After that the father cosigned, and it looks like the rent's been paid faithfully ever since."

"She probably doesn't make much money working in a flower shop," Chapel pointed out.

"True . . . wow. Cool. I've got to remember how to do this."

"You found something?"

"Her résumé is online, with one of those services that helps you get interviews. Interesting. She's worked on and off at the flower shop, on for eight or ten months, off for four or six months. Just about every year she seems to quit, and then comes back and gets rehired a while later."

"That sounds promising. Maybe the job at the flower shop is just a cover, and she takes off long stretches every year to do undercover work for the CIA."

"Watching Canada to make sure those rascally northerners don't try anything?" Angel asked, with a laugh.

"I'm looking for connections here," Chapel said. "I admit that's a stretch."

"Let me take a look at something. Her medical records should be online and easy to get since Canada has nationalized health coverage. Oh."

"What did you find?"

Angel clucked her tongue again. "Let me just check what this does . . . okay. Sure. She's on carbamazepine. That explains a lot."

"What is it?" Chapel asked.

"Carbamazepine is an anticonvulsant," Angel said, "which would suggest epilepsy, but it's also used in the treatment of severe bipolar disorder. Which fits her information pretty well. She can function for most of the year but every so often she probably gets a period of intense depression where she can't get out of bed, so that's why she works sporadically and why she had trouble paying her rent."

Chapel leaned on the balcony railing and closed his eyes. "You're saying she's mentally ill. Just like Christina Smollett."

"Her disease probably isn't as profound, but, yeah," Angel told him.

What could it mean? Why on earth would the chimeras be targeting mentally ill women? It was the one fact of the case that he couldn't comprehend at all. Christina Smollett and Marcia Kennedy couldn't possibly have done any meaningful work for the CIA, or the DoD, or any other governmental agency. They would never have passed the necessary background checks to get clearance. They didn't have backgrounds in genetics research, either. They even lived on opposite sides of the continent . . . it just didn't add up.

"Okay," he said. "Okay. You've already told me there are no red herrings on this list. No false leads. But this is looking just plain weird. I hate to ask, but—Olivia Nguyen. Is there anything there?"

Angel worked her magic for a while in silence. When she came back on the line, she sounded almost afraid to tell him what she'd found.

"Her address is listed as 2600 Southwest Holden Street, in Seattle."

"It's a hospital, isn't it?"

"A psychiatric hospital, yes. She's been a patient there since 1981."

STONE MOUNTAIN, GEORGIA: APRIL 13, T+34:48

Chapel and Julia waddled forward in line with the tourists and sightseers headed to the top of Stone Mountain. Chapel had traded his button-down shirt for a polo that let him fit in a little better. Even this early in the year, most of the people in line for the Skyride were wearing T-shirts and shorts, though most of the women carried windbreakers or sweaters. It was supposed to be cooler up top.

"You still giving me the silent treatment?" Chapel asked.

"Huh," Julia said, not looking up. She read aloud from a brochure she'd picked up while Chapel bought their tickets for the cable car. "I didn't know. This was the first project for Gutzon Borglum. He didn't finish it, though."

Apparently she was talking to him, now. She just wouldn't look at him.

He didn't suppose he blamed her. He'd made a fair share of mistakes with her. He should have told her about the virus. He should have found some way to protect her without bringing her here, without nearly getting her blown up. He should have killed Laughing Boy when he had the chance so she would be safe now.

That was a lot of should haves. It was going to take a while before things thawed out between them, he thought.

"Who's Gutzon Borglum?" Chapel asked, shuffling forward. The line was taking forever. He'd wanted to be on top of the mountain at least an hour before his scheduled meeting with Funt, but it looked like they would have to wait for the next car.

"The man who carved Mount Rushmore," Julia told him. "The monument at Stone Mountain was commissioned by the United Daughters of the Confederacy," she read, "in 1916. It took nearly fifty years to complete."

Chapel leaned to one side to take a look at the mountain. He'd had other things on his mind and hadn't really bothered to check out the sculpture.

"It's the largest bas-relief in the world," Julia read.

Chapel could believe it.

Stone Mountain lived up to its name. It looked like a single piece of enormous rock towering over the nearby landscape, a dome of gray granite almost denuded of trees. From where Chapel stood it rose over him like a sheer wall. Carved into that massive rock face was a portrait of the South's three greatest heroes: Stonewall Jackson, Jefferson Davis, and Robert E. Lee. From a distance the carvings hadn't looked like much, but from the base of the mountain they were colossal and incredibly detailed. It looked like the three giants on horseback were going to leap out of the stone at any moment and go racing across the country, capes flapping in the wind, the heads of the horses rearing, as the three men rode to glory.

Angel snorted in his ear. "What the brochure doesn't tell you is that this is where the modern Ku Klux Klan was officially organized, and where they had their big rallies until the eighties."

"During the Olympics," Julia read, "Stone Mountain facilities were used for the archery, tennis, and track cycling events." She folded the brochure and put it in her purse. "Are we going to have to wait for the next car?" she asked, and a moment later they watched the Skyride lift away from the ground, headed upward across the carving toward the very top.

"Looks like it," Chapel said.

"Chapel," Angel said in his ear, "I know what I said last time, about your being a jerk when you left Julia behind. But I also know you made the right choice, no matter how angry she is with you now. You should leave Julia down here. Just try to say it in a nicer way this time."

"Not a chance," he told her. Julia looked at him for a second as if she thought he was talking to her. Chapel tapped the hands-free unit in his ear and Julia rolled her eyes and turned away.

"Listen, sugar," Angel said, "if Funt is up there and you start asking him questions with Julia around, she's going to hear everything. That's not a good thing. Secrets don't work if everybody knows them."

"The last time I spoke with him I left her behind. Look how that turned out," Chapel said. "No, I can't let her out of my sight anymore."

"Director Hollingshead doesn't want her hearing any of this," Angel pointed out. "You know that, Chapel."

Chapel sighed. He knew it perfectly well. He knew he was exceeding the limits of need to know. He was, frankly, taking a running leap and jumping as far as he could humanly get past those limits.

He glanced at Julia. She was part of this. She had

a right to know. And maybe that exceeded the right of Hollingshead and Angel and the entire government to keep things from her.

He couldn't very well say that, of course. He was a silent warrior. The kind of man who could be trusted to keep his mouth shut.

Or at least, he'd thought that was who he was.

"She's coming with me," he told Angel.

The operator was silent for a long time. "You've been given a lot of latitude on how you work this case," she said, finally. "That latitude can be taken away. If Director Hollingshead needs to rein you in, he will."

"Is that a threat, Angel?"

"It's a friendly warning!" she said, sounding exasperated. "I want you to succeed, sweetie. I want you to win this thing. Why are you fighting me?"

Chapel wasn't entirely certain himself. But he'd begun to suspect something. He'd known for a while that Angel—and Hollingshead—had their own agenda in this. That capturing or killing the chimeras was only part of what they wanted to accomplish.

Maybe it was time he had his own agenda. Maybe it was time to start thinking about what he wanted to get out of this. He looked at Julia again. This time she looked back, a question on her face.

He still didn't know what he wanted to happen. He didn't know how this could end well for anyone. But he was going to make sure Julia came out of this alive. That was a start. Alive, and, if he had anything to say about it, free.

If that fit into Hollingshead's secret plan, so be it.

If not—Chapel would have to start making up his own rules for this game.

He had more important things to worry about just then, though. The time for his meeting with Funt was drawing near. He hadn't counted on having to wait in line to get to the top of the mountain.

"We're going to cut it pretty close," Chapel said, staring at his watch.

The line moved forward again as the next car opened its doors. The tourists, and Chapel and Julia, filed in, filling all the available space. The operator of the Skyride announced that this was the last car of the evening, and that the mountaintop would be closing down in just thirty minutes. The tourists grumbled and booed but good-naturedly, disappointed that they weren't going to have much time at the top.

In compensation, though, they got to see the carving come alive with the sunset.

Red light washed over the face of Stone Mountain, filling in every crack and crevice of the massive bas-relief. The mountain itself seemed to glow like a titanic jewel, a rich luster that only brightened even as the sun faded.

"That's kind of beautiful," Julia said, leaning against the side of the car, pressing her face close to the glass of its windows. Behind her the tourists *ooh*ed and *aah*ed, but Chapel only had eyes for her, this woman he'd dragged out of New York City and taken with him on this mad trip.

"It's exactly the same color as your hair," he observed.

She turned and faced him, her mouth curled

up in a look of bewilderment. "I'm trying to give you the cold shoulder," she said. "You shouldn't say things like that to me right now. It was way too close to being sweet."

"Couldn't help it," he told her.

She shook her head and turned to look at the mountain again. "I know you were just trying to protect me. But not telling me about the . . . about you know what. That wasn't protecting me. That was hurting me."

"It was?" Chapel asked.

"You took away my right to make decisions for myself. That's what I hate about secrets. If I don't know things, I can't do anything about them."

"It's important that some secrets be kept," he said. Because it was what he believed.

"I suppose so. And I suppose that's your job." She sighed. "Chapel, how can I ever trust somebody when I know they lie to me professionally? This is just weird."

"I can tell you one true thing," he said. "When I came out of that hatch in the Underground, and you weren't there, my heart almost stopped. I didn't know what had happened to you. I was terrified you were gone. That I'd lost you."

"As it turned out, I didn't need your protection," she told him, though her voice was softer than the words would suggest. "Thanks. I guess."

"When this is over," he said, "maybe—"

"When this is over, I'm going back to New York. I'm going to live my life the way I choose to. Openly. Honestly. Or—or I'll go . . . where they tell me. The Catskills. Wherever." She shook her head, and her hair swung around in front of the red-stained mountain. He wanted to reach out and put his hands on her shoulders but he didn't dare.

"That's what you want," he said. It wasn't a question. "Just—we part ways, then. And I never see you again."

"Just . . . stop, Chapel. Don't go there."

"I'm sorry," he said.

"It doesn't matter. Listen, I can't give you the silent treatment. We're stuck in this thing together, and if I don't talk to somebody, I'm going to go crazy. So we'll work together from now. Be civil to each other. But that's it. Let's just keep this relationship professional, okay?" She was silent for the rest of the ride to the top.

STONE MOUNTAIN, GEORGIA: APRIL 13, T+35:31

The top of Stone Mountain looked like a patch of the moon transported to earth.

Nothing grew up there save a few scraggly bushes and some lichens. It was bare rock, smoothed out by the wind but broken into ridges and basins where a little rainwater could gather and support the sparse plant life. By that point the sunset was over, though a yellow smudge of light still lingered on the far horizon. The rock was lit blue with deep purple shadows that were fading to black.

There wasn't much to see up top. Just a visitors' center where the Skyride ended, a few radio antennas topped with blinking bulbs to warn off low-flying aircraft—and the view. In the distance

Chapel saw the lights of Atlanta scattered among the darkening greenery of Georgia.

A few of the braver tourists walked out onto the naked rock, perhaps in search of better views of the sunset or the scenery. Park rangers stood around with their hands in their pockets, giving everyone a little time before they had to head back down. There was no sign of Jeremy Funt.

"He must be here by now," Chapel said. "This is right when he told me to meet him. Maybe he's hiding inside."

"I wouldn't blame him," Julia said, rubbing at her arms.

It was cold up top, much cooler than it had been when they boarded the cable car. She took out the pink sweatshirt she'd bought in the Underground and pulled it on, zipping it up to her throat. "This is the ugliest thing I've ever owned," she said, "but right now, it's my favorite."

Chapel wanted to take off his jacket and give it to her, but he couldn't. If he did, everyone would see his holstered sidearm, and the park rangers would definitely have questions. If he was going to make this meeting with Funt, he had to stay inconspicuous.

"Let's walk over to the far side," Chapel said, pointing at a fence on the other side of the mountaintop.

"There's nobody over there," Julia told him.

"I want to make myself as visible as possible so he can find me," Chapel replied. He didn't like this. He'd expected Funt to meet him as soon as he stepped out of the cable car. He'd expected the man to want to talk to him.

Maybe that had been too much to hope for.

"Chapel," Angel said, "I've got bad news. Maybe."

"Go ahead," he told her.

"I've been listening to the chatter on the park service radio channel. They're all checking in, confirming everybody's off the mountain and they can close up shop for the night. Except one ranger hasn't called in yet. They keep requesting he confirm his position, but he's not responding."

"Could be anything. Maybe his radio's battery just died. Or he could have ducked out for a smoke break."

"Maybe," Angel said. "Considering how things have gone since we started with this case, you think that's likely?"

"No," Chapel agreed. He bit his lip. "Damn. If the CIA knows we're up here—" he began, but he was interrupted.

"Chapel," Julia said in a forced whisper, "behind you!"

Chapel swung around just in time for someone to poke a gun barrel in his ribs.

He froze in place.

The gunman wore the uniform of a park ranger, including the Smokey Bear hat. He was grinning maniacally.

"Hi," Jeremy Funt said.

STONE MOUNTAIN, GEORGIA: APRIL 13, T+35:36

"Nice to see you again," Chapel said. He kept his hands at his sides. Funt hadn't told him to put them up, and he didn't want the paranoid ex-FBI agent to think he was reaching for a weapon.

"Give me a second here. Look behind you—there, you see?"

From the visitors' center a park ranger—presumably a real park ranger—made a series of hand gestures, rolling her hands around each other, tapping her watch. Clearly she was suggesting it was time for everybody to head back down. She looked over in the direction where Funt and Chapel were standing. Funt waved his free hand at her, then held up his fingers splayed out as if to suggest he needed five more minutes.

The female park ranger shrugged and headed inside the center.

"In a second we'll have this place all to ourselves," Funt told Chapel.

"You know her? You set this up?"

"Nope. I was up here about a month ago, scouting out new locations for booby traps. I watched the rangers and studied their routine. Half of them are hard-core pot smokers. They invite their friends up here after hours and they get high while the laser show plays on the side of the mountain. The supervisors don't interfere as long as they don't draw too much attention."

The tourists were all herded back into the visitors' center and into the Skyride cable car to head back down to the park below. All the park rangers went with them, including one who turned out most of the lights in the visitors' center before he boarded the cable car. Eventually it departed.

"Okay, just us, now," Funt said. "Why don't you take two steps back, very carefully—the ground here is none too level. And then you can tell me who the hell Red here is, and why you brought her."

"She's someone I'm protecting," Chapel said, nodding in Julia's direction.

"I'm Julia Taggart. I don't work for the government."

Funt didn't look away from Chapel's face. "Who do you work for, then?"

"Cats and dogs," Julia said. She sounded perfectly calm.

Well, Chapel supposed that was easier when you didn't have a gun pointed at your large intestine.

"She's a veterinarian. A chimera tried to kill her in New York," Chapel said.

Funt nodded. "I'll buy it. For now. I did some checking up on you, Chapel. I still have a few friends left in interesting places. You're definitely not CIA." Funt stopped as if he'd just thought of something. "Wait a minute. Taggart?"

"William Taggart is her father. You know William Taggart?"

Funt shrugged. "I met him, a long time ago. Mad scientist type. Liked to clone up perversions of nature in his spare time. Made the chimeras."

"'Made' them. I guess that's not a bad way to put it. What are they, specifically?"

"You don't know?" Funt asked.

"I only know what I've seen. I got no briefing at all, just a warning they were tough. The one in New York was definitely that. He also had funny eyelids. I know what the word 'chimera' means, too. An organism with DNA from two or more sources. Which is more than they're supposed to have."

Funt nodded. "Okay. I'm going to trust you, just a little bit. I can't hold this gun on you all night, after all. So I'm going to put it away. But first, you're going to give me yours. Then I'll tell you what I know, and then we can discuss getting me out of Atlanta. That's the deal. You okay with it?"

"I'd rather hold on to my weapon."

Funt smiled. "I'd rather be married to Phoebe Cates. I'd rather be in Philadelphia right now, eating a cheesesteak. The last fifteen years, I've had to deal with how things are, not how I'd rather they were."

"Fair enough," Chapel said. Very, very slowly he reached into his jacket and removed his weapon. He handed it to Funt by the grip.

"Good," Funt said, shoving it in one of his pockets. He lowered his own pistol, but he kept it in his hand. "*Now* we can talk."

STONE MOUNTAIN, GEORGIA: APRIL 13, T+35:39

"I have a lot of questions," Chapel said. "Starting with what they are. I want to know about the one you called Malcolm, and what your relationship with him is. I want to know when you first encountered them and—"

Funt held up his hands for peace. "Stop. I'll tell you my whole story. That should answer most of your questions. But first I need something from you. I want your promise that when we're done here, we'll go straight to the nearest airport. You'll make sure I get a plane ride to anywhere I want to go."

"Done," Chapel said.

"That easy, huh?"

"I've got carte blanche to deal with the chimeras," Chapel told him. "My boss—at the DIA—just wants to make sure they don't kill anyone else."

"Oh, I'm certain that's not *all* he wants." Funt rolled his eyes. "Whatever. If you get me away from Malcolm, that's all I care about. Okay. Let me think about where to start with this."

"The beginning's always a good place," Julia said.

Chapel looked across at her. She was standing close enough the three of them might as well be whispering. Clearly she intended to listen in on this. Chapel knew that Hollingshead probably didn't want her to hear it, but he figured this time he wouldn't try to stop her. He was in enough hot water as it was. If Funt started revealing state secrets, that would be another thing, of course.

But as far as Chapel was concerned, the chimeras were fair game.

"It started in 1996. I worked for the bureau back then." Funt looked at Julia. "That's the FBI." She just nodded, so he went on. "I wasn't exactly famous; I mean, it's not like I was a household name. But I had cracked some missing persons cases, found some kids who'd been abducted by religious cults or their parents or whatever and I had a reputation as the kind of guy who could find anybody. One day my AD—that's assistant director—calls me into his office and tells me to sign out for the day, then take a train to Virginia and meet with some guy in

Langley. It was all very hush-hush and I wasn't supposed to let anybody know where I was going.

"The guy in question was CIA, which wasn't exactly a surprise—somebody says 'Langley,' that's
what you think. His name was Banks. Asshole.
Giant asshole."

Chapel fought back a grin.

"Tells me," Funt went on, "that he's got a missing
person he needs found. A kid, about ten years old,
named Malcolm. He's been missing for over a week.
I always hated hearing something like that. With
abducted kids, unless it's a parent who took them, if
they've been gone more than forty-eight hours you
think to yourself, I'm not looking for a kid. I'm looking for a body. That's how you approach the case—
otherwise you go insane when you do find the body.
Banks assured me this kid was still alive, though he
wouldn't say how he knew that. And he told me it
definitely wasn't his parents who took him. Then he
asked for my security clearance. He already knew it
by heart, but I gave him what he wanted. He said I
was going to see some things nobody was ever supposed to know about. At the time I didn't realize
that meant I wasn't supposed to know them either,
and I was going on his hit list."

Chapel interrupted. "Why did he bring you in on
this in the first place? The CIA couldn't find the kid
on their own?"

"This was the mid-nineties. There wasn't even an
Internet to speak of back then," Funt pointed out,
"much less the kind of satellites we have now. Back
then when you needed somebody found, you went
to the FBI. I was simply the best man for the job.

"The CIA flew me up to some place in New York State, I never did find out exactly where. They introduced me to William Taggart—your father who, forgive me, miss, was an asshole as well, though not as big an asshole as Banks."

"I'm not exactly offended," Julia said.

Funt nodded in thanks. "He treated me like I was a kid. You could tell when he talked he was translating in his head, from big multisyllabic science words down to the kind of slangy English somebody like me might understand. He said the kid I was looking for was named Malcolm, and he was very, very special.

"They showed me some of the chimeras. Had them come out and speak to me, say, hello, Mr. Detective, isn't the weather nice today. Then one of them took off his shirt. There were a bunch of cinder blocks set up in the room. This kid—his name was Ian, I remember—goes over to them and breaks them, one at a time, by punching them. When he's done, he's breathing a little heavy and his eyes go weird. You know what I mean. An extra black eyelid slides down over his eyes and blinks at me a couple of times.

"When I stopped wanting to scream for my mother, I said, thanks, that was very impressive, but what in God's name did I just see? Dr. Taggart explained they were called chimeras, and they're the next step in human evolution. Ninety-nine percent human, he said, just like you and me. The other one percent was cobbled together from DNA sequences he stole from chimpanzees and rattlesnakes and something called a water bear, which I'd never heard of. They were survivors, he said. They could live through anything, they could survive gunshot wounds, blood loss, hypothermia. They were faster than people, stronger, and, he thought, probably smarter, though they had a hard time testing for that.

"I asked a whole bunch of questions, like how one percent difference could account for everything he'd told me, and why on earth he'd chosen to do this, and whether he thought the devil had a special place for him in hell or if he was just going to get the usual treatment. He got pretty pissed off then and walked out on me. It was another scientist, a woman with red hair like yours but going gray, who showed me the rest."

"That . . . would have been my mother," Julia said.

"Are you going to get mad if I tell you she was kind of an asshole, too?"

"She's dead," Julia said.

"Oh. Crap. I . . . didn't know—"

"She's dead, which is the only thing that keeps me from agreeing with you," Julia told him.

". . . Right. Well, this woman, who didn't even tell me her name, she showed me the place they had the chimeras living. Camp Putnam, they called it. They were all living in a sort of dormitory there. It looked pretty much like a summer camp, except all the kids were exactly the same age and size, and they all kind of looked alike. And instead of hot little counselors in tight T-shirts and short shorts, they had soldiers carrying M4 carbines. The kids didn't seem to think it was weird. They'd never known anything else, your mom told me. They'd been there their whole lives."

"Hold on," Chapel said. "Julia—your parents moved away from the Catskills in, when, 1995?"

"We moved to our house, yeah. For the first couple of years Dad only came to see us on the weekends, and Mom would commute to and from work. She had to get up really early so I had to get myself ready for school in the morning."

"But if the camp was operational then, why wouldn't they want to live closer to it?" Chapel asked. "If that was where they worked—"

"Did you want to hear the rest of my story?" Funt asked.

"Yes. Sorry," Chapel told him. "Just trying to keep the facts straight."

Funt snorted in derision and went on. "Good luck with that. This was the weirdest case I ever saw, and I only got little glimpses of it. Your mom took me to see the fence around the camp. At the time it was just a normal cyclone fence, twelve feet high. They were already building a new one when I was there. Much bigger, and with barbed wire on top. Your mom told me the fence was electrified. They didn't think the chimeras would dare climb it. In this one case, they were wrong. Malcolm had gone right over it. The guards caught him when he landed on the other side."

"They caught him?" Julia asked. "But—"

"They caught him. They couldn't hold him, though. Three soldiers, heavily armed. He killed all three of them, snapped their necks, and ran off into the woods. He was ten years old at the time."

STONE MOUNTAIN, GEORGIA: APRIL 13, T+35:48

"He was . . . ten?" Julia asked, her face pale even in the darkness that had settled over the top of Stone Mountain. "In 1996, he was ten . . . they were all . . . ten?"

"Yeah," Funt said. "That significant, somehow?"

"Just . . . to me. No. I mean, no—it's not significant. Please, go on."

Chapel shot her a glance, but her face wasn't giving anything away. Maybe she had some secrets of her own.

Funt shrugged and went on. He took off his ranger hat and rubbed his arms. "I had my case, anyway. This weird mutant kid had escaped from the camp and I had to track him down. I tried not to think too much about what he'd done to those soldiers, or what the other one, Ian, had done to those cinder blocks. I worked it like any other missing persons. I asked a lot of people a lot of questions, made a lot of phone calls, wore out some shoe leather. I'm guessing the details aren't too important, not now. I spent three weeks looking, and every day Agent Banks from the CIA would call me and bitch me out for not finding Malcolm. Eventually I tracked the kid down to a house outside of Philadelphia. Nice place, just on the edge of farmland. No fence, just a real big lawn he could play on. It was owned by a family called the Gabors. They'd found him walking along the side of a country road outside of Utica, New York, while they were on vacation. Figured he was a runaway so they took him in, raised him like their own. Hippie types—Mr. Gabor worked for a nonprofit feeding homeless people. The Mrs. was a lawyer, but the bumper sticker on her car said No Blood for Oil, so she wasn't exactly the rich kind of lawyer. I'm guessing they were nice people."

"You're guessing? You didn't talk to them?" Chapel asked.

"Nope. What I know about them I got from their daughter. She was a student at Villanova. She came home for Thanksgiving and found them in their bed. Her mom had been strangled. Looked like her dad tried to put up a fight. He was in pieces."

"Oh, God," Julia said. "Don't—please don't explain what you mean."

"I'd prefer not to, myself," Funt said. "I don't even like thinking about what I saw in that bedroom. It was a classic rage killing, from the look of it. What you'd expect if a six-foot-four linebacker came home and found his wife in bed with the mailman. A little more brutal than that, maybe. The daughter was in hysterics, of course, but she gave me the info I needed to find Malcolm. He was in his favorite place, the place he always went to, she said, when he was angry or confused, which happened a lot. He was in this tree fort in their backyard. He was still there when I got to the house. Just sitting up there, staring down at me. He'd been crying. I asked him why he'd done that to his foster parents. Why he'd killed them. He told me. Seems he had been given a cat for a pet, and the cat disappeared. He didn't tell me where it went and I didn't ask. I wasn't in Missing Pets. His foster mom and dad got pretty upset about the whole thing, though, so they must have known what happened to it. He asked if he could have another one, and they said no. Absolutely not."

"What does that have to do with the parents' murder?" Julia asked.

"You're not listening. That was the whole reason. They wouldn't let him have another cat. So he killed them."

"What? That's insane," Chapel said.

"Yeah. Exactly. The chimeras—they're ninety-nine percent human. But that one percent makes a serious difference," Funt told him. "They don't think like us. They look like us, but they don't *feel* like us. To them everything is serious. Deadly serious. When they get frustrated, or upset . . . even just confused, it makes them angry—and when they're angry, nobody is safe. They're not human. They're monsters."

Chapel felt a chill run down his spine. "What did you do?" he asked.

"I asked him to come down from his tree house. I told him I would find him some new parents to live with, that everything was going to be okay. Working in Missing Persons you learn how to talk to kids who are so scared they can't see straight. You learn how to calm them down. You also learn how to get them to climb into a stranger's car. I got Malcolm buckled in and I drove him straight to the local police station. He started freaking out then, but I thought I could handle him. Then Dr. Taggart— your dad—showed up, and Malcolm went ballistic.

"One of the cops at that station ended up on an early pension. Maybe he learned to walk again. I didn't have a chance to follow up. As for me, I was in the hospital for a long time with a broken pelvis and two broken legs. I came real close to putting a bullet in Malcolm's head. Instead, your dad put five tranquilizer darts in him and eventually he fell down and went to sleep. It was the last I ever saw of him."

"You told him he would be safe," Julia said.

"That's right. I lied to him," Funt told her. "I betrayed him. I feel bad about that every once in a while. Then I think about the five people he killed, and what he did to that cop, and to me. He looked like a kid. He sounded like a kid. When he got angry, he was a demon out of hell. I have no idea what they did to him at Camp Putnam when he got back—for all I know they ran Nazi-style experiments on him night and day. Honest to God, I can't say for sure if I think he deserved it or not."

STONE MOUNTAIN, GEORGIA: APRIL 13, T+36:02

Chapel shook his head. Some of this was new information, but he didn't see how much of it helped him. "So the CIA . . . created the chimeras, and then just warehoused them in this camp. But why? Why create them in the first place? What were they supposed to do? What were they supposed to be?"

"You think they'd tell me things like that? I only got to see the camp so I would know how dangerous Malcolm was. How tough my job was going to be," Funt said.

"Okay. Okay." Chapel scrubbed at his face with his hands. He felt soiled just from hearing Funt's story. "Then—"

"The whole time," Julia said. Both men turned to face her, but it was clear she was talking to herself. She had her arms wrapped around her chest and was bending over slightly at the waist. She looked like she might throw up—or start screaming. She shivered violently, and Chapel took his coat off and put it around her shoulders, but it didn't seem to help. "The whole time I was growing up. The whole time," she repeated. She stared into Chapel's eyes. "I was sixteen years old when all that happened. My dad was teaching me how to drive. Then he went and shot a boy full of tranquilizer darts and took him back to prison. My parents—I thought I knew who they were, but—oh God. When I was six, they were just being born. Or made, or grown in vats, or whatever. When I was in first grade, learning to read, my parents were giving birth to little monsters. Chapel. Chapel!"

"I'm here," he said, and reached for her, but she shoved him away.

"Chapel, they're my brothers. Maybe not in, you know, a genetic way. But in every other way that counts. My brothers!"

"No," he said. "No. You can't think like that."

"How can I not?" she asked him. "How can I think about them any other way?"

He started to answer, though he honestly had no idea what he was going to say. Before any words could come out of his mouth, though, a great booming noise ripped through the air and he jumped in surprise. It was followed by a deafening fanfare, and then a haze of light burst over the top of the mountain.

"What the hell?" Chapel asked. He let go of Julia long enough to run over toward the visitors' center and see what was going on.

Then the fanfare resolved into music—familiar fiddle music. It was the Charlie Daniels Band, singing about Georgia. The light came from powerful floodlights that were illuminating the carving on the side of the mountain.

The nightly laser show had begun.

Down at the bottom of the mountain, hundreds, maybe thousands of tourists would be staring in awe up at the carving as the lasers animated the generals and made it appear their horses were galloping across the stone. They were probably gaping in surprise and delight, looking up toward where Chapel, Julia, and Funt stood at the summit.

"Come on," Chapel said. "Right now?"

Nearby someone laughed. Chapel spun around, half expecting Laughing Boy to step out of the darkness. But the figure that moved into the haze of light now was taller than Laughing Boy, and more heavily muscled.

"Funny story, huh?" the figure asked.

"Who—" Chapel began, but he already knew who it was.

"I never heard his version before. Real funny." The haze of light turned red for a moment, then died down to a less diffuse glow. Chapel's eyes adjusted to the sudden darkness, and he could make out the details of the newcomer's face.

His eyes were black from side to side, with no white showing at all.

Malcolm had arrived.

STONE MOUNTAIN, GEORGIA: APRIL 13, T+36:09

"No fucking way," Funt shouted. "Why did you bring him here?"

Chapel could only shake his head in disbelief.

"Nobody else knew where I was going to be," Funt insisted. "I didn't tell anyone. So you must have told him he could find me here! You sold me out, Chapel!"

"No! I didn't tell anyone," Chapel protested.

Except Angel, of course.

He couldn't imagine that she would have told Malcolm where to find Funt. That was just impossible. But her systems had been compromised once before, by the CIA—and the CIA had been trying to kill Funt for years.

But that meant—

A gunshot roared across the top of Stone Mountain, drowning out the blaring music that came from below. Chapel spun around and saw Malcolm looking down between his feet.

"Can't see very well in the dark, can you, Funt?" the chimera asked. "I can."

"Wait," Chapel said. "Just wait." He held his hands up, outstretched, toward the chimera. "It doesn't have to be like this. You've been manipulated, Malcolm. You were sent here like a heat-seeking missile."

"I don't know what that is," the chimera told him.

"Just—just take my word for it. They made you come here. You're doing somebody else's bidding."

"You're talking about the Voice," Malcolm said, nodding.

"Sure—the—the voice. What voice?"

"The Voice on the telephone. The one that told us we would be free, and then the fence came down. The one that told us where to find the ones we wanted to kill. The Voice doesn't make us do things," the chimera said, smiling. "It helps us. It helps us do the things we want to do."

Like killing Funt. Malcolm had a very good reason to want him dead. Just like the chimera in New York had good reason to want to kill Helen Bryant, the woman who made him, the woman who locked him away in an armed camp for twenty-five years.

Malcolm wasn't being manipulated. Used, yes. But he was only being used to do a thing he wanted anyway.

Revenge was a powerful motivator. In Special Forces training they'd taught Chapel it could break through almost any disincentive—you could torture a man, you could take away everything he loved, but in the end you were only making him more re-solved. They'd taught him that the way to fight ter-rorists wasn't to punish them, but to convince them you were really on their side.

"They'll kill you when you're done," Chapel told the chimera. "You do understand that, don't you? They've already sent men to kill you. But I can keep you alive. I can protect you."

"I'm going to kill Jeremy Funt, now, mister. It was nice talking," Malcolm sneered, "but maybe you'll shut up until I'm done."

"No!" Funt screamed, and he fired again. The bullet ricocheted off the rock not three feet from where Chapel stood. He ducked reflexively. "No—

you don't want me. I never hurt you, Malcolm. But he"—Funt stabbed one finger in Chapel's direction—"he killed one of your brothers! Kill him!"

"Wow. You think you know me so well, don't you, Jeremy Funt?" Malcolm said, stalking toward the ex-FBI agent. "You don't know me at all. He killed Brody, yeah. The Voice told me as much. But you know what? Where I come from, if somebody's strong enough to kill a chimera, that's something to respect. Killing us is hard. Apparently fooling us is a lot easier. That's the weakling's way."

Funt raised his pistol again, but before he could pull the trigger Malcolm was running—leaping toward him. Chapel reached for his own sidearm and only then realized he didn't have it. It was in Funt's pocket.

"No!" he shouted, as the chimera collided with Funt. The pistol fired, and a moment later fired again—Chapel could see the muzzle flares as explosions of light between Funt and the chimera—and then Funt's arm flew up, bending in all the wrong places. The chimera stomped on Funt's foot and the man screamed.

"No," Chapel shouted again, as he closed the distance between himself and the chimera. "No!" He locked his fingers together and swung both of his fists down, hard, into Malcolm's left kidney.

The pain of getting punched there was usually enough to incapacitate a grown man. It could cause massive internal bleeding and even death and was an illegal move in boxing and every martial arts competition for good reason. It was a nasty, low blow, and Chapel had been trained to deliver it with devastating precision.

It made Malcolm stop what he was doing for a fraction of a second.

Chapel figured that would have to be enough.

Funt was down on the ground, scrambling away from the chimera like a crab, pushing with his heels and his good arm just to escape. His pistol was gone, probably knocked out of his hand when Malcolm broke his arm.

Chapel decided to stop worrying about Funt, as just then Malcolm was turning around to face him—and smiling wickedly.

"You really want some of this?" Malcolm asked.

Chapel dropped into a defensive posture, his fists raised like they were going to have a nice, friendly boxing match.

"Show me what you've got," he said.

The chimera came at him like a runaway train.

STONE MOUNTAIN, GEORGIA: APRIL 13, T+36:12

There was no way Chapel could stop Malcolm, or even slow him down. The chimera was just too strong, and he outweighed Chapel by a good fifty pounds. So he didn't try to stand his ground. There was no way he could move out of the way of Malcolm's charge, either—he was just too fast.

So he twisted on the ball of one foot and let Malcolm hit him, but he rolled with the bull rush, twisting around to slide over the chimera's back as he went past. Chapel landed on his feet, though not as firmly as he would have liked—the ground was too uneven to stick the landing.

Still, he was suddenly behind Malcolm where Malcolm couldn't see him.

If he'd been fighting a human opponent, Chapel could have ended things then and there. He could have wrapped his good arm around his opponent's neck and put him in a sleeper hold. Block the blood flow to the carotid artery, even for a few seconds, and a human body will simply shut down.

He knew it wouldn't be that easy. But he was out of other ideas.

He brought his right knee up, hard, into the small of Malcolm's back. The chimera didn't even grunt in pain—maybe it felt like Chapel was tickling him—but he was ninety-nine percent human, which meant he had the same reflexes as a human being. He arched his back away from the blow, throwing his head back toward Chapel.

Chapel threw his artificial arm around Malcolm's throat and squeezed.

The prosthetic arm was designed to respond to subconscious commands. Normally Chapel didn't have to think about how the arm should move, it just acted like a real arm. He could override it, though. He could give it conscious commands and it would obey them, even in ways a real arm wouldn't.

He told his arm to squeeze, and it acted like a metal noose around the chimera's neck. It tightened like a vise and stayed locked shut. A living arm could get fatigued. Its muscles were elastic enough to give way as Malcolm bucked and tried to break loose. Chapel's prosthetic arm didn't have those weaknesses.

The chimera gasped and spat in rage as he tried to get free. He tried to reach around behind him, to grab Chapel and hurt him enough to make him let go. His fingers found the side of Chapel's shirt and he tore through the fabric, maybe intending to gouge into the flesh beneath.

Chapel responded by using his good right arm to deliver punch after punch to the side of Malcolm's head.

The chimera screamed in frustration and ducked forward, bending at the waist until he lifted Chapel right off the ground. With his arm locked around Malcolm's throat Chapel had no option but to go along for the ride.

For a second he was airborne and flopping back and forth, like a rider holding on to a bucking horse. Malcolm twisted from side to side, trying to shake him free, but the only way that would happen was if Chapel's prosthetic arm gave out. Chapel forgot all about hitting Malcolm and just tried to hold on, tried to get his legs around Malcolm's waist, tried to grab the chimera with his free hand.

Then Malcolm started to run—straight toward the side of the mountain. Straight toward the laser show still playing out below.

No—no, he wouldn't, Chapel had time to think, as he watched the edge of the stone top of the mountain come rushing toward them. *He'll kill us both!*

But maybe for a chimera, death was preferable to being taken prisoner again. Malcolm ran full speed toward the edge, toward a drop of more than five hundred feet.

A fence ran around the edge of the mountain-top, a chain-link fence that looked about as sturdy as a lace doily from Chapel's perspective. It would catch them if Malcolm threw himself over the edge, but with their combined weight and the chimera's momentum Chapel was certain they would just tear through.

He had no choice. He told his arm to let go.

STONE MOUNTAIN, GEORGIA: APRIL 13, T+36:14

It was exactly what Malcolm had been hoping for. As soon as the pressure on his throat lessened, the chimera dug in his heels and skidded to a stop. But Chapel had no way to slow himself down, and he went shooting forward over Malcolm's shoulders and head to fly through the air, carried along by in-ertia straight toward the fence and the edge.

He slammed into the chain link with a clattering rattle. Lasers and floodlights dazzled his eyes as he felt the chain bend and stretch. It was held up by a series of metal posts spaced about ten feet apart. The posts were anchored in the bare rock of the mountain, but they could only take so much stress. He felt the whole fence jump and dance as one post snapped off at its base, heard another one groan and shriek as the force of his impact bent it down and outward.

He dug his fingers into the chain link, desperate for any kind of purchase. One sharp end of broken chain link dug into his palm, and the pain blasted up his good arm but he refused to let go, refused to even slacken his grip. He felt greasy blood smear his fingers and knew he'd made a mistake.

The chain link began to tilt outward, a whole section of fence collapsing under his weight. He scrabbled to climb up as it bent and twisted, but he couldn't make any headway—it was giving way faster than he could climb up.

Below him the section of fencing slammed against the side of the mountain, draping over the protruding rocks and stunted trees there. Chapel fought with his panicking brain, trying to convince it that the fence was now a climbing wall, that it gave him plenty of hand- and footholds to let him climb back up, onto the mountaintop.

He did one foolish thing and glanced behind himself. There was nothing beneath him but empty air and blazing lights, nothing but empty space between him and the tree-lined lower slopes of the mountain far below. It was not the kind of fall a human body could survive.

Look up, damn you, he told himself, and he forced his head to crane around and peer back up at the night sky and the top of the mountain. He told his artificial fingers to lock on to the chain link, then used his good hand to reach for a grip higher up. His fingers were sore and trembling and they were slippery with blood, but he forced them through the mesh of the fence, forced them to find purchase.

Carefully, slowly, he lifted his right foot and kicked at the fence to find a place to brace it, to support his weight.

Above him, Malcolm walked to the edge and looked down at him.

"You're tough, for a human," Malcolm said.

Chapel couldn't help himself. "Your brother said the same thing right before I killed him," he said, through gritted teeth. He forced the toe of his shoe into a gap in the fence. Pushed himself upward a few inches.

At this rate, some time next week he should reach the top.

Malcolm looked away from him, and Chapel worried the chimera would just leave him there and go finish off Funt. That wasn't acceptable.

"Mind giving me a hand?" he asked the chimera. "So we can finish this like tough guys?"

"No, I don't think so," Malcolm told him. He had something in his hands. What was it? It looked like a black plastic box, about eight inches long. What the hell was it? "At Camp Putnam, the fences are electrified. If you touch them, they can burn your hand. We used to dare each other to go up to the fence and grab it with both hands. Somehow that was worse—if you had both hands on the fence, you couldn't let go. You could feel the electric fire running through your body, but your fingers wouldn't let go. You had to trust your brothers would knock you off the fence with a piece of wood."

"That's some kind of messed-up trust exercise," Chapel gasped. He lifted his left foot, but it just slid off the fencing every time he tried to get a toe-hold.

"Some brothers would do it. Some of them would save you. Others wouldn't. They would just sit there and watch while you cooked like a bird. It was an important lesson to learn. We were brothers, but we were not friends. We did not owe each other anything, even our lives. A chimera can only really trust himself. So when you told me you would help me, you would protect me, that's what I heard. Don't worry. I won't let you cook alive."

"Is there a point to this?" Chapel asked.

Malcolm held up his plastic box. Chapel saw now it had two metal prongs sticking out of one end. As he watched a spark jumped between them.

It was a stun gun. Capable of delivering fifty thousand volts of electricity to anything it touched.

"No," Chapel said. "No, Malcolm—"

"A man in a stupid hat tried to use this on me, down below." Chapel thought of the park ranger who'd failed to radio in. "It didn't work. I'm guessing it must work on humans, or he wouldn't have been carrying it. You're tough, for a human. But humans just aren't much, in the end."

Malcolm lowered the stun gun and touched its prongs to the fence.

STONE MOUNTAIN, GEORGIA: APRIL 13, T+36:21

Chapel had been tased before. It had been part of his training, a ritual everyone in his Special Forces program had to go through. You had to know what it felt like, so if it happened in the field you would be ready.

Except there really was no good way to ready yourself. There was nothing you could do to brace against it. Nothing you could do to stop it taking over your body.

The pain was intense, worse than any kick in the groin, maybe worse, Chapel thought, than getting shot. It felt like your entire body was on fire all at once, like you'd been thrown into a furnace. Worse than that—like you were being burned alive from the inside out. Every muscle in his body twitched and cramped. His spine arched and his teeth slammed together, cutting deep into the side of his tongue. His eyes squeezed shut, and tears burst from under their lids.

It was a horrible violation for a man used to being in total control of his own flesh. He barely managed not to soil himself.

It was all over in a fraction of a second. But after that came the realization. The horror.

His good fingers had let go of the fence. His feet were kicking at air.

He didn't dare open his eyes. The fall would be brief and the sudden impact would probably kill him instantly. A human body falling hundreds of feet had plenty of time to reach terminal velocity. There would be little left of him but a stain on the ground when he hit bottom.

Good-bye, Julia, he had time to think. *I hope you—*

Funny.

Definitely weird.

He didn't feel like he was falling. There was no sensation of weightlessness, no rush of air past his face.

He opened his eyes and saw he hadn't fallen at all.

Looking up, he saw that he was dangling, limp as a rag doll, by one hand. His prosthetic hand.

Of course. The silicone skin that covered his robotic hand was an excellent insulator. The burst of electricity couldn't get through even a thin sheet of the rubbery stuff. The fingers were locked in place, holding him up.

He would have laughed—except he found he could barely breathe.

The clamps on the end of the arm, the clamps that held it on his body, were designed to tighten automatically when needed, squeezing tighter with the more weight the arm tried to lift. At that moment the arm was holding his entire one hundred and eighty pounds. The clamps had compressed so tightly they were crushing his rib cage, making it difficult for him to draw breath.

The arm hadn't been designed for this. It had never been meant to hold so much weight on its own. He had to get his good hand up there, had to grab the fence—

Up above Malcolm screamed in rage and hit the fence again with the stun gun. Chapel barely had time to yank his fingers back from the chain link.

It was then he started to smell burning rubber. He looked up and saw the fingers of his artificial hand were smoking. Molten silicone was rolling down the back of the hand, dripping down his shirtsleeve.

If the silicone melted until the metal finger actuators beneath were exposed, he would have no protection from the electric shocks. The current running through the fence would zap the arm's circuit boards and microchips and short it out. If that happened, the fingers were designed to automatically release anything they were holding. They would go limp, and he would fall.

He couldn't let that happen. "Malcolm!" he shouted, sucking in a deep breath so he could actually be heard. "Malcolm, listen to me!"

The chimera stared down at him with wide black eyes.

"What the hell are you, human?" Malcolm demanded. "Or are you human? Maybe you're like me. Maybe . . ." He shook his head, failing to finish his thought. He grabbed at his hair and pulled until clumps of it came loose.

He was getting frustrated. Which for a chimera could only mean one thing—he was getting even more dangerous than he'd been before.

"Malcolm," Chapel called, "wouldn't you rather kill me with your own hands? Wouldn't that be more satisfying?"

"Shut up!" Malcolm shrieked, his voice suddenly high pitched with rage. "Shut the fuck up! I'm going to eat you, do you understand? I'm going to tear off your flesh and eat it! I'm going to trample Funt until he's paste! Then I'm going to take your woman and I'm going to fu—"

The chimera's head jerked to one side. His black eyes blinked several times. A dark spot appeared on the front of his shirt and started to spread.

He didn't say anything, or make any sound at all. As quickly as it had possessed him, the rage seemed to have flowed back out of him. He raised one hand to touch the spot on his shirt, and his fingers came away dark. A scowl curled across his face.

Then his left eye exploded outward in a miniature cloud of blood.

STONE MOUNTAIN, GEORGIA: APRIL 13, T+36:28

It took as long for Malcolm to fall over as a tree takes to fall in the forest. Chapel could only stare upward, watching in surprise as the chimera died. Malcolm slumped to the ground in a heap, one hand flopping forward over the fence, as if he were reaching out a hand toward Chapel, a final gesture of reconciliation.

Blood rolled down his fingers and dripped on the mountain below.

Eventually Chapel remembered he was about to fall to his death. He stuffed the fingers of his good hand into the chain link, and some of the strain was taken off his artificial arm and he could almost breathe again.

Julia popped her head over the side. "Chapel?" she asked. "Are you—"

"Make sure he's dead!" Chapel called up.

She nodded and disappeared for a moment. Chapel heard two more gunshots. When she came back, she was holding Funt's pistol and the barrel was smoking.

"Can you climb up?" she asked. She looked from side to side. "This fence isn't going to hold much longer."

In that case, Chapel told himself, the answer to her question had better be yes.

He shoved one foot into a gap in the fence and pushed himself upward. His artificial fingers had partially fused to the chain link, but he was able to pull them free. Semiliquid silicone came loose in long thin strands. The fingers were gummed together and deformed but they still worked, it seemed.

"Hang on," Julia said. She pulled off her pink hoodie, then tied one end of it to a fence post that was still holding in the rock. When she lowered the other sleeve down to him, he could almost reach it.

It took him far too long to climb up and grab it. The chain link groaned and started to tear away from its posts, and for a bad, long moment he was certain it would give way. Eventually, though, he managed to clamber up to a point where he could wrap his good arm around a fence post and, with Julia's help, roll back onto the level ground on top of the mountain.

Julia stared at him as if he would disappear if she looked away even for a moment. She reached up and brushed hair out of her face with one hand, leaving a streak of blood on her cheek.

"Blood," Chapel managed to say, pointing at it.

Chimera blood. Full of the virus.

She understood at once. "Oh, God—I checked Malcolm's pulse with those fingers. I didn't even think . . ." Shaking her head she grabbed up the hoodie and used it to scrape the blood off her face and hands.

Would it be enough to protect her? Chapel didn't know. If she hadn't gotten the blood in any cuts or scrapes, if it hadn't got in her mouth—

There was nothing to be done for it.

"Funt," Chapel said. He was still getting his breath back. He didn't know if he could sit up quite yet. "Is Funt alive?"

Julia nodded. "He's in shock, though. I did what I could for him. That's why it took me so long to shoot Malcolm."

"That's the second person you've shot today," Chapel said, with a weak smile. "You're a quick learner." He started to close his eyes.

"I'm getting better at it. Chapel? Chapel, what do we do now?"

"We have to get out of here."

"Definitely. Funt needs medical attention. More than I can give him up here. And the park rangers will probably show up any second. I know *I* don't want to have to explain to them what happened."

"My phone," Chapel said. Very carefully he reached into the inside pocket and found the smartphone. He touched his ear and found his hands-free set was long gone, probably knocked out of his ear when Malcolm threw him at the fence. He dialed Angel and she picked up almost at once.

"I'm here, baby."

"Angel, we need to be extracted, as soon as you can—"

He stopped talking because the sound of the music coming from the bottom of the mountain was drowned out just then by the rotor noise of a helicopter coming over the far side of the summit. It was a civilian chopper, but it showed no lights.

"Anything else I can do for you?" Angel asked.

STONE MOUNTAIN, GEORGIA: APRIL 13, T+36:31

The chopper seemed to take forever to land—the top of Stone Mountain was too rough for it to just set down on its skids. Eventually the pilot found a safe spot, and the aircraft settled to the rock.

The same second it put down, two men wearing Tyvek suits and surgical masks came running over to put Malcolm in a body bag. They didn't even look at Chapel, but Julia grabbed the arm of one of them and asked if he had any alcohol wipes. He handed her a bottle of rubbing alcohol from his kit, and she poured it liberally over her fingers, then scrubbed at her face with the stuff. "We have a wounded man over there," she said, pointing at where Funt lay, dressed as a park ranger, on the bare rock.

"Sorry, ma'am, we're just cleanup. But there's a stretcher in the bird," he told her. She started to protest, but Chapel grasped her shoulder and then ran to the chopper. The pilot was already pulling the stretcher out of the back compartment. "I have orders to take you wherever you want to go," he told Chapel. "But I'll need to file a flight plan before we take off."

"The closest airport is fine," Chapel told him. "Help me get this man onboard," he said, pointing at Funt. "Are we taking the body as well?"

"No, a second craft is coming for that. The two medics I brought will guard the body until it arrives. I don't suppose you can tell me what's going on here? I'm not even supposed to be on this shift."

"Where are you stationed?" Chapel asked.

"Fort McPherson, sir," the pilot told him.

"Oh, so you're army," Chapel said, nodding. "So you'll understand when I say no, I can't tell you anything."

"Sir, yes, sir," the pilot said, shaking his head.

Together they loaded Funt onto the stretcher and carried it back to the chopper. The ex-FBI man didn't wake up. His face was bright with sweat, and when Julia came over and pulled one of his eyelids back, the eye underneath failed to track. "His body knows best," she told Chapel, when he asked if Funt was going to be all right. "When he wakes up, he's going to be in incredible pain—that arm is shattered. So his body put him to sleep. We should leave him that way if we can, though we need to keep him warm. His body temperature is very low."

Chapel nodded and put his phone to his ear. "Angel, we've got Funt and he's alive but badly hurt. This chopper's going to take us to an airport nearby. Can you have an ambulance waiting?"

"I'm on it," Angel said.

Julia jumped into the back of the chopper where she could sit with Funt and keep an eye on him. Chapel ran around the nose of the aircraft so he could take the copilot seat. Before he got in, though, he took one last look at the top of Stone Mountain— and the body of the second dead chimera he'd seen in two days.

"Angel," Chapel said, "what are they going to do with Malcolm?"

"A quick cremation. That's all," Angel told him. "The men I sent you are trained in bacteriological warfare protocols. They'll be safe."

Chapel nodded. There wouldn't be any ceremony for Malcolm, he knew. No prayers, no weeping mourners.

Maybe it was for the best. The chimera had been a killer, through and through. He'd lived for nothing but revenge. After the story Funt had told, though, Chapel couldn't shake an image from his head: a ten-year-old boy, sitting in a tree house, scared and very, very alone. Not knowing what kind of future waited for him. Barely aware of where he was.

Enough. Chapel's job was to hunt down four chimeras, and he was half done.

He climbed into the helicopter and pulled on a crash helmet. "Let's go," he told the pilot.

IN TRANSIT: APRIL 13, T+36:48

The chopper set down—much more smoothly this time—on a helipad at DeKalb-Peachtree Airport, only a few miles away from Stone Mountain. An airport medical team was waiting to take Funt away in an ambulance that sat waiting on the tarmac. Angel had timed everything perfectly, as usual.

Julia ran over to the ambulance to tell the paramedics what she knew about Funt's condition. The medical team didn't waste any time getting him out of there. When Julia came back to the helipad, she was frowning. "Will he be safe if they take him to the hospital?" she asked. "Laughing Boy may be out of the picture, but—"

Chapel nodded. The CIA had been trying to kill Funt for years. This was the perfect chance. They could even make it look like a natural death, like he had died of his injuries. "They're not taking him to a civilian hospital," he told her. In fact he'd been in touch with Admiral Hollingshead and arranged for Funt to be taken to a military hospital where he could be guarded night and day until he recovered. "As long as they keep him alive until he's conscious, I'm okay with this. Once he's awake, well, we saw how good he is at keeping one step ahead of them."

Julia shrugged. "I guess it's all we can do. What's next?"

Chapel nodded toward a nearby runway. Hollingshead's personal jet was already taxiing toward them. "Say good-bye to Atlanta."

"Gladly," Julia said. Her red hair whipped in the breeze. "I'm about ready for another of those goat cheese and mandarin orange salads, too. How can I be hungry at a time like this? I should be sitting in a corner crying my eyes out, begging for somebody to make everything okay. Chapel, I killed a man. I don't feel bad about it. I don't feel scared right now. I don't even feel mad at you anymore."

He knew the look in her eyes. He'd seen it often enough when he was fighting alongside the Rangers. "It's going to hit you, eventually. But right now your body knows you aren't safe. It knows you need to keep fighting. It's flooding your brain with endorphins."

She put a hand over her face and laughed. "This is not how I thought my week was going to go."

He put his good hand on her shoulder and squeezed. She didn't push him away. Probably because she was in shock.

They had to wait a few minutes while boarding stairs were moved into position, but when they climbed up into the jet, Chief Petty Officer Andrews was waiting for them with hot towels. The jet's main door was closed and suddenly they were in silence, sitting in comfortable chairs, and nobody was trying to kill them.

Chapel had to admit it was a nice change of pace.

"We're cleared for takeoff right away," Andrews told them. "Fasten your seat belts until we're in the air, okay? Our flight time to Denver will be a little under three hours. I'll dim the cabin lights now, and—"

"Denver? We're not going to Denver," Chapel said.

"Oh. I'm sorry," Andrews told him. "I was informed you were. Was there a last-minute change?"

"There needs to be. We're going to Chicago." He needed to check in with Eleanor Pechowski. Make sure she was safe.

And find out everything she knew about chimeras and Camp Putnam.

In his pocket his phone began to ring.

IN TRANSIT: APRIL 13, T+36:54

Chief Petty Officer Andrews smiled warmly and went to talk to the pilot. Julia looked at Chapel expectantly. His phone kept ringing.

Finally he couldn't take it anymore, so he answered it.

"Sweetie," Angel said, "I filed your flight plan for Denver—"

"I need to make sure Eleanor Pechowski is safe," he told her.

"Of course you do. Which is why I've been calling her every two hours and sending police around to keep an eye on the place she's staying. But Franklin Hayes's people have been calling *me*, about every fifteen minutes, wanting an update on where you are and how soon you'll be arriving in Denver."

Chapel glanced at his watch. "We have at least eleven hours before a chimera could even possibly reach Denver," he said.

"More like fourteen, because of the time zone difference," Angel confirmed. "That gives you plenty of time to get to Denver and set up your defense for when the chimera comes for Hayes."

"Hayes will be fine. He's surrounded by security. I have no doubt a chimera is going to try to kill him, but even one of them can't realistically break into a federal courthouse full of cops. As far as I'm concerned, Hayes is the safest name on the list. I've finally got some breathing room here, Angel. I finally have time to follow up on some leads, and the last thing I need is to babysit some judge who's in no real danger."

"Sweetie—"

"Unless you know something you're not telling me, Angel, I've made my decision."

She was silent for way too long.

Chapel closed his eyes. "What does Admiral Hollingshead say about this?"

Angel sounded sincerely apologetic. "He suggested to me—without actually saying anything directly, of course—that your next stop would be Denver."

"He suggested that, huh? Which suggests to me," Chapel told her, "that he knows exactly where the chimeras are going."

"I'm not sure I like what you're implying," Angel said, caution thickening her voice.

"Angel. I'm going to tell you something plainly now. No suggestions, no implications. Somebody knew we were going to Stone Mountain. Somebody told Malcolm where to find us."

"I'm not sure I follow," Angel said.

He was damned sure she did. She just wanted him to say it out loud. Maybe so when things went bad she could cover her posterior. Maybe she just wanted a record of him defying official orders.

Chapel didn't really care anymore.

"Someone told Malcolm where Funt would be. They wanted Funt killed. Malcolm told me he was getting orders over the phone from someone he called the Voice. I don't know who this Voice is, but it had to be somebody who can access your line,

Angel. Because the only people who knew about Stone Mountain were Funt, me . . . and you."

Angel sounded panicky as she responded to that. Chapel wondered how good an actress she was. "You think my system's been compromised again?" she asked. "Oh my God—should I move to different servers *again*?"

"I don't think there's any point. I think the Voice can get to you anytime he wants to. Which means the Voice might be Director Banks. Or it might be Admiral Hollingshead."

"You can't mean that," Angel said.

"Someone's been setting me up for a while now, Angel. They tried to get me to run out to Denver while I was still en route to Atlanta. That's why Hayes was able to break into your line. They must have known Malcolm was on his way to kill Funt, but they tried to keep me from saving him. They wanted him dead. Now the same mysterious person wants me to rush out to Denver rather than check up on Eleanor Pechowski."

"I promise you she's safe," Angel said. "I checked in with her just an hour ago and—"

"I'm sure she's safe. I'm not worried about her health. But I'm very interested in what she might be able to tell me—and why this Voice wants to make sure I don't hear it. I'm going to Chicago, Angel. If Hollingshead won't let me take his private plane there, I'll walk over to the terminal and buy a ticket on a Delta flight with my own credit card."

It was a bluff, and one that could cost him. He knew perfectly well that if Hollingshead or Angel truly wanted him in Denver, he'd have no choice. With one phone call they could cut off his credit card—or put him on a no-fly list. They could make it impossible for him to go anywhere *but* Denver.

There was only silence on the line for a long while. "Angel?" Chapel called, but she didn't respond.

By his watch, three minutes passed before she came back. "I've changed your flight plan," she said. "You're cleared to go to Chicago. But Chapel—"

"What is it, Angel?"

"You don't have a lot of friends. It's probably best if you don't start making any new enemies, now."

It was a cryptic threat but he got it. He understood exactly what he was being told. He was on a leash, a short leash, and he would be choked if he strayed too far.

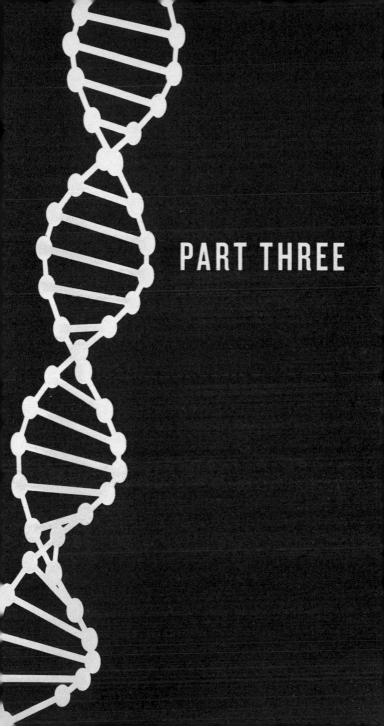

PART THREE

Chapel knew he should take a nap on the flight from Atlanta to Chicago, but Julia was still wired, still a little freaked out that she'd killed Malcolm, and she kept getting up from her seat and walking up and down the aisle between them. Chief Petty Officer Andrews turned the cabin lights back up so Julia wouldn't trip over anything.

"Come help me with something," he told her, just to get her mind off things. She walked over and gasped when she saw what he was doing.

He had rolled up his sleeve and had used a steak knife to cut into the silicone flesh around his artificial wrist.

"What on earth are you doing?" she demanded.

"Look at the fingers," he told her. They were half melted, some of them fused together by the electrical shock he'd gotten back on Stone Mountain. "The motors and actuators underneath are fine, but the artificial skin has to go."

She stared at him in horror but when he kept cutting at the fake flesh, she eventually shook her head and grabbed the knife away from him. "I do this for a living. Kind of," she said. She neatly cut away the synthetic hand and then stripped it back like she was peeling off a glove. He lifted the artificial hand and flexed its various joints, listening to the soft whine of the motors.

He spent the rest of the flight putting the hand through various exercises, getting used to how different it felt. If anything, the fingers were stronger now—they didn't have to work against the silicone. Julia seemed fascinated by the robotic hand, which cheered him up a little. He'd expected her to be repulsed by this reminder that he wasn't like everyone else. He should have known she was tougher than that.

The plane set down in Midway airport in Chicago a little after nine thirty. When they'd taxied up to the terminal, Chief Petty Officer Andrews went to open the main cabin door. "Brace yourselves," she said. "Chicago in springtime can be a shocking thing." The door popped open and a blast of frigid air rushed inside the plane. Julia immediately reached for her pink hoodie.

"It must be forty degrees out there," Chapel said, rubbing at his good arm with his robotic hand.

"The local temperature is closer to thirty-seven Fahrenheit," Andrews told him with a perky smile. "Don't say you weren't warned."

"We'll freeze to death out there," Julia said. She shook her head. "Chapel, I'm not dressed for this. Maybe I should stay in the plane."

Angel had thought of everything though, as usual. A pile of cardboard boxes were waiting on the tarmac, having been delivered even while they were taxiing in from the runway.

Julia got the boxes open and started pulling winter coats out of their wrapping paper. "This one's yours, I think," she said, holding up a black coat with a lot of pockets and zippers. "Plenty of room for all your spy gadgets." The next box held a woman's coat in a shade of grayish blue. "Oh, there's a note with this one," she said, and picked it up. "'I thought this color might suit you more than hot pink,'" she read. She pulled on the coat and zipped it to her neck. Almost instantly she looked happier. "Wow. The coat I have at home isn't this nice."

Chapel took a second to appreciate the way the color worked with her hair and the way the coat's lines suited Julia's slender frame. He'd never cared a fig for fashion, and definitely not for women's coats, but he had to admit that Angel had picked the perfect one for Julia. He smiled. His life might be in danger and there might be homicidal lunatics on the loose, but at least he had attractive company. "What's in the other two boxes?" he asked.

The remaining boxes were much smaller. One held a hands-free unit identical to the one he'd lost in Atlanta. He wasted no time putting it in his ear. "Angel," he said, "nice work here. Julia loves the coat you got her."

"You're welcome, sugar. I know what it's like to be a woman in a cold climate," the operator responded, as if she'd been sitting on his shoulder the whole time. "What do you think of the gloves?"

The final box held three different pairs of black leather gloves. "I wasn't sure what size you would need now that your hand is thinner," Angel told him. "I hope one of them will work."

"Thanks, Angel. You did great." Chapel tried the gloves on until he found one that fit comfortably over his robotic hand. He held it up and showed it to Julia. She nodded in approval.

He went to the cabin door and started wrestling it open again, prepared now for the cold. "Come on," he said. "We have to go meet an elderly school-teacher, and there's no time to lose."

CHICAGO, ILLINOIS: APRIL 13, T+39:44

They caught a cab and fought traffic all the way through the center of Chicago. Chapel checked his watch constantly as they struggled through the streetlights but there was nothing for it. He had to do this, and it didn't matter how long it took.

"You were almost relaxed, back on the plane," Julia told him. "I was so wound up I kept wondering how you could be chill at a time like this. Now you're just as keyed up as you were last night when we landed in Atlanta."

He watched the streetlights and the shadows alternately paint her face. "It's an army thing. Our unofficial motto is 'Hurry up and wait.' You spend a lot of time in the army sitting around somewhere wondering when you're going to be called up, when the next firefight is going to happen. Eventually, if you're lucky, you learn to compartmentalize. You recognize when you're safe and you can let your guard down. It happens so infrequently that you have to take advantage of it when it does happen."

"I feel like I'm never going to relax again," Julia said, pulling her shoulders in. "I keep expecting to fall down. I know that everything that's happened, everything I've done is going to catch up with me. I'm just waiting for the hammer to drop."

Chapel nodded. He'd seen what extreme stress could do to people. He'd seen soldiers come back from firefights whooping and hollering with adrenaline, and before they'd taken their boots off they were already lost, dropped down a hole into their own thoughts. Sometimes they never climbed back out of that hole.

"The only treatment for what you have is to keep moving," he told her. "Your body's smart. It knows how to keep you alive, if you listen to it. Right now it's telling you not to lie down, not to rest."

Julia frowned. "That's not a great solution either. That'll give you ulcers and migraines and who knows what else."

"Hang in there," he told her. "This will be over at some point. Then you can figure it all out for yourself." It was the best comfort he had to offer her.

The cab took them up Lake Shore Drive to a neighborhood called the Near North Side. It was a region of mansions and town houses, everything covered with a sheen of old money. And ice. Some of the houses still had icicles hanging from their eaves.

"It felt like summer was right around the corner, back in Atlanta," Julia said, like she was talking to herself. Maybe she just wanted to change the subject.

The cab pulled up in front of a town house, and they stepped out into a knife-edged wind. Lake Michigan filled half the world around them, and gusts that rippled its surface buffeted them almost constantly.

"Coat or no coat, I want to get inside," Julia told Chapel.

"I'm with you there," he said. He went up to the door of the town house where Eleanor Pechowski was staying and rang the bell. The door was answered almost instantly by an older man wearing thick glasses and a sweater vest.

"You must be Captain Chapel. Please, come inside," the man said. He kept one hand hidden behind the door while he looked out at the street, scanning up and down the rows of parked cars.

"What have you got there?" Chapel asked, nodding at the concealed hand.

The man frowned in embarrassment. He opened the door wider and Chapel saw he held a long sword. "Just come in, please. I'm Julius Apomotov, and this is my house."

CHICAGO, ILLINOIS: APRIL 13, T+39:52

Chapel and Julia stepped inside and Apomotov closed the door behind them, struggling to shut it against the wind.

The house's foyer was all polished wood and sparkling glass chandeliers. Tapestries hung on the walls and a suit of armor stood next to a stairway leading up. The sword clearly belonged with the armor.

"The best I could find, under the circumstances," Apomotov said, lifting his weapon. "I've never believed in guns." He squinted, his eyes magnified by his thick glasses, and then shook his head. "That is,

I believe they exist, but—" He shook his head again, in frustration. "Never mind." He glanced down at the sword in his hand as if he didn't know where it had come from. For lack of anything better to do, he dropped it in an umbrella stand. "Come in, come in. Eleanor is waiting for you. She's holding up remarkably well, under the circumstances."

He took their coats and hung them in a closet near the door. Then he stood there for a while, one hand lifted in front of him as if he was going to point at something. He snapped his fingers. "Chapel. Chapel. I had a student named Chapel once. Mark Chapel. Quite gifted. Any relation?"

"I'm not sure," Chapel said. "My family's from Florida."

"Oh good God, no, no relation then," Apomotov said. "Mark wouldn't be caught dead beneath the Mason-Dixon line. Through here, please. He was a Connecticut boy, bled Union blue if you cut him." Apomotov stopped in place and turned to look at them. "Not that I ever cut him. You understand."

"Of course," Chapel said.

Apomotov led them into a wide parlor behind the stairs. It was tastefully decorated, except for the hundreds of crossbows hanging on the walls, each of them suspended on individual wires from the crown molding. "There," he said, waving at a couch on the far side of the room. An elderly woman there was struggling to stand up and greet them.

"Eleanor Pechowski, I presume," Chapel said.

"You must, absolutely must, call me Ellie," the woman said, coming over to take Chapel's hand. "You're Chapel, of course, the one that very nice young woman keeps saying is my shield against trouble in these dark times. And who's this? Who's this?" she asked, looking at Julia.

"She didn't introduce herself," Apomotov said. "I thought it best to let her in anyway, under the circumstances."

"I'm so sorry," Julia said. "I'm Julia Taggart."

"Ah!" Eleanor Pechowski—Ellie—said. "Aha! Your name precedes you, dear."

"I, uh, I take it you knew my father," Julia said, looking uncomfortable.

"And your mother as well. Come, sit. Have some refreshment. Julius, be a dear and fetch more cups."

The elderly man nodded and headed off deeper into the house.

"An absolute gem of a man," Ellie said when he was gone. "One of the leading lights in Russian medieval studies, a scholar of no small renown. Demented now, of course, quite as crazy as a moth meeting its first lightbulb but still a stellar human being. Took me in when I was told my own—far more modest—apartment wasn't safe anymore. Why aren't you two sitting down?"

Chapel hurried to take a place on a divan near a roaring fire. Julia joined him, sitting closer than he'd expected.

"You'll take something to drink, of course," Ellie said, sitting down herself and lifting a teacup from a table near her. She tucked her legs up under herself on the couch. Chapel saw she wasn't wearing any shoes, and that there were holes in the toes of her pantyhose.

"Tea would be . . . lovely," Chapel said.

Ellie snorted in derision. "At this hour? It's whiskey or nothing. Now tell me—exactly—why you are here."

She fixed Chapel with eyes that could have bored through steel plate. Even if he hadn't known, he would have guessed right away she'd been a schoolteacher once.

"Well," Chapel said, "I wanted to make sure you were safe, and—"

"'Rock-bottomed and copper-sheathed,'" Ellie said.

"I beg your pardon?"

"It's an old phrase from *The Devil and Daniel Webster*. It means I'm just fine. There's been no trouble and I'll have Julius to protect me if need be."

"I'm sure he's loyal, but—"

"Then there's the squad of plainclothes policemen sitting in a car out front, where they've been for nearly two days now," Ellie added. "I must remember to send Julius down with some sandwiches and a thermos of coffee later. Cold duty this time of year, and this is a cold year even for Chicago." She clucked her tongue. "Captain Chapel, I'm old. I know I'm old. I do not believe I am yet an old fool. I know the danger I'm facing. I also know you wouldn't be here, sitting and chatting with me, just to be cordial. I take you for a man with far better things to do than comfort spinsters. So why don't you ask the question that you've been holding on the back of your tongue since you walked in the door?"

"All right," Chapel said. "I need you to tell me everything you know about the chimeras, and Camp Putnam."

In his ear Angel sounded very worried. "Chapel, sweetie, she's not necessarily cleared to talk about—"

He pulled the hands-free set out of his ear. When his phone began to ring in his pocket, he switched it to vibrate. "Excuse me," he said.

CHICAGO, ILLINOIS: APRIL 13, T+39:53

"Hee. Ha heh. Ha."

Tyrone Jameson had been a trauma nurse for twenty-two years. He'd seen his share of horrors in that time, working in the ER at Piedmont Hospital in Atlanta. He'd seen people come through the doors who looked like they were chopped in pieces—and who had eventually walked out again under their own power. He'd seen people gone out of their mind on drugs take gunshot wounds to the face and not even feel it.

This asshole took the cake.

"Ha. Heh . . . ha," the man said. He swung his injured foot off the bed and put it down on the floor. Put his weight on it.

The man screamed—and laughed at the same time.

"Jesus, buddy, just—just lie down for me, okay? Will you do that for me?" Tyrone asked, his hands reaching to grab the guy's shoulders and push him back down onto the bed.

The look the patient gave him made Tyrone's blood turn to icy slush.

"Ha."

The jerk had lost two toes. The front half of his

foot looked like hamburger when he came in. Now it was encased in a hard cast and a metal brace just to keep the foot from falling off. And he was putting *weight* on it.

And laughing about it.

"Hee hee ho," the man said, standing up on wobbly legs. He grabbed for his shirt, which was hanging on a chair next to the bed.

"Look, I can see in your face, you think you're some kind of badass tough guy," Tyrone said, not sure what to do. He should call for security, get some orderlies in here and a doctor to sedate the man. But he was scared. He was honestly scared of what his patient would do to him. "But if you try to walk out of here, you're going to undo all the good the surgeon did. You're going to wreck that foot permanently."

He could only watch as the man got dressed, one painful button at a time. He never stopped laughing.

As he headed for the door, clearly intending to check himself out against medical advice, Tyrone just shook his head. "You need to lie down, buddy. You need to spend the next six weeks in that bed. Or you're doing yourself a real disservice."

"Ha. Hee. Can't wait," the patient said. He turned around to give Tyrone a nasty look. "I've got a body to find, and burn. And then I've got to kill a bunch of people. Ha. Hee ha hee. It's going to be a full day."

Tyrone shook his head. "No, seriously. Seriously—"

The man's smile was worse than his laugh. It was the kind of smile you would expect to find on a corpse.

"Doesn't it hurt?" Tyrone asked, because he couldn't find any other words.

"Hee ha ha ha! Like you can't imagine," the patient admitted. "Now. Where—hee ha hee—do I go to find a taxi out of here?"

CHICAGO, ILLINOIS: APRIL 13, T+40:07

"The chimeras. Well," Ellie said, "that is quite an interesting thing to be asking about. You do understand I'm absolutely forbidden to speak of that with anyone? I signed more than one nondisclosure agreement."

"I wouldn't ask if the need wasn't great," Chapel told her.

"I have no doubt," Ellie said. "And I'm sure you know more about security clearances and needs to know and the like than I do. One hates to break the law, though. You're in some kind of trouble, Captain, I can see it in your eyes."

Julia glanced over at him in surprise.

"I'm beginning to think so, ma'am. I'm beginning to think my own people are using me as a pawn in a game I can't see yet. And since those same people don't seem to want me to talk to you about this, I'm thinking I definitely need to know whatever information you have. I understand your reluctance, but I have to insist."

"Hmm," Ellie said, watching him closely.

"There are lives at stake," Chapel tried.

"Of course," Ellie said. "There always are."

Chapel saw in her eyes that she was waiting for

him to say the right words. She wanted to talk to him, but she wasn't going to give up what she had for free. He took a deep breath. He was making a big leap of faith, he knew. But he needed this information. "The chimeras are loose. They've left their camp and are at large, with a list of people they want to kill. Your name is on that list. Julia—Dr. Taggart here—wasn't on that list, but they tried to kill her anyway."

"They are quite dangerous, yes," Ellie said, still giving nothing away.

"Not just them. Somebody helped them escape."

"Ah," Ellie said, leaning forward. "Now that's interesting."

Chapel nodded. "I intend to find out who it was. And make sure they're punished," he told her. "Somebody is using the chimeras, somebody has turned them into his personal death squad. I won't let him get away with it."

She smiled, and he knew he'd won her over. She sat back and looked up at the ceiling as if gathering her thoughts. "Have you met any of the chimeras? Ian, perhaps?"

"Not Ian. Malcolm and another one, who I'm told was named Brody," Chapel said.

"Oh, my. Oh, my my. The look on your face tells me something," Ellie said, leaning back on the couch. She took a deep sip from her teacup full of whiskey. "That's the look of a soldier. Are they . . . ah?"

"Yes," Chapel said.

"At least they're at peace, then. For once in their lives." Ellie sighed deeply. "I was their teacher. I disciplined them when need arose, and I daresay I was stricter than they would have liked. But I did care for them. You can't not love your students, even the stupid ones."

Julia gasped in shock.

"Oh, young lady, did you think a teacher wasn't allowed to call someone 'stupid'? Part of our job is to evaluate them, you know. And there were a few of the boys who were stupid, quite as dumb as the proverbial rocks. Others were brilliant. They all possessed what we used to refer to as *animal cunning*."

"You were a teacher with UNESCO, weren't you?" Chapel asked, prodding her to go on.

"Oh, yes, back in the eighties, back when I thought I could still save the world by teaching it not to end sentences in prepositions. I was rather more idealistic back then. I specialized in children with developmental and emotional issues. That was why the Defense Department wanted to hire me. That and my security clearance."

"I'm sorry," Chapel said. "You worked for the DoD? I thought the chimeras were a CIA project."

"I wouldn't know anything about that. I know the man who recruited me was wearing a uniform, that's all."

Chapel nodded. No need to jump to conclusions. "So the DoD approached you about a teaching assignment. When was this?"

"Nineteen ninety," Ellie said.

"So they would have been pretty young," Chapel said. "Did anyone ever tell you why they were created—or why they were detained?"

"Absolutely not. Before you ask, yes, I *did* wonder.

I burned with curiosity about that for a long time, but when you ask the same question a hundred times and are routinely told you don't need to know the answer, you eventually give in and stop asking. I'm sure you can understand that."

"Yeah," Chapel said. "Yeah, I can."

"Captain, the word 'yeah' does not belong in the English language. The word you want to use is 'yes.' As in, 'yes, ma'am.'"

Chapel felt himself blush. "Yes, ma'am."

Ellie frowned and picked up her teacup again. "I think this will be a very long night if I make you guess which questions to ask and then tell you what I think you should know. Why don't I just go through the story as I remember it?"

"All right," Chapel said.

Ellie knocked back her cup in one gulp and began.

CHICAGO, ILLINOIS: APRIL 13, T+40:12

"It was 1990 when they first approached me. A captain of the navy whose name I don't remember—I never saw him again—came to my school on Roosevelt Island in New York. He asked if I had any experience administering intelligence tests, specifically culture-neutral IQ tests. I explained that I had been doing just such a thing for more than ten years. I asked why he wanted to know, but of course he didn't answer. A few months later, during my summer break, I was asked to come up to the Catskills for a weekend and to bring anything I needed to administer such a test to a group of two hundred children, all of them four years old, all of them boys. In exchange I would be paid handsomely for my time, but I had to agree not to tell anyone where I was going or why.

"Back then I was just a little older than you are now. Still young enough to think an adventure sounded fun, rather than exhausting. So I went. I was certainly not expecting what I saw. Camp Putnam was about a hundred acres of ground enclosed by an electric fence. There were guard towers and quite a number of soldiers. Inside the fence were the boys. They were adorable, and even when I noticed what was so strange about their eyes, I couldn't help but feel they were the healthiest, most curious bunch of four-year-olds I'd ever met. I'm sure I asked a thousand questions that day, but I did not receive any answers, as you can imagine.

"I did the job I'd been brought in for, administering the tests. Julia, dear, your parents were really quite interested in the results. They kept asking me if I would stay and tabulate the results then and there. They offered me more money. It was summertime, when every teacher needs more money, so I did as they asked. As it turned out, I ended up staying at the camp for eight more years.

"The boys were incredibly healthy and most of them had quite high IQs. They never seemed to get sick, and when they fell out of trees or skinned their elbows, they healed with astonishing speed. The soldiers played with them and treated them very well—at that time—but nobody, no one at all had considered they needed to be educated. In the end I had to volunteer to be their teacher. The prospect of these boys growing up in that camp, unable to read, unable to do basic math, was just startling to me. I was under the impression, you see, that they were orphans or something. That they were being raised there by the military but that when they were old enough they would go forth into the world, that they would get jobs and marry and have happy lives.

"I sometimes think your father, Julia, hired me on simply because it was easier to do that than to disillusion me.

"In many ways that was an idyllic time and I was quite happy. The Catskills are a beautiful place, and I fell in love with country living. In the summer I would hold class in a field of wildflowers deep in the camp. In the winter we would all crowd into a cozy little schoolhouse, the boys wrapped up in blankets around woodstoves. Beyond that—I was electrified. It was an incredible opportunity for someone like me. There were no televisions in Camp Putnam. No radios or newspapers. I could teach these boys to become men, to become upstanding gentlemen without any of the distractions or temptations of modern life. I imagined the papers I could write based on my observations, the awards and grants I could win with the data I collected. I will admit I was not above the scientific impulse that drove people like Taggart and Bryant.

"That changed, though, in 1993. That was the year of the first death.

"The boys had always fought among themselves. They were quick of temper, though at the time we thought that was just a product of their environment. Boys will be boys, we said. They squabbled over any little thing that one of them had and the others lacked. If a guard gave one of them a candy bar, we knew it would end in a fistfight as one of the other boys decided it by rights belonged to him.

"When one of them—his name was Gerald—failed to show up in my class one day, I assumed he was just playing hooky or that he was sick. When he was gone for a week, I began to worry. Eventually Dr. Bryant took me aside and explained. Gerald was dead. He had been attacked by three other boys, and they had broken his neck. She made it sound like an accident. A tragedy, but nothing unnatural. The three boys who killed Gerald would be punished, she said, but I didn't need to worry about it.

"Three months later it happened again. Two boys went into the woods, just playing, exploring, doing what eight-year-old boys do. Only one came back. He refused to tell us what happened to his friend and so guards had to go out looking for him. The missing boy's name was Marcus. They found him impaled on a tree branch. When his friend, Tyrone, was questioned, he admitted they had fallen out over whether Huckleberry Finn or Tom Sawyer was smarter. It was a question I had asked in class that day, and they had debated it at some length before Tyrone decided he could settle the question once and for all. He had made a kind of spear out of the tree branch and he ran Marcus through with it, puncturing a lung.

"I had plenty of training in dealing with emotionally confused youths. I offered my services in helping Tyrone, but Dr. Taggart said that wouldn't be necessary. I did not see Tyrone again. I assumed he had been taken to another facility, separated for the safety of the population. What actually happened to him is something I don't like to contemplate.

"It became rapidly apparent, however, that we had a real problem on our hands. The violence escalated each month. Fistfights turned into boys throwing rocks at each other, which turned into horrible beatings and boys using makeshift weapons against one another. The scientists tried all manner of ways to settle things down, from putting drugs in the boys' food to splitting them up into small groups and forbidding them from being alone with each other at any time. The number of guards in the camp was doubled, and then tripled.

"It did not help. A guard was killed, in 1994. It was a horrible time. The other guards swept through the camp looking for the culprit. They were not . . . gentle in their interrogations. For a while things quieted down as the boys were put under a draconian sort of lockdown. They were forced to stay in their cabins at all times, not even being allowed out for exercise. That couldn't last, though, not if we wished to keep the boys healthy. I imagine some of us believed the rash of violence had been a fad. A phase the boys would grow out of.

"This was not the case.

"The boys continued their lessons through it all. The only time they saw each other, for a while, was in my classroom. Which meant that their anger at each other found no other outlet. I had to break up fights constantly. I had guards rush in and restrain my students in the middle of my lectures. If I called on a boy and he didn't know the answer, the others would jeer at him mercilessly. If he did know the answer, they would mock him for being a show-off. Then one day a fight broke out that I couldn't stop. One of the slower boys, but one notorious for his incredible strength, attacked another boy right in front of me. The attacker—his name was Keenan— broke the other boy's arms in the time it takes to say it. He was jumping on top of his victim, smashing him with his feet. I tried to pull him away and he lashed out at me. His nictitating membranes—his third eyelids, I can see you don't know the term— were down, and when their eyes were like that I knew they weren't going to stop. They were going to hit and bite and scratch until everything in front of them was destroyed. Keenan came at me with nothing in his heart but pure, animal rage. I had thwarted him, and he would tear me to pieces."

Julia gasped. "What did you do?" she asked.

Ellie inhaled deeply. "I drew my sidearm and I put him down like a mad dog. Three bullets in his skull, that was enough. Did I not mention that I was carrying a pistol while I taught? We all were, by that point. Every human being in Camp Putnam went armed at all times. It just wasn't safe otherwise."

CHICAGO, ILLINOIS: APRIL 13, T+40:51

The fireplace by Chapel's right side crackled and popped. Apomotov came in and poured more whiskey into their teacups. Outside the wind from the lake battered at the house, but inside all was quiet.

No one spoke a word as they waited for Ellie to continue her story.

"The level of aggression we saw," she said, looking only into her teacup, "was far beyond anything we'd expected. Anything we'd planned for. These were children! You've only seen them as adults. At that age they looked like little seraphs, angels with black eyes. When they turned on each other, or on us, they turned to demons in a moment. We tried so many things. I recommended individual counseling—bringing in a small army of psychologists, child development specialists, social workers. My request was roundly denied. It was too great a security risk.

"The boys kept fighting, and every time they hurt a guard, things just got so much worse. In 1995, they killed one of the researchers, a Dr. Harkness."

Julia gasped.

"I'm . . . sorry," Julia said, when Chapel looked at her. "Just—I knew her. Dr. Harkness. She was really sweet. She used to bring me magazines, *Tiger Beat* and . . . and *Seventeen*. She said being raised by scientists, I needed to see what the real world was like. They killed her? Oh my God. Oh my God . . . Mom just told me she moved away."

She shook her head, and Chapel saw a tear roll down her cheek.

"Please," Julia said. "Just—go on. I'll be okay."

Ellie gave her a sympathetic frown, but she clearly wanted to get back to her story. "After that the guards were told to shoot any boy acting violent. They were human beings, those guards, and they rarely did as they were told. At least, at first. In 1996, things changed."

Ellie drew her feet up underneath her as if they were cold. She took a moment to catch her breath and drink some more whiskey. "I made a mistake. A bad one. It has occurred to me, more than once, that what happened was my fault.

"I know I'm being overly hard on myself. But it happened because of what I did. Or rather, what I didn't do.

"A group of the boys came to me. Just four of them, a little cabal. They were the smartest of the lot, my best pupils. And they knew what was happening. They understood that normal children—human children—weren't like this. They said that if they could just get out of the camp, see the world beyond and live like normal children, then they would settle down. That they would overcome their impulses. The leader was a boy named Ian. The smartest of them all, and one of the strongest. You could see in his eyes he was a natural leader. Well, when his eyes weren't covered by those horrible membranes, you could see it. He had organized this little committee. He came to me because he knew I was the most sympathetic adult in that camp, and the one who was the least tied to the military. He asked me for my help. They had a plan, but they needed certain things to make it happen. They needed to know where the guards would be at a certain hour. And then he told me he needed my sidearm.

"I told him it was impossible, and I refused to help. He saw at once I wouldn't budge and that he'd made a mistake asking for my gun. So instead, then, he pleaded—begged, on bended knee—that I not tell anyone what he'd asked. He promised that he would forget all about the plan, that he would devote himself to stopping the violence.

"So I kept my peace. Two nights later they rushed the fence. They had no weapons and no idea what they were doing; they simply thought they could climb over an electrified fence and run away. The guards killed one of them and restrained Ian. Two more of them did get over the fence, believe it or not. They fought the guards who came for them. One of them was tranquilized and taken away and I never saw him again. One of them actually got loose, and it was months before he was returned to us."

"That was Malcolm," Chapel said, remembering Funt's story.

"Yes. Malcolm. They caught him again, eventually. The camp he came back to was not the one he left," Ellie said.

She shuddered but went on. "There had been a gate in the fence, originally. A wide gate you could drive a jeep through. The guards sealed that up. They added a new, outer fence. And in between them they laid mines. Land mines. There would not be a second escape attempt."

"Wait," Chapel said. "They sealed the fence? There was no gate after that?"

"I believe I spoke clearly, Captain. After 1996, the fence was complete. After that date no human being ever set foot in Camp Putnam. The guards had decided, you see, that it wasn't safe. Not even for armed men. Anyone attempting to go in or out was to be shot on sight. And believe me, this time the guards obeyed their orders to the letter."

CHICAGO, ILLINOIS: APRIL 13, T+41:06

Chapel's phone started to ring. It surprised him enough he jumped in his seat. He took it out of his pocket and saw that it was still set to vibrate, but apparently Angel could get past that. "Forgive me," he said. He yanked the battery out of the phone, and it went silent again.

"Someone doesn't want you to hear this," Ellie said, looking frightened.

Chapel didn't blame her. "That's all the more reason why I *need* to hear it," he told her. "A lot of people have spent a lot of time and effort keeping this secret so long. But secrets have a way of festering. This one's old enough and dangerous enough that people are dying for it. I have to stop that."

"I suppose someone must," Ellie said. "There's not much more to tell, though, I'm afraid. My involvement with Camp Putnam didn't last much longer."

"You said you started there in 1990, and that you worked there for eight years," Chapel told her.

"Yes. Those last two years were . . . terrifying. My safety was guaranteed, but the boys were trapped in there. They were abandoned. Left to their own self-destructive impulses. When I took the job, I had thought I was working at some kind of high-tech summer camp. By the time I left, I felt like I was a schoolteacher at Auschwitz."

"I'm sorry you had to go through this," Chapel told her.

"I stayed, Captain. I stayed even after they sealed the fence. I'm not asking for your pity." Ellie finished her drink. "Perhaps I thought I could still help in some way. It can be hard to remember why we *did* things, later on. I've often suspected that human brains are more susceptible to inertia than we like to think. I had been the boys' teacher. I kept teaching. The soldiers built a platform, a kind of stage that rose above the level of the fence. The scientists and I would go up there whenever we wished to observe or address the boys. We were separated from the boys by twenty yards of no-man's-land, so we had to use megaphones to talk to them. The scientists kept asking them questions. The guards would throw food and clothing down to them. I tried to teach them. I tried to stick to my lesson plans. Each day fewer and fewer of them came to listen. I told myself they had decided what I had to impart wasn't worth hearing. I think I knew the truth, though. There were fewer of them all the time because there was nobody stopping them from acting out. No way to dissuade them from killing each other. When I began, there had been two hundred boys in that camp. When I left—when it became clear that I wasn't helping them—there were perhaps thirty of them remaining."

Chapel's heart skipped a beat. Thirty, in 1998. According to Hollingshead, only seven had still been alive when the fence was blown open and they escaped. Seven—out of two hundred.

"The last of them I ever saw was Ian," Ellie said. "He kept coming. My star pupil, he was always there when I went on that stage. He would shout questions up to me, and I would answer them the best I could. When he asked when I was coming

back inside, when the gate would be reinstalled—"
She stopped for a moment. "When he asked when
he would be free, I had no answer for him. I could
only pretend I hadn't heard him. Captain, you told
me earlier about Malcolm. Malcolm survived all
this time. He got to be free again. That makes me
strangely happy. I'm not surprised Brody made it as
well. He was the most thoughtful of them. The one
who tried to think things through, to understand
why things were the way they were. Quinn almost
certainly made it. He was the strongest of them by
far. But I am certain—absolutely certain—that if
even one of them is still alive out there, it's Ian. You
say you haven't met him yet. When you do, I think
you'll understand."

She fell silent then. She wasn't looking at Chapel
or Julia, just at her own memories. When Apomotov
came in to announce someone was persistently trying to call them on the telephone, Ellie glanced up.

"Well, who is it?" she asked.

"A young lady who won't give her name. I told
her we couldn't accept any calls now. Under the circumstances."

"Quite right," Ellie said. "Captain Chapel. I've
told you all I know. I find it has distressed me more
than I expected, saying it all out loud after all this
time. I think I'd like to go to bed now. Was there
anything else you required?"

"Just one more thing, ma'am. I hate to impose."

Ellie lifted one hand in resignation. "I can hardly
refuse now."

Chapel leaned forward on the divan. "I need directions on how to get to Camp Putnam," he told her.

CHICAGO, ILLINOIS: APRIL 13, T+41:27

Apomotov fetched them their coats and Chapel thanked him profusely. Julia just stared at the door like she couldn't wait to leave. Before going back out into the cold, though, Chapel decided he needed to do one thing.

He put the battery back in his phone. It started ringing instantly. He put the hands-free unit in his ear and said, "Hello, Angel. What's new?"

Any trace of the sultry vixen he remembered was gone from the operator's voice. "Captain Chapel. I have new orders from Director Hollingshead. Will you listen to them and acknowledge receipt?"

"Sure," Chapel said, with a sigh.

"The director orders you—and I am told to phrase this as a direct order—to proceed immediately to Denver, Colorado, where you will take charge of the security detail around Judge Franklin Hayes. Do you acknowledge?"

"You can tell the admiral I received him loud and clear," Chapel told her.

"Chapel," Angel said, her voice warming up by maybe a tenth of a degree, "you're headed down a dark path."

"I know it, Angel."

She clucked her tongue. "You're not supposed to know any of this. I'm not supposed to know anything about Camp Putnam. That's a top secret DoD installation, and just the fact of its existence is need-to-know information."

"I know."

"I can't help you if you disobey these orders, Chapel. I can't help you with the consequences of your actions. You'll be on your own. I want to go on record as saying—no—begging you to reconsider your next move. You have your orders."

"Understood," he said. He put the phone and the hands-free unit in his pocket. He left the battery in the phone for the moment, just in case. Just in case of what, he couldn't say. He glanced at Julia, but she was still staring at the door.

Ellie had come up to the foyer to see them off. "Stay warm," she said.

"Thank you for everything," he told her. "You've been more help than I expected." He thought of something. "You don't know Franklin Hayes, do you?"

"The federal judge? The one who's supposed to become our next Supreme Court justice? Just from what I've seen on the news."

"What about the names Christina Smollett, Marcia Kennedy, or Olivia Nguyen?"

Ellie just shook her head.

Chapel nodded. It had been a long shot. "Okay. Thanks again—and stay safe, please. I hate the fact I'm leaving you here alone when you're in danger."

Ellie's face fell. "Captain, I could have done more for them."

Chapel shook his head in incomprehension.

"I could have fought harder. I could have helped Ian and his cabal. I could have . . ." She let the thought trail away. "I could have made their lives a little easier, in some way. Been kinder to them." She was starting to cry.

Was she looking for forgiveness? Chapel would have given it if he could, but he sensed that nothing he said would matter. He tried anyway. "They came to you for a reason. You were probably the only human who ever really cared for them," he said.

She shook her head in negation. He'd been right—he couldn't offer her any forgiveness, not now, if she couldn't forgive herself.

"If they do come here and . . ." She lowered her head. "If they came here," she said, "I don't think I would blame them."

Chapel had no words for that. He disagreed, but it didn't matter, not to Ellie. He pushed open the door and stepped out into the night, Julia following close behind.

"I need to borrow your phone," he told her.

Julia looked up at him. Her eyes were blank. "My whole life," she said, her voice a flat monotone. "My whole life that was going on and they never told me. My parents were doing that. They were doing all of that."

It had finally happened—the endorphins and adrenaline were gone, and she'd fallen into the abyss of her own thoughts. Just as she'd said she expected, it had become too much for her to bear. Without another word she handed over the phone.

Chapel dialed from the piece of paper in his pocket. "Chief Petty Officer Andrews," he said, "I'm coming to you right now, and I have a flight plan to file. The destination is anywhere in the Catskills Mountains, in New York State."

LANGLEY, VIRGINIA: APRIL 13, T+41:46

On the phone, Franklin Hayes was livid. Tom Banks toyed with the idea of just hanging up on him.

But no. The judge was too important to Banks's plans for the future. Especially the next few days.

"He's headed where?" Hayes demanded.

"The Catskills. You know what he expects to find there. Don't make me say it, even on an encrypted line."

Hayes was silent for a second. "You think he'll learn anything?"

"It's hard to know. My jurisdiction stops at the fence. What may still be inside there, if anything, is Hollingshead's business. It doesn't matter."

Hayes wasn't about to be diverted from his previous ire. "Whatever. I need him here, in Denver. I need him here now."

Banks agreed. Chapel needed to be in Denver as soon as humanly possible. This jaunt to Camp Putnam was going to slow down a lot of plans. Not for the first time, Banks wondered how much Chapel had figured out. Whether he was starting to guess what the real game was here, and what the stakes were.

It seemed unlikely. Chapel had proved he was tougher than nails, but he'd also made a lot of dumb mistakes—like dragging the cute veterinarian around with him. A smart operative would have left her behind.

He couldn't just assume Chapel was an idiot, though. And he definitely couldn't just ring him up and tell him what to do. The one-armed asshole had to be led around like a bull with a ring in his nose. If you pulled too hard on the ring, he would just plant his feet and refuse to move. You had to be subtle about it. Make him think he was still in charge of his own destiny.

"I've got to go," Banks told Hayes. "I think I can solve our mutual problem, but it means making a very delicate phone call."

"To whom?" Hayes demanded.

The judge had no need to know, but for once Banks relented. "Rupert Hollingshead. I've got to light a fire under his ass." Chapel trusted his boss. Time to exploit that particular mistake.

IN TRANSIT: APRIL 14, T+43:07

They landed in the Catskills with no fuss. The airport there was little more than a short runway between two forested hills, a place for hobbyist pilots to park their Cessnas. It was just big enough to accommodate the jet.

"There are some pretty rich people up here, in the middle of nowhere," Chief Petty Officer Andrews told Chapel. "This isn't the first G4 to land on this strip. What do you want me to do now?"

"Hmm?"

"Me, the pilot, this plane. Do you want us to wait here for you?"

Chapel thought about that for a second. "What are your orders from up top?"

Andrews studied his face for a moment before

answering. Perhaps she was trying to decide what his security clearance was. "I've received no new orders since I picked you up in Atlanta. Though—there was one thing. I was told to watch you closely and provide an update on your psychological state." She was being careful, he saw, choosing her words precisely. She hadn't told him *who* was supposed to get that update.

"Okay. Don't get in trouble on my account," he told her, knowing perfectly well she wouldn't. If orders came in to leave him stranded in the Catskills, she would take her plane up and away on a moment's notice. "If you don't get any other orders, stay put. Refuel if they have the right facilities here. We might need to leave in a hurry."

"Sir, yes, sir," she said, and saluted him. Her way of saying she would follow her orders—wherever they came from. Reminding him, perhaps, of the chain of command.

He returned the salute anyway, then went to wake Julia. She'd just managed to fall asleep and she was surly getting up, pushing his hands away and pulling her hair down over her eyes as if she wanted to block out the light. She didn't say anything, though, as he led her down the stairs to the ground.

It was cold out, though not as frigid as Chicago. What Chapel hadn't been expecting, though, was how dark it was. There were a few lights on the airstrip's sole building, a hangar about five hundred yards away. The jet behind them showed its own lights that blinked on its wingtips. Otherwise the world was wrapped in a thick blanket of dark cloud that only a few stars could penetrate. The moon was down, and Chapel couldn't see more than a dozen yards in any direction.

No one was waiting for them on the tarmac. Not a soul.

That was a good thing, of course. It meant Chapel wasn't about to be arrested—or worse. It meant Hollingshead wasn't ready to reel him in, not quite yet. Maybe the admiral wanted to give him a chance to come in on his own. Or maybe he wanted to see just how far Chapel would push.

The darkness was also a bad thing, though, because they had a ways to go yet in the middle of the night. "Angel," he said, "what are the chances of getting some transport out here?"

"Sorry, Captain," the operator said in his ear. She sounded like she had better things to do. "You can turn around and get back on that plane. Follow your orders. Otherwise, you're on your own."

"Understood," Chapel said.

Crap. He'd gotten used to Angel's help. He'd gotten used to having cars waiting for him everywhere he went, and helicopters when the cars weren't fast enough.

Well, he still had his training. Army Rangers didn't have angels sitting on their shoulders when they were dropped behind enemy lines. They were taught to improvise as necessary.

A little parking lot sat on the far side of the hangar. Three vehicles were parked there—two compact cars and a pickup truck. Chapel glanced through a window on the side of the hangar. There was an old man sitting in there, applying daubs of paint to a canvas the size of a barn door. Chapel saw no sign of anyone else—most likely the man in the hangar was simply a night attendant, there to make sure nobody ran off with the row of private planes parked inside the cavernous hangar. Loud music came through the window, something wild and classical. The attendant probably hadn't even heard the G4 land on his runway.

So far so good.

The compacts were most likely stored there for the use of people flying in for the weekend—people who lived somewhere else but wanted to be able to drive around when they got up here. The pickup probably belonged to the painter, but it was the best choice for where Chapel was headed. It would also be the easiest vehicle to acquire. The doors weren't locked. He stuck Julia in the passenger seat—she did as she was told without complaint or acknowledgment. Then he bent down under the dashboard and pulled some wires away from the fuse box. "You can't do this on modern cars," he told Julia, who didn't even look at him. He was talking to fill up the silence. "The computers in them know better. But the older models were designed to be fixed by their owners, so everything's out in the open." He found the two wires he wanted. With his fingernails and teeth he stripped a little insulation off them, then rubbed them together until the pickup coughed to life.

As Chapel threw the truck in gear and rolled through the open gate of the airfield, there was no sign the painter was even aware he'd just been robbed.

PHOENICIA, NEW YORK: APRIL 13, T+44:19

The night was impenetrably dark. The skeletal branches of trees loomed over the road on either side, blocking out even starlight. The truck's headlights could illuminate no more than a few gray weeds sticking up through the gravel of the road. Chapel had to take it slow, consulting the GPS in his phone every time the road branched or turned.

Occasionally they passed by an open field and the silver light of the overcast was just enough to see by. Old wooden buildings crouched on that open land, barns and farmhouses. Few of them showed any lights of their own.

Suddenly Julia sat up straight in her seat and peered through the truck's window, her hand on the glass.

"I know this place," she said, as he slowed the truck down to a crawl. "I remember this."

Chapel couldn't see anything but darkness and more trees. "You sure?" he asked.

"We're on the road to Phoenicia," she said. "I grew up there."

Chapel had forgotten that much of Julia's youth had been spent on these back roads. Her parents had lived here, working by day at Camp Putnam where they were raising a small army of genetic misfits, coming home at night to check her homework and take out the trash. He shook his head. "What was it like?" he asked.

She shrugged and made herself small in her seat again, withdrawing once more. For a second he thought she wouldn't answer, that that would go beyond the bounds of their new professional relationship. Then she made a small noncommittal noise and said, "It was all right, I guess. I went skiing a lot in the winter, and in summer my friends and I would steal some beer and go tubing."

"Tubing?" Chapel asked.

Julia actually smiled a little. "It's the local sport, I guess. You get an old inner tube from a tractor tire and you throw it in the river, then you sit with your butt in the hole and your legs dangling in the water. The current takes you downriver while you lie back with the sun in your face and the water splashing you to keep you cool. The river keeps the beer cold for a long time."

"Sounds pretty idyllic," he said, to keep her talking.

"Now, yeah. When I was a teenager, I thought it was boring as hell. I used to dream about when I grew up and I could move to New York City. I was going to be a reporter, for a while, until I realized that newspapers couldn't compete with the Internet. Then I was going to be a famous blogger." She laughed, a welcome sound in the dark cab of the pickup. "There are some things I really miss about this place. In Phoenicia there's a restaurant called Sweet Sue's. They make the best pancakes in the world."

"I've had some pretty good pancakes," Chapel told her. "Down in Florida we used to get *panqueques* from street vendors. They served them with fruit and honey on top."

"No comparison," Julia said. He could almost hear her roll her eyes. "At Sweet Sue's the pancakes are like half an inch thick, and lighter than air. Except they fill you up fast. I could never eat more than one of them at a sitting, but my dad would order *four* of them, which is the equivalent of saying you want to eat an entire birthday cake all at once. He never managed to finish and Mom would scold him for wasting perfectly good carbohydrates. Then she would pull out a pen and work out how many grams of fat he'd just eaten and how many calories he would burn if he walked all the way home."

"You really were raised by scientists," Chapel said. When she didn't respond, he nodded at the road. "You know this road? You know where it heads?"

"Yeah—out to nowhere. There are some farms on the far side of the mountain, but from here it's fifty miles of just trees and little creeks and crazy people."

Well, he couldn't disagree. They were only a few miles from Camp Putnam.

CAMP PUTNAM, NEW YORK: APRIL 14, T+44:37

Chapel parked the pickup well clear of the camp. Based on Ellie's directions the fenced-in area was surrounded on most sides by mountains and hills, but a one-lane gravel road snaked alongside a river for a while and then ended at a guardhouse very close to the perimeter. It was the best guess Chapel had for where the fence had been breached when the chimeras were released.

He stepped out of the truck and into a chaos of stars.

The overcast had cleared away while he drove, and now the sky was a blanket of light. He could clearly make out the gauzy trail of the Milky Way, but he had trouble figuring out the constellations because there were just too many stars up there he wasn't used to seeing. As he watched, a meteor streaked by overhead, silently burning in a trail of fire that was gone so fast he thought maybe his eyes were playing tricks on him.

"Beautiful," he said.

"Yeah," Julia replied, coming to stand next to him. "Funny place to put something straight out of a horror movie, right?" She opened the truck's glove compartment and rummaged around inside until she found something. She pulled it out and Chapel saw she'd found a flashlight, a big heavy Maglite of the kind security guards used. He realized he hadn't thought of that. He hadn't considered what it would be like tramping around in the dark woods with no light at all.

Not for the first time, he felt lucky he had her with him.

He inhaled deeply. He needed to focus. He had to smuggle a civilian into a compromised facility. Well, he'd been trained for this. "Okay. There shouldn't be too many guards down there. The place is empty, now—they just need someone to keep curious people from coming in and taking a look around. We do need to be careful, though. From now on we need to be silent and keep our heads down. Just follow me, and don't switch on that light until I tell you it's safe."

She nodded to indicate she understood.

Together they moved out, staying as low as possible. Chapel kept them under trees or near bushes when possible. He had no idea what kind of surveillance equipment the camp boasted, nor did he want to find out.

He led Julia down the side of a hill toward the end of the road. There was enough cover to screen them but not as much as he would have liked. Anyone with night-vision goggles or—worse—active infrared would have spotted them in a second. As the minutes ticked by and no one ordered him to halt he forced himself to keep his fear at bay.

At the end of the road stood a single sentry post, and beyond, the fence—or what was left of it.

Twisted chain link had been pulled down and stacked in heaps by the side of the road. It looked like it had been torn out of the ground by the hands of giants. Beyond lay a wide stretch of open ground scored here and there by roughly circular patches of bare earth. That must have been where land mines had exploded—Chapel figured the patches were just the right size to have been craters before someone had filled them back in.

Beyond the zone of tortured ground lay trees and darkness. This was definitely the way in. The only way in, since he was certain the rest of the fence remained intact.

He saw no sign of working cameras or floodlights or machine-gun nests. All good. The one thing between Chapel and his goal was that sentry box. It was a narrow little box the size of a tollbooth. Inside sat a single soldier reading a magazine. A single lightbulb over his head provided light—but it would also make it hard for the soldier to see outside, to see anyone sneaking up on him until they were lit up by the same bulb he read by.

Sloppy, Chapel thought. The light should be outside the box, illuminating the approach of the road. Of course, the soldier had no reason to expect anyone now. Camp Putnam was empty, a forgotten relic of a history no one knew. And it was unlikely anyone would hike up here in the dark, especially at this time of year. If anyone did come up here, say a lost motorist, they would be showing headlights that the soldier would see coming from half a mile away.

Chapel led Julia in a wide path around the box, getting as close to the remains of the fence as he could without giving away his position. A stand of trees had grown almost right up to the fence. It would give them good visual cover. When he'd picked the right spot, he hunkered down and put a hand on Julia's shoulder, keeping her down as well.

And then he waited.

Julia never said a word while they waited. She didn't fidget, except to shift her weight from one foot to the other now and then. She kept her eyes on the sentry box, just like Chapel. For someone with no military training she had an incredible amount of patience and that most important talent of a covert operator: the ability to sit still.

Chapel knew she would eventually lose her cool, that she would have to move to alleviate cramped muscles or just to keep from falling asleep. It would happen to him, too. He had no idea how long it would take.

In the end they got lucky.

The soldier in the sentry box was keeping himself awake by drinking caffeinated soda. He had a big two-liter bottle of cola that he sipped at from time to time, wincing at its bite or maybe because it had gotten warm. The problem with using soda to keep yourself alert was that it was a diuretic. Less than half an hour after Chapel picked his hiding spot, the soldier was forced to answer the call of nature.

He lifted a radio to his lips and said something Chapel couldn't hear, then climbed out of the box and waddled toward the trees on the far side of the road.

Chapel wasted no time. He tapped Julia on the shoulder, then sprang up and moved quietly across the cratered earth and through the gap in the fence.

They were in.

CAMP PUTNAM, NEW YORK: APRIL 14, T+46:22

The camp comprised a hundred acres of woods surrounded by a fence. A hundred acres can be an interminable wasteland if you don't know what you're looking for and you have to search every corner.

For the most part the camp was exactly what it looked like—uninterrupted forest, an endless stretch of trees that grew so close together the two of them were forced to stick to winding, cramped trails that twisted between them. Occasionally they would cross a chattering creek, the icy water bright in the starlight. Very seldom they found an old shack or lean-to, beaten down by years of wind and weather until it was little more than bare lichen-smeared planks sticking up from the broken remains of a concrete foundation.

Those were the only signs that anyone had ever lived in Camp Putnam. Chapel found himself wondering if the shacks had been built by the chimeras, or by mountain men who lived up here a hundred years ago. It was impossible to tell just by the wan light of Julia's flashlight. Some of the shacks had latches on their doors, while others had more modern doorknobs. Beyond that they all looked the same. They were all empty save for a few scraps of fabric in one, the remains of a campfire in another. Everything inside them was sodden and bristling with mushrooms.

"It looks like this place has been abandoned for years," Julia said at one point.

"The chimeras were here less than two days ago," Chapel said, though he had to agree with her.

They found no sign of habitation for nearly an hour, until they stumbled on a pond in the middle of the forest.

The water stretched away from them as far as they could see, black and full of stars except where mist snaked across its surface. A stout rope hung down over the water, perfect for swinging out over the still pond. Nearby a row of changing stalls had been built back in the trees. The door of each stall had been torn from its hinges and lay shattered on the ground. Julia shone her light into one of the stalls, and Chapel saw a splash of bright red on its back wall.

He stepped closer, intending to take a closer look, and nearly crushed a skull under his shoe.

The skull was half buried in the dirt, only one

eye socket looking up at them as if its owner had been disturbed in his bed and wanted to go back to sleep. Nearby the remains of a rib cage could be seen. The limbs were missing, perhaps dragged off by animals.

"Jesus," Julia said. "If a guy with a chain saw and a hockey mask shows up, ask him for directions. He'll be the *least* creepy thing in this place."

Chapel squatted to examine the skull. It was fractured in a couple of places, but otherwise it seemed normal enough. "Looks human," he said.

Julia shook her head. "But . . . look at those ribs—they're too thick, and too close together."

When he knew what to look for, Chapel saw it at once. This was the skeleton of a chimera. The thickening of the ribs explained, perhaps, how they could take multiple gunshots to the chest and not even slow down. The skull was human enough that when you shot them in the head they tended to die. It matched what he'd seen in the field.

"Looking at this," Julia said, "I'd say he came here to hide. Someone was chasing him. He went into the stall to hide, but it didn't work. The pursuer tore the stalls open one by one until he found him. After that the cause of death looks to be multiple traumas to the head with a blunt weapon."

Chapel felt his jaw fall open. "Impressive analysis, Doctor," he said.

Julia shrugged. "When your patients can't tell you what's wrong, you have to get all kinds of CSI on them. You learn to spot the signs of abuse and trauma."

"That's no poodle," Chapel pointed out.

She shrugged. "I'm about to wet myself with fear. Acting like a professional helps."

"Then please, keep it up," he told her. "Look over there, on the far side of the pond," he said, pointing.

She swept her light across the water, but it couldn't reach that far. It didn't matter. Something big and shadowy was hidden in the trees there, something made of right angles, which suggested a building.

"Ellie mentioned a schoolhouse, big enough for her and two hundred students," Julia said.

Chapel nodded. "Let's take a look."

CAMP PUTNAM, NEW YORK: APRIL 14, T+46:31

It proved difficult to get around the pond. The trees grew right down to the water, and all the paths seemed to wind away into dark groves, farther and farther from where they wanted to go. Eventually, though, they stumbled out into a massive clearing full of buildings, some small and haphazardly built, some massive and made of durable brick. The building they thought was the schoolhouse was the largest, a two-story edifice with lots of broken windows, but it looked mostly intact. Other buildings had been burned down to cinders. Directly in front of the schoolhouse lay a broad patch of open grass that had grown knee-high. On the other side of this lawn lay a little church with a cross on its roof.

"It's like Smalltown, USA," Julia pointed out, letting her light play over the broken windows of the nearest buildings. "After the bomb dropped."

Chapel took in a tall flagpole in front of the

schoolhouse. A tattered rag hung lifeless from its top. In the starlight he could almost make out its stripes. "You see anything that looks like a laboratory? Or maybe a cloning facility?"

"That could look like anything, but . . . no," Julia said. She shrugged. "You'd expect it to look clean, I guess. Maybe to have its own fence so the boys couldn't wander in and disrupt the experiments. Everything I see here is kid-friendly. I mean, if the kids in question are superstrong and violent."

Chapel had to agree. There was nothing resembling a scientific facility in the clearing. He approached one of the bigger buildings and peered inside. It was mostly dark, but part of the roof had fallen away and he could see a line of steel cots with no mattresses. "Dormitory," he called.

Julia had gone to look at a low, long building with multiple chimneys studding its roof. "This is a kitchen. Like the kind you'd see at a school—big enough to feed two hundred people every day."

Chapel nodded. "Come on," he said. "Let's check out the schoolhouse."

If Ellie hadn't told them there was a schoolhouse, he might have given the building a different name. Maybe "town hall" or "auditorium." A pair of double doors had once stood at its entrance, but one of them was missing now. Debris—broken wood, bits of glass, a pile of leaves—clogged the entry, but he kicked it out of the way and stepped inside.

Julia followed with her light, which she shone around the interior of the building. It turned out not to be two stories after all, just one big floor and most of that open space. Starlight streamed in through high, filthy windows but showed Chapel little. He could only take the place in piece by piece as the flashlight moved across its surfaces. A yellow wooden floor—cracked and scored now—stretched away to a raised stage at the far side. A podium stood on one side of the platform, and at the back of the stage stood a massive blackboard, scrawled with obscenities and doodles of—

"Oh my God," Julia said, and nearly dropped the flashlight.

Its light had just illuminated the four bodies tied to the blackboard, their arms twisted up over their heads, their feet dangling just above the floor.

They were in bad shape, heavily decomposed, but not as far gone as the skeleton they'd seen by the pond. Their flesh looked dry and leathery, like the flesh of mummies.

They weren't boys when they died. They were adults with beards on their chins and hair on their chests. If these were chimeras, they must have died recently, when they were fully grown.

The stench hit him then, and he nearly threw up. He fought to control himself. This was as bad as anything he'd seen in Afghanistan. Maybe worse.

To one side of the bodies the blackboard had been washed clean, then someone had written a final message there:

we did this
together

"What does that mean?" Chapel asked, though he knew Julia was just as in the dark as he was.

"Four bodies, partially mummified. Their throats were slit," Julia said, and he could hear her fighting back her own urge to vomit. "That's probably how they died. But—but there are other cuts, on their arms; those are defensive wounds; they were—they fought, hard. They were attacked with . . . with knives . . . Chapel, I can't do this. I have to go outside."

He started to nod, but then he heard something. A creaking sound, as if weight was being applied to floorboards, just above his head.

Julia must have heard it too. She swiveled around, pointing the flashlight like a weapon. Chapel saw there was a balcony running around the walls above them, a mezzanine looking down on the main floor of the place. Something was up there, moving fast. It was out of the light before he could get a good look, but—

"Chapel, someone's here!" Julia gasped.

CAMP PUTNAM, NEW YORK: APRIL 14, T+46:52

Whoever it was, he moved too fast for Chapel to get a good look at him, dashing out of the light almost before Chapel had registered his presence at all. Julia tried to move the light to keep up, but Chapel heard the sound of footsteps coming down an iron stairwell in the corner of the room. He drew his sidearm and pointed it into the darkness, having no idea what was coming for him.

"Over there," he said, pointing at a corner of the massive room. Julia swung the light around and it scattered over a pile of folding chairs, some of them twisted and bent out of shape. A bird fluttered its wings near the door, and Julia stabbed the light at it, even as the figure in the dark came running right at Chapel.

He could hear its feet pounding on the squeaking floorboards, hear it breathing heavily. He would only get one shot, once chance to—

But before he could fire his weapon, it was on him, knocking him sideways. His jaw stung and he knew he'd been hit, but everything happened so fast he barely had time to drop his pistol and put his hands out to catch himself before he hit the floor.

Chimera, he thought, which was impossible—all the chimeras had been accounted for. But the strength in that hit, the speed with which the figure moved couldn't be denied.

He dropped to one knee, threw his artificial arm up to protect his head, knowing it was futile. He hadn't been ready for this. He'd thought he was safe here, that the place was deserted. That lack of planning was going to get him killed. Would he end up hanging on the blackboard, his throat slit, his feet turning black with congealed blood?

He had time to shout for Julia to run. Not that it would make any difference.

In a second he would be dead, as soon as the chimera hit him again.

He braced for it.

Waited for it.

Eventually he opened his eyes.

"He ran out there," Julia said, pointing her light at the doors of the auditorium.

Chapel squinted at the light. A starling hopped

across the debris there, turning its head from side to side.

"Did you get a look at him?" Chapel asked.

"His eyes," Julia said. "When the light hit them, they turned black. All black."

Chapel grabbed his pistol from the floor, then rose to his feet. "Okay," he said. "Stay behind me. Point the light where I tell you."

She brought the light up under her chin, sending deep shadows upward from her nose, obscuring her own eyes. But he could see the terror in her face. "Chapel, maybe we should just go. Head back to the fence. This isn't one of the chimeras you were supposed to track down, is it? Why would they come back here?"

"If there are more of them—"

She lowered the light. "I know. I just—I guess I'm just scared."

"I am too. But we have to do this," he told her.

He led her to the door and out onto the lawn between the buildings. The starling scampered out of their way.

Outside the starlight made everything silver and gray. A chimera could have been hiding anywhere and they wouldn't have spotted him until they were right on top of him. Chapel forced himself to hold his pistol in a loose grip. The last thing he wanted to do was discharge it because he was so jumpy his finger slipped.

He looked forward, directly across the lawn. The little church stood there. It looked more intact than the other buildings—some of its windows hadn't been broken, and the paint on its door hadn't peeled or been scratched off. Of all the buildings on the lawn it looked most like a place where someone might find shelter from the elements.

He whispered when he spoke to Julia. "I want you to turn the light off. We're going to the church. When I get to the door, we'll stand to one side of it. I'll cover the door with my weapon. When I say 'freeze,' you turn on the light and shine it inside. Okay?"

"Okay," she whispered back.

They moved forward faster now. If Chapel was wrong about this, they might both be dead. The chimera could be lying in wait anywhere on the lawn, ready to spring up and attack them. It was the best idea he had, however.

The door of the church was raised up on a narrow porch. Two steps went up to the porch. Their feet sounded on each step, but there was nothing to be done about that. On the porch Chapel pressed his back up against the front wall of the church and Julia did the same. He checked his weapon, made sure it hadn't been decocked when it fell from his hand. Then he nodded to Julia and swung around to point his pistol inside the church door, into the darkness inside.

"Freeze!" he shouted, though he could see nothing. Almost instantly the light burst into life behind him. Its beam speared inside the church and lit up a carved wooden crucifix on the far wall. The eyes of the figure on the cross had been blackened with a permanent marker.

At first Chapel thought he'd made a terrible mistake, that the church was empty and the chimera was probably right behind him. But then something moved among the pews inside, and he swiveled around to cover it with his weapon.

The chimera stood up very slowly, his black eyes wide in the light. He had a full, bushy beard, and his long hair was tangled up in the rags of a shirt he wore.

"Put your hands up!" Chapel demanded, expecting the chimera to jump right at him. At least this time he had a chance to shoot before he got knocked down and slaughtered.

Amazingly, though, the chimera obeyed him. Both hands came up and lifted above the chimera's head. Chapel kept his eyes on the chimera's face, looking for any sign he was about to be attacked.

"Chapel," Julia said, "his hands!"

Chapel glanced upward and saw what she meant.

The chimera had no fingers.

CAMP PUTNAM, NEW YORK: APRIL 14, T+47:01

The chimera started to lower his hands, as if he were ashamed of them.

"Keep them where I can see them," Chapel told him, and the chimera obeyed.

This made no sense. Based on what he'd seen for himself and what Ellie had told him, chimeras were impulsive and aggressive, unable to bear any kind of frustration or anger. This one acted like a human with a gun pointed at him.

"Chapel, he's terrified. Don't be such a man," Julia said.

"Seriously?"

"Look at him. He's half starved and he's shivering." Julia took a step forward. Chapel held out his free arm to stop her. At least she didn't run over and give the chimera a hug. "What's your name?" she asked.

The chimera looked at Chapel as if for permission to answer. When it didn't come, he said in a halting voice, "I'm Samuel. Are you going to kill me?"

"No," Julia said. "No. We're not going to hurt you at all. We're just trying to be careful. When was the last time you ate, Samuel?"

Now that he knew to look, Chapel saw the chimera's cheeks were sunken, and he was much smaller than the chimeras he'd seen outside the camp. His wrists were like sticks coming out of the sleeves of his tattered shirt.

"It's been a while. They used to throw food to us over the fence but . . . now I just get what I can catch, and it's not easy," Samuel said. "I can find some mushrooms, sometimes. But sometimes they make me throw up, and that's worse than eating nothing. There's tree bark, and every now and again I catch a fish. I have a net."

Julia lowered the light and Chapel expected Samuel to bolt, but he didn't. Julia rummaged around in her purse for a while, then brought out a half-eaten protein bar. "Here," she said, but Chapel stopped her from walking over to hand it to the chimera.

"Throw it to him," he said instead.

She tossed it underhand. He might be half dead with starvation, but Samuel was still a chimera. He caught it effortlessly between his two palms and tore the wrapper off with his teeth. He shoved half of it in his mouth all at once.

"I'm afraid that's all I have. The other half was my breakfast two days ago," she said, glancing at Chapel.

"That was when the fence came down," Samuel said, nodding. "When Ian and the others left, to follow the Voice."

"The Voice—" Chapel began, but Julia put a hand on his arm to stop him.

"Samuel, what happened to your fingers?" she asked.

"Frostbite. Six winters ago," the chimera said, his mouth full of granola and molasses. "I got in a fight with Mark, which—no fooling—I won, I totally killed him, but I was beat up pretty bad. I fell asleep in the snow and didn't wake up for three days. When I did wake up, I couldn't feel my fingers or my toes. Ian cut them off for me with an axe, so I didn't die from rotting."

Jesus, Chapel thought. The fence would already have been closed off by then. There would have been no medical care in the camp at all. Samuel was lucky to have lived through that. If he hadn't been a chimera, maybe he wouldn't have.

"That must have made it hard to fight, afterward," Julia said, her voice calm and soothing. Chapel realized she must be using the same voice she used when she spoke to dogs and cats.

"Sure did. Some of the others, they picked on me; they would beat me up just for fun because I wasn't a threat anymore. But Ian stopped that. He took me on as a mascot. He protected me and made sure I got some food, though not as much as the others. That's how come I'm so small."

Another chimera. Impossible—they'd all been accounted for. Hollingshead had said as much in his briefing. There had been six detainees when the fence came down, two who were killed in the escape and four who made it out.

No—wait. Hollingshead had said there were seven, but that the seventh was presumed dead. Why he'd been presumed dead had been something Chapel didn't need to know.

"Why are you still here?" Chapel asked. "If Ian liked you so much, why didn't he take you with him when he left? Or later, you could have just walked out on your own."

Samuel shrugged. "Where would I go? I don't know nothing about the world. I know the camp pretty good, but that's it. And anyway, the Voice didn't want me."

"You mean the Voice didn't tell you who to kill?" Chapel asked.

"Yeah. The Voice said I was useless. It told Ian to kill me before they left, and he said he would. I got so scared. But Ian just took me out to the baseball field, that's a ways north of here. He told me what the Voice said, and that he wasn't going to do it. He said the Voice wasn't like Miss P, or like the doctors, and he didn't have to do what it said. That he was his own master. He cut me a little, and wiped my blood on his hand, so he could show the others and tell them he'd killed me. Then he told me to run into the woods and hide until they were gone. I did what he said. Ian was like Miss P. I always did what he said. I'm a good boy."

Miss P had to be Ellie Pechowski. Their teacher. Chapel was certain the doctors he meant were Helen Bryant and William Taggart.

"You heard this Voice?" Chapel asked. "It spoke to you?"

"Sure," Samuel said, licking the wrapper from the protein bar. "It spoke to all of us. You want to see it?"

See the Voice? "Very much so," Chapel told him.

Samuel went over to the church's altar and picked something up, using both hands. Chapel knew how hard it could be to manipulate small objects with one good hand. He could imagine it must be much harder with no fingers. But Samuel held the object easily, then tossed it toward Chapel.

He managed to catch it with his free hand. "Give me some light," he told Julia.

She shone it on the object he held. It was a cellular phone, a cheap prepaid model with a black case. One side was badly scuffed. Chapel tried to turn it on, but the battery was dead. He put it in his pocket.

"Hey, you can't have that! That's the Voice!" Samuel said, and took a step toward them.

Chapel raised his pistol. Samuel's face contorted and his fingerless hands shook and Chapel wondered if he would finally revert to form, change into one of the violent, aggressive chimeras he had met before.

But slowly, and with visible effort, Samuel calmed himself down. "I get it," he said. "You're like Miss P, too. Or Ian. I'll do what you say. I'm a good boy."

"Okay, then," Chapel said. "Why don't you sit down, and tell me a story."

CAMP PUTNAM, NEW YORK: APRIL 14, T+47:25

It took a while for Samuel to get started. Chapel had to prod him, ask leading questions, and finally take him all the way back to when Malcolm escaped, back when they were still just children. Once Samuel got started, though, he seemed to almost fall into a trance. The words he spoke sounded like an oft-repeated history lesson, a text he'd memorized.

"When the fence was closed, when they took the gate away, things changed," he said, looking into the middle distance. "They brought Malcolm back to us. Many were jealous of him, and angry. They said it was his fault the fence was closed. They said because of him, we would never leave here.

"Many of them wanted to kill him. They thought that would make it easier to bear. Ian said no. Ian had many friends, even then, though no one thought of him as their leader. Not yet. Ian said he would talk to the humans. He would talk to Miss P and she would get us out. She would free us.

"He went so many times to her platform. He begged her for help, for forgiveness. He spoke with the doctors, too. He listened when they spoke to him through their megaphones and he shouted back, he shouted back all kinds of promises.

"The rest of us were close by, hiding in the trees. We listened to the things he said. He had an idea, a vision he called it, of what we could become. Not everyone agreed with it. When he couldn't make the humans change their minds, some of them decided it was his fault. Ian's. After all, he had come up with the idea, the plan, that let Malcolm get away.

"Some of them, they tried to kill Ian on their own. They challenged him or ambushed him in the trees, or tried to steal his food and starve him. He beat everyone who came for him. He killed them if he had to. So his enemies, they got smart, and they joined together. They made the first gang.

"That was called the Blame War. It was our first war. It was bloody and many died. The worst was the Battle of the High Oaks. Ian had retreated to a place on a hill, northwest of here. Malcolm was with him and swore oaths to him. Quinn was with him, too, Quinn who was always the strongest.

"The gang came for them on a rainy night. Nobody could see. The gang was led by Franklin, who was almost smart as Ian, and almost strong as Quinn. But not enough of either. Quinn was the great hero then and killed many. But in the morning, Ian was our leader. He told us what to do."

Chapel's eyes went wide listening to the story. It was amazing to him—this little world had its own history, its heroes and its villains. Walled away from the world, the chimeras had created their own struggles, their own nations.

"He had a way for us to live," Samuel went on. "A way to survive. We would each go and make our own place, our own house, as far away from each other as we could stand. We would come together only when the food was thrown over the fence, and then only to share it out. It was too dangerous for us to be together.

"It worked, for a while. Winters were hard. It gets

so cold here, and the snow is so deep, and it's hard to stay warm. Some of us made new gangs and slept all in a house together, even though Ian said not to. Some of the gangs thought Ian was no good, and they wanted a new leader. There were more wars then. But Ian always won. When they challenged him, he fought back, though always he tried not to kill. Already there were so few of us left. He said the humans wanted us to kill each other off. To destroy each other, so they wouldn't have to think about us anymore."

Julia shot Chapel a glance, and he knew what she was thinking. From the sound of it, and what Ellie had told them, that probably wasn't too far from the truth.

"Ian said we couldn't give the humans what they wanted. Too long, we'd tried to be good boys. We did what Miss P and the doctors told us. We listened when the guards talked. Ian said they'd turned their backs on us, and now we had a duty to be better on our own. A duty to live.

"Still, we were chimeras. And that meant we fought. Chimeras always fight. So Ian made new rules. He made rules about how fights could go, and what you could and couldn't do. No weapons. No killing someone who was already unconscious. No killing a chimera who couldn't fight back—that rule was about me," Samuel said, looking glum. "He had to make that rule so I could live."

He shook his head and went on. "Most times, we followed his rules, and we lived. Nobody died for many years. We ate what was thrown over the fence. We lived in our own little houses in the woods. We stayed apart. Sometimes, one of us would steal food or take something from another's house. Then we had to come together. The two chimeras who disagreed, the one who claimed he'd been stolen from and the one he said did it, they would fight. Only with fists, that was the rule. And then Ian would say who won, and it was the one who followed his rules better. We would stand in a circle, with the fighters in the middle, and the one who broke a rule first we would grab and pull away and beat until he was unconscious, and that was that.

"It worked. For years it worked. Until they made the last gangs.

"Alan was the leader of one gang. Him and his three, they said they were done. That Ian wasn't a doctor, and he wasn't like Miss P, and they didn't have to do what he said. It started because there was less food; there were times, whole weeks, when no food came over the fence. What did come, Ian split up among us all, but Alan said no. He said only the strong should have food. He said I should be left to starve. Ian challenged him to come to the ring, to send the best man of his gang to stand in the circle and fight it out with Ian's best man, but Alan said that was stupid. Ian had Quinn, who could beat anybody in the ring. Alan took a bunch of food that wasn't his and said it belonged to his gang, and they were going to go live out by the pond, and if Ian wanted the food back, he could come and get it.

"Ian went alone, just to talk. He said, if Alan and his whole gang would come here, to the church, he would give them a bunch of stuff he'd been hiding. He said he had a radio and some books and a lot of medicine, and he would share it. It was a lie, but they didn't know that.

"Ian waited for them here. He was waiting with Quinn, and Brody, and Malcolm, and Stephen, and with Harrison. They waited here in the church and they had knives they made from broken windows. Alan and his gang came, all four of them, and when they weren't looking, Ian and his gang cut them and killed them."

Chapel gasped. "The four in the schoolhouse," he said. "The bodies hanging on the blackboard—"

"That's them," Samuel agreed. "He put them there and told me he did it for me. So I could eat and not starve. I keep the animals away from those bodies and make sure they don't fall down."

"The words next to them," Chapel said. "It says 'we did this together.'"

"Sure," Samuel said. "Ian wrote that. Him and his gang, they broke the rules, they used weapons when they did it. They broke Ian's own rules. But he said that was all right because they did it together. If they worked together instead of against each other, then the rules didn't apply."

Sharing the guilt, Chapel thought. Ian didn't want them to turn on him so he'd made sure they were all implicated.

"This can't have been that long ago," Julia said. "Those bodies weren't that old."

Samuel nodded. "This was just last fall, when the leaves were red. Just before the Voice came."

CAMP PUTNAM, NEW YORK: APRIL 14, T+47:59

"Some of them, some of Ian's gang, they thought the Voice was a sign. They said the doctors had been waiting and watching, that they had wanted us to prove ourselves. That we'd passed some test, and that's why the Voice came. Some of us just thought it was because there were so few left. The Voice needed us and wanted to reach us before we were all gone. All dead." Samuel shook his head. "I don't know. I just know when it came, it changed things. It changed everything."

"How did the Voice come, Samuel?" Julia asked. "Where did it come from?"

"From heaven," he told her.

"It came down from the sky," he went on, when she wrinkled her nose in distaste. "You can call it what you want. It came on a parachute, a little parachute that got caught in a tree near here. It came down and it was talking already, even before we found it. It was saying the same thing, over and over. It said 'Press the green button.' It said that for hours while Ian and his gang, they stared at it, wondering if it was a trick, wondering what would happen. Quinn thought if he pressed the green button, they would all die. Brody thought it would make more food come. There was hardly any food then, and there's been none since, so I guess Brody was wrong.

"In the end it was Ian who pressed the green button. Who made the Voice come.

"It spoke to them all by name. It knew who they were, and it said it would give them the thing they wanted most. It would make them free. For most of a day it talked, making promises, telling them how strong they were, and how smart. How they were better than humans. Ian spoke back to it, and it answered him. He asked what the Voice wanted in exchange for freeing them. And it told them.

"Eight humans had to die. That was all. Eight humans and then they would be free forever. It would even help them do it. At first Ian thought it had to be a trick. Miss P and the doctors always said if we killed humans we would be punished. How could that be wrong back then, back when Miss P said it, but right now, when she was gone? But the Voice kept talking.

"It said the eight humans were people Ian and his gang wanted to kill anyway. It said they had to kill Jeremy Funt, who caught Malcolm when he ran away. It said they had to kill the doctors and Miss P for abandoning us. There were other names, too, names I didn't know."

"Christina Smollett," Chapel said. "Olivia Nguyen. Marcia Kennedy."

Samuel bobbed up and down in surprise and excitement. "Yes! I don't know who those are. The Voice said they were responsible for us being here, for us being locked up. It said they deserved to die like the rest."

"What about Franklin Hayes?" Chapel asked. "You must know that name."

Samuel shook his head in the negative. "No. I don't know him. But the Voice said he was the worst of all, the one who deserved to die the most. It said Quinn had to kill him. The others could choose who they went after, but Quinn had to kill Franklin Hayes. The Voice told them it would help them, it would show them where these humans lived, and make it easy. And then they would be free."

Chapel frowned. He'd hoped that Samuel would have heard something more useful. He'd hoped the Voice might have told them its own name, or why the mentally ill women were on the kill list, or something. But he supposed that had been too much to wish for.

"The Voice told them the fence would come down. They might have to fight a little to get out, but they were chimeras and that shouldn't worry them. It told them it would always be with them, as long as they did what it asked, and it would help them.

"And they listened. They listened, and they did what it said.

"Except—Ian wouldn't kill me. He disobeyed the Voice in that," Samuel said, and he sounded confused. He sounded like he couldn't understand why he was still alive.

"They left you here all alone," Julia said. "Ian left you here."

Samuel shook his head violently. "No, he—he said he would come back for me. He said I would be okay!"

"It's all right," Julia soothed. "It's okay. You're going to be fine, now. We'll take care of you."

We will? Chapel thought. Didn't she hear what Samuel had said, what he'd told her about wars and gangs and constant bloodshed? Samuel might have a childlike mind and a naiveté born of isolation but he was still a killer. He was still a chimera.

"Isn't that right, Chapel? We'll take him with us, make sure he's okay?" she asked.

Chapel looked up, realizing suddenly that he'd been lost in thought. "We'll figure something out," he said.

"No," Samuel told them. "No, I'm fine here."

"Oh, sweetie, no," Julia told him. "I can already tell you're half starved to death, and it's too cold here to—"

"I said I'm fine! I'm staying!" Samuel shrieked. He jumped up and loomed over Julia like he was about to attack her.

It had come out of nowhere. Chapel should have expected it, though—he knew what the chimeras were like. They were implacable killing machines. He raised his pistol to point right at Samuel's face—

—but before he could fire, Samuel had smacked the flashlight out of Julia's hand and dashed into the shadows. Chapel tried to track him, sure he would flank them and attack where they weren't expecting him. He swung around wildly, pointing his weapon into every corner of the room, trying to cover all angles while Julia groped around on the floor for the light.

By the time she had it, Samuel was gone.

He'd simply vanished without a trace.

"It's broken," Julia said.

Chapel turned to look at her. She was holding up the flashlight and flicking its switch back and forth. "It's broken," she said again.

Chapel wondered how they would find their way back to the gap in the fence without it—but then he realized he could see her face, even in the darkened church. A little pink light lit up her cheek. It made him think of the sunset on Stone Mountain, the day they'd made love.

He turned around and looked at the door of the church. Its frame glowed with the same pink light. He staggered outside, tripping on debris, and saw a haze of light over the tops of the skeletal trees.

He'd been so wrapped up in Samuel's story that he hadn't noticed the sun coming up. It was dawn light streaming in, dawn light he'd seen.

Which meant he had a major problem on his hands.

CAMP PUTNAM, NEW YORK: APRIL 14, T+48:20

"Samuel!" Julia called. "Samuel! Come back!"

Chapel reached for her arm. "Julia, you have to let him go."

"He needs help," she told him. "Medical help. Or are you going to tell me he's a chimera and he doesn't deserve it? Because one of them killed my mother?"

"I'm going to tell you we're screwed. The sun is up."

"It tends to do that this time in the morning," she told him. She looked angry, but he was pretty sure she wasn't angry with him. He guessed she was angry at her parents, who had created Camp Putnam and populated it with sad monsters. So angry she couldn't help but express it, and he happened to be standing nearby.

"Listen, we'll come back for him, I promise. But

there are people out there who need to be saved right now." Like Franklin Hayes. Chapel still didn't know why Hayes was on the kill list. But it sounded like he'd been singled out for special consideration. Banks and Hollingshead had both told Chapel that Hayes was the most important target on the list; he'd assumed they just thought that because he was politically connected. It looked like the Voice—and the chimeras—had their own reasons to hate him.

Chapel glanced at the sky again. "We need to get out of here now. Once the sun is up, sneaking past that guard will become impossible. We barely made it in the pitch dark. And if he catches us—"

"I see your point," she said.

Together they raced for the trees. Finding their way back wasn't going to be easy—they had wandered quite a ways in the dark, just following the forest paths, because they hadn't known what they were looking for. They'd had a working flashlight, too. Even with dawn coming up, the trees screened out most of the light and it was still almost midnight dark under their groping branches.

Chapel headed southeast, his best guess at where the gap in the fence lay. He knew there was almost no chance of reaching the exit before the sun was fully up, but he had to try. Any amount of cover could make a difference. Every beam of light that hit the gap would make it harder to escape unnoticed.

The path wound and snaked about, and he cursed every time they had to double back because the trees were just too thick to pass. Growing up he'd spent some time in Florida's swamps and he knew all about undergrowth and how it could tangle you up. He knew forests like this and he knew they were death traps—even if this one didn't have any alligators in it, or sucking bogs so deep you could fall in and never be found. This forest had its own dangers.

He tried not to think about that. He tried to keep one eye on his feet, watching for exposed tree roots or piles of leaf litter that could hide all kinds of obstacles. But the forest just wasn't built for running.

"There," Julia said, finally. She was out of breath, but she grabbed his arm with one hand and pointed with the other. "That shack. I remember it."

Chapel could see why. It was a collapsed hovel like all the others they'd seen, maybe one of the places the chimeras had retreated to when Ian told them to split up. Only one wall remained intact, the roof having collapsed and taken the other walls with it. But the intact wall was decorated with hundreds of tiny skulls. They looked like fox skulls to Chapel.

"My God, it's even creepier in daylight," she said.

Chapel grunted in frustration. He looked up and saw the sun had fully risen. It was too late to try to just sneak out.

Even though they were so close to the gap in the fence. "That was the first shack we saw when we came in, wasn't it?" he asked.

"Yeah," Julia said. "The fence is just a little ways over there." She pointed at a stand of woods that looked like every other group of trees.

"It is?" Chapel asked. "How can you know that?"

"We came north by northwest when we entered. We'd gone less than a quarter mile when we saw this place."

Chapel could only stare at her.

"What?" she asked.

"How could you know that?"

She just stood there for a while catching her breath. "Girl Scouts," she told him. "Orienteering award."

"You," he said, "keep surprising me with just how incredible you are."

"Sweet," she told him. "Now. How do we do this without getting shot?"

Somewhere nearby someone stepped on a pile of pine needles.

Somebody who wasn't one of them.

Chapel whirled around—and saw motion between two trees. It still wasn't light enough for him to see what it was. Maybe an animal. Maybe Samuel.

He put out one hand to signal to Julia that she should stay very still and not speak. She seemed to get the point. Chapel closed his eyes and just listened for a moment. He heard more footsteps, coming closer. Very slowly.

"Damn," he said, very softly. Mostly to himself. Then, much louder, "I am a federal agent. I am armed, but my weapon will remain in its holster. My companion is a civilian, and she is not armed."

Julia stared at him like he'd gone crazy—at least, until a few seconds later, when soldiers poured out of the trees and surrounded them.

IN TRANSIT: APRIL 14, T+49:06

They took away Chapel's phone, his hands-free set, the scuffed-up phone Samuel had called the Voice, and of course, his pistol. They left him his arm, even after one of the soldiers pulled the glove off his left hand and found what lay beneath. They handcuffed him with his hands behind his back, then forced him at gunpoint through the gap in the fence and into the back of an old M35 truck—a "deuce and a half," a two-and-a-half-ton truck of the kind the military used all over the world.

What happened to Julia he didn't get to see. None of the soldiers hit him or mistreated him in any way, so he could only hope they'd extended her the same courtesy.

He did not ask any questions or speak at all except when they demanded he identify himself. He gave them his name, his rank, and his serial number. They didn't ask for anything else.

He got a good look at their uniforms and saw they were navy—most likely they'd been drawn from the Naval Support Unit at Saratoga Springs. Sailors, then, seamen rather than soldiers. They weren't SEALs, he could tell that much, but they were well trained and efficient. They carried M4 carbines—but not M4-A1s, which meant they probably weren't Special Forces.

Observing little details like that helped him keep his cool. Just like Julia had dealt with the horrors of Camp Putnam by falling back on her medical training.

Besides, he had little else to do while he waited to find out what was going to happen to him.

The back of the truck was cold and drafty—it lacked a hard top, instead just having a canvas cover. It smelled like grease and old boots. That was a comforting smell to Chapel—it reminded him of his early days in the army. It also made him think he wasn't being detained by the CIA.

That was something, anyway. He consoled himself while the truck bounced and rolled over gravel roads, carrying him away from Camp Putnam.

In time the truck stopped and the engine was switched off. Chapel closed his eyes and listened to every sound he could hear. He heard the sailors moving around the truck, heard them click their heels as they saluted someone. He heard other vehicles moving around. And yes—there—the sound of a helicopter's rotor powering down.

He heard boots crunching on gravel outside the truck. Heard sailors come closer, and he knew they were coming to get him. He had no idea what to expect.

He was unable to keep his jaw from dropping when Rupert Hollingshead jumped up into the back of the truck and stared at him with a cold and angry eye.

NAVAL SUPPORT UNIT SARATOGA SPRINGS, NEW YORK: APRIL 14, T+50:21

"Admiral," Chapel said. "Please forgive me for not saluting."

Hollingshead just glared at him for a while. The DIA director was wearing an immaculate suit with a perfectly folded handkerchief in his breast pocket. His bow tie had a pattern of anchors on it, but otherwise he looked very much the civilian, just as he had the last time Chapel saw him, back at the Pentagon.

He was carrying a stool, a folding three-legged stool that he assembled and set down next to him. Eventually he sat down on it and crossed his legs, his hands gripping one knee. He said nothing, but he kept looking at Chapel, utter disappointment on his face.

The silence between them took on its own life. It made Chapel want to squirm. It made him want to explain himself. He did not do these things.

Eventually it was Hollingshead who broke the silence. "The life of an officer is quite lonely, at times. You see, son, an officer can't afford to have friends."

Chapel stayed at attention. He had not been put at ease.

"An officer always has a superior to whom he must report. No friends there, I assure you. Then he has men and women under his command. A good officer will have good people—if they aren't good people when they are assigned to him, he turns them into good people. That's what I was taught by my commanders, anyway. He learns to respect them, their hard work, their sacrifice; these things make them special in his eyes. They make him proud, and he comes to, ah, love them, in his very special way, I suppose. But he can't ever forget he's responsible for them. That their actions, in a very real, very concrete way, are his actions, and so—when it becomes necessary—when he must—he has to punish them. In accord with their offenses. When they break the rules, you see."

When Chapel was sixteen he'd been caught, once,

sneaking out of a girl's bedroom window. The man who'd caught him was the girl's father, who didn't approve of her seeing Chapel. The girl's father had been carrying a pistol at the time.

At that particular moment, listening to Hollingshead describe the burdens of leadership, Chapel remembered that long ago summer's night with exquisite fondness. As scared as he'd been, as ashamed, it wasn't a patch on this.

"I'd like you to answer some questions, Captain, just so I can sleep better tonight. So I can be content in knowing I did the right thing, here."

"Sir, yes, sir," Chapel said.

"When Angel relayed to you my direct order that you were not to come to the Catskills, but to instead proceed directly to Denver, was your equipment functional? Your telephone and your—your—hands-free unit, I believe it is called?"

"Sir, yes—"

"Just yes or no, please."

Chapel bit his lip. "Yes," he said.

"So you did hear her correctly? The order was received without transmission errors? You understood the order and acknowledged it?"

"Yes."

Hollingshead nodded. "All right. Let's try another question. Were you at any time under the impression that Julia Taggart had a security clearance that would allow her to know—oh, anything—about your current mission?"

"No, sir, but—"

"Just yes or no, Captain."

"No."

Hollingshead sighed. "So when you interrogated Jeremy Funt, say, or when you spoke with Ellie Pechowski—oh, I heard everything she told you, I'll be having words with her as well. Oh, my, yes. And let us not forget, when you infiltrated a Department of Defense secure facility with Julia at your side, were you in any way operating under the delusion that Julia had a need to know what you found?"

Chapel supposed he deserved that. What he didn't deserve was to be spoken to like a child. But he held his tongue. "No," he said.

"No. No, I don't suppose you would have been that foolish. You were recommended to me as a man who actually understood secrecy and the importance of national security. I might ask you many more questions, son. I might sit here all day asking them. I might also have you brought up on charges of espionage and treason, which—while perhaps not the best descriptions for the very, very foolish things you've done—are the best words I have to describe them. You—"

"Sir. Permission to speak candidly," Chapel said. Interrupting Hollingshead was insubordination, but compared to espionage and treason it wasn't much of a crime.

"Oh, but of course, son, I'd never dream of anything else. I so very much want to hear your explanation for what you've done."

Chapel inhaled sharply. "She had no need to know, as we define that term in the intelligence community. But if anyone on earth had a *right* to know, it was her."

Hollingshead waited, a patient expression on his

face, as if he expected Chapel to say more. Chapel chose not to do so.

"Let's put her aside for a moment," the admiral eventually said. "We'll also put aside the utter na- iveté and silliness of your last statement."

Chapel bit his lip to keep from responding. The shame he felt had kept his anger under wraps until then. It had kept him from even feeling it. But there was a time to just accept that you were being chewed out, that you deserved to be called a fool. And there was a time when that stopped.

He was getting pretty close to that moment.

Hollingshead sighed and continued. "Let's in- stead talk about how I failed you. How I made an utter mess of this thing."

"Sir?"

"I said something to you just before you left the Pentagon. I told you to follow the clues. To figure out what was really going on here."

"Yes, sir, you did, which is exactly what I've been—"

Hollingshead lifted one hand.

Chapel fell silent.

"I meant, you see, and—now this is where it be- comes my fault—I meant that you should figure out what the CIA wanted out of all this. Why, say, they were so anxious to handle it themselves. I don't be- lieve you've done much in that regard, other than shooting the toes off a special agent. Instead of the investigation I wished you to complete, you took it upon yourself to dig up the secrets of a very old, very moribund project that it behooves no one—no one at all, son—to know about. About which you certainly have no need to know."

"My orders were to catch or kill the chimeras, sir. To know how to do that I needed to know what they were," Chapel said.

Hollingshead's eyes sparkled.

Which made Chapel think he'd made a mistake.

"Ah! Finally! We have some insight, a little window into the soul of James Chapel and why he chose to do all this. But that doesn't make it all better. Or does it?"

"No. Sir," Chapel said, though it made his teeth grind.

"No, no, because you found nothing in the camp. Because, of course, there was nothing to be found but some very old, very sad secrets. You wasted all that time, son. You wasted it for nothing."

Chapel opened his mouth, but then he closed it again quickly.

Hollingshead didn't know about Samuel. He didn't know Samuel was still alive.

It was probably best for Samuel that it remain that way.

But after what Chapel had seen in Camp Putnam—after what he'd learned—he could not remain silent. He had taken a vow to serve his country. To obey his superior officers. But there were times when even that vow had to be broken.

"You're wrong, sir. I did find something there."

It was gratifying to see Hollingshead look surprised for once. The man who knew everything, the spider at the center of the web of secrets, looked like he'd been punched in the face. His eyes were very wide as he waited to hear what Chapel said next.

"I found evil," Chapel said. "What happened in that camp was nothing short of criminal. What was done there—what happened to those boys—"

"Boys who grew up to be killers," Hollingshead interjected.

But Chapel wouldn't be derailed. Justice was at stake. "Maybe. Maybe we made them that way. We talk about the chimeras as if they're monsters. And I won't deny that they do monstrous things. But they're still ninety-nine percent human. And I figure that means they should have had the same rights as you and me. But they weren't given those rights. They were tortured in there, starved, neglected, and abandoned."

"I won't speak to this," Hollingshead sputtered. "And if you're wise, you'll—"

"No, sir, I won't shut up. They were children. And they were tortured. That's not something that can just stand. Someone's going to have to pay."

NAVAL SUPPORT UNIT SARATOGA SPRINGS, NEW YORK: APRIL 14, T+50:31

Hollingshead was quiet for a very long time. He took off his glasses and folded them carefully. Put them in a pocket of his vest. Chapel couldn't read anything in his face or his body language. He couldn't tell what Hollingshead was about to do.

Not that it mattered. Chapel knew his career was already over. That he'd be lucky not to be arrested and thrown in prison for the rest of his life, after what he'd done.

He didn't regret a single word he'd said.

"I . . . see," Hollingshead said, finally. "Have you . . . well. I suppose I should ask what you think you're going to do now. How you intend to attain this hypothetical justice. Are you going to go to the media? Reveal classified information to the public? Write a book about what you've seen and go on Larry King to talk about it?"

Chapel frowned. That was one thing he hadn't considered. Something had to be done. But what? "No, sir, I don't suppose I will," he admitted. "I did take an oath not to do that sort of thing."

"Then . . . perhaps you'll try to get justice from within the DIA? File reports with some oversight committee or other, make a nuisance of yourself? Will you write a carefully composed e-mail to the president?"

Chapel felt the wind go right out of him. That was more in line with what he *could* do. But he also knew that it would achieve exactly nothing. There were people out there who were responsible for Camp Putnam, but they were people in positions of influence, and people like that didn't respond well to being called out. They would go into damage control mode. Shift blame. Implicate Chapel in the whole thing and make sure he took the fall for what they'd done. It was how any bureaucracy worked.

"No," Hollingshead said, "I can see it in your eyes. You're too smart to throw your life away like that, either. If it will accomplish nothing. Well"—he sighed—"son, maybe you should think more on what you're going to do. But perhaps you can wait on that until you're done with your assignment."

"I—sir?" Chapel was deeply confused. Hollingshead couldn't mean what he'd just implied, could he?

"I'm sending you to Denver, right now," Hollingshead said. "Come now, Captain. You look honestly surprised."

"I suppose I didn't expect that after . . . what I said," he tried.

"Oh, Captain, I assure you. I have not yet begun to chew you out, as the men say. This conversation will continue at some future date. But I need you in Denver because there is a chimera there about to try to kill Franklin Hayes. Quite clearly, I have no time to brief or ready anyone else. Director Banks and I agree that what we need, right now, is boots on the ground—not stewing in a cell in some loathsome brig. So you will go to Denver and you will continue the job we assigned you."

"Sir?" Chapel asked. And he knew it was over. He wasn't going to get his moment of righteous indignation after all. It burned inside him still, but Hollingshead had moved on. Cut the floor out from under Chapel's feet and gotten back to what mattered to him.

"There will be a chimera attack in Denver, and it will happen today," Hollingshead said. His tone told Chapel this was not speculation. "The judge's security team will not be prepared to defeat it. If you aren't there, son, loaded for bear and knowing what you know—it will succeed."

"It . . . will," Chapel said. He knew he would not

be allowed to know how Hollingshead could be so certain.

"And if that happens, Tom Banks will win."

"Win," Chapel said. Because he couldn't think of what else to say.

He had been mistaken, it seemed. He had been mistaken all along. He'd thought Hollingshead had given him this mission so he could protect the people on the list.

That had been foolish, it seemed. Apparently, to both the CIA and the Pentagon, this was a *game*.

Hollingshead rose stiffly to his feet, then pulled back the canvas cover at the back of the truck. "Follow me, please," the admiral said.

Chapel followed him out of the truck and down onto a concrete surface that he thought he recognized. He looked up and saw that he'd been brought to the same airport in the Catskills where he'd landed the night before. Hollingshead's jet was sitting on the runway, ready to take off. Nearby was the helicopter Chapel had heard—it must have brought Hollingshead here.

A sailor came up to unlock Chapel's handcuffs. The same sailor returned his phone, his hands-free set, and his sidearm. He checked the action and the magazine and saw it had been cleaned and reloaded for him.

He had begun to suspect that Hollingshead wasn't on his side. That the admiral was working against him in some nefarious way. He lacked any real proof or any good reason to believe that other than a hunch and a few scraps of half-certain information.

Now this—all this, the guilt trip, the threats of criminal charges, the sudden reversal and reinstatement . . . was it all part of the deeper game? Was it just a way to make Chapel step back in line?

That was intelligence work for you. It was impossible to ever really know who you could trust.

Hollingshead met Chapel's eye one last time before sending him away. "You will protect Franklin Hayes to the utmost of your ability," the admiral said. "When that is done . . . we will address your future. But for right now, Chapel, I need you—God protect us all."

Chapel climbed inside the jet, and Chief Petty Officer Andrews closed the hatch.

When she'd finished, the CPO turned to give Chapel a long and questioning look. "I've got new orders, now," she said.

"I know. You're taking me to Denver."

She nodded. "And if you try to divert the plane, I'm supposed to shoot you. Are you going to push it, or do you want to sit down and wait until I have the towels heated and your breakfast cooked?"

Chapel hadn't eaten or slept in quite a while. "I'll be a good boy," he said.

She nodded and headed toward the back of the cabin. "It's almost four hours to Denver from here. Get comfortable."

Chapel nodded and headed toward one of the seats, intending to sit down and promptly pass out.

Before he could even pick which seat looked the most comfortable, though, one of them swiveled around and Julia jumped out of it, rushing over to put her arms around him.

He was surprised to see her there, to say the least. After what Hollingshead had said to him in the truck, he assumed he would never see her again. "Are you all right?" he asked her.

She nodded, her head against his shoulder. "They asked me a million questions, but nobody beat me with a rubber hose or anything, if that's what you mean. Then that nice old man—your boss, right?—he told me to get on the plane. He said I was your responsibility now, and you'd have to figure out what to do with me."

None of this made any sense, Chapel thought. Not a bit.

He knew he was glad to see her, though. He lifted his hand to stroke her back.

And just like that the moment between them was over. She pushed him away, and when he looked in her face again, he saw she had recovered herself, that she was back to their professional relationship.

But for a second there, when she'd first seen him, there'd been something more. She had looked to him for something not professional at all—comfort. She must have been terrified when the navy men interrogated her. She must have wondered if she would ever see daylight again. So when she saw Chapel, she'd known that she was going to be okay, and she had run to him in relief. Maybe that was all there was to it. But maybe . . .

He shook his head and forced himself not to think stupid thoughts.

IN TRANSIT: APRIL 14, T+51:07

Julia was exhausted enough that she fell asleep soon
after they took off, but Chapel still had some work
to do. He would try to take a nap before they landed
in Denver—his body was certainly ready for it—but
he needed at least some information on what he was
getting himself into.

So he plugged the hands-free set into his ear.

"Angel," he said, "are you online?"

"I'm here, Captain," she said.

Chapel closed his eyes. This wasn't going to be
fun. "So it's Captain, now. Not sweetie, or sugar?"

"Do you have any idea how much trouble you've
gotten me in?" Angel asked. She didn't sound particularly angry, though. More concerned.

"I'm sorry, Angel. I truly am."

"Apparently—and I have this from on high—I'll
be listed as a conspirator when they charge you for
espionage. That means I could face the same penalty you do. Do you know what the penalty is for
espionage?"

"All too well. Listen, Angel, it won't come to
that. Conspiracy charges are just a way to get ac-
complices to provide information on the principal
in any investigation. Which means if you tell them
everything, they'll let you off."

"You mean, if I throw you under the bus."

"It's not a betrayal if I tell you it's okay," Chapel
said. "I don't want you to suffer because I made
some bad decisions."

Angel sounded a little less upset, but she still didn't call him sweetie. "Okay, okay, enough. We can have a blame party later," Angel said. "Tell me what you need now. And I'll let you know if you're approved for it."

"I just need to know about Franklin Hayes. Is he still alive, at least?"

"Yes. And just as ornery as ever. He's been calling me constantly, or at least his office has, demanding updates on when you're going to arrive. Right now I have you down for landing in Denver about half past eleven, local time."

"What about the chimera?" *Quinn*, he thought, *it's Quinn who will be there.*

"He might already be in Denver. By the time you land, he'll have more than a five-hour head start on you."

That wasn't good. But it was encouraging to know that Quinn hadn't already struck. "What do you know about security on-site?"

"It's pretty solid. Judge Hayes is surrounded by Colorado Highway Patrol officers. That's the closest thing they have to a state police force. He has some private bodyguards as well. I've seen their dossiers. They've all got security clearances, though nothing near what they would need to be told what's coming for the judge. They're all former Blackwater or Halliburton guys. Most of them were civilian contractors in Iraq."

Private security. Civilian contractors. Mercenaries, to give them their proper name. Chapel had met plenty of those in Afghanistan and had never had a high opinion of them—they weren't military but liked pretending they were. Well, at least they'd be likely to know how to shoot straight.

Not, apparently, that it would matter. Hollingshead had been clear on that—the judge's security team wouldn't be enough. "Are they ready for me to take over when I arrive?"

"Not quite. A man named Reinhard is the head of security there, one of the private bodyguards. He sent me an itinerary. Once you reach Denver and meet with the judge, they're going to move him to a safehouse somewhere outside of the city. He'll turn over all authority to you once Hayes is installed there."

"Huh," Chapel said. "That's a weird move. He'll be vulnerable during the transfer. The chimera could attack his car."

"I worried about that, too. Especially since we know somebody is telling the chimeras where their targets are. I haven't forgotten what happened at Stone Mountain. That probably explains why they won't tell me the location of this safehouse."

Chapel's eyes went wide. "So I can't know in advance where I'll be protecting the judge." He shook his head. "This has catastrophe written all over it."

And he was going to be the man who took the blame if it went wrong.

IN TRANSIT: APRIL 14, T+52:10

Chapel sighed and sank back into his chair. "I need to know about Franklin Hayes. He's a federal judge, I know that much. He's supposed to become the next Supreme Court justice as well. Beyond that, what's his story?"

"He worked for the CIA, you already know that," Angel replied. "He became a judge in 1994 in Denver—he was appointed by the mayor of Denver to oversee a county court. In that position he would mostly have heard cases relating to traffic citations and misdemeanors. It's not a very glamorous position, but it was a stepping-stone for him, a way into the judiciary. He worked his way up to the Colorado Supreme Court by 2003, and then switched over to his current position as a federal judge. As for becoming a Supreme Court justice, I'm not sure he'll make it."

"No?" Chapel asked. "Every time they talk about him on CNN or Fox News it sounds like he's a shoo-in."

"The president's appointment went through just fine, and the judge's record is squeaky clean. But he still has to get past the Senate, and given the political situation right now, he's facing a pretty tough confirmation hearing."

"He's some kind of activist judge?" Chapel asked. "Or is it the other side that doesn't like him—is he rabidly antiabortion or something?"

Angel worked her keyboard for a while. "Nothing like that, nothing that simple. He's a pretty solid moderate when it comes to politics—which is a tough thing to be in these partisan times. It takes a really slick judge to avoid ruffling everybody's feathers, but Hayes has managed to avoid the usual pitfalls. Except once. His Achilles' heel is a single motion he ruled on in 2002. It was a domestic terrorism case. The guy in question set fire to a federal building, and three people inside burned to death. The federal government wanted him remanded to the custody of the Justice Department—they wanted to interrogate him and find out who he had worked with. Hayes threw out the request on a minor technicality. The terrorist stayed in a state prison, served out his term, and was released seven years later."

"He did that in 2002?" Chapel frowned. "Back then everyone in the country was still pretty gung ho about anything that even resembled terrorism. It must have been an unpopular decision."

"Worse still, Hayes refused to explain why he did it."

Chapel sat up straight. There was something in her tone that had got his attention. "You think you know, though, don't you?"

"It could just be a coincidence. There's nothing like real evidence here. But during the hearing, the terrorist claimed he should be set free because he'd been given his orders by the CIA. Obviously, at the time people thought he was crazy."

"That is an interesting coincidence," Chapel agreed.

"It was just a minor scandal at the time, but now it's coming back to bite him. There are senators on both sides of the aisle who are muttering that Hayes is soft on terrorism."

"So you think the Senate will refuse to confirm him to the Supreme Court?" Chapel asked.

Angel clucked her tongue. "I'm not an expert, Chapel. That's just my opinion. But a lot of pundits are starting to suggest it. He looked great when he was first nominated, but now the buzz is against him. And the current problem, the chimera problem, isn't helping him any."

"What on earth does that have to do with his confirmation?"

"Supreme Court nominees don't just sit back and wait to hear if they've been accepted or not. They lobby hard to get the votes they need like any other kind of politician. Hayes has a PAC working for him in Washington. He's supposed to be there right now meeting with members of the Senate Judiciary Committee, but instead he's locked up in his offices in his courthouse."

"No wonder he got so angry with me," Chapel said.

"He's not a good guy to mess with," Angel told him. "He's connected, at every level. I mean, the president likes him. They know each other personally. And clearly he's still connected to the CIA through Director Banks. Even just as a federal judge he has a lot of power to ruin your life if he wants to. Chapel, when you meet this guy, if I were you I would lick his boots. No, wait, he might not like that. You should ask him if you're *allowed* to lick his boots."

"Maybe I'll just try saving his life," Chapel suggested. "See how he likes that."

IN TRANSIT: APRIL 14, T+54:13

Chapel did finally manage to get some sleep, after that. He put his head back on the seat and pulled a blanket over himself and he was out like a light.

But he must have dreamed.

He would never remember the dream. But he would remember waking up with one fact firmly in his mind, one thing that had nearly escaped his conscious mind, but which his subconscious mind had carefully filed away.

"Ellie," he said, as his eyes opened.

Admiral Hollingshead had chastised Chapel for going to talk to Eleanor Pechowski. Except he hadn't called her that. He'd called her Ellie Pechowski.

She'd told Chapel to call her Ellie when he met her. Probably she said that to everyone who met her. Which meant Rupert Hollingshead knew Ellie, had at least made her acquaintance.

Maybe they were even friends. Chapel had wondered why she was allowed to remain at large, knowing what she knew. Having as much exposure to the virus as she must have had. Hollingshead must have been protecting her this whole time.

She had told Chapel something else, as well. She'd told him she'd been originally hired to work at Camp Putnam by a man in a uniform. A captain in a navy uniform.

"Did you say something, Chapel?"

It was Angel's voice in his ear.

"Angel," he said, "can you tell me something about Admiral Hollingshead? Nothing secret. Just—when was he promoted to admiral?"

"I doubt he'd want me answering that," she said, "but . . . you could just Google it yourself, so, okay." She worked her keyboard for a moment. "It was after Operation Desert Storm, in 1991."

Ellie had been recruited in 1990. Back then Hollingshead would have been a captain. In the navy.

"Okay," Chapel said. "Thanks."

He settled back into the seat and closed his eyes again.

In his head the pieces fit together, revealing more of the picture.

IN TRANSIT: APRIL 14, T+55:21

The plane set down at Denver International Airport and before it had even finished taxiing to the terminal, cars were already moving on the tarmac, headed to meet them. There were three cars, all black late-model sedans with tinted windows. Anybody who saw them would know instantly they were full of security for some VIP.

When the cars reached the plane, a trio of men in black suits and sunglasses poured out and took up defensive positions surrounding the cars. Each of them carried a shotgun in plain sight. They made a good show of tapping their ears and calling out status updates to each other.

"They're not bothering with a low profile," Chapel said, as he and Julia watched the convoy approach. "That's probably a mistake. A chimera on his own might not know what all this signifies. But the Voice will."

"You think that Quinn will attack during the transfer," Julia said, because he'd filled her in on what he'd learned of Hayes's itinerary.

"I would, if I were trying to kill him. It's when he's most at risk. But there are ways of avoiding that—or even using this kind of display to our advantage. We could put the judge in a nondescript car, let Quinn attack the security detail and then have the judge's car speed away in the middle of things." Chapel threw up his hands. "But it's not up to me. I don't take charge of security until we reach this undisclosed location. I can't give any orders until then, so I'll just have to play this straight."

"I'll keep my eyes open," Julia said.

"Ah." Chapel turned away from the window and looked at her face. "About that."

Julia sighed. "You're not taking me with you, are you?"

Chapel tried to pick his words very carefully, this time. "No. I want you to stay here, on the plane. So you can be ready to get out of here at a moment's notice. Chief Petty Officer Andrews is armed. I've already spoken with her, before you woke up. She knows that the CIA may attempt to get at you. Her orders are to try to get the plane out of here before they arrive—or to defend the aircraft if anyone tries to board it."

"Chapel—"

"You'll be safe here. This plane looks like a normal corporate jet, but it's actually been uparmored. It's designed to resist small-arms fire. I know that every time we separate something bad happens, but—"

"Chapel, okay! I get it. You can't take me with you this time."

"It would be kind of hard to explain to the judge

what you're doing here. I can't really pass you off as my secretary."

Julia rolled her eyes. "I said I get it. I'll stay here."

"You don't seem very happy about it," he pointed out. He'd expected that, of course. "I know you don't like being left in the dark. The last time I left you behind . . . I can only say I'm sorry about that. I promise this time is different."

"It's not that," Julia said.

"No?"

"No." She reached over and put a hand on his cheek. That he hadn't expected at all. "It's not that at all."

"What happened to our professional arrangement?" he asked, before he could stop himself.

"Chapel, for a guy whose job is to keep secrets, sometimes you don't know when to shut up," she said. He saw in her eyes then that she was upset, definitely—but for once she was *not* upset with him.

"What's going on?" he asked, softly.

"It's what I see in your eyes. You're leaving me here because you don't expect to come back, yourself." She looked down at her lap. "You think you're going to die here."

"It's not like I want to," he tried.

She pressed her face against his chest. "You could just say no. You could quit. You could tell them all to fuck themselves and then run away. We could run away."

Chapel stroked her hair. For a while he just held her.

Then he whispered, "No. No, I can't."

That wasn't who he was.

She nodded against his chest. "Chapel. You go do what you have to do. When you're done, I'll be here, waiting for you so we can fly off on our next big adventure. Okay? I'll be right here."

They waited together in silence while CPO Andrews opened the hatch and readied the debarkation stairs.

DENVER INTERNATIONAL AIRPORT, COLORADO: APRIL 14, T+55:36

One of the black-suited men was waiting for Chapel when he came down the jet's stairs. The security guard did not offer to shake his hand. "Captain Chapel," he said, in a flat voice, "welcome to Denver. We're to take you directly to His Honor."

"Sure," Chapel said. "He's at the courthouse, right?"

"My instructions are to take you to him," the guard said.

"Are you Reinhard?" Chapel asked.

"I'm just here to take you to him," the guard repeated.

"Fine." Chapel walked over to the nearest car. The guard at least held the door for him. "You've been given orders not to answer any questions, right?"

"I've been given orders to escort you to His Honor," the guard told him.

After that Chapel kept his mouth shut.

The three cars headed out of the airport and up a

major highway toward the city. Outside the airport, broad fields cut by irrigation ditches lay yellow and bedraggled in the sun. The sky was huge. Chapel had been out west before, and should have known to expect it, but still it was always a surprise. The flat land of the prairies meant you could see for miles in every direction, and that made the sky just look bigger than it did back east.

The effect wasn't diminished much even when the cars rolled through a zone of strip malls and old box stores, auto parts warehouses and colossal Laundromats, all of them looking dusty and worn. This part of Denver had no trees, just broad roads laid out in a perfectly square grid. The car rolled down Colfax Avenue, through a zone of strip clubs and bars, and soon enough Chapel could see the city's handful of skyscrapers sticking up from the flat ground ahead of them.

At the courthouse the cars pulled into an underground lot, and Chapel blinked as they left the sun behind. Someone opened Chapel's door, and he stepped out onto concrete that stank of old motor oil.

"This way," the security guard said. He wore his sunglasses even indoors.

Chapel was ushered up an elevator and through a small office where a dozen State Highway Patrol troopers were drinking coffee and talking about football. This must be the security detail he was supposed to take over, but none of them would even meet his eye. His black-suited escort didn't let him linger in that office but directed him through and into a larger office beyond.

Judge Franklin Hayes was waiting there for him, looking almost exactly as he had when he'd broken into Angel's line to demand Chapel's presence. The judge hadn't shaved in a day or so and steel-colored stubble had broken out on his cheeks. He looked just as angry as he had when they'd spoken.

"Took you long enough," Hayes said.

DENVER, COLORADO: APRIL 14, T+57:01

Hayes steepled his fingers in front of him and glared at Chapel. "You're seven hours late, Captain." He turned to his security guard. "This is Reinhard, my head of security. He's been in charge here since you refused to come earlier."

Reinhard was a big guy, broad through the shoulders like a linebacker, though not much taller than Chapel. He had a crew cut and a strong jaw, but his eyes were hidden behind dark sunglasses. Even without seeing his eyes, though, Chapel could tell the man was giving him the once-over.

"Doesn't look like much," Reinhard said.

Hayes chuckled. "Oh, Chapel's got his qualifications. Director Banks was happy to send them along. He's a war hero, Reinhard. Lost his arm in Afghanistan, fighting for your freedom."

"A cripple, then," Reinhard said.

"All the best military training. He served with the Army Rangers, that's quite an elite force," Hayes went on, smiling. The judge had the look of a career politician. He'd probably had acting lessons to be able to look so jovial and friendly. But his eyes gave him away. They were like chips of glass in his face. Hard and cold. "Of course, that was several years ago."

"He does look pretty old," Reinhard agreed.

"Come, come. He's had plenty of time to mature and gain wisdom, let's say." Hayes put his hands down on the desk. "Plenty of time for that. He hasn't seen much field service since he lost his arm, of course . . ."

"So they sent you a desk jockey," Reinhard grunted. "Huh."

"Are you suggesting he isn't the best man for the job?" Hayes asked, a look of fake shock creasing his face. "Are you suggesting they could have sent someone better?"

"Maybe one of the rent-a-cops who works over at the mall," Reinhard said.

Chapel fumed in silence.

He understood this game. He knew what Hayes wanted to get across but was too slick to say outright. The judge hadn't gotten as far in his career as he had without knowing how to lay on a good line of bullshit, but still make himself understood.

He was saying he didn't trust Chapel. He was also saying he *did* trust Reinhard, his own man, and that he wanted to keep Reinhard in charge and let Chapel play second fiddle here.

Time to fix that.

"Your Honor," he said, "you'll want to move to your left."

Hayes didn't have time to ask why before Chapel's pistol was out, held tight in his right hand and pointed at Reinhard's throat. The security guard was smart enough to keep his hands visible and not flinch.

"Take off your sunglasses," Chapel said.

"I'll be damned if—"

"Take them off now," Chapel insisted, using his best officer voice.

Hayes scooted to the left in his rolling chair.

Slowly, using both hands, Reinhard reached up and took off his sunglasses. His eyes were a cold blue. They narrowed as he stared at Chapel. "You just bought yourself some trouble," he said. "And you were already fully stocked."

"Shut up," Chapel told him.

A lamp with a brass shade sat on Hayes's desk. Chapel grabbed it and shone the light directly in Reinhard's eyes.

"—the fuck," Reinhard said, squinting, turning his face away from the light.

"Okay. He's clean," Chapel said, and put the lamp back on the desk. "Reinhard, you go outside and find your men. Tell every one of them to remove his sunglasses and keep them off. Nobody's wearing sunglasses today. You got it?"

"Why the hell should I—"

"The judge knows why," Chapel said.

Reinhard turned to look at Hayes, who just nodded. The security guard shook his head in disgust and stormed out of the office.

Chapel holstered his weapon, then went over to close the door.

"Huh," Hayes said. "I hadn't thought of that. If he was a chimera, his nictitating membranes would have closed, by reflex."

Chapel nodded.

"I've known Reinhard for years," Hayes pointed out. "You think I'm dumb enough to let one of the monsters join my team?"

Chapel inhaled sharply through his nose. "I haven't made up my mind yet how dumb you are," he said.

Hayes's face started to turn red, but Chapel wasn't about to let him talk. He would just spout more insults or threats, and that wasn't getting them anywhere.

"I'm here to do one job, which is to keep you alive," Chapel pointed out. "Sometimes you may want to doubt my methods or to question my orders. Don't. I've taken down two chimeras in the last two days. I know how it's done. Reinhard clearly doesn't even know what they are. He doesn't know what to expect. He doesn't know how dangerous they really are."

"He knows how to shoot," Hayes said.

"No. No, he doesn't. Not this time. I don't know where he got his training—if he's ex-military or he just took a six-week correspondence course out of the back of *Guns and Ammo*. It doesn't matter. Whoever taught him to shoot told him to always aim for center mass. That doesn't work with chimeras. They have reinforced rib cages. You can put six slugs in a chimera, right over his heart, and it won't even slow him down. You have to aim for the face. Their skulls are just like ours."

Hayes opened his mouth. He looked like he was going to say something nasty. But then he closed it again and just nodded.

"Okay," the judge said. "We've got a little time

before the convoy is ready to move out. Why don't you have a seat, so we can talk?"

DENVER, COLORADO: APRIL 14, T+57:12

"First off, let's talk about why I'm here. The chimeras," Chapel said. He kept one eye on the window. It was unlikely that Quinn would climb up the side of the courthouse to get to the office, but you never knew. "I'm sorry I'm late getting here. But I wasn't wasting that time. I've learned a great deal about them in the last two days."

"Oh?" Hayes asked.

"I don't know how much you're cleared to know," Chapel said. "But you do need to know what's coming for you. It's a chimera named Quinn. He's supposed to be the strongest of them, and one of the most vicious."

Hayes turned around and got a bottle of bourbon out of a sideboard. He offered Chapel a glass, but he turned it down. "Maybe I don't want to know some of this," he said, pouring himself a healthy drink. His tough guy act had evaporated like summer rain on a hot sidewalk. Interesting.

Chapel shook his head. "I'm not trying to scare you. But you need to understand how serious this is. The chimeras were given a list of victims. A kill list. For the most part they were allowed to choose their own targets. But this Quinn was given specific orders to come here. For you."

"Okay," Hayes said. He sipped at his liquor. "Okay, but—why?"

"That's exactly what I'd like to know." Chapel sighed. "Some of the names on the list make sense. The scientists who created the chimeras are there. People who worked at Camp Putnam. I notice you aren't asking a lot of questions here. You know about Camp Putnam."

Hayes set his glass down. "Tom Banks is a personal friend of mine," he said, meeting Chapel's eye. "He gave me a briefing. One I'm definitely not cleared for. But he agreed with you—I needed to know."

Chapel nodded. He'd assumed as much, though he'd hoped there was another reason Hayes knew so much about the chimeras. "Some of the names on the list don't make any sense at all. There are three people on that list who couldn't possibly have been involved in the project. People with no connection to Camp Putnam. And then there's you."

"Me?" Hayes said. "I've never been to that place."

Chapel shrugged. "Your link to the chimeras seems pretty tangential. But it's real. You worked for the CIA at one point. You did yearly debriefings of people the agency wanted to keep an eye on. Specifically, you debriefed William Taggart and Helen Bryant."

Hayes blinked rapidly. "Sure. They were a couple of scientists. Biologists, I think. A little creepy, as I recall. I always assumed they worked in germ warfare."

"You debriefed them but you didn't know why they were being checked up on?"

Hayes frowned. "That was common practice back then. CIA practice. Everything was cutouts;

nobody knew anybody else's business. That's why they got a lawyer to do the debriefings in the first place. I wasn't privy to anything truly sensitive, so they could trust me not to give away any secrets by accident."

That jibed with what Chapel knew of the CIA and its culture of compartmentalized information, but he was still surprised. "How did you even know what to ask them?"

"I had a script," Hayes said. "'In the last year, have you met with or spoken by telephone with anyone who identified themselves as an official of a foreign nation? Has anyone you don't know approached you in a social situation and asked questions you felt uncomfortable answering?' That kind of stuff. It was really just a checklist—they would say no to every question, I would make marks on a form, and then I would go home. I debriefed a lot of people. Scientists, defectors, former radicals who claimed to have gone straight. It was just part of my job."

Chapel nodded. That wasn't helpful at all—he'd really hoped Hayes might have known something about Taggart and Bryant that he didn't—but at least it was one small mystery cleared up. There was another one, though. "You were also counsel when Christina Smollett sued the CIA."

"Who?"

Chapel gritted his teeth. "A mentally ill woman in New York City. The suit was probably brought by her parents. She claimed the CIA was sending people into her bedroom at night to sexually assault her."

Hayes made a disgusted face. "There were always

cases like that. I hated them. Those people were obviously suffering, but it wasn't our fault. It was my job to get rid of them as quickly as possible. Preferably without spending any money."

"You don't remember this case in particular?" Chapel asked.

"No. I could go through my old files," he offered.

Chapel held up a hand. "No need."

"Why her?" Hayes asked. "Why did you bring her up?"

Chapel leaned to the side and tilted his head a little to the left. Was there sweat on Hayes's forehead? Just a trace. Not enough he would even notice it. And his pupils were a little dilated, Chapel decided.

Interesting.

Extremely interesting.

"Her name came up in one of my investigations, but it's probably nothing," Chapel said. No point in telling the judge that Christina Smollett was on the kill list.

Not when Hayes was lying to him about not knowing who she was.

Hayes was a good liar. He'd been a lawyer, once, so it made sense—he'd been trained how to keep his cards close to his vest. But Chapel had been trained in military interrogation techniques. He could spot the telltales. He knew when someone was withholding facts from him.

Hayes knew exactly who Christina Smollett was, Chapel was sure of it. And he knew why she was on the list.

DENVER, COLORADO: APRIL 14, T+57:36

"All right, let's move on," Chapel said, because he knew better than to push—if he started demanding information now, Hayes would just shut down and refuse to talk at all. There might be time to ask more questions later. "Talk to me about this itinerary. I understand you plan to move to a different location. Somewhere I'm not allowed to know about until we get there."

"I've already seen that your systems can be hacked," Hayes told him. "And Tom—Director Banks—told me that whoever released the chimeras has access to military technology. Apparently they used a Predator drone to break open Camp Putnam."

Chapel hadn't known that. He filed it away for later review. Right now he had to focus on keeping Hayes alive.

"I think it's a bad move to change locations now. You'll never be more vulnerable than when you're in transit."

"Whoever is giving the chimeras their instructions already knows I'm here. What they don't know is the new location."

"Which is?" Chapel asked.

Hayes surprised him by actually telling him. "I have a house up in the foothills of the Rockies. A little place outside of Boulder."

"Is it secure? Can it be secured?"

"It's six acres of land, mostly forested. All of it fenced. There's one private road leading to it so we don't have to worry about traffic. It's hard to find if you don't know where to look, and it's not listed under my name—technically it belongs to my ex-wife, but she's in Washington State now and won't be dropping by."

So, Chapel thought, it's distant from the local police, and if they needed help it would be a long time coming. One road leading in meant only one escape route if they needed to flee. Forested land was Quinn's favored terrain—it was where he'd grown up. Add to that the usual problems of a rural location: spotty cellular coverage (if any), frequent power outages, and it would be pitch-dark at night.

But Hayes did have a point. The Voice, the author of the kill list, wouldn't know where they were going. And he'd been right to keep the information from Chapel as well—the last thing they needed was a repeat of Stone Mountain.

"Okay. We'll leave tonight, about two in the morning—"

"The convoy is gathering right now," Hayes said. "Reinhard has overseen everything. We'll leave as soon as the lunchtime rush hour is over."

Chapel sat back in his chair. He had pushed Hayes hard enough already. Maybe it was time to ease up a bit. Still, it wouldn't hurt to try reasoning with him. "It would be safer at night. I'd also like to get you in a nondescript car. The black sedans your people use will make good decoys, but if you're in a different car, then even if Quinn attacks during the transfer you'll be safe."

"I'm taking my limousine," Hayes said, in a voice that wouldn't brook disagreement.

Chapel sighed. "I've been trained in how to do this," he said.

"So has Reinhard."

Chapel shook his head. "I was flippant about it before, but really, whoever trained him had no idea what this situation was going to be like."

"I've known Reinhard for nearly ten years," Hayes said. "I trust him. He's kept me safe through riots and protests and death threats from some of the most hardened criminals in Colorado. You, Captain Chapel, I've known in person for less than an hour. When we get to the house, he'll accept your command. You can see to security there as you please. But right now I'm putting my life in his hands."

"Okay," Chapel said. "At least let me oversee the embarkation. The absolute most dangerous time is when you move from this office to your vehicle. I'll feel better if I'm watching you while you make that switch."

"As you wish," Hayes said.

IN TRANSIT: APRIL 14, T+58:39

Chapel managed to get the judge into his limo and moving out without incident. If Quinn was nearby, he didn't show himself. Chapel supposed that was the best he could hope for, at the moment. The sedans, several troopers on motorcycles, and a highway patrol vehicle formed up in a loose convoy, headed north.

Hollingshead had said it wouldn't be enough. Hollingshead had been certain of that.

Chapel rode with one of the troopers, in the patrol cruiser, at the back of the convoy. Out on the road, under the big western sky, an attack could come from any direction. He strained his neck trying to look every way at once.

The mountains off to the west were wrapped in the green majesty of heavy pine growth, dappled here and there by the shadows of clouds that streamed across the big sky as fast as trailing smoke. It was a spectacle that might have taken Chapel's breath away any other time.

"Are we likely to hit much traffic?" Chapel asked his driver, a grizzled old state trooper named Young.

She shrugged. "Could be. The road to Boulder is pretty heavily traveled all times of day. I've had no reports of congestion so far, but if there's an accident . . . well, these roads really weren't meant for all the people on 'em. There's four million people in the entire state of Colorado, and two million of 'em live in this corridor, between Fort Collins and Colorado Springs."

"Great," Chapel said. He watched civilian vehicles go whizzing by on his left. They were moving fast enough he couldn't get a good look inside any of them. Quinn wouldn't know how to drive, himself, but the chimera in New York had proven how easy it was for one of them to commandeer a vehicle.

If Quinn was coming from the north, headed toward them, it would be easy enough to veer into oncoming traffic and ram the limo. Even a chimera would know the long car was where the judge would be. At highway speeds, that kind of collision might kill the judge outright.

Chapel touched the hands-free unit in his ear. "Is the judge wearing a seat belt?" he asked.

"No, he is not," Reinhard called back. "Keep this channel clear, Captain. My men might need it in an emergency."

Chapel shook his head. There was something wrong here. Reinhard was acting like this was just a Sunday drive and Chapel's paranoia was irritating him, rather than reassuring him like it should.

"Get the judge belted in. If someone rams the limo, he'll go bouncing around in there like a pebble in a tin can, otherwise. And keep that screen of motorcycles tight in his front left quadrant."

"We're doing good, Captain. I want this channel clear. If you have any more suggestions, keep them to yourself."

Chapel watched a civilian car try to overtake them. A motorcycle drifted out to their right to block its advance. The civilian honked his horn but eventually got the point.

"If it's any consolation, I think you were right," Young said.

Chapel glanced across at the driver. "About what?"

"About the seat belt. You know how many people we have to scoop out of wrecks every year? That's half our job in the summer," Young said. "If people would actually wear those belts, a lot of them would survive."

"Colorado doesn't have a mandatory seat belt law?" Chapel asked.

"Well now, we do, but we can't pull you over unless there's some other reason," Young told him.

"Unless you're under seventeen, we don't even make you wear a helmet when you're riding a motorcycle."

"I guess things are a little different out west," Chapel said.

"Sure are. We all think of ourselves as having a little cowboy in our souls, still. So we don't much like the government treating us like children who have to be told what to do." Young clucked her tongue. "Does make you think twice, though, when you get a report of some family of vacationers in a crashed car, and all you find is raspberry jelly all over the dashboard."

Chapel laughed, despite himself. "That's gruesome, Young. Truly gruesome."

"Oh, I'm sorry," she said. "I guess that's what we call dark humor. Helps us get through our job. You know. You ever want to see gruesome for real, you come out for a ride along with me up in the mountains."

"If I ever decide that yes, I want to see gruesome for real, I'll do just that," Chapel told her. He turned his head and saw one of the sedans full of Reinhard's goons just ahead of him and to one side. "What about those?" he asked. "Tinted windshields. I thought those were illegal, too."

"It's a kind of iffy thing. You're allowed to tint them down to twenty-seven percent, which means twenty-seven percent of available light gets through. I'd say those sedans are pushing the limit."

"Only twenty-seven percent of available light? That's ridiculous," Chapel said. "How can they expect to see anything? They're missing three-quarters of their visual perimeter like that."

"I have a feeling, now, that Mister Reinhard figures, if you can't see in, you can't tell who's in the car. So you can't tell which car the judge is in."

"Unless you notice that one of the cars is a limo, and the rest are sedans," Chapel pointed out.

"That *is* what we might call, in my line of work, a clue," Young agreed.

Chapel touched his hands-free unit. "Reinhard, your people can't see anything through those tinted windows."

"Captain Chapel? I told you to keep your thoughts to yourself," Reinhard replied.

"Have them roll down their windows. It'll be windy but they'll survive," Chapel ordered.

"Those windows are bulletproof, Captain. They're up for a reason."

Chapel grimaced. "Our guy isn't a shooter. That's not his style. Roll down the damned windows."

"Chapel, I swear, if you don't clear this—"

Reinhard's transmission cut off in midsentence. At first Chapel thought something had gone wrong, that Quinn had somehow disrupted their communications, but then he realized Reinhard had just muted his microphone, presumably so he could talk to the judge.

"All right, Chapel," Reinhard said, after a while. "The judge says I have to play nice with you. I'll make you a deal. If I have them roll down their windows, will you promise to stay off this channel?"

"Cross my heart and hope to die," Chapel said.

"I'll hold you to that," Reinhard replied.

Young laughed. "That boy does not like you, he surely does not," she said. "You'd think the two of you might get along, being in the same line of work."

"Oil and water are both liquids, but they won't mix," Chapel pointed out. He craned his head around, watching all the sedans. One by one they started lowering their windows and he could see the black-suited security guards inside. The guards blinked and squinted as the pure mountain sunlight hit their eyes.

"Tell the truth, now. Did you do that just to annoy 'em all?" Young asked.

"I think I'd like to have my lawyer present before I answer that—"

Chapel stopped talking, then.

"Something wrong?" Young asked.

"Yeah," Chapel said.

One of the security guards, up in a sedan just ahead of Young's car, didn't squint or blink in the sun. No, he didn't need to.

His third, black eyelid just slid down to protect his eyes.

Quinn had been with them the whole time.

IN TRANSIT: APRIL 14, T+58:51

"Angel? Angel, can you hear me?" Chapel called. There was no response. "Angel, come in! I need you to patch me through to the walkie-talkie system Reinhard's people are using. Angel!"

Trooper Young glanced over at him. "Maybe we're just out of cell range. Reception is still kind of spotty out here," she suggested.

"Maybe," Chapel said. Though he'd assumed that Angel's signal was carried by the satellite network, not by cell towers. She'd reached him in all kinds of strange places.

He tried the leader of the security guards. "Reinhard, come in. Reinhard—the assassin is riding in car three!" There was no response. Just as there hadn't been since he'd first called the man. "Damn it, Reinhard—I know you can hear me!" The head security guard wasn't responding. Maybe he'd been serious about clearing Chapel off his radio frequency. Maybe he'd turned off his walkie-talkie.

The timing suggested that was more than a coincidence.

He grabbed the handset of the radio unit built into the car's dashboard. He tried to raise anyone and heard only static in response.

"That can't be right," Young said. "I ran a radio check not ten minutes before we left the courthouse. It was working just fine."

"Somebody's jamming it," Chapel said. It was the only thing that made sense. Except it made no sense at all. "We have to let them know. There has to be some way to communicate with them." Two of the sedans were way up ahead, one in front and one in back of the limo. Car three, with Quinn in its backseat, was just ahead of Young's car, which was trailing at the back of the convoy. "Short of yelling at them—"

"There's a thought," Young said. Chapel looked at her, having no idea what she meant. She laughed and gripped the steering wheel with both hands. "I guess I've been doing this longer than you. I remember back before we had cell phones, before we had wireless Internet, before—"

"Young? What are you talking about?"

"Just hold on," she said, and floored the accelerator.

The patrol cruiser shot forward, swerving to narrowly miss the rear bumper of car three. The sedan made way for them, though the driver flashed his lights and honked his horn. Young ignored him. "There's a pen and paper in the door pocket by your right hand," she told him. "Write a message, quick."

Chapel scrabbled for the items—a ballpoint and a citation book. He scrawled out the words *ASSASSIN IN CAR THREE CALL REINHARD* while Young pulled up alongside car two, directly behind the limo.

"Here, give me it," Young said, and grabbed the citation book. She flicked her siren on and off until the guard in the passenger seat of car two looked over in their direction. She held the citation book up to her window. "Is he looking?"

"Yeah," Chapel said, watching the passenger's face. "Yeah, I think he's got it. He's shouting something but I can't hear him."

Young rolled down her window. Air burst into the car, ruffling the pages of the citation book.

"I said," the passenger shouted, "are you nuts?"

Chapel grimaced in frustration.

"Our radio is out," Young shouted back.

The passenger in car two rolled up his tinted window.

"I don't think they're taking us serious," Young

said. Her face was impassive, but Chapel knew she must be thinking the same thing he was.

They were a guard detail for a man who had been targeted by an implacable assassin. They might doubt what Chapel had to say. They might think he was trying to sabotage the detail. But there was no excuse for not being cautious and heeding what he said.

"We have to assume a few things," Chapel told her, picking his words carefully. "We have to assume they have orders not to listen to us."

"I'll go that far," Young replied.

"We have to assume they're not going to take any action," he went on.

"That's what I'm seeing," she said.

Chapel nodded. He had a couple more assumptions he wasn't going to say out loud. He had to assume that Reinhard—and his entire security crew—already knew that Quinn was in car three, and that they were on his side. On the side of the Voice and the chimeras. They were in on the assassination plot.

Chapel also had to assume that Young wasn't in on it, too. If she was, this was going to be over very quickly.

"The judge is in danger," Chapel said.

"Yep."

"Are we going to do something about that?" he asked.

"We sure as hell are." Young flipped on her lights and sirens and stamped on the brakes.

IN TRANSIT: APRIL 14, T+58:59

The sedans—cars two and three—shot past the cruiser as Young maneuvered them back to the rear of the convoy again, straddling the two lanes. Chapel saw her plan immediately—she was leaving the right lane open so car three could move across to the shoulder, but not leaving any room for them to fall back. As soon as the cruiser was clear of car three's bumper she picked up speed again, until they were separated by only a single car length's distance.

She grabbed the microphone and switched on her loudspeakers. "Car three, break off from the convoy immediately," she said, and Chapel heard her voice repeated so loud outside the car it made the windshield rattle. "Move to the shoulder and stop your vehicle. You have ten seconds to comply." She switched over to the radio, but held her palm over the microphone. She glanced over at Chapel. "I know I can trust my fellow troopers. I've worked with some of 'em for years."

Chapel remembered the judge saying he'd worked with Reinhard for years, too. But they needed allies. There were three troopers on motorcycles in front of the limo, screening its advance, and two more well behind them keeping an eye on their tail. "Call them," he said.

Young flipped some switches on the radio and got on a state police restricted channel. "This is Sergeant Young, calling all motorcycle units. Have identified that car three is a threat, repeat, car three."

"Tell them to screen the limo and get it off the road if they can," Chapel told her.

"Forward units, protect the principal, and get it to safety," Young said into her microphone. "Rear units, close this road to traffic! Fall back and deploy flares. Calling headquarters, calling headquarters. We have an immediate need to close the north-bound lanes of I-36 south of Broomfield. Repeat, we need an immediate road closure of I-36 north-bound south of Broomfield." Almost instantly the units ahead of the limo called in to report they had received Young's orders and would do what they could. At least the troopers were paying attention.

Chapel leaned forward to peer through the wind-shield. Car three hadn't changed its speed or posi-tion at all. Neither had the other sedans. All three of them had rolled up their windows, though. He couldn't see anything through the tinted glass.

"Do we hail 'em again, give 'em another chance?" Young asked. "I don't want to start shooting out tires or running anybody off the road if we don't have to."

"I think—" Chapel said, but he didn't get to finish his thought.

Up ahead the rear passenger-side door of car three popped open, and a man in a black suit flew out. He bounced off the asphalt and came caroming straight toward the patrol cruiser.

"Mother Mary!" Young shouted, and whipped her wheel over to the side, narrowly avoiding roll-ing right over the security guard.

Chapel spun around in his seat to watch as they raced past the man. He was struggling to get to his feet in the middle of the fast lane of the highway. It looked like he had a broken leg.

Chapel guessed immediately what had happened. Quinn must have panicked. The other guards in car three must have tried to mollify him.

Chimeras didn't take well to attempts to calm them down.

"Shotgun, mounted behind your head," Young said, her voice tight with worry.

Chapel looked for and found the shotgun where it was held behind the headrests by a pair of metal clips. He grabbed it and broke it open. "Shells," he said.

"Glove compartment. Grab the blue ones, those are slugs," Young told him. Her eyes were all over the road.

Chapel yanked open the glove compartment and found the box of shells. Half of them were shot packed in red paper. The other half were solid slugs mounted in blue plastic casings. She was right—they would be far more effective against vehicle tires than the shells full of buckshot. He loaded two in the shotgun and nodded at her.

"Aim for the right rear tire," she told him. "That'll make 'em slew over to the left, into the median. It's the safest—Jesus!"

He looked up to see what had her attention. The rear window of car three erupted in shards of glass. Chapel could see Quinn using his fist to clear the remaining glass. The barrel of a pistol emerged from inside the vehicle and started to track them.

"Head down!" Young shouted, as she veered to the right. Chapel was thrown up against the passenger-side door, jarring his good shoulder. The box of shotgun shells burst open and spilled all over his lap, the shells rolling down into the leg well.

The windshield of the patrol cruiser cracked from top to bottom as a pistol round tore through its cabin, narrowly missing Young's ear.

"I'm fine," she shouted, and he nodded, snapping the shotgun closed and rolling down his window. "Take your shot, quick!"

Chapel caught a flash of motion ahead of them and saw car two drifting back toward them. Either they'd come to see what was happening—or to help. Whether they wanted to help Chapel or Quinn was an open question.

"I've got this," Young told him. "Take that shot!"

IN TRANSIT: APRIL 14, T+59:03

Chapel rolled down his window and unbuckled his seat belt. Cradling the shotgun in his arm, he got his knees up on the seat and leaned out the window. The wind of their velocity tried to tear him out of the car but he braced himself and held on. Young shouted something at him but he couldn't hear. He could barely keep his eyes open as the air slapped him in the face over and over, but he managed to get the shotgun clear of the window and brought it up to his shoulder.

Then a second pistol shot struck the hood of the cruiser, and Young had to veer to the side. Chapel flopped like a rag doll as the car shifted under him. He had to grab for the car door with his artificial hand, and nearly lost the shotgun. A third shot took off the wing mirror on the driver's side.

At least Quinn—or whoever it was shooting from car three—wasn't aiming at Chapel. They clearly intended to incapacitate Young so she couldn't continue the pursuit. Chapel had to end this before that happened. He raised the shotgun and tried to find an angle to get the rear tire of car three. Normally with a shotgun you didn't need to aim—you just pointed and fired. This shotgun was loaded with slugs, though, solid projectiles that acted similar to rifle bullets. He needed to make his shot precise and clean.

That wasn't going to happen with him hanging out of his window. He was firing across the car and the hood was in the way.

There was only one thing for it. He reached forward with his left hand and grabbed the windshield wipers so he could pull himself forward. He was going to have to climb out onto the hood.

Up ahead car two had fallen back in the right lane, boxing car three in. Were they trying to help? Their windows were up, and he couldn't see anyone inside the car. They weren't shooting at him, which was nice, but they were preventing car three from complying with Young's instructions. Not that Quinn was likely to let the driver of car three just pull over and surrender.

No, it was on Chapel. He dragged himself forward, compensating every time Young veered or drifted into one lane or the other, trying to make it as hard as possible for the shooter in car three to get a bead on her. He could hardly blame her for not wanting to stand still, even if it did make it next to impossible for him to move out onto the hood. He glanced through the windshield and saw her sitting up in her seat, trying to see over him. Her eyes were firmly on the road. Either she knew what he was trying to do or she figured it was his own neck at risk.

Stop stalling, he thought. He tried to channel Top, tried to hear his old physical therapist's voice in his head. This wasn't exactly a situation Top had prepared him for, though, and no words came.

It didn't matter. He knew what Top would want him to do.

Chapel kicked his legs out of the window and flopped down hard on the hood of the cruiser. Inertia tried to yank him up over the windshield and onto the roof of the car but he kept his center of gravity down and hugged the hood, the mechanical fingers of his left hand grabbing at the grill on the front of the car because it was the only thing to hold on to. Heat from the engine seared his chest and groin. The buttons of his shirt soaked up that heat and scorched his flesh, but he could only ignore it. With his right arm he reached around and brought the shotgun to bear. He braced it against the hood, angling the barrel down toward the tire of car three.

That was when Quinn erupted out of the shattered rear window, howling in rage, hauling himself through the broken glass. The chimera pulled himself onto the trunk of car three. His mouth was wide open, virus-carrying saliva forming long strands between his massive white teeth. He stared at Chapel with eyes as black as the bottom of a well.

Quinn had a pistol in his hand.

Chapel had the shotgun.

Quinn lifted his weapon and pointed it straight at Chapel's face. There was no way Chapel could dodge the bullet, no safe place he could move to.

His weapon was already aimed.

He took his shot.

IN TRANSIT: APRIL 14, T+59:07

The sound of the rear tire of car three exploding was the loudest bang Chapel had ever heard. Shreds of hot rubber and steel belting blasted outward in a cloud of stinging, slapping chaff. Chapel looked up and saw Quinn's pistol discharge. He could have sworn he saw the bullet come out of the barrel, that he watched it travel in slow motion straight for him. He dropped the shotgun and let it clatter away between the two cars. Car three was already turning, swerving over into the grassy median strip, dust and pieces of torn-up vegetation rising in a plume from its front tires.

Chapel couldn't tell if he'd been hit or not. Quinn had fired from point-blank range. He'd been aiming right at Chapel. Had the car started to swerve before or after Quinn pulled the trigger? Chapel knew from past experience that you could be shot and not know it for long seconds, that the brain under stress could delay pain reactions for a surprisingly long time.

Was he already dead, but his body hadn't realized it yet?

He wanted to look down at himself, check himself for wounds, but he didn't dare. Car three had rumbled to a stop, nose down in the median, and was rocking back and forth on its suspension. Young hit the cruiser's brakes, though she was careful not to decelerate so hard that Chapel went flying. When he decided she'd slowed down enough, when he could look down at the asphalt and see the grain in it, the texture of the road surface, he scrambled forward off the burning hot hood of the cruiser and rolled down to the ground, taking the fall on his artificial left arm. In a moment he was back up on his feet. He felt like he was floating, like adrenaline lifted him up into the air and then he was running, dashing full tilt back down the highway toward where car three sat, lifeless and unmoving.

On the far side of the median civilian cars went by so fast they were just blurs of color in the air, red, bottle green, gunmetal gray. He heard the sirens of Young's cruiser but only as if they were far away, as if they were in the next county. He heard the breath surging in and out of his lungs. He heard his own heartbeat.

His right side felt wet and cold. That was probably blood. Not a good sign, but he still didn't feel any pain, and he definitely didn't feel like it could slow him down. Quinn was back there, Quinn—a third chimera, one of his targets—

His head was vibrating, like he'd taken a punch to the temple. His brains felt like they were quivering Jell-O inside his skull.

Black cars were moving all around him, slotting themselves into place. Men in black suits were jogging across the asphalt, guns and walkie-talkies in their hands. He glanced back and saw the limo almost right behind him, pulled across both lanes of the highway, standing across the road.

"The judge," he shouted. He couldn't hear his own voice. That wasn't a good sign. It could mean a lot of things, though, anything from a concussion to a gunshot wound to the head. "Get the judge out of here! Get the limo out of here!"

Up ahead car three stood in the median. Beyond it he could see something black and white moving, thrashing around.

It was Quinn. They'd dressed him in one of their suits, made him look like a member of the security detail. They had cut his hair neat and professional, made him look like an ex-soldier or maybe an ex-football player. The kind of man who would work for Reinhard. If his eyes weren't covered by those nictitating membranes, Chapel would never recognize him. Quinn was staggering back and forth on the median like he was drunk. Like he was trying to walk on the deck of a heaving ship.

Someone was shouting at Chapel. One of the troopers, one of the motorcycle troopers, was shouting at him, but Chapel couldn't hear the words, he could only see the man's lips moving. Chapel waved him away and ran toward Quinn.

Around the median there was a ring of black suits. Men in black suits. Their eyes were normal, at least, but why were they standing there? Why were they just standing there?

Quinn saw Chapel and pulled himself upright. He pounded at his ears with his palms as if they were full of water and he was trying to clear them. Was he deaf too? Maybe—maybe the noise of the tire blowout had deafened them both.

Chapel had no time to think. He couldn't think. He drew his sidearm. Stood sideways to make a smaller target of himself, pointed his weapon at Quinn. "Lie down! Lie down on the ground and put your hands behind your head!" Chapel shouted. He could just hear the words, though they sounded distorted and weird.

Quinn scrubbed at his face with his hands. His jacket was torn all up one side, and the white cuff had frayed down to torn ribbons. The skin of his palm on that side was pink and bloody. He must have gone flying when car three veered into the median. He must have been thrown clear and slid twenty feet on his hand and side. No wonder he looked so disoriented.

He was still a chimera, though. Even as Chapel watched Quinn seemed to regain his composure. He pulled himself up to his full height. Tilted his head back and roared like a lion.

Tell me who the Voice is. Tell me why the Voice wants you to kill Hayes. Tell me why you were created.

There were a million questions in Chapel's head, questions he wanted to ask Quinn. He dearly wanted Quinn to surrender, wanted him to stand down so Chapel could take him into custody and interrogate him.

Quinn was a chimera. He was hurt, and angry, and scared. He wouldn't be taken without a fight.

He rushed straight at Chapel, his head down, his arms out like he would grab Chapel around the waist and knock him to the ground. Like he was going to crush Chapel's life right out of him.

Chapel breathed out, aimed at the top of Quinn's head, and fired until Quinn dropped to the ground, dead as meat.

IN TRANSIT: APRIL 14, T+59:10

Chapel holstered his gun and closed his eyes, trying to clear his head. His ears rang with the noise of his own gunshots. He could hear the sirens of Young's cruiser better now.

Slowly he opened his eyes. He was looking down at his feet. He was standing in a patch of dry, dusty weeds in the median strip. Quinn was nearby. Covered in blood.

"Nobody touch him," Chapel called out. "Stay away from the blood, especially."

He could hear his own voice a little better, now. That was good.

Without even thinking about it he moved his good hand to his side. He could feel the wetness there. He lifted up his jacket and saw his whole side slick with blood.

Not so good.

Quinn had shot him. Chapel couldn't tell if it was a flesh wound or if the bullet had pierced his abdominal cavity. There was an awful lot of blood. His blood. Quinn's blood. His head started to spin again.

You hurtin'? Top asked him. In his head, that voice was just in his head, he forced himself to remember that. *You feelin' the burn? You know what that means.*

"Means I'm still alive," Chapel said, because they'd been through this so many times it was like a litany. Every time Chapel flagged or slowed down during their workout sessions, every time he wanted to take a break, Top would say the same thing.

And if you're still livin'—

"Then there's still work to do," Chapel said, out loud.

He opened his eyes again. He didn't remember closing them. He kept them open, looked around himself.

The security guards were standing in a circle around him, around him and Quinn's body. Some of them looked shocked. Maybe they'd never seen a man's head blown off before. Maybe they just couldn't believe Chapel was still standing.

One of them was holding a walkie-talkie. It squawked and Chapel heard something, heard Reinhard's voice come through, though he couldn't make out the words.

Reinhard—who was in the limo with Judge Hayes. Reinhard—who maybe wasn't quite as trustworthy as the judge thought.

"Out of my way," Chapel said, as he ran through the circle of black suits. They didn't try to stop him. He got back up on the asphalt, started running as his feet hit solid highway pavement. The limo was still sitting there, across the lanes. It hadn't moved at all. Chapel ran up to the back door, tried the handle. It was locked at least.

"Your Honor," Chapel shouted. "We need to move you out of here now. The assassin might have had backup." That wasn't how the chimeras normally worked, but this kill was different. The judge had been singled out by the Voice. It was possible the Voice had a contingency plan. "Your Honor?"

The door lock clicked open. Chapel grabbed the handle and pulled at the door. Inside the limo it was dark and cool, and Chapel saw two men, Reinhard and Hayes. He leaned inside the door, blinked as his eyes tried to adjust to the darkness inside.

"Well done, Captain," Hayes said. "Get in."

"Your Honor, it isn't safe here," Chapel said, stepping inside the limo. He plopped down on a leather seat and wondered why he hadn't thought about sitting down before. It felt so good, so good to get off his feet. "I, uh—I need to—"

"Relax," Hayes said. Reinhard rapped on the partition between them and the driver. Chapel felt the limo's engine rumble to life and felt them moving. "Relax. It's all over, and you did exceedingly well."

Hayes reached inside his jacket and pulled something out.

It was a pistol.

He shot Chapel twice in the chest.

DENVER INTERNATIONAL AIRPORT, COLORADO: APRIL 14, T+59:17

"Julia," Angel said.

"I'm here," Julia said. "I'm just . . . still trying to understand what you told me. It's a lot to take in."

"I know," the operator told her. "But something's happened. There's no time to talk about Marcia Kennedy right now. Chapel—"

Julia's body froze. In an instant she felt like a solid block of ice. "Is he—?"

"He's in trouble. He's moving north toward Boulder. I've been tracking him by satellite, watching over him as best I could, but someone up there has been jamming my signal. I'm sure of it now. They're actively jamming me. Or they were."

"What? I don't understand. They stopped jamming you?"

"I have no way of telling. He's in a car moving north. Someone just threw his phone and his hands-free set out of the window."

"Do you think he's . . . still alive?"

Chapel had known. He'd known he was walking into a trap. A setup. He'd expected to die here in Denver. He'd gone anyway. Julia had been doing her best not to think about it. Now she felt like she might throw up.

"Normally I can track his pulse and his blood pressure through sensors in his artificial arm, but right now I'm not getting any readings. They could be jamming my signal still, or—"

"Angel!" Julia interrupted. "Just tell me. Do you think he's dead?" she forced herself to ask.

It was a long time before Angel answered her.

"I don't know," she said, finally.

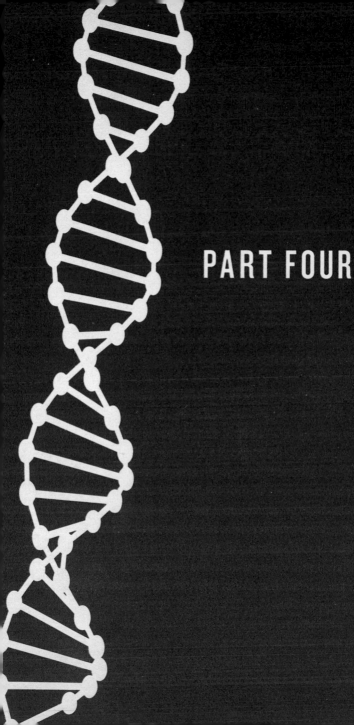

PART FOUR

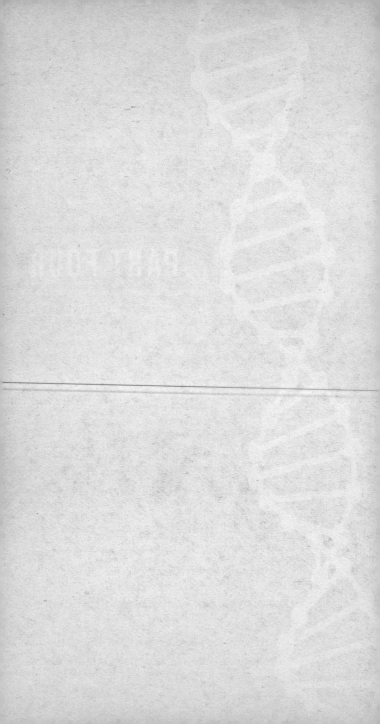

WASHINGTON, D.C.: APRIL 14, T+60:04

Rupert Hollingshead had always liked the Jefferson Memorial best of Washington's many landmarks. It was far enough from the Mall that the tourist crowds were always thinner there. In spring it was a wonderful place to enjoy the cherry blossoms. He'd always been a devotee of Jefferson the man, as well, and it was good to sit in the midst of all that neoclassical marble and look up at the man's wise bronze face and imagine what he would have done in a given situation.

After today, though, he imagined he would feel differently about the place. He would remember it as where he'd been forced to concede defeat.

Tom Banks was waiting for him when he arrived. The CIA director looked pleased with himself, of course. No matter what kind of horror show this had become.

"Your man failed," Banks said, with barely disguised glee. "He's dead, dead, dead."

"He got three of the four," Hollingshead said, when the two of them were close enough that they could speak without being overheard. "Really, all in all a good show."

"For a cripple, sure," Banks said, with a chuckle. "Rupert, old boy, old chum, old pal. You *do* know how to pick 'em."

Hollingshead fumed in silence.

"So go ahead. Say the words," Banks insisted.

"Really? Here, and now? Is that proper protocol?"

"Maybe not. But for my personal satisfaction I've got to hear it from your lips," Banks insisted.

Very well.

"I, Rupert Hollingshead, do affirm that as of this moment the CIA should have full jurisdiction over all secret projects resulting from or evolving from Project Darling Green. The Central Intelligence Agency shall be fully responsible for all further activity, oversight, and secrecy concerning said projects and the Defense Intelligence Agency will have no access to any work product or intelligence product resulting therefrom or associated therewith without the CIA's prior approval and knowledge. There. Is that enough? Or must I sign something in blood?"

Banks grinned like a feral cat. "I've been waiting years for this, Rupert. This project of yours should never have happened in the first place. No sane mind could have approved it, and keeping it going this long was utter stupidity. And now I get to clean up after you."

"You don't seem very put out," Hollingshead observed, "for a man whose workload has just increased."

"Because it gives me a chance to do something else I've wanted to do for a long time. Hang you out to dry. When the president hears about what you did—what you signed off on—he's going to demote you down to ensign at the very least. He'll be fucking pissed, to be blunt about it. And you and your stupid bow ties will never darken my doorstep again."

"All of this. All of this, because you hate me," Hollingshead said, shaking his head. "Because our two agencies don't get along. All the deaths, all the misery—"

"Spare me, you old fuck," Banks said. He turned on his heel and walked away, then. He didn't even bother with the traditional handshake. Hollingshead watched him go.

Then he turned and with a sigh settled his bulk onto a marble bench where he could look on Jefferson's face. Maybe for the last time.

He took his cellular phone from his pocket and put it to his ear.

"It's done," he said.

Angel's voice on the other end sounded downcast. Perhaps she'd come to have high hopes for Chapel as well. "He just took over? Just like that?"

"Bought Camp Putnam for a song, yes," Hollingshead replied. "No questions asked. He seemed anxious to get on with things." The ghost of a smile touched his lips. "It's almost enough to make me feel sorry for him. He has no idea what he's just inherited."

"Director Hollingshead? I'm not sure I understand," Angel said.

"Give it time." Hollingshead ended the call.

BOULDER, COLORADO: APRIL 14, T+64:54

There's two kinds of people who get to just lie in bed all day, Top said. *Babies and cripples. Babies are cute, so they get away with it. Cripples ain't cute.*

"I can't open my eyes, Top."

You want to be a cripple, that's fine. Nobody expects anything from a cripple. They just lie there, being a drain on everybody else's hard work. But that's fine. Because you're a war hero, right? You earned the right to do nothin' all day but feel sorry for yourself. You made that sacrifice. Don't matter you got two perfectly good legs. You're all depressed. You're traumatized. So you're crippled in the head.

"I got shot. I got shot three times," Chapel told him.

He did not know if he was speaking out loud.

Darkness surrounded him. Darkness filled his body, an aching kind of darkness he couldn't understand. He desperately needed to go to the bathroom.

A man whose body's crippled, sure, people can look at that and pity him. They can feel sorry for him. A man who's crippled in the head, people can't see that. They don't understand it. Now you and me, we both know about trauma. We both know what it's like to wake up in the middle of the night and be back there, back in the mud and the fire and hearing the screams. We understand that. Nobody else ever will. They'll see you lyin' in this bed, with two perfectly good legs, and they'll say, he's just lazy. He's just milking it. Our tax dollars are payin' for him to sleep all day and eat Jell-O.

Chapel was lying in a pool of something wet. Had he soiled himself? The shame of it was too much to bear. He wanted to just curl up and go back to sleep. He wanted to sleep forever. He had a feeling that was an attainable goal.

Open your damn eyes when I talk to you, boy.

"Top," Chapel said, the start of a protest he didn't know how to finish. He tried to open his eyes, tried to obey orders. It was so hard, though. His eyelids felt like they had been cemented shut. "Top . . ."

I'm gonna keep yellin' at you. I'm not gonna stop. Because I'm no cripple. I got one arm, one leg, and one eye, but I refuse to be a cripple. Cripples don't work no more. I still got work to do, and you're it.

"I'm trying, Top."

I know you are. But my boys don't accept that just tryin' is enough. My boys—and don't you dare forget you are one of my boys now—my boys only accept victory. They only accept one hundred percent success. How's those eyes comin' along? They open yet?

It took every ounce of his strength. It was like trying to rip a phone book in half. But Chapel opened his eyes.

He couldn't see much, just blurry shapes and shadows. The light hurt when it hit the back of his eye sockets. It felt like each individual beam of light was drilling into his skull. But his eyes were open.

Some of the blurry shapes were moving. They moved around him, bent over him. They were people, looking down at him.

"Jesus," someone said. "He's awake!"

"How the hell is he still alive?" someone else asked. "He must have lost a gallon of blood already."

"He can't last much longer," the first voice said, though it didn't sound sure.

"Get Reinhard. If we have to kill him ourselves, Reinhard will know how."

BOULDER, COLORADO: APRIL 14, T+65:12

Chapel was lying on a cement floor in a pool of his own blood. It ran down his side, under his legs, and into a drain in the floor. He could hear it dripping away. He could feel it oozing out of his gunshot wound.

His shirt was off. He could look down and see the wound, caked in gore. He had two smaller wounds in his chest, just tiny pinpricks.

His artificial arm had been removed. It lay on a table on the far side of the room. The silicone skin had been completely cut off, revealing the complex assemblage of pistons and actuators underneath.

His good arm was handcuffed to a pipe that ran along the wall behind him. The cuff around his wrist was loose enough that it didn't cut off the circulation to his good hand, but not so loose he could slip out of it. He wasn't going anywhere, even if he did feel strong enough to stand up. Which he didn't.

Those were all facts.

As for anything else, all he had were suppositions and theories.

The judge had shot him twice in the chest—that must have been where the pinpricks came from. The judge must have hit him with a tranquilizer gun. Chapel remembered Jeremy Funt's story of how Malcolm was recaptured after his escape. William Taggart had taken him down with a tranquilizer gun. Most likely, Chapel thought, the judge had been given such an unusual weapon in case he needed to use it against Quinn. The judge would have known about the unpredictable nature of chimeras and been armed accordingly. The fact he hadn't been given a high-powered revolver instead meant that the judge had wanted to make sure he kept Quinn alive—at least long enough to serve his intended purpose.

So the judge had known about Quinn's presence in his security detail. He'd known everything.

The wound in Chapel's side was serious. It would eventually cause him to bleed out. It was only a flesh wound, though—Quinn's bullet had cut through his skin and muscle but failed to penetrate his abdominal cavity. If it had hit any major organs, Chapel would already be dead. He'd gotten off pretty easy, actually. If the wound had been properly treated and bandaged, he would be on his feet and ready for action even now.

No one had treated it or bandaged it in any way. He'd been handcuffed in this little room and left to bleed.

There were four men in the little room with him. Security guards in black suits. They wore their sunglasses again—apparently they were done with following Chapel's orders. When he begged them for help, for a bandage, for water, they didn't even glance in his direction. Two of them were playing cards. The other one just stared out the room's sole window.

Chapel had to fight constantly to stay conscious. He did not know if he was always successful—he might have blacked out once or twice by the time Reinhard came into the little room and checked on him.

The head of the judge's security detail poked and prodded at the wound in Chapel's side, reopening the crust of blood there. Chapel could feel fresh blood leak from the wound.

"Where's the judge?" Chapel asked, not expecting any kind of answer.

Reinhard surprised him. "He's in Boulder, at a press conference. Covered in blood—your blood. But otherwise fine."

"Press conference?"

"Earlier today, the judge was attacked by a mysterious assassin, didn't you know that? Hundreds of people on the highway saw it. If it wasn't for a brave war hero who was guarding him, the judge would have been killed."

Chapel forced words out of his dry throat. "Awful shame, though, that the war hero who took the bullet for the judge died before they could get him to a hospital."

Reinhard nodded, looking impressed. "You've figured most of this out, haven't you?"

Chapel took a deep breath before saying anything more. "This was all a false flag operation," he said.

"Yeah?" Reinhard asked.

"The judge is up against a tough confirmation hearing in the Senate because he's supposed to be soft on terrorism. An assassination attempt by some domestic terrorist group would give him a great platform to wave the flag around and talk tough, make himself look bloodthirsty. But you and I know better. We know this whole thing was a setup. But you can be trusted not to talk. As for me, the judge doesn't know what I would do. So he's going to make sure I don't ruin this for him. You can't kill me yourself, though. That would look wrong when they did the autopsy. So you're going to let me bleed to death, then turn my body over to the local coroner. Nobody will think to look for traces of tranquilizer in my blood, because there won't be enough blood left to test. The cause of death will be obvious so no uncomfortable questions will be asked."

Reinhard laughed. "You're smarter than we thought. When you just walked into this, we kind of thought you were an idiot."

Chapel tried to shrug. Hard to do with only one shoulder, and that arm handcuffed. "No. Not an idiot. Just predictable. It was my job to track down the chimeras. I would go wherever they did." He rested for a while before speaking again. "Tell me one thing. Are you working for Banks? Or for Hollingshead? Which of them is the Voice that gives the chimeras their instructions?"

Reinhard sighed. "You know, all this talking is going to drain your strength. Why don't you just try to sleep, now? Just close your eyes and drift off. You've earned it."

The reverse echo of Top's remembered voice in his head made Chapel smile. "I've slept enough. Let's talk some more."

"I've got things to do," Reinhard told him, shaking his head.

Chapel's only chance was to keep the man engaged. To talk him around. "That's a pretty sweet posting you're looking at, huh? Head of security for a Supreme Court justice. It's too bad you won't live to see it."

Reinhard sneered. "Idle threats, now? That's what you've been reduced to?"

"Oh, I'm sure I'll die first. But I'll have the satisfaction of knowing you'll go with me. Or didn't they tell you about Laughing Boy?"

"Who?"

Chapel smiled. Reinhard was still listening. That was good. "I don't know his actual name. Creepy guy, with a scar on the back of his head. Laughs all the time. Have you met him? If you're working with Banks, I'd bet that Laughing Boy was your go-between. He cleans up after the chimeras."

"What do you mean, 'cleans up'?"

"You know the chimeras are carrying some kind of germ warfare virus. I mean, come on. They must have told you that much. Laughing Boy finds everybody who's been in contact with one of them. He kills them and burns the bodies."

"Bullshit. You're just trying to scare me. It won't work."

"Sure. Believe what you want. Did you have much physical contact with Quinn, though? Did you shake his hand? Maybe pat him down at some point? Laughing Boy doesn't take any chances." Chapel looked over at the black-suited men playing cards on the far side of the room. "What about you guys?" he called out, raising his voice as much as he could. "Did any of you touch Quinn? Were any of you in car three when he went berserk? I bet they didn't tell you about the virus."

One of the guards looked up and stared at Chapel. "Reinhard," he said, "what's he on about? Nobody told us about a virus."

Reinhard scowled. "Shut up," he said. "Williamson. Hand me that duct tape."

Another of the guards tossed a roll of tape to Reinhard.

"Enough bullshit," Reinhard said. Then he tore off a generous piece of tape and pressed it tight over Chapel's mouth.

So much for talking his way out of this.

The guards went back to their game. The one who had spoken kept staring at Reinhard and at Chapel, but he didn't get up from where he sat.

Chapel wondered how much longer it would take to bleed out.

BOULDER, COLORADO: APRIL 14, T+65:48

There was nothing but darkness outside the room's little window.

Tools hung from hooks on the walls—saws, hammers, mattocks, and hedge clippers. A toolshed, then. Most likely Chapel had been taken to the judge's wife's place in the mountains above Boulder. The judge had said that was the undisclosed location, the safehouse where he would wait for Quinn.

There didn't seem like a lot of point in figuring out his location, but he couldn't just lie there and wait to die. He was an intelligence operative, so he spent the last of his time trying to gather information.

There were three guards in the shed, as well as Reinhard. The guards were named Williamson, Reynolds, and Hook. Hook kept winning whatever game they were playing. Apparently Reynolds owed him a fair amount of money. Chapel thought Hook might be cheating.

If he could talk, he could have tried to drive a wedge between Hook and Reynolds. Convince Reynolds he was being taken by a cheat. Get them to fight each other. It would make a great diversion.

Except he couldn't talk. He couldn't create the diversion. And even if he had a diversion, what then? He was handcuffed to a pipe. He still had some strength in his body—he hadn't succumbed to anemia quite yet—but even at his strongest he would never have been able to break the pipe or pull his hand free of the cuffs. They were designed to hold stronger prisoners than him.

If Reinhard would leave the room, Chapel could try to catch Williamson's attention somehow. Maybe he could convince the guard to remove his duct tape, convince him that Chapel had a cure for the virus, that he could save Williamson from Laughing Boy . . .

But Reinhard wouldn't leave the shed. And as long as he remained, Williamson was more afraid of his boss than he was of the virus.

If he could . . .

If things were just slightly different . . .

If . . .

Reinhard's walkie-talkie crackled with loud static

that ramped up to a nasty whine of feedback. Looking annoyed, the chief guard grabbed the unit out of his jacket and switched it to a new channel. He started to put it back in his pocket, but it crackled to life again.

". . . say again," Chapel heard, "say again."

"Movement . . . the trees," a new voice said on the walkie-talkie.

"What the hell is this?" Reinhard asked.

Reynolds looked up from his game and shrugged. "Sounds like Praczek, kind of. Isn't he out by the road?"

Reinhard grunted in frustration. He put the walkie-talkie to his ear. "Praczek, come in. Praczek, this is Reinhard. Report right now."

Only static answered him. Reinhard set the walkie-talkie down on the table next to Chapel's artificial arm.

"Sounded like something, maybe," Hook said. "Sounded like there was somebody out in the trees. If Praczek saw something—"

"Shut up," Reinhard said. "We hear something more, I'll worry about it then. There's nobody out there. Praczek was probably just jumping at shadows." He grabbed the walkie-talkie again. "Praczek, report in. Everybody, report in."

For long tense seconds all the guards stared at the walkie-talkie, but nothing but static came through. Reinhard repeated his request for reports, but still there was nothing.

"So there's a fault in my set, that's all," Reinhard said, while his guards stared at him. "Maybe my battery is dying. Reynolds, give me yours."

Reynolds took his own walkie-talkie out of his jacket pocket and handed it over. Reinhard played with it for a while, adjusting its various knobs and dials. Every time he switched it on, however, it got nothing but static.

"If there's somebody out there, maybe they got to Praczek and Foster," Hook said, rubbing at his chin.

"Maybe this Laughing Boy guy," Williamson said.

"Shut up!" Reinhard shouted.

In Chapel's head a little fantasy played out. He saw Army Rangers parachuting into the woods, scrambling to take up positions. He saw them moving in to take out the guards Reinhard had stationed around the house. He saw them breaching the door of the toolshed, bursting in with battering rams and flashbangs and M4 carbines at the ready. He saw them come to rescue him. To take him home.

It was a nice little fantasy. It was also bullshit.

Chapel was a silent warrior. He knew that Hollingshead wouldn't send Rangers in to rescue him—if Hollingshead even knew he was still alive. If Hollingshead even wanted him to be alive, which Chapel had come to seriously doubt.

This was probably nothing. He hated to admit it, but Reinhard was probably right—it was most likely just a radio malfunction. Praczek's original message, about movement in the trees, was probably about some animals he'd seen moving around.

"Praczek, damn it, report now," Reinhard said into his walkie-talkie.

Static.

Suddenly red light flicked across the shed's window. Just a glimmer. Then a moment later it came back, much stronger, bright red light illuminating the trees as if they'd caught fire.

Everyone in the toolshed jumped at the sight.

Reinhard's eyes were wide. He visibly regained control of himself. Then he pointed at the others. "You three go check that out."

"You want us to go out there?" Williamson asked.

"Yeah. Yeah, I do." Reinhard drew his pistol. He didn't point it at anybody, but the message was clear. "Go on, now."

Hook and Reynolds headed for the door. Williamson held out a moment longer, but he must have known better than to anger his boss. Eventually he went, too.

Leaving Chapel alone with Reinhard.

Reinhard didn't even look at Chapel. He sat down next to the table and started playing with his walkie-talkie again. He looked nervous and jumpy, but not nearly scared enough to do something stupid. As far as Chapel was concerned that was both good and bad. It meant Reinhard wasn't going to go rushing out himself—leaving Chapel with a chance, no matter how slim, to escape. It also meant he wasn't likely to shoot Chapel just because he was scared.

Chapel supposed you had to take the good with the bad.

He tried to listen for any sound coming from outside the shed. He could hear nothing, though. The static coming from Reinhard's walkie-talkie was the only sound inside the shed.

Whatever was going on, it wouldn't take long to resolve. Hook, Reynolds, and Williamson would go figure out what that light meant. Then they would come back and explain how it was all a false alarm. Maybe one of them would go and check on Foster and Praczek, and find out that sunspots or an electrical storm in the mountains or something else had caused the radio problem. Everything would be explained, and then the situation would return to normalcy, and Chapel would be right back where he'd been: bleeding to death on the toolshed floor, with no hope of escape.

This was the closest he was going to get to a diversion, he knew, and he couldn't make any use of it.

Except—

On the table behind Reinhard, something was moving. It was Chapel's artificial arm, and it was moving on its own volition.

BOULDER, COLORADO: APRIL 15, T+66:01

The arm wasn't supposed to be able to do that. It was supposed to power down automatically when it wasn't attached. If it didn't detect skin contact through its electrodes, it shut down to save battery power.

But its fingers were definitely moving.

It couldn't get the leverage to move very far. But it bent at the elbow, and the index finger whined softly as it extended to its full length. Chapel, who was used to that sound, heard it clearly, but Reinhard didn't react. Maybe he couldn't make out the sound above the static coming from his walkie-talkie.

Chapel tried not to stare. He knew who was controlling the arm—the only person in the world, as far as he knew, who could. He remembered when he'd first heard Angel's voice. She had wanted to convince him she could hack into any system, so she had briefly taken over his arm and made it wave at him. He had been massively disturbed by her ability to do that. He'd been horrified she had the ability.

But now, when what she was doing was infinitely creepier, he was glad for it.

Reinhard was too busy playing with his walkie-talkie to look at the arm. But after a moment, he turned the radio off in disgust and threw it down on the table. And then he must have heard the motors squealing behind him. The mechanical sound of the robotic fingers clenching and unclenching.

His reaction was immediate and violent. He jumped off his chair and squawked like a parrot, spinning around to stare at the arm. "What the hell?" he demanded.

The arm bent slowly at the elbow, looking for all the world like a living thing. Its fingers flexed rapidly, waggling back and forth as the motors made their high-pitched whine. It was impossible to ignore now. Reinhard made a nasty noise in his throat.

What was Angel trying to achieve? Did she want to make it choke Reinhard to death? But no, that was impossible. There was no way she could even see the arm or where it was—there were no cameras in the toolshed for her to hack into. She must just be triggering the various motors at random. But why?

Because, Chapel realized with a start, she thought the arm was still attached to his shoulder. She wasn't trying to get Reinhard's attention. She was trying to signal Chapel, to send him a message.

Too bad Reinhard was the one to receive it. He reached for a mallet that hung on the wall. With three vigorous swinging motions he smashed the arm into bits of flying metal.

No, Chapel thought. *No! Do you have any idea how expensive that thing is? Do you have any idea what it's meant to me?*

For Chapel, it was like watching someone shoot his pet dog.

Reinhard spun around and stared at Chapel with wide eyes. "What the fuck do you think you're doing?" he demanded. Clearly he thought Chapel had some way to make the arm move remotely. "Answer me, damn it!"

Chapel tried to shrug. Then he stared downward as best he could, toward the gag of duct tape over his mouth.

Reinhard's reaction was immediate and unthinking. He rushed across the room to grab the gag and tear it off Chapel's face. His own sweating red features were only a foot or so from Chapel's mouth.

So Chapel only had to whisper when he said, "That was dumb."

Reinhard's features didn't change. Maybe he didn't realize what he'd just done. Or maybe he just had no idea what Chapel was capable of.

Chapel swung his legs up fast and wrapped them around Reinhard's neck. He was weak from blood loss and lying at a bad angle. But he had strength enough left to put pressure on Reinhard's carotid arteries.

They'd taught him this move in Special Forces training. If you can cut off blood flow to a man's brain, even for a few seconds, he will see a flash of white light . . . and then he will fall unconscious and collapse in a heap.

Reinhard obliged nicely, falling across Chapel in a sudden rush of weight.

"Thank you, Top, for making me swim again and build up my leg muscles," Chapel breathed.

Using his knees, he rolled Reinhard off and onto the floor. The next part took a lot of work, and Chapel had to stop several times to catch his breath. But eventually he managed to move Reinhard around until he could reach into the man's jacket pocket. Just as he'd expected, there was a handcuff key in there.

He uncuffed himself and got to his feet. His head spun for a while and he saw red spots in his vision, but he managed. Fresh blood started flowing from his wound. He shoved a hand over the hole in his side, but the blood dripped through his fingers.

First things first. He found the roll of duct tape and wrapped a generous swathe of it around his midriff. It was hardly sanitary and would never work as well as real gauze, but it made a passable bandage and kept him from bleeding out there and then. Next he searched Reinhard's pockets until he found what he was hoping for—his pistol. The P228 that Hollingshead had given him. Reinhard must have picked it up when the judge surprised Chapel in the limo.

He looked down at the arm where it lay on the table. It was a total loss, sadly. Reinhard had smashed it to pieces. It moved spasmodically, its few remaining intact actuators whining and moving pointlessly.

The hand had been damaged almost beyond recognition. It felt weird, but all the same Chapel picked it up with his good, living hand and gave it one last squeeze. It could be tough, saying good-bye to an old friend.

But it was time to get out of there.

BOULDER, COLORADO: APRIL 15, T+66:06

Chapel felt woozy and nauseated even before he opened the door of the toolshed. Cold night air swept in and nearly knocked him off his feet. It made the waxy sweat on his face and chest feel like ice. But he managed not to fall down.

He didn't know how long Reinhard would remain unconscious. He didn't know what he would find outside of the shed. He desperately wanted to sit down and rest for a while. But a lot of things had come together to give him this one chance. He could not afford to waste it—he definitely would not get another one.

He stumbled outside, trying to keep low. It was hard to bend from the waist without blacking out. The pain from his wound was excruciating, and his duct tape bandage constricted his chest and made it hard to breathe. So he squatted down and duck-walked around the side of the shed to try to get his bearings.

What he saw was more confusing than revelatory. The shed stood about twenty yards away from a big house, a pile of fake log cabin construction with lots of windows. Most of them were dark. Between the house and the shed was a wide patch of gravel where four cars sat, unattended. Surrounding the gravel and the buildings were tall dark trees, mostly pines. A single break in the forest led down to a road about two hundred yards away. That had to be east, since the rough shapes of mountains loomed over the trees on the other side, which must be west.

The entire scene was lit by a flickering red light, as if the forest were on fire. Chapel soon saw that wasn't accurate, however, as a new red light burst into life high over the trees to the south, a light that sank slowly toward the forest. A flare, fired from a flare gun. It was impossible to say where the flare had come from.

The moment the flare appeared, Chapel heard gunfire open up—automatic fire from at least three light machine guns, maybe Uzis or Mac-10s judging by the sound. The muzzle flashes came from over by the house, and he heard men shouting over there as well. That must be Reinhard's men, shooting indiscriminately into the trees. But who were they shooting at? They were acting like they were under invasion by a full-scale assault, but Chapel heard no return fire, saw no movement at all to the south. Just the flare, slowly settling to earth.

Whatever—it didn't matter. He had to get away.

Chapel ran east as fast as he could, ducking into the trees, headed straight for the road that lay beyond. He heard shouting behind him, but he didn't stop, didn't look back.

Just up ahead the trees gave way. The road appeared, a single lane of blacktop painted a dim red by the distant flare. Chapel broke through onto the road surface and smelled fireworks, the distinct sulfurous tang of spent gunpowder.

Then a soft shoulder rammed into his armpit, and he smelled Julia, felt her body press up against his. She was moving, running, and she supported him as he hobbled along. They headed down the road toward an SUV parked fifty yards away, showing no lights. As they got closer he saw Chief Petty Officer Andrews standing next to the open driver's-side door. She had a smoking flare gun in her hand.

The rear hatch of the SUV swung open, and Julia shoved him inside, into the rear compartment. Chapel realized he could barely keep his eyes open, that he was so weak he was likely to pass out at any second.

The hatch swung down to close him up inside the vehicle. He heard feminine voices talking in a low whisper. Heard the engine of the SUV turn over.

Enough. He let go of consciousness and sank into darkness.

BOULDER, COLORADO: APRIL 15, T+68:14

Reinhard stared down at the puddle of blood on the floor of the toolshed. He rubbed his throat where the bastard had choked him. His hand came away stained with red, and he shook drops of semicoagulated blood from his fingers. "This is where I woke up. Just before you arrived. My men were still out in the woods, shooting at flares."

He shook his head. "They weren't trained to handle that kind of Special Forces shit. They were trained to work as bodyguards for celebrities and CEOs. Not to guard against an attack by Army Rangers."

He bent down and looked at the set of handcuffs lying on the floor, one cuff open with the key still in the lock.

"I'll admit it, I wasn't ready for this either. Maybe I should have known better. I saw what Chapel was like on the road, when he took down Quinn. But I also saw how much blood he lost. There was no way a man in that kind of condition could do what he did, not without help. You're telling me there was nobody here. Just a stewardess and a veterinarian out in the woods." He shook his head again. "No way. I'm telling you, there had to be a whole company of Rangers involved. Otherwise . . ."

He didn't want to turn around. He didn't want to look at the man who had come to debrief him. He didn't want to admit he'd failed. "We did our best. We followed the script, did exactly what we were told. I've worked for the judge a long time. I knew I had to give this my all, and I did. I honestly don't see how we could have done any better."

"Ha," his debriefer said. It was almost like a little laugh. Not that there was anything funny here.

"Are you going to tell me I'm fired?" Reinhard asked. "Shit. I know you are. You're here to tell me I screwed up and I'm off the payroll. Gonna lose my pension, too. I had fifteen years in that. Well, I don't know who could have done better."

"Heh. Hee ha hee," the man behind him said. "Nobody's saying otherwise."

Reinhard felt his heart skip a beat. Was it possible he was going to walk out of this with a job? He knew what a mess this was. He knew how many kinds of hell the blowback would be. Was it possible?

He started to turn around to look at the man. "So am I—"

"Fired? Ha ha ha," the man laughed. "No."

Which would have been good to hear, except the debriefer was holding a silenced pistol in his hand. And the barrel was pointed at Reinhard's side.

"One—ha—problem, though. The plan was, Chapel would—hee hee—die while protecting the judge. Ha hee. We were going to present his body to the coroner and—heh—say that Quinn killed him."

The gunshot was louder than Reinhard expected. Silencers always were. You expected a flat little cough, like when somebody fired a silenced pistol on TV. Real silencers just muffled the sound of the gunshot a little. He looked down and saw a stain of red spreading across his side. Exactly in the same place where Quinn shot Chapel.

"See—ha—we still need a body, to make it look right," the debriefer said. "Heh ha ho. Gotta stick to the—ha—script. That left arm's going to have to come off, too."

SUPERIOR, COLORADO: APRIL 15, T+69:33

It was a lot easier opening his eyes, this time. Chapel felt warm and comfortable, like he was waking up after a good nap in a soft bed. He felt a dozen times stronger than before. Something was jabbing him in the arm, but it was easy to ignore. He looked up and saw a stucco ceiling above him, and a light fixture that was a little too bright for comfort. So he closed his eyes again and fell back asleep.

The pinpoint irritation in his arm woke him again, a little later. It was exactly in the crook of his right arm and it felt like a mosquito bite, maybe. He reached over with his left arm to swat it away.

His left hand passed right through his right arm, meeting no resistance. That made him open his eyes again. He looked over to his left and saw that his arm was gone.

Oh, yeah, he thought.

He did not find the fact particularly distressing. He had woken up so many times before, expecting to find himself whole and intact. The first few months it had been a horrible sensation to have to wake up and remember he was an amputee. Eventually he'd gotten used to it, or at least it had stopped waking him up with the cold sweats.

Leisurely, knowing there was no rush, he turned his head to the right.

Chief Petty Officer Andrews was lying in the bed next to him. She looked pale and slightly disheveled, but she was smiling.

Damn, Chapel thought. *Julia's not going to like this. And I don't even remember getting into bed with the CPO. Or anything we might have done.*

"You're awake," Andrews said.

Julia's face appeared over Andrews's shoulder.

Oh, wow, Chapel thought. *What exactly did I miss?*

But Julia wasn't in the bed. She was standing next to it, leaning over Andrews. Julia wasn't smiling.

"Try not to move your arm," she said. "If that needle comes out, it's going to make a hell of a mess."

Keeping his shoulder immobile, Chapel tilted his head to look down at his arm. A needle was buried in the flesh there, a needle attached to a plastic tube full of blood. The tube ran to an IV bag, and another tube ran to a needle in Andrews's arm.

Andrews laid her head back on her pillow. "Type O negative," she said. "I'm a universal donor."

"You lost a lot of blood," Julia told him. "I had to give you a transfusion or you probably would have died." She checked the blood bag and the tubes. "The CPO is going to be tired for a while, but otherwise she should be fine. You, on the other hand—"

"Where are we?" Chapel asked. His voice sounded hoarse and reedy, but he felt good. He felt better. He wanted, suddenly, to get up and get back to work.

"A motel room outside of Boulder," Andrews told him. "It was the closest place that Angel felt was safe. Actually, she advised us to keep going, to get out of Colorado altogether, but Julia decided you needed to be treated immediately if you were going to make it. She started barking orders and Angel had no choice but to listen. Julia would make a great combat medic, you know."

"She's fantastic," Chapel agreed. "But Angel—"

He stopped. He'd been about to say they couldn't trust Angel. But he shouldn't be able to trust Andrews, for the same reason. They both worked for Hollingshead. The man who'd sent Chapel to Denver so he could die just to make the judge look good.

He didn't want to speak his suspicions out loud,

however. Not when it was clear that Andrews had just saved his life.

"Angel was the brains behind this whole rescue," Julia said. "She tracked you by satellite to that house. She guided us there."

Angel had made his arm scare Reinhard as well, and that had certainly helped. What did it mean? Angel had to have been in on the setup. She had steered him toward Denver just as strongly as Hollingshead and Banks.

"What about the flares?" he asked, trying to piece things together.

"That was her idea, too," Andrews said. "I keep a sidearm on board the jet, in case I need to act as an impromptu sky marshal. But one pistol-packing CPO wouldn't have a chance against a small army of security guards. So she told me to take the flare gun from the emergency kit on the plane and told me how to use it—where exactly to shoot the flares so it would look like a bunch of Special Forces types were storming the compound."

"Most of the medical equipment I'm using came from that same emergency kit," Julia told him. "Angel told me to bring it along. There was a full suture kit in there, as well as some antibiotics and painkillers. You owe her, big time."

It made no sense.

Angel had led him right to the trap and told him to walk in. Banks and Hollingshead had come up with this scheme to make the judge look good by staging an assassination. Angel must have known something of the details.

So why, now, was she helping him? Part of the

plan had been for him to die at Quinn's hands. Hayes had presumably announced to the world that Chapel was dead. If he showed up in public now, alive and with a story to tell, it would ruin the entire plan. Angel should have been helping to kill him, not helping to save him.

He looked over at Andrews. She was beholden to Hollingshead, certainly, but he doubted she'd known any details about the plan. The fewer people who know a secret, the easier it is to keep. That was the entire rationale behind need-to-know information. So it was highly unlikely she was his enemy.

He would just have to trust her. "Angel betrayed me," he said aloud. "She was told to get me to Denver no matter what it took. Because I was supposed to go there and get myself killed while fighting Quinn."

Neither Andrews nor Julia looked particularly shocked.

"It was a setup, do you understand? She was in on the scheme to kill me."

Chapel nearly jumped when Angel answered him directly.

Her voice came from the motel room's telephone, which must have been set to speaker so Julia and Andrews could consult with her. She must have been listening the whole time.

"That's partly true," Angel admitted. "Chapel, Hollingshead and Banks did collude in sending you to Denver. And, yes, I knew you were walking into danger and I didn't tell you everything I knew."

Chapel glared over at the phone. If she was admitting that much—

"I thought I was doing my duty. My job. I thought keeping secrets from you, and operating on a secret agenda, was important. It was a matter of national security, and even if I wanted to be honest with you, I couldn't be. I'm sure you understand that. But then things changed," Angel said.

"Changed how?" Chapel demanded.

Andrews and Julia both looked away. This was between Chapel and Angel, and they didn't want to be part of it.

"First, I need to tell you something."

Chapel grimaced. "What? You're going to apologize?"

"In a way. Chapel, I want to tell you something about myself. Something I'm not supposed to reveal to anyone. I was a hacker, once. Back when I was a teenager, I was pretty good with computers and I had nothing better to do than to try to hack into the Pentagon's servers. I thought it would be funny."

"Why are you telling—"

"Just listen. I was a high school kid. I didn't know any better. It was easy, almost too easy to get in. I never saw anything important, really. I didn't understand any of the data I found. I think it was all just payroll records. So I logged out and forgot about it. Until the next morning when a bunch of soldiers broke down my bedroom door and arrested me.

"Long story short, I was looking at a lot of jail time because I'd been bored and fooled around where I shouldn't. I got passed around to a lot of people, psychologists and intelligence analysts and military lawyers, all of them wanting to know how I did what I did. I tried to explain, but none of them understood. They were convinced I was a domestic terrorist, and they were talking about espionage charges. I could have gone to jail for life, Chapel. But then they took me to this one office, in the sub-basement of the Pentagon. You know that office. It used to be a fallout shelter for the Joint Chiefs."

"You're talking about Hollingshead's office."

"Yeah," Angel said. "Director Hollingshead was there. He was nice to me. He was the first person who'd been nice to me since I was arrested. He said I shouldn't worry, that they knew I was just fooling around. I was so relieved! I asked if I could go, and he got really sad and told me, no, it wasn't that easy. What he could do for me was give me a job. They would find a job that would use my particular skills. He said it would give me a sense of purpose. It would give my life some meaning.

"And he was right. I love my job, Chapel. I love being able to make things happen and help agents in the field. I love the fact that I get to do good things.

"But there's one problem. Sometimes, I find out that the government isn't always . . . good. Sometimes I learn things I wish I never had to know. And that makes me wonder where my loyalties really should be."

She fell silent. Chapel took a deep breath.

"Okay," he said. "Well, we've seen plenty of evidence of that lately, haven't we? So what are you telling me, Angel?"

"I'm trying to say I'm on your side. That I'm all yours, Chapel, from now on. No more secret agendas. No more withholding information."

"I'm supposed to trust this sudden change of heart?" he asked.

"Yes," Angel told him. She sounded like she expected him to say that in that case all was forgiven and they could go back to being best friends forever.

"Really? And what, exactly, made you switch allegiances?"

Angel was silent for a long moment. "I spoke to Marcia Kennedy," she said.

SUPERIOR, COLORADO: APRIL 15, T+70:03

"I wasn't supposed to talk to her, of course," Angel said. "Director Hollingshead was quite clear about that. You weren't supposed to continue your investigation. I wasn't supposed to help you dig up any more secrets. But I had already called her and left a message on her voice mail, asking her if she could help. Asking if she could shed any light on why her name was on the kill list. She called me back, shortly after you were picked up at Denver International Airport. I tried to tell her that I'd made a mistake and that I didn't have any questions for her, but she wanted to talk about it. She'd been wanting a sympathetic ear to listen to her story for more than twenty years. I couldn't stop her once she got going, and then, I couldn't bear to stop her. I had no right to stop her." Angel's voice was thick with emotion. "I recorded the call. I record all of my calls. Do you want to hear it?"

Chapel looked around the room. Julia and CPO Andrews were both staring at him, watching his face. He couldn't quite read their expressions. He couldn't tell if they were judging him or just waiting to hear his reply.

"I'm starting to think maybe I don't," he said, and Julia started to turn away. "Angel. Go ahead and play it anyway."

Angel said nothing more. She just let the recording play.

"This is about the—the experiment. I know it is. What? No. No, I want to tell you. I need to. It started in 1984."

Marcia Kennedy's voice was thin and whispery. It sounded like her mouth was dry when she spoke, like getting the words out took real effort. Even distorted by the speaker of the motel room phone, the urgency in the voice was plain.

"Please, just—please. Please let me talk, I have to get through this in one go or I'll start—

"1984, like I said. I was in a hospital then, a hospital in Oregon. I was in one of my depressive phases at the time. It was a bad one. I . . . I tried to hurt myself.

"They took me to this hospital. They pumped me full of lithium, which is the best drug they have to treat my disease. It works, I guess. It makes me feel normal again. It also makes me so thirsty I feel like I'm going to die, and it makes me gain all this weight, and . . . I don't like it. I don't like the way it makes me feel. I complained about it. They took me to see a doctor I'd never met before. I thought he was going to admonish me for complaining so much, but instead he was very kind. He said he understood that the side effects of lithium were bad, but that I had to take something. He said there was something else they could try. Some new kind of drug that the army had developed.

"I jumped at the chance. I mean, why wouldn't I? He said it was experimental, that they weren't sure what the side effects would be like, but I was so thirsty. I was so thirsty. I had to beg my father to sign the papers, the, the consent forms or whatever, but he did it. He looked so hopeful. He thought they were going to cure me. I just wanted to get out of that hospital so I could go home.

"They started me on the drug right away. They said it might make me gain weight, and I might have some problems with memory. They weren't kidding. The trial for the drug ran nine months. I don't remember more than a handful of days in that time. I remember sitting in a day room at the hospital, playing chess with somebody. She was schizophrenic and she cheated. She cheated at chess; she would just, just make up new rules, and say I had to play by them, but they didn't make sense. I got really frustrated and I could barely breathe. I remember looking down and there was my stomach. It was huge. I felt like I'd swallowed a bowling ball. I started to cry because I'd gotten so fat. Weight gain was one of the side effects of lithium, too. I guess I thought they must be related kinds of drugs.

"Except this one didn't make me thirsty. It made me nauseated. I don't remember much of those months. But I remember always wanting to throw up. I remember my hair thinning, and my sweat smelled funny. I have little glimpses, sometimes. Little recollections. I remember the pattern of light on a wall, or I see myself in a mirror, and my skin was so clear. It had never been that clear in my life.

"At the end of the nine months I woke up in this bed, there was blood on the sheets and I had no idea what I was doing there. The doctor, the kindly doctor was there and he held my hand. He held my hand for hours because I was crying, except I didn't know why I was crying. I felt like something had ended. Like something had been taken away from me but I didn't know what. He told me I wasn't thinking straight, that the drug had unexpected side effects. One of them was that it made me hallucinate some things, except I couldn't remember any hallucinations. He told me it had also interacted badly with my digestive system, which explained the nausea. He said that because of the drug my appendix had become inflamed and that they had to remove it. I had a scar on my stomach, this huge scar right at the bottom of my stomach, right at my bikini line. He said that was where they took out my appendix.

"They stopped giving me the new drug, which was fine, I didn't want it anymore. I figured lithium was better. Anything would be better. I got to go home. The weight came off pretty fast and I guess—I guess I just went on with my life. I didn't think about it too much. I didn't want to. It was like I went to sleep and had a nightmare, and when I woke up, it was nine months later.

"I had dreams sometimes but they were just . . . dreams. For years I had them and I told myself they meant nothing. When you're bipolar, you learn to make a lot of excuses. That's what my therapist tells me. You make excuses for your behavior. When you're manic and people tell you you're acting crazy, you just tell yourself they're jealous because you're having more fun than they are, or that they just can't keep up with you. When you're depressed, on the other end of the cycle, you make up excuses why you need to spend the day in bed, or why the rent is late . . .

"So every time I thought about that drug trial, every time I would remember something, I would just tell myself none of it was real. That the things I was thinking were just disordered thoughts, or misinterpreted memories, or whatever. Nothing really happened to me in that hospital except I went a little loopy, and wow, how fortunate was it that I couldn't remember what I did all that clearly. I didn't want to remember. I wanted to put it behind me.

"Sometimes people would ask me about my scar. You know . . . boyfriends, mostly. I've had a few, and they always ask where it came from. I tell them I had my appendix out a long time ago. In 1985. Usually nobody asks twice. But there was one guy, once. He asked and he said his mom had a scar like that. I said she'd probably had her appendix out, too, but he said no. He said she'd had a cesarean section when he was born. He was upside down in her womb and they had to cut him out.

"I don't . . . I don't want to say what I think. It sounds crazy. It just sounds crazy. But you know, don't you? You're a woman. You know what I think.

"You know what I think they took from me."

SUPERIOR, COLORADO: APRIL 15, T+70:31

CPO Andrews wiped a tear from her cheek. She had turned her face away from Chapel's, so he couldn't tell what she was thinking, though he could guess.

Julia got up without a word and left the room.

"Angel," Chapel said, "I didn't know."

"No, Chapel, of course you didn't. None of us did. We never stopped to ask where the chimeras came from."

Chapel had imagined they must have been grown in vats somewhere, fetuses floating in glass tubes in some dark laboratory. When he thought about it now, that seemed ridiculous. That kind of technology didn't even exist. Whereas even in 1984 it would have been child's play for a scientist like William Taggart to implant embryos in unsuspecting women all over the country.

The thought made him gag a little.

"I suppose we can assume Olivia Nguyen and Christina Smollett underwent the same . . . procedure," Chapel said. He stopped talking then. He wanted to ask more questions, but with CPO Andrews lying next to him it felt like it would be in bad taste to continue his line of thought. "Maybe we should talk about this later," he said.

CPO Andrews turned to face him again. Her mouth was set in a hard line. "No," she said. "No. This is inexcusable. You're a man, and I don't expect you to understand the level of violation we're talking about."

"I guess you're right about that," Chapel admitted.

"But even worse," Andrews said, and she pressed her lips tightly closed for a moment as if she couldn't bear to speak, but then went on, "even worse than what the government did—would be to just keep it secret. To not do something."

Chapel nodded slowly. "This isn't about hunting down the chimeras anymore. Not for me. It's about finding out what was done back in 1984 and 1985, and finding out who's responsible."

"Good. You find them. And you make them pay," Andrews told him. "Go on. Talk to Angel. Work this case. I insist."

He watched her eyes for a second. Then he said, "Angel, there were two hundred chimeras born in 1985. Why do we only have three names on our list?"

"I've been wondering that myself," Angel said, over the speakerphone. "I don't have a concrete answer. My best guess is that only these three women represented a threat to the project's secrecy."

"I don't follow," Chapel said.

"It's ugly to think about, but it makes sense why the CIA chose these women to be the mothers of the chimeras. The project was always top secret, but they needed two hundred women of the appropriate age and relative health. That's a huge security risk. They picked women with emotional problems because they were less likely to understand what was happening to them, or to talk about it afterward—and even if they did, nobody would believe them. Christina Smollett, for instance, or maybe her father figured out some of it and sued the CIA. The case was thrown out because the judge assumed she was just . . . crazy. That she'd hallucinated the whole thing, or whatever. The secret was safe, but still, it meant she was enough of a threat to get on the list. Marcia Kennedy is a relatively lucid woman. She guessed what was done to her, and maybe I wasn't the first person she talked to about it. So that gets her on the list, too. As for Olivia Nguyen, I looked up her records and she suffers from paranoid schizophrenia. She has long stretches where she appears to be perfectly healthy—that's common with her diagnosis—but she has a habit of keeping knives under her mattress, and sometimes she thinks the songs she hears on the radio are a government plot to drive her crazy."

"A government plot—"

"Yeah," Angel said. "I don't think she's aware of what was done to her, or who did it. But she writes a lot of letters to the editor of the local newspaper talking about the government. A few of them even get printed. They're quite well written, and it takes a while before you realize they're the product of a disordered mind. They never contain anything specific enough to endanger the secrecy of the chimera project but maybe the CIA doesn't want to take the chance that someday she'll get more focused, more coherent."

"So they want her dead just in case," Chapel said. "Even though she's never done anything to hurt them. So she's on the list."

"Chapel, there's one thing I don't understand. Why the chimeras?"

"You mean, why were they created, or—"

"No," Angel said. "I mean, why send the chimeras to kill their own mothers?"

Chapel hadn't even considered that before. "Because they know the chimeras will do it," he said, at last. "The people who are running this plot, they don't care about who gave birth to who. They just know how to manipulate the chimeras. They know the chimeras hate the people who created them, and then abandoned them. It wouldn't take much to convince a chimera to kill his biological mother. Even if she never knew he existed. They can't think through their emotions."

"But why even take that chance? Why not just send Laughing Boy to kill these women?"

Chapel frowned. "Plausible deniability," he said. "There's always the risk somebody will see Laughing Boy shoot the people on the kill list. Some chance someone will put two and two together and realize the government is assassinating its own citizens. But if it's just some big, obviously crazy guy who kills these people, well, the world knows that happens sometimes. No one will investigate too deeply."

"I don't want to think about this. I don't want to know these things," Angel said. "Chapel—what's your next move?"

"I don't know yet," he told her. "Let me think about it."

SUPERIOR, COLORADO: APRIL 15, T+72:14

Eventually Julia decided that the transfusion had gone on long enough. Chapel was still short on blood, but CPO Andrews could only donate so much before her own health was at risk. Julia came back into the motel room and removed the needles from their arms. CPO Andrews got up slowly from the bed and then excused herself to go in the bathroom and wash her face.

Julia checked Chapel's pulse and looked into his eyes, checking the response of his pupils. She rubbed his arm down with an antibacterial solution and then put a small adhesive bandage over the puncture. "How do you feel?" she asked.

"Better. A lot better, thanks to you."

Julia nodded and looked away. He reached over and took her hand.

"You saved my life. Again."

"I had a lot of help." She started to pull away.

"Julia," he said, "just talk to me for a second. Okay?"

She made an irritated noise and pulled her hand away. But she didn't move away from him. "What is there to talk about?" she asked.

"I need to know if you're okay," he told her.

"No one shot me and left me to bleed out. I'm fine."

"Physically, sure. But you've learned a lot of things recently that I'm sure you didn't want to know." He leaned over and put his arm around her. She didn't push him away. "I know about emotional trauma. A lot of the guys I served with in Afghanistan came back suffering from PTSD. They couldn't just return to their normal lives, not with what they'd become over there. They couldn't sleep. They couldn't talk to their wives or children without getting angry, without blowing up. Some of them just shut down, stopped talking or stopped getting out of bed."

"I'm not—I'm handling this as best I can," Julia said. "Chapel, this was my family doing all these things. My mom and my dad forcibly impregnated all those women. They raised the chimeras like their own children, and then they locked them up and threw away the key."

Chapel pulled her closer. She laid her head on his shoulder.

"When I was a teenager, sitting in my room listening to Nirvana on my headphones and wondering which boys at school liked me, they were . . . they were out at that camp. They were there looking after their other kids, their *two hundred* sons. Training a whole generation of psychotic killers. I don't . . ."

She stopped because tears had crowded up in her eyes and she couldn't seem to speak until they'd all squirted down her cheeks.

"It's like my entire life was a lie. A cover story. I was their cover story. Their alibi. That was the whole reason I existed." She rubbed at her eyes with the balls of her thumbs. "I don't understand it! I don't understand any of it! I don't know who I am anymore. Last week I was a veterinarian in New York City, with a crummy little apartment and an OkCupid profile I checked every once in a while and a standing date to have lunch with my mother every week. Who am I now?"

"You're the same person," Chapel said.

"I shot a man's foot half off! I killed one of my brothers. My mom is gone, and my dad is probably going to die, and honestly—honestly, Chapel, and it bothers me, absolutely disgusts me to say this, but I think maybe he deserves it. I kind of want him to die to pay for what he did. How can I feel that way about my father? This isn't Julia Taggart, DVM! This isn't me!"

Chapel held her for a long time without saying a word. She was done with tears, but she rocked back and forth slowly, clutching her hands together in front of her. Clearly she'd needed this, needed to vent like this, for a long time. He'd been too busy chasing his mad quest to give her the chance.

Eventually she slowed her rocking and she just leaned into him, crowded up against him until they fell back on the bed and just lay there together. He stroked her hair, and she just breathed, breathed and did nothing else.

"I know how you feel," he told her.

"Come on," she whispered.

"Every soldier knows how you feel."

"I'm no soldier," she moaned.

"No. But listen. When you enlist in the military, you're just some kid. You grew up, went to high school, maybe you got in some trouble or maybe you just didn't know what else to do with your life, maybe you wanted to serve your country but frankly, a lot of soldiers I know just were looking for something to do. So they go to boot camp and everything about you is broken down. Everything you think you know about yourself is challenged and tested and evaluated. Then you get shipped overseas right into a war zone. People are trying to kill you all the time. Sometimes you have to try to kill other people. Everything you ever learned in church or in school or from your friends has to be put aside, put on hold, just so you can survive through another day. You give up every shred of who you were, who you thought you were, so you can be something else. Something that can fight, and will fight. Something that will survive no matter what."

"Jesus," Julia said. "Why would anyone choose that?"

"It's hard to explain, but . . . you're surrounded by other people just like you. People going through the same thing. They watch your back and keep you alive. You do the same for them because there's nobody else who can. You get through every day because if you fail, if you lower your guard even for a moment, your friends might die. Friends isn't even the right word. They're more than that. There's no good term at all for what your buddies become. But that's the compensation. It's the consolation for all the horror you face. You get these people in your life, these people who mean everything to you, and you know they feel exactly the same way about you. You'd never say it. They would tease the hell out of you if you did. But you love them."

"You . . . do?" Julia asked. Maybe because she understood what he was trying to say to her.

"Believe it," he told her. "Believe it. When you're a soldier, you're not alone. You are never alone."

She pressed her face against his chest, and he just held her, held her close, because he knew that was exactly what she needed.

SUPERIOR, COLORADO: APRIL 15, T+73:21

After she'd rested for a bit, CPO Andrews went out and got some food and other supplies—some antibiotic cream for Chapel's various wounds, new clothes for both Chapel and Julia, some toiletries for all of them and three disposable cell phones so that they could all stay in touch with Angel. Andrews and Julia both had their own phones, but they were afraid to use them. None of them were sure what was going to happen to them, whether CIA agents were hunting them down even then.

"Laughing Boy could be coming here, right now," Julia pointed out.

"I'm actually more worried about Hollingshead," Chapel told her.

CPO Andrews found the idea shocking—that was her boss he was talking about—but she'd worked for the Defense Intelligence Agency long enough to know it wasn't impossible.

"He sent me to Denver," Chapel explained, "and I'm sure he knew what was waiting there for me. I pushed him too hard when I investigated Camp Putnam. I wasn't supposed to see that place. Now I'm a liability. Angel," he said, because she was always listening via the speakerphone, "I don't know how you left things with him—"

"I told him you're dead," she answered.

"Oh," Chapel said.

"Judge Hayes had announced as much in his press conference. He claimed he had your body and was going to turn it over to the Denver county coroner.

Director Hollingshead sounded pretty upset when I confirmed it."

"I'll just bet he did," Chapel said, frowning. Hollingshead was an excellent spymaster, and that meant he had to be an excellent actor, sometimes.

CPO Andrews shook her head. "I don't get it. Why would he want you dead? He chose you to track down the chimeras. There's still one at large. Why would he want you dead now?"

"Because while I was so busy digging up CIA secrets—which suited him just fine, since he's at war with Director Banks over there—I accidentally turned up one of his." Chapel sat down on the bed and reached for a plastic container full of roasted chicken. He was starving. Blood loss could do that to you, he knew. "Rupert Hollingshead was in on the chimera project from the beginning. I'm pretty sure he ran the whole thing."

No one spoke. The two women in the motel room stared at him. He was sure Angel was listening intently, too.

Chapel took a bite, chewed, swallowed. Wiped his hands on a napkin. "In 1990, Ellie Pechowski was recruited to teach the chimeras. She was recruited by a captain in the navy. It's funny how ranks work—I'm a captain in the army, but that's not the same rank. In the navy—"

"Captain is O-6, one rank below O-7, a one-star rear admiral," CPO Andrews said. "You're talking about my branch, now."

Chapel nodded. "*Captain* Hollingshead was the one who recruited Pechowski. When we talked about her, he called her Ellie Pechowski, not Eleanor. Only people who know her call her Ellie." He took another bite. "I can't prove it. But I think he probably recruited William Taggart and Helen Bryant as well. I think he was the commanding officer at Camp Putnam. I think the chimera project wasn't a CIA project at all. I think it was a Department of Defense project all along."

"That's—that's—" CPO Andrews couldn't seem to accept it.

"It makes sense. It makes a lot of sense," Angel said. "It explains why Camp Putnam is a DoD facility, and why Hollingshead was the one who captured you when you went there, not Banks."

Chapel nodded. He didn't like this much. He wished it weren't true. But the evidence kept mounting. "I think he's been lying to me—to us—all along. For one thing, I don't think there even is a virus."

"What?" Julia asked, laughing as if the idea was ludicrous.

"Think about it," Chapel said. "Ellie Pechowski and your parents had constant exposure to the chimeras for years. But nobody ever treated them like Typhoid Mary. They were never quarantined, and until now nobody tried to kill them."

"No virus," Julia said, staring at her hands. "But . . . Laughing Boy . . ."

"They claim he's tracking down anyone who might be exposed. That's a great cover story. It lets him kill anyone who might be a witness—there won't be any serious oversight if Banks can claim that Laughing Boy is just controlling the outbreak of a weaponized virus. Even the president would sign off on that. But it also means Laughing Boy can kill anyone who even saw a chimera. Hollingshead and the DoD started this thing. Banks is trying to erase it from history. That's what this has all been about. I understand the kill list now. I know why those people were chosen to die. They're the only ones who know what happened. The only people who could bear witness to what Hollingshead did."

"Which means," Angel pointed out, "that everyone in this room is on that list—and I am, too."

"They want to kill us," Julia said.

"Yes," Chapel told her.

"Okay. How do we stop them?"

SUPERIOR, COLORADO: APRIL 15, T+74:22

Chapel gave her a warm smile. "I have an idea about that. It means getting your father—alive—to someone who'll listen. Congress, maybe. Or the media if that's not an option. We make this thing part of the public record. Expose the secret. Tell the world what they did to those two hundred women."

Julia and CPO Andrews both seemed to like the idea. Chapel wasn't as crazy about it, himself. It was treason. It was breaking every rule he'd ever learned as a spy. But it was the only way out of this.

"We have one advantage," Chapel said. He reached for the new shirt Andrews had bought him and started pulling it on. "They think I'm dead. Angel, what did you tell Hollingshead about Julia?"

"He thinks she's on a train headed back to New York City. I considered telling him that CPO Andrews was taking her back on the jet, but it would be too easy for him to track that. She has to file a flight plan every time she moves to a new location."

"If you're headed for Alaska, I'll take you, of course," Andrews said. "But by that same reasoning he'll know right away that you're alive, as soon as he checks the flight records. There would be no other reason for me to take the plane to Alaska."

"We'll just have to risk it. Hope that he's preoccupied and doesn't check those records, at least not until we've got Taggart. It puts even more time pressure on us, but I don't see any other way to get there in a hurry. How soon can you have the jet ready?"

"Hold on," Julia said.

Chapel stopped buttoning his shirt to face her.

"You lost nearly half your entire blood volume," she said.

"And got it back, from the transfusion. I feel fine," he insisted.

"I'm sure you feel great. People always do after getting new blood. You're still weak, regardless of how you feel. You were shot, Chapel. You have a gunshot wound. You shouldn't be going anywhere except a hospital."

"We don't have time," he told her.

"Believe me, I get it. All our lives are at stake. And I hear what you're saying, that we have to move quickly before they come for us. But if your wound reopens in the middle of a firefight, or you just collapse from anemia . . . I don't know how I'll feel about that. I can't just let you kill yourself, Chapel."

"'First do no harm,' right? That's the oath they made you swear?"

"I'm not a people doctor. My oath said something

about only using my skills for the benefit of society. Whatever. I'm not saying this as your veterinarian. I'm saying it as your . . . buddy."

Chapel reached out and put his hand on her arm. She didn't shy away.

For a long moment they just stared into each other's eyes.

"Angel," CPO Andrews said, "can you book these two a room? Another room, I mean?"

Julia and Chapel turned to face her as one. "What?" they both asked.

The CPO just smiled knowingly.

"Are you going to try to stop me from going to Alaska?" Chapel asked Julia.

"I guess not. Just consider it to be against medical advice." Julia turned around and started gathering up her things. "It'll be cold in Alaska. It's probably still winter there. Angel, can you order us some parkas? And maybe some nice, warm boots."

"I'll have them sent to the plane," the speakerphone told her.

IN TRANSIT: APRIL 15, T+75:37

There were no mandarin oranges or goat cheese salads left on the jet—the tiny galley had never been meant to be used so often. Besides, it felt wrong to ask CPO Andrews to act like a stewardess now that she was part of their conspiracy. The three of them waited for takeoff together and ate cold chicken, the remains of the meal Andrews had gathered in Boulder.

On the table between the jet's seats lay a cell phone, a cheap disposable flip phone that they left open so Angel could join their conversation. There was no need for hands-free sets now, since Chapel wanted Julia and Andrews to hear everything that was said.

"It's five and a half hours in the air to reach Fairbanks International," CPO Andrews told them. "That's the closest airport to the address we have for William Taggart. Probably another hour in ground transport. That probably means snowmobiles, of all things. My weather data says it's still very much winter up there—the snowpack won't melt until May—and there are drifts five feet deep in the surrounding areas."

"Snowmachines," Chapel said. "In Alaska, they have snowmachines, not snowmobiles."

"What's the difference?" Julia asked.

"In Alaska, they're called snowmachines. Everywhere else they're called snowmobiles."

Julia stuck her tongue out at him and he laughed. It was good to see her smiling again. He'd worried that the trauma she'd endured might have broken her spirit. Of course, every time he'd thought the woman must surely be at the end of her rope, she'd surprised him by coming back stronger. He should have expected no less.

"Angel," Chapel said, "assuming Ian was traveling by train, how long would it take him to reach Fairbanks?"

"It's hard to say. There's no direct rail service— Amtrak only takes you as far as Vancouver," Angel answered. Chapel could hear her clacking away at her keyboard. "If he was driving a car, it would take three days and nine hours, but of course, he won't know how to drive. So it has to be longer than that, given the weird ground transportation options he's looking at. How much longer I can only estimate. Say, a minimum of three and a half days."

Chapel checked his watch. "So we'll still arrive before him. It'll be close, but we'll make it."

Everyone sighed a deep breath of relief.

"What about Laughing Boy?" Chapel asked. "Have you had any luck tracking him?"

Angel sounded apologetic. "No. He checked himself out of the hospital in Atlanta shortly after you left Stone Mountain. Since then he's been a ghost. I did find out one thing you're not going to like. There was a fire at the visitors' center on Stone Mountain. A bunch of park rangers died. I think we can assume that was no accident."

Chapel leaned forward in his seat. "What about Jeremy Funt?"

"Still in a hospital in Georgia. Still under armed guard—guards sent there by Director Hollingshead," Angel pointed out. "Banks may very well want him dead, but Hollingshead is protecting him."

Chapel nodded. He had a sudden hunch. "What about Ellie Pechowski? Have you been in touch with her at all?"

"She's very much alive, if that's what you're asking. Do you want me to go down the list? Ellie, Marcia Kennedy, Olivia Nguyen, and Christina Smollett are all fine; there's no sign they've been visited by the CIA or anybody else who might wish them harm. I got a phone call from Marcia Ken-

nedy just an hour ago, asking if it was still dangerous for her to go outside. I told her yes, but I think
you were right, that Laughing Boy needs to have
proof someone's been exposed to the virus before
he can kill them. I think they're safe, as long as Ian
doesn't come to see them."

"That's what we're going to try to stop, now,"
Chapel told her. "I almost hate to ask, but what
about Franklin Hayes?"

"Perfectly healthy," Angel told him, "and giving
nonstop press conferences. He's still reporting that
you're dead, that you died saving him from Quinn."

"Wishful thinking," Chapel said. "He's probably
assuming Laughing Boy will kill me before I can
prove him wrong."

"In the press conferences, whenever he talks
about the 'assassin,' he always uses the term 'domestic terrorist.' There's been no release of information
concerning Quinn's identity—or the fact that he
wasn't quite human. The media's going crazy with
the story, though, trying to link Quinn to everyone
from Timothy McVeigh to the Unabomber to the
Earth Liberation Front. Both sides, Democrats and
Republicans, have been quick to blame the lunatic
fringe of the other party. I'm guessing that Franklin Hayes won't be getting any tricky questions at
his confirmation hearing when he goes before the
Senate. If they stop short of giving him a Bronze
Star, I'll be surprised."

"Civilians aren't eligible for that medal. You can
only earn it during wartime."

Angel laughed. "Honey, they're already calling
him a frontline veteran of the culture wars."

Chapel fumed, but he had worse enemies to face yet. Maybe someday, when the case was broken wide open, he'd have a chance to tell the real story and take Franklin Hayes down a peg.

Maybe.

IN TRANSIT: APRIL 15, T+76:06

Once they were in the air, CPO Andrews brought a bottle of Scotch and three tumblers out of the galley and they all shared a drink. "This is good stuff. Sorry you can't join in, Angel," Chapel said, as he sipped at the brown liquor.

"I've got a Red Bull here and some leftover Chinese food," Angel told him over the phone that lay on the table. "Works for me."

Chapel exhaled deeply and lay back in his seat. "We should all try to get some sleep," he said, and the women agreed. CPO Andrews helped them recline the seats so they became full, comfortable beds. She dimmed the cabin lights and then headed back toward her galley.

"You're not going to sleep in one of these things?" Julia asked.

"I have a bunk back there and a little TV set," Andrews said, shrugging. Chapel thought she might have winked at Julia, but he couldn't be sure. "I'll be fine."

Before she left, Chapel had one question for her. He glanced toward the front of the cabin, toward the jet's cockpit. "I've never seen the pilot of this plane," he said.

"No, and you won't," Andrews told him. "He has his own exit from the cockpit, and he never needs to come back here. Hollingshead wanted it that way—he holds all kinds of meetings in this jet, and the things he has to say aren't for everyone's ears. Don't worry about the pilot. He has no idea what we're up to, and he doesn't want to know. He's cleared to receive my orders about where we fly to and that's it. If we need to communicate with him or vice versa, there's an intercom system, but it's only used in emergencies."

Chapel nodded. It was for the best, of course. CPO Andrews had probably wrecked her career already by conspiring with him and Julia. There was no need for the pilot to be implicated.

"Good night," Andrews said, and she headed aft.

"Good night," he told her. He lay down in his seat-turned-bed and grabbed a blanket. Before he could pull it over himself, though, Julia came and lay down next to him, spooning up against him in the seat. He didn't ask why. Frankly, he was glad for her warmth lying against him.

Julia said nothing. She pulled a pillow around to support her head, pulled the blanket up over their shoulders, and was probably out like a light. Maybe she was learning a few things, like how to sleep anywhere and whenever she was given the chance.

He regretted that she'd had to learn that. Or what it felt like to kill a man. But he was grateful she'd been there—grateful that she'd saved his life so many times, but also just grateful that he'd gotten a chance to know her. To be with her.

For a long while he just lay next to her, watching

her red hair stir in front of his face, blowing this way and that with his breath. Eventually he lifted his arm and gently placed it around her waist.

"Mrmph," she muttered, and snuggled back against him some more. The smell of her, the presence of her, filled his senses. It was like they were alone, floating on a cloud high over the mountains, high above the world.

He couldn't help it. He leaned forward and kissed the back of her neck. In response she brought her hand down and placed it over his. He kissed her neck again and she shivered, then laced her fingers through his.

"Can't sleep?" she whispered. She wriggled back against him again and gasped in surprise. He had a pretty good idea what she'd just felt. "Apparently not," she said. She turned her head so she could look at him over her shoulder.

"I'm just glad you're here," he told her.

She twisted around enough to kiss him on the lips. "Me too," she told him. She rearranged herself to spoon him again as if she planned on going back to sleep, but she stroked his thumb with hers, and he knew she was at least half awake now.

He kissed her neck again, and this time her back arched. She let out a pleased sigh and pulled his hand up to her mouth. She kissed each of his fingers in turn. "This might be our last chance," she said, and he knew exactly what she meant, but he waited for her to make the next move.

She did so by bringing his hand down to cup her breast. He squeezed it gently and she sighed again. Through her sweater and her bra he felt her nipple begin to harden and he stroked it with his fingers. He kissed her neck more passionately now, and she squirmed against him, rubbing up and down on him until he couldn't stand it. He moved his hand down between her legs and felt the heat there, heat and a little dampness, even through the thick fabric of her jeans.

"Ohhh," she said. "Chapel . . . last time, in Atlanta, it was about comfort. This time it's more. Right?"

"Yes," he told her, and he pressed his mouth against her neck, her back. He unbuttoned her jeans and unzipped them. She moved his hand down inside her panties and he slipped a finger inside of her, feeling how wet she was.

With her help he pushed her pants down, then unzipped his own fly. Her hand found him and guided him into her from behind. Their bodies fit together effortlessly. She was more than ready for him and he grabbed her hip, ready to thrust deeply into her, but she pushed back. "No," she said. "Take it slowly. In fact, don't move. You shouldn't be exerting yourself."

"Oh," he said. "Should I . . . stop?" He moved his hand against her body, his fingers making circles through her damp pubic hair, finding the right spot.

"No," she told him. "No, I didn't say that. I didn't say that at . . . all." Her ass slid back and forth against him in tiny movements that were going to drive him insane. "Just . . . stay there. Oh, yes. Right there." She ground against him and he started to gasp. It was torture, utterly sweet torture, and he desperately wanted to grab her and just fuck her, but he knew how to obey orders. The tip of his index finger made tiny circles on her clitoris and she moved with her own rhythm, her own pace. He could feel her body shivering, feel her rising toward climax. Deep inside her, he felt his own body surging with blood as she took him along for the ride.

"Right there," she said again, and pushed her hand down over his, crushing his fingers against her body. "Right . . . yes . . . there . . . yessss . . . Don't you dare stop," Julia told him, and pushed his hand back to where it had been. The whole time her ass shifted against him, rubbing up and down in tiny increments until he complied. He forgot all about—whatever it was that had made him stop— and moved his finger in quicker, ever smaller circles until Julia was bucking against him, thrusting backward with her ass again, and again, and again, and—

"Chapel, I'm going to come," she told him, and looked back over her shoulder at him. "I'm going to—I'm going to—" Her lips were slightly parted and her hair had fallen down over one of her eyes. "I want you to come with me," she begged, and he kissed her deeply even as their bodies jerked and ground together, and he felt himself surging, passing the point where stopping was even an option. She pushed herself back against him one last time and then put her free hand up over her face as her body squeezed him inside of her, as they came together. He pulled his hand free of hers and lifted her fingers away from her face so he could watch her, watch her eyes as she came. He stared deep into her eyes and saw what he was looking for there, even as his own body released all his tension into her. He cried out and she covered his mouth with hers and they kissed, just kissed for the longest time as they rode out the wave of their shared orgasm.

Eventually she relaxed and dropped back against him, her back wriggling against his chest. She turned her face toward the pillow and just breathed, breathed in the same rhythm as his own breath. She took his hand in both of hers and used it for a pillow and in a moment he realized she was falling asleep, spent and in perfect comfort with him there, still inside of her.

IN TRANSIT: APRIL 15, T+80:49

Chapel woke later to find the cabin lights slowly coming back on. He blinked his eyes and gently stirred Julia. "I think it's time to get up," he said.

CPO Andrews's voice over the intercom was soft and pleasant. "Good morning. We'll be landing soon. I have a simple breakfast of leftover chicken and vegetables, and a little bread. I'll come into the cabin in a few minutes to serve it."

Julia looked up groggily. She smiled when she saw Chapel's face and leaned in to peck him on the lips. Then she squirmed around to pull her pants back up and zip them. Chapel did the same.

When CPO Andrews entered the cabin, she carried their breakfast on a tray, which she set down on the table between the seats. "It's a little before eleven in Fairbanks," she said. "The current temperature is hovering around thirty-six degrees and it's snowing, but just a little. It won't interfere with our landing. I'm going to the galley to prepare for landing, so you won't see me again until we touch down," she said.

"Uh, thanks," Chapel told her, reaching for a glass of juice.

This time, Andrews definitely winked before she headed aft.

Julia dropped her fork. "She—she must have heard us," she said.

Chapel watched her face. She was blushing, and with her fair skin her whole face turned red, as well as her ears.

"It's a small plane," Chapel said, apologetically.

"But I was trying to be quiet!" Julia put a hand over her mouth. "Oh God. I am so embarrassed."

Chapel bent over his breakfast and ate heartily. He had no comment to make.

IN TRANSIT: APRIL 15, T+81:21

Fairbanks International Airport might have been huge and cosmopolitan or it could have been a tiny airstrip. There was no way to tell. The snow had picked up while they taxied across the runway, and now the whole sky had turned featureless white. Fat, wet flakes landed on Julia's blue-gray parka and collected in her unbrushed hair. Chapel squinted through the snow and tried to make out the terminal.

CPO Andrews hugged herself in the cold. "Are you sure you don't want me to come with you?"

"No," Chapel told her. "I need you here, ready to take off again as soon as we get Taggart."

Andrews shook her head. "Listen, at least—Julia, you take this." She reached inside her jacket and drew her sidearm. It was a snub-nosed revolver. She handed it over to Julia, who held it as if it were a poisonous snake.

Then Andrews wished them luck and closed the door behind them.

They walked across to the main terminal building. At the ground transportation desk, Chapel learned it was easier to rent a snowmachine than it was to rent a car.

"The roads here are treacherous all winter," the clerk explained, showing them to their vehicle. "Snowmachines are the best way to get around. Now which of you is driving—" He stopped suddenly and stared at the way Chapel's left sleeve hung loose from his shoulder. "Here you go," he said, handing Julia the keys.

Chapel looked at the snowmachine. It was bigger than he'd expected, a long, sleek model with skids in front and big, powerful-looking tracks in back. It had room for two, a high windshield, and a spare gas can mounted behind the rear seat. It was no racing model—this was a utility vehicle, meant for getting around over rough, snowy terrain. A workingman's snowmachine.

Steering it, however, meant holding on to a pair of handlebars. That was beyond him now that he'd lost his artificial arm.

"You ever drive one of these before?" he asked Julia as she climbed into the front position. He remembered she was from New York City. "You ever drive a car?"

"Back in the Catskills, sure," she said. "Admittedly, that was fifteen years ago." She shrugged and reached up to touch the new hands-free unit in her ear. Angel had made sure they each had one so she could talk to them both. "I have someone to walk me through it," she said. She gunned the throttle, and the machine roared underneath her. "Ooh," she said. "I might like this."

Chapel climbed on behind her and wrapped his arm around her waist. They leaned forward together, and she steered the machine out onto the open snow, and they were off.

DENALI NATIONAL PARK AND PRESERVE, ALASKA: APRIL 15, T+81:45

The first mile on the snowmachine made Chapel consider seriously just jumping off and walking to their destination. Julia kept goosing the throttle when she thought she was going too slow and stamping on the brake every time the machine fishtailed on a patch of ice, and it was all Chapel could do to hang on. But he should have known by then that she was a fast learner, and she rarely made the same mistake twice. After a while she was driving like a pro, keeping her speed steady and her treads well in contact with the ground. He had to admit he was impressed. He wondered if he could have taught himself to drive the machine as quickly.

The snow made no sound as it fell, and the afternoon sun melted it nearly as fast as it accumulated, but it never stopped. Julia stayed close to the roads where she could, but they were already slick with ice and she had an easier time cutting across open fields. They headed south of the city, across the Tanana Flats, a vast frozen plain that ran unbroken as far as Mount McKinley and the Alaska Mountains.

Chapel thought that William Taggart could have chosen a more hospitable location for his lab. Ahead of them, at the far edge of the Flats, lay a maze of twisting canyons carved by glaciers, a landscape of nothing but snow and dark rock. It would be way too easy to get lost back in those canyons if you didn't have Angel whispering in your ear. Visitors weren't even allowed into the more mountainous parts of the park except on special buses. It was rugged terrain even in summer, and now, with winter only slowly loosening its grip on Alaska, it seemed like a great place to get yourself killed.

They started to see signs warning them that the park was off-limits to snowmachines, but Angel told them to turn off and head west anyway. They entered a narrow canyon between two high ridges and headed south again, skirting the highway as it bent around to follow the river that formed the northern border of the park. Down here in the shelter of the mountains more trees grew, and the only path they had to follow was the road, which they had to cross every once in a while to avoid obstacles.

"You're close, now," Angel said, and Chapel was glad for it. It felt colder and darker by the river, and the snow was falling heavier. They headed away from the road, north along an old logging trail. The ground was broken by permafrost and general disuse, and the snowmachine bounced and shook even when Julia slowed them down to a crawl. "We never would have made it this far in a car," she shouted back over her shoulder. "What the hell does my dad do out here?"

"I thought you might have some clue," Chapel shouted back.

"What?" she asked.

Angel repeated his words, but Julia just shrugged. "I haven't spoken to him in years. I knew he was in Alaska, but I didn't even know which city."

An even rougher path split off from the logging trail. It wound through a stand of pine trees that looked like new growth—few of them were more than ten feet tall. The darkness of the place grew, even though somewhere overhead, through the cloud cover, the sun was shining.

Up ahead, in the lee of a high cliff, stood a small cluster of unremarkable buildings. There was no fence, nor any sign, but Angel was sure of it.

"You're here," she told them.

DENALI NATIONAL PARK AND PRESERVE, ALASKA: APRIL 15, T+83:01

Julia switched off the snowmachine and an incredible silence settled over the clearing in the trees. After a few seconds Chapel could hear the individual snowflakes falling on the ground around him.

He climbed off the back of the machine and took a few steps toward the main building. It was a squat, windowless structure, built of heavy brick that looked like it could survive being buried in snow every year. A metal stovepipe stuck up from one end, pushing white steam or smoke into the air that was the same color as the snow, the same color as the sky. A snowmachine not unlike theirs sat parked near the single door. The machine looked like it had seen some heavy use—duct tape had patched a crack in its windshield, and the skids were scuffed and pockmarked.

Chapel looked back and saw Julia still straddling their snowmachine, her hands on the handlebars as if she might start the vehicle up and drive away.

"You coming?" he asked her. "You don't have to."

She nodded. She was looking at the building as if she could see through its walls. "Give me a second," she said.

He understood. Her father was in there, a man she'd never gotten along with. A man who had done terrible things. He waited in silence. He could feel his nose hairs freezing, but he just gave her the time she needed.

"Okay," she said, finally. Just as he'd known she would. She got off the machine and came up to the door with him. Reaching out one hand, she knocked hard on the door. There was no bell or intercom or any other way to summon the inhabitants.

Nor was there any answer to the knock. They stood together, their breath frosting the air between them. Snowflakes settled on Julia's eyelashes. She knocked again.

Chapel tried the knob. It turned easily—the door wasn't locked.

They stepped inside, out of the snow. The room

beyond the door was wide and open, only a little warmer than the outside air. The inside of the building was even less impressive than its exterior. The interior was lined with row after row of cinder blocks, and one wall of the room was a big rolling door, like a more secure version of a garage door. If it were opened, the building would offer no shelter at all from the elements. There was little furniture inside except for three waist-high aluminum slabs.

On top of each slab lay a grizzly bear, curled up and sleeping, their enormous bodies rising and falling slowly as they breathed. Electrodes were buried in their thick fur and attached to wires that hung from the ceiling. Where the wires came together they were gathered into thick cables.

Chapel put his arm out to hold Julia back. "Watch out," he said.

The bear closest to them had opened one eye. It watched them with a dull indifference. The bear moved its forelegs a few inches, sliding them across the slab as if it would start to get down at any moment. Then, as Chapel held his breath, the bear tucked the foreleg in, closer to its body, and its eye closed again.

"This is not what I expected," Julia said.

"No," Chapel agreed. He tried to think of something else to say.

Before any words came to him, Julia approached one of the bears—one that had not stirred—and walked slowly around its slab, examining it without touching it. Chapel wanted to drag her back, to get them both out of there, but he didn't want to risk making any noise.

"They don't appear to have been ill-treated," Julia said, bending low to examine one bear's nostrils.

"Are they drugged?" Chapel asked, whispering, though she'd spoken at conversational volume. Having grown up in Florida, he'd learned a healthy respect for animals that could maul and eat him without much provocation. You didn't mess with alligators if you wanted to live to go to high school, and he had a feeling grizzly bears belonged in that same category.

Of course, she was a veterinarian. Maybe she knew what she was doing.

"They're hibernating," Julia told him. "Actually, 'denning' is the preferred term. Bears don't really hibernate."

"No?" Chapel asked.

"No, their body temperatures never fall low enough for that, and they can be woken up a lot more easily than, say, a hibernating bat or hedgehog."

"Then maybe you should keep your voice down," Chapel told her.

"Aren't they gorgeous? You just want to curl up with them and pet their fur," she said, almost touching a bear's two-inch-long claws. "Not a good idea, though. They're way stronger than they look, and a hell of a lot faster. They can run faster than us. And they're highly aggressive—it doesn't take much to set them off."

"Like the chimeras," Chapel pointed out. Meaning, she should get away from them and the two of them should leave. As cold as it was, the air in the room was humid and full of the smell of the bears, and he was feeling distinctly uncomfortable. Give Chapel a squad of heavily armed Taliban screaming for his death and he knew how to react to that. This was wholly outside his sphere of knowledge.

"My dad's not here," Julia said. "He must be in one of the other buildings." She took one last look around and inhaled deeply. "Come on. Let's go."

"Okay," Chapel said. He backed toward the door slowly, not wanting to take his eyes off the bears.

When the door opened behind him, he jumped and nearly shouted in panic.

A man in a heavy parka stood there, looking in at them. He looked like he was in his midtwenties, and he had a calm, unexceptional face. "Who are you?" he demanded. "What are you doing in here?"

"We're looking for William Taggart," Julia told him. "He's my father."

The man's expression didn't change. "He's over in the lab. You shouldn't be in here. We can't risk exposing the bears to anything you track in. What do you want with Dr. Taggart?"

Julia looked confused. "I told you, he's my father. And he's . . . in danger. I've come to find him and take him out of here."

The man turned to face Chapel, as if expecting him to introduce himself. Chapel stayed silent. There was something about this guy he didn't like. He *felt* wrong, even though Chapel couldn't have said why.

"Dr. Taggart can't leave. Not now," the man said. He was still staring at Chapel. When Chapel didn't say anything, he held out one hand for Chapel to shake.

Chapel grabbed him by the wrist and twisted around to get the stump of his left shoulder into the man's stomach, knocking him off balance. Chapel pushed hard, and the man fell backward out of the door, into the snow, with Chapel almost on top of him.

A look of sudden rage passed over the man's face. But that wasn't what Chapel was watching. When the man staggered out into the daylight, the sun hit him right in the eyes. Just as Chapel had expected, black nictitating membranes slid down over the man's eyes to protect them from the sudden light.

Chapel rolled off him and up to his feet, drawing his sidearm in the same motion. He pointed the weapon right at the man's face.

"Ian," he said, "don't you fucking move."

DENALI NATIONAL PARK AND PRESERVE, ALASKA: APRIL 15, T+83:16

The chimera blinked and spat some snow out of his mouth. He put his hands down on the ground as if he might spring up at any second, jump up and right at Chapel.

"Where's Taggart?" Chapel demanded. "What have you done with him? Did you kill him? I don't know how you got here so quickly, but if you killed him, you're going to pay. And don't get any crazy ideas about trying to trick me. I've met your brothers. Malcolm, and Quinn, and the one who went to New York. The one who killed Helen Bryant."

"Brody," Ian said.

"Brody, fine. He's dead. They're all dead, except for you. And I don't think you're going to last much longer."

"Brody killed her," Ian said. "He actually did it." He shook his head. His body was tense on the ground, a steel spring ready to be triggered.

Chapel took a step back, his aim on Ian's forehead never wavering. He should just do it, he knew. He should shoot now and end this. He'd tried to convince Malcolm to come in peacefully and look where that had gotten him.

Ian started to sit up.

"I told you, don't move," Chapel said.

Julia appeared in the doorway of the building where the bears were hibernating. She looked scared.

"Stay back," Chapel told her, and she nodded.

"You killed them," Ian said. "All of them?"

"Three of them. Yeah," Chapel said. "I had to. They would have killed me, otherwise. They would have killed a lot of people. You need to realize, right now, that you've already failed. That getting up right now, that fighting me, will get you exactly nothing. Just because I killed them doesn't mean you need to fight me."

"You must know a little about us," Ian said. He held himself perfectly still. Probably biding his time. "Maybe you know how we feel about someone who can kill a chimera in a fair fight. We respect that."

Chapel thought of Camp Putnam. Of four corpses mounted on a blackboard, and the words scrawled beside them. He remembered what Samuel had told him, about the gang that Ian had ambushed and destroyed. "I know about Alan, and what you did to him and his gang," Chapel said. "So I know your respect isn't worth a whole lot."

"You probably also know I won't make this easy on you. Why don't we both back down? You leave here. I won't kill you."

Chapel squinted at Ian, wondering what to do. Then, over to his left he heard feet crunching on snow. He didn't move, didn't look away from Ian's face.

Julia stepped out of the doorway. "Dad?" she said.

Chapel couldn't help himself. His eyes flicked sideways, and he saw another man, an older man, standing twenty feet away. William Taggart. Alive and apparently unharmed.

"What are you doing with my new lab tech?" Taggart asked.

DENALI NATIONAL PARK AND PRESERVE, ALASKA: APRIL 15, T+83:26

"Everyone just stay calm," Chapel said, once they had relocated to the lab.

"Young man," William Taggart said, "that would be a lot easier if you weren't holding that gun."

Taggart was in his midsixties but looked younger to Chapel. He had a wild shock of red hair that stuck up almost straight from his receding hairline, and bright eyes that never stopped moving. He talked elaborately with his hands and always seemed excited about something.

His lab was little more than a shack, much smaller and more cramped than the building that housed the three bears. Much of it was filled with equipment—centrifuges, racks of test tubes, piles of computer towers tied to laptops by thick bundles of cables. The rest was filled with cages. Cages full of bats and hedgehogs and squirrels in three different colors. Every animal in every cage was fast asleep, breathing so slowly it was hard to realize they weren't dead. They were all hibernating, and like the bears they were being constantly monitored by electrodes buried under their fur.

"What—exactly—are you studying here?" Chapel asked. "And why is the CIA funding it?"

Taggart's eyes went wide, and his smile lit up the room. "I've found the DNA sequence that codes for hibernation," he said, grabbing a nearby cage and peering down at the sleeping hedgehog inside. "It's so simple! For a long time we've understood the metabolic pathways involved in hibernatory behavior, but we've lacked the genetic understanding to know why some animals do it and some don't. Just imagine what we could achieve if humans could hibernate. Can you grasp how useful that would be, to be able to program yourself to sleep that deeply, any time you wanted? The possibilities are enormous, from spaceflight to military applications—"

Chapel shook his head. "I don't think the CIA has manned missions to Mars planned for this."

"Well . . . no, probably not," Taggart admitted. "They probably want to use it to torture people or something; that's what they're good at. But what if I could put you to sleep for four months, at the end of which you would have lost twenty-five percent of your body weight? We could end obesity and curb the diabetes epidemic!"

"Or turn Guantanamo Bay into a warehouse full of people the government doesn't like," Julia said, "asleep for as long as we wanted."

"That's a horrible thought," Taggart admitted.

"The CIA is famous for taking horrible thoughts and making them realities," Chapel pointed out. "Like, say, the chimeras."

Taggart threw his hands in the air. "I knew it would come to this! That's why you came here, isn't it? To accuse me of doing bad things. Maybe you thought I would get all ashamed and start apologizing."

"It would be a start," Julia said. "Dad, we found out what you did to all those mentally ill women. We found out about their—their mothers."

Every eye in the room turned to look at Ian.

The chimera was sitting quietly in a chair at one end of the room. He'd allowed Chapel to tie him to it with lengths of computer cable. Chapel had no doubt that when Ian was ready he could break those bonds without much trouble. But tying Ian up made him feel marginally better.

"Apologies and the like can wait," Chapel insisted. "We actually came here to save you. From him."

"As you can see," Taggart said, "that wasn't necessary. Ian's been quite pleasant company, actually. He just showed up here about three days ago, and since then he's been helping me with some of the more mundane tasks. Cleaning the place, at first, but now I've taught him to titrate samples and prepare them in a centrifuge. He's an amazingly quick learner and—"

"Three days?" Chapel asked. "He's been here three days?"

"Yes. He showed up even before I got that phone call saying I was in danger."

Chapel's eyes went wide. There was no way Ian could have gotten to Alaska that quickly on trains or even in a car. He must have flown directly to Fairbanks after escaping from Camp Putnam. The Voice must have helped with that. This whole time Chapel had been racing against the clock, trying desperately to get to Alaska before Ian could . . . and the chimera had been here the whole time.

But then something else occurred to him. "When Angel called you to warn you someone was coming here to kill you, you didn't even mention to her that someone—that a chimera—had already arrived?"

"Ian and I had already come to our arrangement by then," Taggart pointed out.

"Arrangement?" Chapel asked.

It was Ian who answered. "I had questions. I had a lot of questions. I needed to know why I'd been created, mostly. I needed to understand. So I made a deal with Dr. Taggart. I promised I would control myself, that I wouldn't hurt anyone, if he would tell me what I wanted to know."

"You're a chimera," Chapel pointed out. "You can't make a promise like that. Any kind of frustration, any small thwarting of your will can set you off. I've seen it—I've watched your brothers go from reasonable to homicidal in seconds. You can't control it!"

"Any kind of frustration," Ian said, smiling. "Like, for instance, having a gun pointed at my face and being threatened with death right when I'm about to find out the answer to the most pressing question of my life? You mean a frustration like that?"

Chapel had to admit that Ian had already proven him wrong. "It's just a matter of time," he said.

"It's a matter of will," Ian told him.

Chapel shook his head. "No. I've tried to reason with chimeras. I know where that gets you. You're a time bomb, Ian." He turned to face Taggart. "Doctor—back me up here. I don't know why you created the chimeras, but I know they were a failure. You had to lock them up in Camp Putnam, seal them off from the world because they were too violent. Maybe you thought they could be something else, but their level of aggression was more than you could handle. They—"

"I beg your pardon," Taggart said, sneering. "There was no failure. The chimeras were—are—exactly what I meant them to be."

"You meant them to be so aggressive they killed each other off while the U.S. military could only stand back and watch?" Chapel demanded. "You meant for them to be violent psychopaths?"

"I wouldn't put it that way," Taggart said. "But the answer is yes."

"Good God!" Chapel exclaimed. "What the hell did you think you were playing at? Why on earth did anyone authorize you to make these things?"

Taggart took a step backward and leaned against a stack of cages full of sleeping bats. "As an insurance policy, of course."

DENALI NATIONAL PARK AND PRESERVE, ALASKA: APRIL 15, T+83:37

"Insurance policy?" Chapel asked, deeply confused. "Against what?"

"All this is top secret, Captain," Taggart said. "Are you sure you're cleared to hear this? I know my daughter isn't."

"Dad," Julia said, "he has a gun."

Apparently that was enough. Taggart shrugged and inhaled deeply before beginning his story. "It was 1979 when I was first brought in to consult on what became the chimera project. It had a code name back then—Project Darling Green—which thankfully was abandoned later, when we actually realized we could do it, we could solve the problem."

"What problem?" Chapel demanded.

"Nuclear winter," Taggart said. "You're young. You might not remember what it was like back then, during the Cold War. We were locked in a stalemate with the Russians for so long. They hated us, wanted to conquer us. And we would do anything—anything—to stop them from taking over the world. After the Cuban Missile Crisis we understood that if either side started a war, it just wouldn't stop. Nuclear missiles would launch. The world would be reduced to ashes. There were generals back then, smart men, really, who thought we could still win. That even after a nuclear exchange America could prevail. By the seventies, though, we scientists had figured out that was wrong—simply untrue. A thermonuclear exchange on a global level wouldn't just turn cities to rubble and give a few people cancer. It would fill the sky with dust that would linger for years. It would change the planet's climate and make human survival—not just American survival but the future of the human race—next to impossible. If the Russians launched against us, it would be the end of humanity."

"But the Russians knew that, too," Chapel pointed out. "That's why they never launched."

"It's why they didn't launch when they could still control their people," Taggart said. "Even then, even in '79, we could see the Politburo wouldn't last forever. The Soviet Union was crumbling. The Pentagon was convinced, absolutely convinced, that if a coup or a popular uprising began in Moscow, then the Kremlin would start a war just as a last-ditch attempt to consolidate their power. At the time it was taken as gospel—a nuclear war was coming and could happen at any time.

"The generals came to me with an idea. A crazy idea, I thought, though it had potential—and they had money to make it happen, more grant money than I'd ever seen before for a project like this. What they wanted was . . . visionary. They wanted to create a new human race, a new phenotype based on good American DNA. A race of men and women who could survive even through a nuclear winter. People who were highly resistant to radioactive fallout, who were strong enough to live on polluted water and whatever food they could dig out of the ground. People with the immune systems of gorillas, people with the healing factors of lizards, people with the vision and the resistance to ultraviolet light of hunting birds. People to survive the apocalypse."

Chapel glanced at Ian. "You gave them chimeras."

"If you want to skip ahead, then, yes," Taggart said. "The work was fascinating. It was incredible— Helen and I invented whole new fields of genetics and even basic biology. We had the money, the equipment, anything we wanted, anything we needed to do work that would have been unthinkable at the time. No one back then had even considered transgenics. The idea of splicing together disparate genomes to create a functional organism was pie in the sky, it was science fiction. Nobody understood homeotics at the time, work on atavisms was partial and hesitant at best, and we had barely begun to experiment with plasmids and gene therapy. But we knew it could work."

"'We,'" Julia said, softly. "You and mom both signed off on this."

"Helen . . ." Taggart's face grew wistful. "She was a genius. She and I together were . . . something more." He shook his head. "We would stay up all night, hurling ideas back and forth, tearing holes in each other's hypotheses, spinning out new trains of thought, building on each other's brilliance. It was—it was the most satisfying relationship any two human beings could ever have. She understood what we were really doing. We weren't just working for the Pentagon. We were working for the future. Both of us should have gotten Nobels out of that work. But it had to be kept secret, utterly secret." He shook his head, but then he smiled as if he was reliving a happy memory. "DNA sequencers were so primitive back then, it was like coding genes by hand, like writing computer code on a legal pad." He laughed. "We had to do all the basic research ourselves, compile our own library of sequences. There was no Human Genome Project to consult. I remember the night we finished writing down the final strings. When we had the recipe for what would become Ian and the others. It was well past midnight. We were tired, but we were also so full of As and Cs and Gs and Ts that we couldn't sleep. We were talking in code, in genetic code, making jokes about our favorite proteins and dreaming of ribosomes hard at work. We went outside and looked up at the stars. We watched the moon set. It was like *we* had become something more than just human beings. Like we were little gods, at the dawn of a new creation."

"And then you created two hundred embryos, which you implanted in the wombs of mentally ill women without their consent," Chapel pointed out.

"Hmm. Yes. All right, we did," Taggart admitted, waving his hands in front of him as if he'd like to argue the moral niceties but didn't have time. "We ended up with two hundred perfect little organisms."

"Babies," Chapel said.

"Hardly. These weren't like human infants. They could walk within weeks of being born—almost as fast as horses. They had teeth and they could eat solid food after a few months. No, these weren't babies. They were the children of a new race. A new species, almost."

"You locked them up in a camp in the Catskills.

You gave them basic medical care, a little education, and nothing else," Chapel said. "You raised them like children, but then they started killing each other." He looked over at Ian. The chimera's face was totally passive, unreadable. "They tore each other to pieces. They were too aggressive. Too violent. So you sealed up the camp and abandoned them."

"Is that what you think we did?" Taggart asked, looking offended. "You think we made a *mistake*? That we were surprised and horrified that they were dangerous? Please. The world they were created for—the world under nuclear winter—was going to be a harsh and dangerous place. We made them aggressive so they could rule it. So they could own it. That was always part of the plan, Captain. They were always supposed to be that way."

Chapel's blood went cold. He couldn't believe it.

"You wanted us to kill each other," Ian said. It was the first time he'd spoken since Taggart began.

"We wanted you to be fighters. And when you fought each other—well." Taggart made an expansive gesture. "That was just Darwinian selection. The strongest survive. The most fit. We needed you fit."

"Not everyone agreed with you," Chapel pointed out. "Dr. Bryant seems to have changed her mind about things. She left you and went on to spend the rest of her life trying to make amends for what she'd done."

"She lost her detachment, yes," Taggart agreed. "She started thinking of the chimeras as humans. As children. Well, she was a woman. She was genetically coded for that kind of sentimentality."

Julia leaped up, her face red with anger. "Dad—" she began, but Chapel gestured for her to wait a moment.

"Not just Dr. Bryant. The CIA didn't like it, either. They decided at some point, maybe when Malcolm ran away, that the project was too dangerous. Especially since there was no more Soviet Union, and no real possibility of nuclear winter. They decided to shut you down. Kill everyone involved to keep it secret. They've spun a cover story, claiming the chimeras are infected with some kind of virus. They're killing anyone who might possibly be infected, even though we've figured out there is no virus."

Taggart said nothing.

He didn't need to. His face went white. His hands stayed frozen in the air.

"There is no virus," Chapel repeated.

"Dad," Julia said. "Dad—answer him! Tell him there's no virus!"

Taggart slowly shook his head. "I can't do that," he said.

DENALI NATIONAL PARK AND PRESERVE, ALASKA: APRIL 15, T+83:44

"There *is* a virus," Chapel breathed.

He'd been so sure. He'd been certain it was a ruse. But they'd told him the truth all along. The chimeras were carrying a virus, a man-made pathogen, and they could infect anyone they came in contact with.

Laughing Boy wasn't using it as an excuse. He was cleaning up a very real mess.

Ian leaned forward against the cables that bound him. He looked very interested. On the other side of the room, Julia let out a little whimper.

"There had to be," Taggart said, softly.

"What do you mean?" Chapel demanded.

"It's . . . it's how it's done. There was no other way. We wrote the code, the one percent of the genome that had to change to create a chimera from human gametes. We assembled the code in a virus. A virus doesn't reproduce on its own. It needs a host. It latches on to a cell and injects its DNA into the cell's nucleus. The cell has no defense against this; it can't tell one strand of DNA from another. So it replicates the viral DNA exactly. Over and over again. The virus we used to create the chimeras was designed to target egg and sperm cells only. It takes over the normal egg, say, and turns it into a chimera egg. When the egg is fertilized, it develops into something like Ian here, not a human embryo. Look, this is all very basic stuff, it's the foundation for gene therapy and—"

"Then skip to the part where the chimeras are still carrying the virus," Chapel told him.

"Well . . . they have to. To do what they're designed for. The chimera DNA has to be copied exactly, or the much more robust, more proven human DNA will take over. The chimera virus has to spread so that any normal human who reproduces with a chimera will bear a chimera child."

"Wait—you wanted them to reproduce?"

"Yes, of course," Taggart said, blinking. "Oh. I

see. You thought our insurance policy was supposed to survive on its own. You thought our two hundred male specimens were supposed to be the entire batch, that they would survive when the rest of us died." He seemed to find the idea amusing. "That wouldn't do us much good, would it? They're all male. They would only last one generation."

"Wait," Julia said. It looked like she'd figured this out. "Just wait."

"In the event of a nuclear war, the chimeras would have been released into the survivor population," Taggart explained. "They would have mated with female survivors—human female survivors—and produced chimera offspring, which would breed true. We couldn't afford to have their children be human. So the virus remains in their systems. It looks for other hosts, hosts that can allow it to reproduce. It looks for human sperm and egg cells."

"And it spreads through any bodily fluid contact," Chapel said.

"Well, yes. It would be nice if it only passed on through sexual contact, that would be more elegant, but—"

"Anyone who gets infected has chimera babies?" Julia demanded. "Anyone? And all their babies are chimeras like him?" She jabbed a finger toward Ian. "Dad—you fucked up. You really fucked up!"

"Julia, sit down and watch your language," Taggart commanded.

"No. No, I will not," she said, striding toward him.

Chapel grabbed her arm. "Dr. Taggart. You and your wife, and Ellie Pechowski, all had constant contact with the chimeras at Camp Putnam. How is it you were able to avoid becoming infected? Is there a vaccine against the virus?"

"Not exactly a vaccine," Taggart said.

"Then—what? A cure? A treatment?"

"You could call it that. I had a vasectomy and Helen had her tubes tied. Ellie was already in menopause when she came to work at the camp."

A chill ran down Chapel's spine. So that was the nature of the virus. Angel had been told it had a long incubation period and it was hard to detect. She couldn't have known the whole truth. The virus would sit dormant in the body of anyone it infected, lie there waiting for them to have children. Only then would it manifest itself. There would be no symptoms, no warning. Just, one day, a little baby would be born . . . and blink its nictitating membranes. That would be the only way to know you had it.

"Dad, I always knew you were an asshole, but—"

"What are you going on about, Julia? Why are you talking this way?"

"Because I probably have it, Dad. I probably have your fucking virus! Tell me, were you looking forward to having grandchildren? How about grandmonsters instead?"

"What? I . . . what?" Taggart said, his face as white as the snow outside.

DENALI NATIONAL PARK AND PRESERVE, ALASKA: APRIL 15, T+83:44

"Enough," Chapel said.

They all turned to stare at him.

"This isn't getting us to where we need to be. So there is a virus. That's good to know, but it doesn't change anything. We still need to get you out of here, Dr. Taggart. I have no doubt the CIA is sending men here right now to kill you. They're trying to shut up anyone with knowledge about the chimeras or Camp Putnam or Project Darling Green. They're done trying to pay you off with grant money—the virus, and the escape of the chimeras, has given them the excuse they need to just kill you. Julia and I are in the same boat."

"So you came here to protect me?" Taggart asked.

"I came here to extract you," Chapel said. "We need to move you to a safe location. The problem is, we're still not sure exactly where that might be. The CIA has a long reach. Moving you to Canada won't be enough . . . I need to talk to somebody."

"Angel?" Julia asked.

"Yeah," Chapel said. "Excuse me." He holstered his weapon and took out his phone. "Julia—you watch Ian. If he tries to get free, just shoot him."

"I guess I don't get to be protected," the chimera said. He didn't sound particularly offended.

Chapel ignored him and walked over to the door of the shack. He dialed Angel's number and put the phone to his ear. Waited for the cheap phone to find a signal.

And waited. And waited. Eventually the phone beeped at him three times to say his call had failed.

"You won't get reception out here," Taggart said, looking mildly amused. "The mountains are in the way of the nearest cell tower."

"This is Angel we're talking about. She's very

good at getting around obstacles." Chapel tried the call again. "Huh," he said, when the call failed again. The third time, he said "Damn," instead.

It took him a while to realize that the phone in his hand was just a cheap disposable. He'd been working with Angel so long he'd come to think she was magic. That she could communicate with him anywhere. But that hadn't been the case, had it? In Atlanta, when he'd gone too far underground, she couldn't reach him. In Denver, her signal had been jammed.

Crap. He'd lost his arm. He'd lost the backing of the DIA. Now he'd lost his guardian angel. He'd been reduced to just his own, natural resources. He had to think this through. Pick his next step very carefully.

"Okay," he said, walking back over to the others. "Okay. We just have to do this the old-fashioned way. I'm going to go outside and scout the road, make sure we have a clear route out of here. Then we're all going to get on the snowmachines and head for the nearest town."

"That's Healy, back at the highway," Taggart told him. "It's just a little tourist trap of a place, though. They sell things to the tourists who come to see Denali."

"If we can just get to civilization, any kind of civilization, we can hide in the crowd there. That'll help," Chapel told him. He looked at Julia—then at Ian. He didn't like the idea of leaving her in the shack with the chimera. The alternative wasn't great, but it would have to do. "You," he said, pointing at Ian. "You're with me."

"Okay," the chimera told him.

"You try anything, I will have to kill you," Chapel said.

"Understood. Just make sure *you* understand— that deal goes both ways. You try to execute me, and I'll twist your head off."

"I don't doubt it," Chapel told him.

Chapel untied the chimera and let him grab his parka. Then he went to the door and cracked it, peering out into the afternoon light. He saw nothing but snow out there—it had been falling the entire time they'd been inside talking. A thick layer of snow sat on top of the snowmachines, and more snow had fallen against the door so it tumbled inside around his shoes and started to melt instantly. The weather could be a problem, he thought. If they got back to Fairbanks only to find the airport shut down while it was snowing, they could be stuck, vulnerable and alone, waiting for the CIA to show up.

Nothing for it.

"Come on," he said to Ian. The two of them pushed their way outside, shoving the door open against the new-fallen snow. Outside, visibility was cut down considerably by the snow in the air. Their feet made loud crunching noises with every step. If someone was out there, waiting to ambush them, they would never know it.

DENALI NATIONAL PARK AND PRESERVE, ALASKA:
APRIL 15, T+83:55

Chapel's feet sank deep into the snow with every step, slowing him down to a crawl. If he'd had snowshoes, maybe it would have been different. "Why did it have to be Alaska?" he asked.

The question had been rhetorical, but Ian answered anyway. "For the grizzlies. If you're going to study hibernation, you need to understand why small animals do it so well but large animals have a hard time with it. And why grizzly bears, which are very large, can do it while primates can't. And if you want to study grizzlies in anything like their natural habitat, you need to be right here."

"Taggart told you all that?" Chapel asked. He headed through the clearing, intending to make it as far as the road before he turned back. "You and he are getting along pretty well. Considering you were supposed to kill him."

"The Voice wanted me to do lots of things," Ian replied. "But I'm not a machine. I don't do things just because someone tells me to."

"The Voice got you out of that camp," Chapel pointed out. "Some people would think maybe you owed it."

"People, maybe. Not chimeras. We know better than that."

"How did you get here so fast?" Chapel asked. "You can't have come over land. You must have flown. The Voice must have arranged things for you."

Ian stopped in place and seemed to have to think

about it. "I stowed away in the cargo hold of a plane that brought me as far as Fairbanks. From there I walked. The Voice gave me directions. As long as it was helping me, sure. I did what it said. When it wasn't helping me any more, I stopped listening."

"Stay in front of me," Chapel said, gesturing for the chimera to walk ahead of him on the path.

"You don't trust me," Ian said. "I don't blame you. You met some of the others. Malcolm, and Quinn, and Brody. I'm different."

"I met your old gang," Chapel pointed out. "The ones who helped you kill Alan and his gang." Ian said nothing. For a while they just kept wading through the snow, headed south, toward the road. Chapel thought about Samuel. The Voice had told Ian to kill Samuel, and Ian had refused. Maybe—just maybe—there was something to what Ian claimed. Maybe he was different from the others. Maybe he could control his impulses. Maybe that meant Chapel couldn't treat him like the others. Couldn't treat him like a monster.

That was a dangerous line of thought. But if Ian really was able to control himself, to act like a human, then Chapel had to treat him like one, too.

"I met Ellie Pechowski, too," Chapel said, finally.

"Miss P," Ian affirmed.

"Yeah. She said you were different. And I'll admit, you showed a lot more leadership potential than the others. A lot more emotional stability. But you're still a chimera. You're still genetically programmed for violence and aggression."

"You're still a human," Ian said. "You're still programmed for mercy and compassion. It didn't stop you from killing the others."

"I did that to protect other humans," Chapel said. "You did what you did—why? So you could escape from Camp Putnam? See the real world for once?"

"Would that be an unacceptable reason to you?" Ian asked. "Would you have done any differently?"

Chapel thought about it. The chimeras had been created for a purpose they didn't understand. Then, simply because of what they were, they'd been locked away from the world forever. In that situation, yeah. He would have done almost anything to get his freedom. But he would have wanted something else, too.

"They gave you books to read in there. Did they ever give you *Frankenstein*?"

Ian shook his head.

"I read it after I lost my arm. I felt like I was made out of spare parts, then, and I thought maybe I'd find some answers there. It's the story of a man, a scientist, who creates a new life form. In the book he builds it out of parts of dead people. Dead humans. Then he animates it with life, but he's so horrified at what he's done that he runs away from his own creation. Refuses to accept it. The creature ends up killing everyone he loves, and then pursuing him halfway across the world to hound him to his death."

"Why are you telling me this?" Ian asked.

"If I was that creature, I'd want to kill my creator, too."

Ian was quiet for a while. The two of them waddled through the snow, not covering much ground.

There was no sound but the crunching of the snow. No smell in the air but the smell of snow.

Maybe the weather would help them, in the end. Maybe it would slow down the CIA even more than it slowed down Chapel.

When Ian spoke, it was like the air had frozen and his words broke the ice. "But that's not true. You don't want to kill God, do you?"

"What?" Chapel asked. "That's insane."

"You were created by God, weren't you? Do you want to kill him? Look at what he's done to you. He took your arm."

"That wasn't God. That was the Taliban."

Ian shook his head as if it didn't matter. "This creature, in your story. He's upset because his creator was horrified by what he'd done. His creator hated him. Your God loves you, I'm told. He created you and he loves you for it. Don't you think he's proud of you?"

"I . . . I guess I hope he is," Chapel said.

"Dr. Taggart is proud of me," Ian said. "He sees in me what I am, and to him, that's good. Worthy."

"The reason you were created doesn't exist anymore. You were supposed to replace us in case of nuclear war. But there was no war." Chapel glanced up at the mountains, at the sky. He reached for his cell phone, but that meant putting away his weapon.

Too late he realized he'd made a mistake. Ian was already moving, already rushing toward him.

"I'm sorry," Ian said. "It has to be this way."

Chapel dropped the phone and reached for his pistol. He managed to draw it from its holster—but even as he brought it around to fire, Ian smacked it out of his hand. It went spinning off into the snow.

Ian's other hand was already coming toward his face. It was balled into a fist.

Bright flecks of light exploded in Chapel's head. He could feel the cartilage in his nose snapping, feel the bones of his skull shifting on their sutures. He flew backward, propelled by Ian's inhuman strength, and landed on his back in a snowdrift, dazed and unable to move.

"You would have killed me, eventually," Ian said. "You would have had to."

Chapel waited to die.

But he didn't. Nothing more happened. Eventually he regained enough strength to lift his head, to look around.

He saw nothing but snow, nothing but pure white light reflected back at him by a trillion crystals of ice.

Ian was gone.

DENALI NATIONAL PARK AND PRESERVE, ALASKA: APRIL 15, T+84:14

"What's taking Chapel so long?" Julia asked. She was pacing back and forth in front of the door of the laboratory shack, holding CPO Andrews's pistol in both hands. She'd been doing so almost every second Chapel and Ian had been gone.

Behind her, her father was busy tending to his experimental animals. If he had to leave his lab behind, he'd said, he at least wanted to make sure his pets were healthy and had plenty of food and water in case they woke up. He seemed to think he'd be coming back in a day or two. Julia hadn't bothered to tell him otherwise.

"I wouldn't worry," her dad said. "He has Ian with him."

"That's a reason for me to *not* worry?" Julia asked.

"Ian's quite strong and capable," Taggart replied. "If your friend gets stuck in a snowdrift or falls over and can't get up, Ian will help him. For a chimera he's really quite helpful. Can you hand me that spray bottle?"

Julia looked around and found the bottle he wanted, a plastic spray can half full of something straw colored. She tossed it to him. "You lived with them. For years. You spent every day at Camp Putnam. And then you would come home from work and I'd get back from school and we'd sit down to Shake 'N Bake pork chops or maybe Mom's stew for dinner. And you would ask me about my day and what I was learning."

"I remember that time fondly, dear," Taggart replied. He spritzed a little of the yellow liquid on the wings of a caged bat. "The happiest time of my life."

"I never thought to ask you anything about your day," Julia said. She couldn't believe this. She couldn't believe what her life had become. "I could have asked how many of my brothers died that day. How many of them tore each other to pieces."

"You never had any brothers," Taggart said, with a little sigh.

"It's hard not to think of them that way. You

and Mom spent more time with them than you did with me."

Taggart put down the bottle and dragged a stool over so he could sit and look at her. "You're an adult now, Julia. You're almost thirty."

Her eyes went wide. "I've been thirty for a couple years, now," she said. "You can't even remember how old I am?"

"Old enough, I am certain," Taggart said, "to stop blaming everything in your life on your horrible parents."

Julia wanted to scream. She wanted to throw something at him. "I'm not allowed to blame you? I'm not allowed to blame you because one of your experiments killed Mom? I'm not allowed to be angry that one of them tried to kill me, and maybe infected me with his tiny weird-eyed babies?" She put the gun down so she didn't accidentally shoot him in her rage. "I'm not allowed to be upset that now the CIA wants to kill my entire family?"

"I assure you, if I'd known any of that in advance—"

"Oh, no. Oh, no, you don't get off that easily. Let's put aside what you've done to my life. I know what you did to those women, Dad! I know how you took advantage of all those women, those mentally ill women. And I know what you did to the chimeras—studying them, testing them—and then walking away when they got too violent. I've found out all your little secrets. I know exactly what you've done, and now—now—you—"

Tears crowded up in the corners of her eyes and refused to spill over. She was shaking with rage, filled up with excruciating anger. She had to get it out of her body, had to vent it or she would explode.

"What the hell were you thinking?" she demanded. "Why would you do those things? Didn't anybody, even once—didn't Mom ask if what you were doing was moral? Not even once?"

"Your mother was my partner in all of it," Taggart said, in a very small voice. Clearly he'd never expected this. Everything he'd done had been top secret. He'd never expected that anyone would call him on his actions. Much less his own daughter.

But who else had the right, more than she? Julia felt like she was a sword of vengeance wielded by some indignant archangel. She was going to make him pay. She was going to get even for all those women. She would—

"You want to know why I did it?" he asked, finally.

"Yes," she said, blazing with wrath.

"I did it for you," he said.

DENALI NATIONAL PARK AND PRESERVE, ALASKA: APRIL 15, T+84:15

Ian didn't mind the cold.

He ran over densely packed snow, spreading his feet so he didn't sink through the crust, didn't leave footprints. He did this by reflex. There had been snow in the Catskills as well, and he'd spent plenty of time running there. His muscles remembered.

There was much about this place that resembled Camp Putnam. The trees, the rocks, the snow—

all familiar. The birds and even the bears, there had been bears in the Catskills, though they were smaller and not so dangerous. The harshness of this landscape sang to him. It called to him. He had been built for a place like this, a land of winter. This place was a good place for him. He thought of his brothers, of Brody and Malcolm and Quinn. The Voice had led them into cities, into human places. Perhaps that was why they had failed.

Ian didn't mind being alone.

In the camp, he had fought all the time. He had never been at peace in the company of his brothers. He had never had a friend in the humans there, not even Miss P. He saw that now. It had not mattered. His biggest fights, his greatest war, had always been with himself. He had worked so hard, struggled daily, to make himself like the humans. To control his rages, to overcome his emotions. To be worthy of being free. In the end it turned out all that work had meant nothing.

Ian didn't mind that. The futility. Not too much, anyway.

He skidded down a steep hillside, grabbing at tree branches to check his fall. Powdery snow flicked down across his shoulders, danced off his scalp. At the bottom of the slope was a trickling stream. He thought of Samuel and how his fingers had turned black, how they'd died on his hands and had to be taken off. Ian leaped over the stream, not wanting to get his feet wet in that cold, cold water. Even he had limitations.

On the far side of the stream the ground rose again, toward a narrow ridgeline high above. From the trees up there he would be able to see for miles. He would be able to see where he had to go next.

Except . . .

That was the one thing that burned inside him. The question. Dr. Taggart had given him so many answers. He'd explained almost everything. Why Ian had been created. Why he had then been spurned. It made sense. It all made such perfect, crystalline sense in his mind, a graph with clear data points forming a straight line headed . . . headed toward somewhere. Somewhere he couldn't yet see.

He climbed the slope on all fours, grabbing at anything his hands could seize to help him gain more ground. He moved faster than any human could. Any bear. He was so strong. They'd given him that. They had made him strong, and fast. They had made sure the sun glaring on the ice would not hurt his eyes.

They were going to give him a world. A whole world where he would be king.

The last question was like a spiky thing, a worm with sharp-edged armor burrowing through his brain. There had to be an answer. There had to be a final point on the graph, a place where the line came to its end.

But how could he find it now, without Dr. Taggart? Who could tell him what came next? He had worked and fought and bled all his life for freedom. What was he to do with it now?

That was the one thing he minded. And it was tearing him apart.

Just before he reached the ridgeline he stopped. He was about to stand up, to make himself visible on that high ground. But his instincts, the instincts of some predator who had given him some small portion of his DNA, made him stop. He crouched low, cutting down his profile. Making himself invisible against the dark trees.

Perhaps he had heard something in the distance. Something so quiet his conscious mind did not register it. He lowered his third eyelids. He held his breath.

And then he saw it. Movement, very far away. Just now becoming visible. Something—several somethings—moving across the white land.

Others. Other humans, coming this way.

DENALI NATIONAL PARK AND PRESERVE, ALASKA: APRIL 15, T+84:16

Another concussion, Chapel thought.

But no. This didn't feel the same. He'd had chimeras hit him before, and it had been enough to lay him out. This felt like he'd gotten the bad end of a fight in a bar. It felt like he'd fallen off a bicycle and did a face-plant. It did not feel like he'd been hit by a truck, or a jackhammer.

Ian had pulled his punch. He had been trying not to kill Chapel, just stun him a little and buy himself time to get away.

Thank heaven for small favors, Chapel thought and slowly, very slowly, he sat up. He'd been lying in the snow long enough for the flakes to gather on his legs and start to build up a thin blanket there. He shook himself to clear the snow away.

He touched his face, and his fingers came away bloody. He definitely had a broken nose. Well, that was survivable. He used his arm to get up to his feet. He felt shaky, still weak from losing all that blood back in Colorado. He felt like all his joints had been loosened by all the hits and injuries he'd taken over the last few days.

"Damn it!" he shouted, and his voice echoed around the snowscape, knocking small cascades of white off the nearby trees and rocks.

Ian was going to get away.

It took a while for the echoes of his voice to die down. For silence to return to the rocky woods. Except, it wasn't quite silence. There was a sound in the distance, a rumbling, droning sound.

Chapel thought Ian must have left a trap for him. The chimera must have rigged an avalanche, or maybe he'd just set it off himself by shouting like that. He looked up, all around him, looking for where the waterfall of snow and ice and rocks would come from. But as he listened he realized he wasn't hearing an avalanche at all. Instead the sound he heard was more like a swarm of bees, coming closer.

Snowmachines. More than one. Moving toward him at high speed.

He spun around, looking for the lab buildings. They were invisible in the snow, too far away to see. He would never make it back to them in time.

Cursing again, under his breath this time, he threw himself into the snow and used his one arm to cover himself, bury himself in its soft whiteness.

DENALI NATIONAL PARK AND PRESERVE, ALASKA:
APRIL 15, T+84:21

"You did it for *me*?" Julia repeated.

Even to her own ears her voice sounded like a tiny squeak.

"We—your mother and I—did it all for you. Our daughter," Taggart said.

He wasn't looking at her. He was staring at his hands, which lay folded in his lap. She knew him well enough to understand what that meant. Her dad was an excitable, boisterous man who talked with his hands, gesturing for emphasis because words wouldn't come fast enough to keep up with all the ideas in his head. If his hands weren't moving, it could only mean that what he had to say was breaking his heart.

"It was 1979. The year the Soviets invaded Afghanistan," he told her.

"What does that have to do with anything?"

"It was the end of the world. Everybody thought so back then; I mean, everybody in our circle. Fellow scientists. Intellectuals. The military people who asked us to help them only confirmed it. The Soviets were going to take over the Middle East and then India and the president would have no choice but to retaliate with nukes."

"Dad, that has nothing to do with me," Julia pointed out.

"Oh, you're wrong. Because you're not thinking about what else was going on in 1979. That was the year Helen got pregnant. We were so excited when we found out—we knew you would have red hair, we talked about it all the time. We argued about whether you would have my eyes, or her nose. You've never had kids."

"No," Julia said.

"Maybe you can't understand, then. You can't know what that's like. When you start thinking about the future, not just in terms of your own life, of how many years you have left, but in terms of what your child's life is going to be like. What kind of world she's going to live in. What kind of world her grandchildren will have, and what their grandchildren will inherit. And there we were, looking at the future based on the best possible projections. And what we saw was the apocalypse. Civilization, gone. Agriculture, gone. No clean water, no food at all, people in chaos everywhere. That was the world you were going to grow up in."

"That's nonsense. None of that happened."

"Because Gorbachev was actually sane, maybe. Or maybe because Reagan took a hard line with him. Who can say? We couldn't know that at the time."

Julia put a hand over her mouth. She couldn't believe this. "No," she said. "No, that doesn't get you off the hook. What you did was unforgivable."

"If you say so. It's not my place to judge," Taggart admitted.

"It was *criminal*. Dad—you—you can't just—"

She was on the verge of breaking down and she knew it. If he said one more thing, one more word—

"I don't care if it was wrong. I loved my daughter and I wanted her to have a future, that's all. I loved you, Julia, and I still do."

She opened her mouth; she wasn't sure if she was going to say she loved him too or scream in rage or just howl in anguish, but she had to open her mouth to do it, and then—

—closed it just as fast.

"Julia, you don't have to forgive me, it doesn't matter," Taggart said, "because—"

"Shut up," she told him.

"No, you need to hear this," he said.

"No, you need to shut up," she replied. She ran to the door of the laboratory shed and cracked it open. The sound she'd heard was much louder, then. It was definitely what she'd thought it was. The sound of snowmachines coming closer.

"That's not Chapel," she said.

Taggart got up from his stool and joined her.

Together they watched as four snowmachines came roaring up the clearing toward the lab complex. The men on them were dressed in black parkas and goggles that hid their features.

All of them were carrying guns. One of them carried a big shiny revolver. He used it to wave the others forward.

"Oh shit, oh shit, oh shit," Julia said. "Dad, they're going to kill us. We have to fight them off."

"What, make a last stand like the French Foreign Legion?"

"I have my pistol," she said. "You must have some guns in here, right? You live in Alaska. You must own guns."

"I have a tranquilizer rifle," he said. "Huh."

"What is it?" she asked.

Outside, the men were climbing off the snowmachines and spreading out to approach the buildings. She saw that they were making the same mistake she and Chapel had made when they first arrived. They were headed toward the biggest building in the complex, assuming that had to be where everyone was.

"I have a sudden brilliant idea," Taggart said.

DENALI NATIONAL PARK AND PRESERVE, ALASKA: APRIL 15, T+84:33

"Where the hell is Chapel?" Julia breathed, as she watched the CIA men swarm over the little complex. Any second now they would realize where she and her dad were hiding. They would come for them, with their guns, and—

Taggart tapped a key on his keyboard, and his computer flashed a warning at him. He tapped the same key again.

"It turned out to be quite simple, really. A single hormonal pathway that I could manipulate with a very small molecule, something easily synthesized. In the end I could put them into a denning state or wake them up any time I wanted, simply by misting them with a low dose of the chemical."

Julia stopped listening to him. Outside men started screaming, and something like hope burst inside her chest. Because she understood what her father had just done.

In the big building, she realized, the three bears were waking up. And waking up angry—and hungry.

The screams came from inside the big building and they didn't stop. Julia shuddered to think what was happening in there. The man with the revolver—who was obviously in charge—waved more of his men inside, but they looked like they didn't want to go. Julia could hardly blame them.

The leader shot one of his men in the arm.

That got their attention. Two more of them rushed inside the big building. That just left the leader and the wounded man standing outside.

Two too many. Julia had killed Malcolm and shot Laughing Boy in the foot, but she knew better than to think that made her an expert gunslinger. She could hardly expect to get the drop on both those men without getting shot herself.

But if she stayed inside the lab shack, she and her dad were going to die. The bears had bought them a few seconds of grace, but that was it.

Behind her Taggart loaded a dart into his tranquilizer rifle. It was a big weapon, and it looked unwieldy.

"Aim for the one standing next to the snowmachines," Julia told him. That was the leader. "I'll take the other one. You really think that dart will drop him?"

"Every dart is dosed to take down a grizzly," Taggart told her. "It might kill him, actually."

"I can live with that. Okay. When I say go, we go, right?"

"If you're sure about this," he told her.

"I have never been more sure about anything in my life," she promised.

Which was, of course, a lie. She didn't believe this would work, not at all. But she had no other ideas.

"Go," she shouted and kicked the door open. She didn't let herself think about what came next; she just started shooting, barely bothering to aim as she fired three shots in the direction of the wounded man. He looked up and even through his goggles she could see the surprise on his face.

Taggart ran out of the lab shack holding his rifle like it was a club. She started to yell at him, to tell him to shoot, but then he brought the rifle up to his eye, aimed carefully, and squeezed his trigger.

The dart bounced off the side of the snowmachine, a few inches away from the leader's arm. The leader looked down and saw it glinting on the snow.

Then he lifted his revolver and pointed it straight at Julia's face.

She froze in place, paralyzed by fear. Part of her brain was screaming at her to move, telling her how ashamed Chapel would be if he could see this, but her legs wouldn't work. She barely had control of her hands. As if in slow motion she started to bring her own gun up.

The leader aimed his revolver and started to squeeze his trigger.

And then his hand exploded in a cloud of blood.

"Over here," Chapel shouted, firing round after round at the men staggering around the clearing. He was running toward her as fast as he could, his feet digging deep into the snow with every step. He waved toward the old, dirty snowmachine that was parked outside of the large building. He jumped on the back of it and pointed his pistol at the leader's head.

He needn't have bothered. The leader was too

busy just then, down on the ground searching for his severed fingers.

"Come on," Julia said, and grabbed her father's arm. She dashed across the flattened snow between the buildings and jumped on the snowmachine. It started up as soon as she turned the throttle. She glanced down and saw the keys were in the ignition. She hadn't thought to check before.

Other than the leader, the rest of the men who'd come to kill them were down on the ground, dead or wounded. She didn't have time to check each one. She saw that one of them had three big slashes across the front of his parka, exposing the white stuffing inside. She remembered the sleeping bears, how sweet they had looked when they weren't dangerous, and she shuddered.

She glanced back just once to make sure that both Chapel and her father were on the snowmachine. Then she put it in gear and roared out of the clearing as fast as she could go, even as bullets started whizzing all around her.

DENALI NATIONAL PARK AND PRESERVE, ALASKA: APRIL 15, T+84:37

Trees and rocks flashed by as Julia sped them down the trail toward the road. Chapel held on as best he could with one hand while constantly looking back, trying to see who was coming after them. He could hear nothing over the roar of the snowmachine's engine, but he was certain they weren't in the clear yet.

Up ahead the trail headed down a steep slope toward a creek. It looked like the surface had frozen over. Chapel didn't want to have to find out if it was solid or not.

Behind him a black snowmachine came into view, the man driving it struggling to control his vehicle with one wounded hand while fumbling with a pistol at the same time. It was their leader, the one he'd shot before he could kill Julia. Apparently he'd gotten over the shock of his wound. Chapel had a bad feeling about that—he was pretty sure he knew exactly who that man was.

"Into the trees," Chapel shouted, "lose him in the trees!"

Taggart shook his head. He couldn't hear a word.

Luckily Julia seemed of the same mind as Chapel. She powered away from the slope, then slid around in a tight bend until they were racing between trees, pine branches smacking off the windshield and making Taggart duck. It was all Julia could do to keep them zigging and zagging between trees and avoid a collision.

Behind them the black snowmachine appeared, lifting up on one skid as it cut the turn too sharply. The driver rose up off his seat, bracing his pistol on the top of his windshield.

Chapel saw a small animal trail up ahead on their left. "Left!" he shouted, over and over, but Taggart was shrugging and Julia didn't seem to hear him at all. Instead she plowed straight on, weaving and darting through the trees. One branch was low enough to ruffle Chapel's hair and dump a pound of snow down the back of his collar. The trees seemed to be growing closer together now, the room to maneuver between them even tighter. A bullet scored the paint on their machine, leaving a bright oval of silver as it exposed the metal beneath.

Chapel reached for his pistol, hugging the machine with his knees so he wasn't thrown clear. He swiveled around at the waist and fired wildly, not worrying about conserving ammunition. It didn't seem like it mattered much now. With the snowmachine bucking and jouncing under him, he failed to hit the pursuer at all, but at least he made the man duck and kept him from shooting.

"We've got to lose him somehow," Chapel shouted, but no one bothered replying. It was painfully obvious to all three of them. They needed some kind of miracle, some lucky break, or they were all dead.

Too much to hope for.

Directly ahead he could see the trees gave way altogether. So did the ground. The snow ended abruptly and beyond was only sky. They were racing full throttle straight toward the edge of a cliff.

"Julia!" he shouted. "Julia, look out!"

She didn't even turn around. Didn't she see what he saw? How could she not? And meanwhile, behind them, the pursuer was lining up another shot. Chapel was pretty sure he wouldn't miss this time.

There was nothing he could do but watch as the world went into slow motion, as the cliff edge raced toward them and the gunman behind took careful aim. It was going to be close—it was going to be—

The snowmachine hit the cliff edge and for a second, a sickening, horrible second, they were airborne. Weightless. Chapel saw the sky all around him, white and featureless. He felt Taggart rise up from the snowmachine's seat, felt him start to come loose and go flying off on his own. Chapel hugged at the snowmachine with his knees, using every muscle in his swimmer's legs, and tried to pull the scientist back down.

And then the snowmachine hit the earth again, hard enough to rattle every bone in Chapel's body.

They had only fallen about ten feet. On the other side of the cliff was a gentle slope headed downward into a narrow canyon.

Taggart hit the seat hard and nearly spun off. It was all Chapel could do to hold him on to the snowmachine. Julia had lowered her head under the dubious protection of the windshield, and now she raised it again and gunned the throttle.

The snowmachine underneath her gave a whining, coughing sputter. It lurched forward a few dozen feet and then stopped. The engine died. The fall must have damaged something.

The machine was dead.

Chapel craned his neck around to look behind them. Up there, on top of the cliff, the pursuing snowmachine had come to a stop just before the precipice. Its driver stared down at them through his goggles as if he couldn't believe what they'd just done.

"I was kind of hoping he would follow us over and break his neck," Julia said, softly.

"What about *our* necks?" Taggart asked.

"It was the best idea I had at the time. Anybody have a better one, now?" she asked.

Chapel watched the black snowmachine spray ice from its tracks as the driver turned his vehicle and headed away from the cliff edge, presumably so he could find a safer way down and continue the chase.

"How about now we run?" Chapel suggested.

DENALI NATIONAL PARK AND PRESERVE, ALASKA: APRIL 15, T+84:59

The canyon was only a few hundred yards wide, surrounded on every side by high jagged cliffs that Chapel knew he would never climb with only one arm. It stretched out ahead of them, curving gently to the north. There were no trees in the canyon, nowhere to hide except for a few big rocks. A broad but shallow stream ran down its exact middle, glittering in the wan sunlight, rippling over a bed of smooth, moss-covered stones. Away from the stream the snow lay three feet deep over the entire canyon floor.

They had no choice. They ran.

The stream took them around the bend of the canyon quickly enough, even though to Chapel it felt like they were just strolling along, taking their time. He could occasionally hear the whine of a snowmachine up on the cliffs as the assassin searched for a good way down into the canyon.

They came around the final bend and Chapel nearly screamed in frustration.

The canyon dead-ended in a little tarn, a glacial lake surrounded on three sides by cliff. There was no way forward.

They stopped running. There was nowhere to go.

Chapel ejected the magazine of his weapon, wanting to see how many rounds he had left. He got a bad shock when he saw the clip was empty. There was one round in the chamber, still, but—

The sound of the snowmachine grew louder and louder . . . and then stopped abruptly. They could hear the engine wind down and then ping as it cooled in the frigid air. There was no other sound.

"He could be right around that boulder," Chapel whispered, pointing at a giant rock that shielded the bend of the canyon from view. "Find some cover."

There were plenty of smaller rocks to hide behind, scattered around the edge of the waterfall. The three of them each found a good sheltering spot and hunkered down.

And waited.

"Where is he?" Taggart whispered.

"Shh," Chapel said. His eyes scanned the big rock and the ground around it. It was half buried in the side of a massive cliff. A few scrubby pine trees had found anchorage near its top, where scree from the cliff had gathered to form a kind of rudimentary soil.

Along the edge of the boulder a shadow moved. He glanced across at Julia and saw her still peering over the edge of her rock, trying to spot the assassin. He gestured for her to get her head down.

Chapel heard the sound of a foot crunching on snow. The barrel of a revolver peeked around the edge of the boulder. Sunlight glimmered on its silvery metal.

Julia reared up and fired a shot that knocked chips

off the boulder. The revolver barrel drew back, out of sight.

The echoes of the gunshot faded away slowly. Only to be replaced by another sound. A kind of dry, wheezing laughter.

"No," Julia said, louder than she'd probably meant to.

"Ha ha heh," Laughing Boy chuckled. "Hoo! Ha ha."

He had followed them all this way. He'd come personally to make sure they were dead. Banks must have wanted to be certain.

Chapel remembered something that gave him a tiny flicker of hope. "You really think you can hit us firing left-handed?" he shouted.

Back at the laboratory complex he'd ruined Laughing Boy's shooting hand.

"Hoo ha hee heh," Laughing Boy spluttered. It might have sounded like a laugh, but it had plenty of anger in it.

"No toes," Chapel said. "No fingers. Pretty soon you'll look like me."

"I'm no fucking—ha ha—cripple!" Laughing Boy shouted, and he leaned out from behind the boulder to fire three rounds at them, one after another. Chapel shouted for Julia not to take the bait—he could visualize Laughing Boy dropping into a roll, lowering his visual profile, making himself almost impossible to hit—but it was too late.

She fired wildly, squeezing her trigger until her hammer clicked on an empty chamber. Wasting all her bullets. She screamed in frustration and stared down at her weapon, then dropped behind her rock just as Laughing Boy started firing again. Chapel dropped into cover as well, throwing his arm over his head to protect it.

The shooting stopped. Chapel risked a glance over the top of his rock. Laughing Boy was gone. He'd exhausted the six rounds in his revolver. Chapel was certain, absolutely certain he had more, and had just gone back into cover to reload.

"Jul . . . ia," Taggart said.

Chapel looked over and saw the scientist slumped behind his own rock. Blood slicked Taggart's neck. He'd caught a round.

"Dad," Julia gasped, and ran to him before Chapel could tell her to stay in cover. Maybe she could do something for him.

Maybe Chapel could do something for both of them. He jumped up from behind his rock and ran toward the boulder as fast as his legs could carry him.

"Hee heh ha," he heard as he ran.

DENALI NATIONAL PARK AND PRESERVE, ALASKA: APRIL 15, T+85:06

Ian saw it all. He saw blood explode from Dr. Taggart's neck. He rose halfway to his feet in terror. If Dr. Taggart died—how would he ever learn the final answer? How would he ever know what his life was to become? No one else could tell him.

He had followed the snowmachines, crept after them, keeping himself out of sight. Knowing if he showed himself one human or another would kill him. He had followed and stayed close on the off chance there would be one more opportunity, however unlikely, to talk to Dr. Taggart. To ask the final question.

Even if he was beginning to think he knew the answer. Even if he was terrified of what it would be.

Indecision was not a trait common to the chimeras. Their rages led them on, made everything simple. But Ian had mastered his rages. Mostly.

He crept closer, careful not to show himself, and watched.

DENALI NATIONAL PARK AND PRESERVE, ALASKA: APRIL 15, T+85:07

Chapel kept his head down as he ran, knowing that at any second Laughing Boy could start shooting again. The boulder loomed overhead. Its irregular shape made a hundred deep shadows, a dozen good hiding places. Smaller rocks lay tumbled against it, creating natural cover. Laughing Boy could be anywhere in there.

Up ahead he heard rocks patter and fall. He raised his pistol. Kept his trigger finger loose. He couldn't afford to snap off a hasty shot. He had one bullet left. He had to make it count.

He ducked low under an overhanging ledge of rock. Padded across bare stone and came upon a patch of snow that glared in the sun. The sky was clearing, and light was streaming down in thick golden beams that lit up every patch of lichen on the rocks, made every crevice a vein of impenetrable shadow.

Click. Click. He heard the sound and knew what it was. He'd heard it before. Laughing Boy was loading shells into the cylinder of his revolver. It was taking him a while.

"I don't know—ha heh—how you do this one-handed," Laughing Boy said, not shouting now. At a conversational level. He knew Chapel was close enough to hear him.

"You learn to do all kinds of things. You want the chance to learn them? You can put that weapon down and come out with your hands up," Chapel said, because there was no point in stealth now. Laughing Boy was right around the side of the boulder. He couldn't be more than ten feet away. "I'll let you live."

"Oh—ha—will you? Wonderful! Except, heh heh, that's a terrible, heh, deal for you. You kill me, you—ha ha ho—let me live, doesn't matter. They'll send—ha—more like me."

"There's no one else like you," Chapel said.

Laughing Boy seemed to find that amazingly funny. He laughed and chuckled and guffawed. "Guess you'll—heh—find out!"

Chapel dashed around the side of the rock, his arm held out straight, the pistol an extension of his arm, his eyes focused on where his shot would go, his—

Laughing Boy was crouched among some rocks, looking right at Chapel. Revolver shells lay scattered on the ground around him. The cylinder was full, with the brass casings of six new shells loaded into its chambers. All Laughing Boy had to do was snap the cylinder shut and he'd be ready to fire.

Chapel took his shot.

The noise of it was enormous. It blasted around the rocks, came caroming back from the cliffs to deafen him. The stink of the gunsmoke filled his nostrils and he had to blink as it stung his eyes. He forced his eyelids open, forced himself to see if he'd fired true.

He'd aimed for Laughing Boy's center of mass, just like he'd been trained to do. The heart lay just to the left of the sternum, but it was a thick mass of muscle and it was not unknown for a bullet to just graze it, to be turned by its knotty texture, and leave the target alive. You shot for the aorta, the swollen blood vessel just above the heart. Pierce that and death was almost instantaneous.

A red dot appeared on Laughing Boy's parka, just left of center. Blood welled from the wound. But it didn't spurt.

Laughing Boy screamed and gurgled and choked on his pain.

But he didn't die.

His eyes stared into Chapel's, as if he couldn't believe it either. But the light didn't go out of those eyes.

"Must have—heh—missed it by . . . by a—he heh—hair."

"Guess so," Chapel said.

Laughing Boy flicked his wrist, and the cylinder of his revolver snapped shut. He cocked the hammer and was ready to fire again.

Before he could, though, Ian dropped from the rocks above them, to land in a catlike crouch.

His eyes were black from side to side.

DENALI NATIONAL PARK AND PRESERVE, ALASKA: APRIL 15, T+85:10

Chapel could only stare in utter surprise as Ian rose slowly to his feet.

He didn't think he had the capacity for any more shock, but then it happened and he was left reeling.

"Good," Laughing Boy said, "you're—heh—here. Kill this fucker for me."

Ian turned to face Chapel. His nictitating membranes were still down, and his eyes were unreadable. "You didn't know, did you? You didn't know who the Voice was."

"He—you mean—" Chapel had no idea what to say.

"He freed me from Camp Putnam. He showed me how to get here." Ian turned to look at Laughing Boy. "He told me what to do."

"Yeah. Heh ha hee. Yeah," Laughing Boy said. His face was turning pale, and sweat was forming beads on his forehead. He was hurt, and badly, by Chapel's shot. But he wasn't bleeding out. He would live through this, Chapel knew. Laughing Boy was going to survive. And Ian—Ian would—

"I was supposed to be the father of a generation," Ian said, softly. "Instead they made me a weapon. I was supposed to live on after the greatest war, and instead, I am a foot soldier in this petty little squabble."

"Ian, just—let's talk about this," Chapel began.

The chimera lashed out with one hand and knocked Chapel away, sent him flying. The empty pistol leaped from Chapel's hand as he threw his arm back to arrest his fall.

"Good, yeah, heh," Laughing Boy said. "Good. Looks better—ha ah ha—this way, if you do him. Heh."

"You used me," Ian told the CIA assassin. "But I used you, too. I used you to get my freedom. I thought I could be something more, but no. You humans. You can't understand us. You're too limited to understand. All you see in us is death. Well, so be it."

Laughing Boy frowned. "Wait. Heh. What?"

Ian took a step toward Laughing Boy. Another step.

Laughing Boy was no fool. He brought his revolver up. Pointed it at Ian's chest.

"Dr. Taggart made me promise I wouldn't hurt anyone anymore," Ian said, stopping in place. "But he broke so very many promises he made to me. Humans break promises all the time. We can, too."

Laughing Boy fired as fast as he could pull the trigger, pouring lead into Ian's chest and face. He got off five bullets of his six before Ian snapped his arm like a piece of dry wood.

He broke Laughing Boy's other arm with a punch. Another punch took him in the throat and stopped his laughing. After that—

After that it was largely superfluous. When Ian was done, there wasn't much left of Laughing Boy.

Then he turned to face Chapel.

Chapel had no weapons left. He knew he couldn't fight Ian hand to hand. Trying that had nearly gotten him killed when he faced Malcolm—only Julia had saved him then. He tried to scramble away, tried to fend Ian off with his arm, but it was impossible, there was nothing he could do. Ian grabbed Chapel by the throat and just picked him up off the ground and held him in the air. Chapel grabbed at Ian's wrist with his hand, tried to force him to let go, but it was like trying to free himself from an iron manacle.

Chapel couldn't breathe. He couldn't speak.

"No," Ian said, but he didn't let go. "No, I don't have to do this!" He was arguing with himself, trying to step back from the all-consuming rage that ruled him. "No, I will not. I will not!"

He threw Chapel away from him like a piece of garbage.

Chapel rolled through the snow, his whole body racked with pain. He thought he had broken some ribs. Maybe his shoulder, too. He could barely breathe, couldn't think at all. He opened his mouth and tried to talk. Tried to reason with Ian. "Ian, it's over—no one wants to kill you now, you—"

"I had a question," Ian said.

He sounded perfectly calm.

Chapel struggled to sit up. To get back on his feet. Ian was different from the others, maybe. But he was still a chimera. He could still kill them all without any real effort. And he was bleeding. Even if he didn't kill them, if he got his blood on Taggart—on Julia—

Chapel would die before he let that happen.

He forced himself upward. Forced himself to stand. Walking was probably out of the question. But he dropped into a fighting crouch. Got his arm up. Made a fist.

"I had one question left to answer," Ian said.

"What—is it?" Chapel asked. If he could keep Ian talking, maybe Julia could get away. Get her father back to the lab, to the snowmachines there.

"It doesn't matter. I found my answer. I found it while I watched you fight among yourselves."

"Try me," Chapel said.

Ian came closer. One big stride and he was almost close enough for Chapel to touch. It was hard to read his eyes, covered as they were, black from side to side. But the way Ian kept twisting his mouth around, the way he held his hands, spoke volumes.

All his control, all that self-restraint that made Ian different from the others, was just a veneer. A surface. Underneath he was still a chimera, with all that meant.

"I wanted to know what I'm supposed to do now," Ian said. He closed his mouth with an audible click. His blood was draining away, cascading out of him to stain the snow. He didn't seem to be weakening, though. He would never be weak enough that Chapel could take him in hand-to-hand combat. "What comes next for me?"

"You can come south with us," Chapel said. "You can tell the world what they did to you. You can make sure the people who did this to you pay."

Ian studied Chapel's face with his black eyes. His nostrils were flaring. He was one wrong word away from turning into a machine with tearing hands and pummeling fists, a machine that could only kill. "That's what you want from me?"

"Isn't it what you want? Revenge?" Chapel asked. "Killing us won't do it, but you can—"

The chimera grabbed Chapel again and threw him down on the ground. Raised one foot high in the air as if he would stomp Chapel to death, there and then. Chapel closed his eyes and threw his arm across his face, for all the good it would do.

The foot didn't come down.

Slowly Chapel opened his eyes and looked up.

"In another life, I would have been a great man," Ian said. He glared down at Chapel with those black eyes. "I would have been a hero. A king. And you want to give me revenge. You want to make it all better by punishing the guilty. That's not how it works."

The chimera looked down at himself. Blood covered the front of his parka. He tore it away with hands like claws, tore away the shirt beneath. Four massive wounds like red roses had blossomed on his chest. A fifth marred his cheek.

"This world," Ian said, "isn't my world. My world was to be cinders and dust. My world was a place where I could build something new. In this world I have no place." He bent down and sorted among the ruins of Laughing Boy's body and picked up the assassin's revolver.

Chapel was on his back in the snow, still gasping for breath. He tried desperately to get up, to run toward Ian, but it was too late.

Ian pressed the barrel of the revolver under his chin and fired.

UNDISCLOSED LOCATION: APRIL 15, T+85:14

Angel saw it all on the satellite feeds. She couldn't reach Chapel without a cell signal, but she could still watch him from orbit. She saw Ian die.

In a corner of one of her many computer screens she had a clock running, a timer that she'd started around six ten on April twelfth. The moment the fence of Camp Putnam came down and the chimeras walked out into the world. It had been counting up ever since then, telling her how much time had expired, measuring the length of their escape.

She stopped the clock now, at eighty-five hours and fourteen minutes.

All four targets had been neutralized. The mission was complete.

EPILOGUE

Rupert Hollingshead was sitting on a bench with a good view of the Capitol building. He was eating a sandwich from a paper bag, and he had a laptop computer sitting on the bench next to him.

Chapel watched him from across the street. "What am I missing, Angel?" he asked. "Where are the soldiers waiting to arrest me as soon as I show my face?"

"I guess anything's possible, sugar, but it looks like he actually came alone. I don't see any SEAL teams hiding in the bushes. He did say he would meet with you one-on-one."

"And you trust him?" Chapel asked. He had a baseball cap pulled low over his face. He was relatively certain no one had followed him to this meeting, but he'd gotten pretty paranoid over the last month as he made his way back to Washington. When Hollingshead had asked for this meeting, he'd just assumed it had to be a trap.

"About as much as you do," Angel admitted. "But I also want to hear what he has to say."

Chapel grunted in frustration. This was a stupid

move. Coming out of the cold like this, even for just a few minutes in a public place, meant putting himself at enormous risk. They could take him at any time. And once they had him they could get him to talk. He had no doubt about that. He would hold out as long as he could, but eventually he would tell them where Julia was hiding.

But if he didn't go down there and talk to Hollingshead, he would never know what the admiral wanted to say for himself.

"Okay," he said. "I'm going in. Let me know the second you see any suspicious movement near my location."

"You got it, honey."

Chapel strode quickly over to the bench and sat down. He did not look at Hollingshead. The admiral seemed slightly surprised to see him.

"Is that a mannequin arm in your sleeve there, son?" he asked.

"Your people would be looking for a one-armed man," Chapel said. "My artificial arm was destroyed in Denver, so I had to improvise."

"Clever."

For a while they sat in silence. Chapel waited to see armed soldiers come running at him, weapons ready, but none appeared.

Hollingshead continued to eat his sandwich. He said nothing.

"Banks was behind it all," Chapel said, finally, though he was relatively certain Hollingshead already knew that. "I can't prove it, though. He used Laughing Boy as a cutout. Laughing Boy was the Voice. That disposable phone I found in Camp

Putnam that you took from me. It would have told you as much."

"Indeed," Hollingshead said.

"He released the chimeras. Gave them the kill list and sent them out to murder everyone on it. If they failed, he would still have the excuse the targets had been exposed to the virus, so he could kill them anyway. It was all about cleaning up a mess. Your mess. Fixing the chimera problem, and fixing it quietly, will earn Banks some favors in the White House. And meanwhile he'll have a pet judge on the Supreme Court, in Hayes. The CIA is going to come out of this looking like a bunch of heroes."

"You've figured it all out," Hollingshead agreed.

"Not all of it. I thought you were on my side, but then you betrayed me."

"Interesting. That's how you saw it?"

"How else can I see it?" Chapel asked. "You knew what was going to happen in Denver. You knew it was a suicide mission. But when I started to figure it out, when I started to ask questions, you shut me down. And then you threw me under that particular bus. You all but sent me to Denver at gunpoint."

Hollingshead took a bite of his sandwich. "I suppose I did."

"I know why you picked me. I get it now. You said you didn't pick my name out of a hat. That was true. Banks would have vetoed anyone you chose for this mission, if he thought they had a chance to succeed. So you called up a semiretired one-armed guy in his forties, long past his prime. Me. You needed to sacrifice somebody and I was expendable. I understand that. Obviously I don't like it."

"Obviously."

"But I understand it. I just can't figure this one thing out, though. What did you stand to gain from this?"

"I beg your pardon?"

Chapel shook his head in disgust. "It was a game. The CIA and the DIA were playing a game, with Camp Putnam as the chessboard. Right?"

Hollingshead nodded. "Darling Green was a DoD project, and for a long time we owned it lock, stock, and barrel. That changed when Malcolm escaped. That wasn't supposed to happen. The CIA was brought in to cover external security on Camp Putnam. Ever since then they've been trying to take over the whole thing."

"Why would they even want a mess like that?"

Hollingshead smiled warmly. "Until you can answer that question, you'll never truly understand politics, son. Why did the U.K. go to war over the Falkland Islands? Because they thought it belonged to them, and people with power will never give up power voluntarily."

Chapel laughed, a short, bitter laugh. "So to take over Camp Putnam, Banks had to blow part of it up. Wow. By letting the chimeras out, they became an external security problem. His bailiwick."

"But his mole failed. I was called in before he was. So I retained some oversight on the recovery effort." Hollingshead put his sandwich down. "I was allowed to bring you in, as a last attempt to save myself from disgrace."

"Except—you didn't. You had every chance to make that work. But you threw the game. You could have warned me not to go to Denver. If I didn't go, there would never have been an attempt on Hayes's life. Hayes needed a martyr for his cause, and until I arrived he couldn't play out his false flag operation. You could have ruined all of Banks's plans by just telling me not to go. Instead you sent me in with a pat on the back. Certain that I would get myself killed just like Banks wanted."

"No," Hollingshead said.

"No?"

"That's where you're wrong."

"Admiral. With all due respect, sir. Don't lie to me now. It's not going to get you anywhere."

Hollingshead sighed. "You think so little of me. Are you armed, Captain? Did you come here to kill me? Let me tell you a little story first if you'd be so, ah, kind. Don't worry. It's quite short."

"I'm listening."

"About two years ago I fell down a flight of stairs. Terrible bother of a thing, broke my femur if you can believe it. When you're as old as me that can happen, apparently. I had to have a hip replaced, too, which—son, be glad you aren't old enough to know this yet—is one of the most debilitating surgeries there is. After the replacement I needed lengthy and quite, oh, decidedly unpleasant physical therapy."

Chapel frowned. Where was Hollingshead going with this?

"I went to Walter Reed for it. And there I met a man who was going to become a very good friend of mine, despite the fact that I cursed his name every day. A physical therapist, a fellow with one arm, one leg, and one eye."

"Wait—you're talking about Top," Chapel said.

"I'm talking about the meanest son of a bitch I ever met," Hollingshead confirmed, "and the man who made sure I am not in a wheelchair today. A man who, despite my advanced age, insisted that I consider myself one of his 'boys.'"

"You're definitely talking about Top."

Hollingshead nodded. "Top had one bit of conversation he kept coming back to. Just how lucky I was. I certainly didn't feel that way. But he would continuously point out that while I had lost a hip, my new one was a perfectly good replacement. I was far luckier, he kept telling me, than boys of his who had lost arms and legs. He occasionally mentioned one of his boys who had lost an arm. A boy from Military Intelligence with one arm who had somehow taught him—taught Top, that is—how to swim. He was unabashedly proud of this particular boy."

Chapel didn't know what to say.

"When Tom Banks came to my office and I could see in his eyes he would never accept a young, strong, whole man for this mission, I rejoiced, honestly. I finally had the chance to activate the operative I'd wanted to meet for so long. I most certainly didn't pick your name out of a hat, son. I'd been following your career for months, waiting until I had the perfect opportunity to bring you into my personal fold. When I discovered what Banks had planned for my operative in Denver, I didn't hesitate for a second to recommend you for that particular mission."

"Now you're losing me," Chapel said.

"I didn't send you to die there, son. You're one of

Top's boys. I sent you there because I knew nobody else could live through it."

Chapel could only stare in disbelief.

"It had to happen that way. It had to come to all this. It is a sad fact of our particular line of work that the pieces on the game board can never be allowed to know all the rules of the game they're playing out," Hollingshead said. "Perhaps most sad is the fact they rarely know if they're winning or losing."

"You—you think you won this?" Chapel asked.

"Not entirely. We lost Helen Bryant, who was a good woman, despite what history forced her to do. Many other people died as well, people who were perfectly innocent. I don't consider that a total victory."

"But—but Banks and Hayes got what they wanted—they—"

Hollingshead put away his sandwich and picked up his laptop. He opened it and clicked the trackpad a few times. Then he turned it to show the screen to Chapel. "It looks like I've timed this just right. What you see here is a live feed of what is happening, even now, on the floor of the Senate. It's going out on C-SPAN."

Chapel studied the screen. There was no sound, but the video showed exactly what Hollingshead had described. A panel of senators had gathered to ask questions of Franklin Hayes. Chapel was watching the judge's confirmation hearing.

"I don't understand," Chapel said. On the screen Hayes was smiling. One of the senators said something and everybody laughed. Clearly they were all having a great time. Just as Chapel had expected, it looked like Hayes was going to sail through the hearing and be confirmed with no trouble.

But then the view blurred as the camera was whirled around to point at something else. It ended up focusing on the doors at the back of the Senate chamber, which had just opened. Two people came up the aisle. In the grainy view of the laptop's screen, Chapel couldn't quite make them out. A Senate page led them toward a table next to the one where Hayes sat. A microphone was put on the table and adjusted so the newcomers could reach it. They were given water and legal pads and pens in case they wanted to take notes. Slowly the camera zoomed in until Chapel could finally see their faces.

One of them was Ellie Pechowski. The other he barely recognized—until someone pointed a camera light at him.

Then his nictitating membranes slid down over his eyes, turning them completely black.

"Samuel," Chapel gasped. "You knew he was still alive."

"The whole time," Hollingshead affirmed.

On the screen the Senate floor erupted into chaos as people rushed to get away from Samuel, to pull back from the monster in their midst. Franklin Hayes jumped up and started shouting at someone. The senator in charge of the proceedings banged his gavel for order. Without sound, Chapel could only imagine what people were saying.

"Samuel will give witness to the entire story," Hollingshead promised. "He will expose everything that happened to him. He will tell them about the Voice. He will tell them about the kill list, and how the assassination attempt on Hayes was staged."

"No one will believe him," Chapel said.

"Perhaps not. Does it really matter? Most likely Banks will attempt to spin this against me. He'll expose my involvement in the day-to-day running of Camp Putnam. I may be indicted," Hollingshead said. He was smiling. Beaming. "Maybe I'll pay for everything I did back then. Just as I deserve."

"And that's winning?"

"I've wanted to come clean on this for a very long time, son. I'm willing to pay the piper now. It's unlikely I'll go to jail," Hollingshead said. "I may be removed from my post. But Tom Banks is in much worse trouble, believe me. When everyone was under the impression that you were dead, he forced me to turn over the entire project to him. I gave him full authority on the cleanup of Darling Green, and for maintaining the secrecy of the chimeras and their escape. He bullied me into it, but I conceded with as much grace as I could muster."

Chapel wanted to laugh. "You old son of a bitch. You gave him all the rope he asked for—so he could hang himself with it."

"All the, shall we say, blowback from this little display," Hollingshead said, gesturing at the laptop screen, "will fall squarely on Tom Banks's head. It will ensure he is ejected most forcefully from CIA headquarters. He'll be lucky if they let him back into the state of Virginia. And it will forever and irrevocably make sure that Franklin Hayes is never appointed to the Supreme Court. I may not win, son. I may not come out of this smelling like a rose. But I guarantee you *they will lose*."

Chapel shook his head. "And once the kill list is made public, there's no way Banks can ever hurt anyone on it, not without implicating himself as a conspirator to murder."

"You have put your finger exactly on it. Ellie, a dear friend of mine, will be safe. So will the young ladies who we used so horribly. Jeremy Funt will no longer be persecuted. And you, and your dear Julia, are perfectly welcome to come out of hiding now. You are safe, son. Everyone is safe."

"I—I don't know what to say," Chapel said. "I thought, coming here today, you were going to have me arrested. Or killed."

"Hardly. In fact," Hollingshead told him, "if you're willing to put up with me awhile longer . . . I'd like to offer you a job. A permanent position. The Cold War was a long and dark time, full of secrets. There are plenty of skeletons in that particular closet I'd like yanked out into the light of day. Assuming I still have a job tomorrow, I promise you'll have one, too. Oh, and I'll see about getting you a replacement for that arm of yours. Least we can do, really."

Chapel put a hand over his mouth. He couldn't help it.

He laughed long and hard.

WASHINGTON, D.C.: JUNE 5, 14:28 EDT

"So it's official? You're working for Hollingshead now?" Julia asked

"I'm getting a W-2 form and everything," Chapel told her. They were walking down a Washington street on a sunny day and no one they saw was armed, no one was looking to kill them. "I get two weeks' vacation a year, though, and I'm starting my first one immediately."

"Maybe we can go someplace quiet," Julia said, taking his arm.

Neither of them was exactly sure what they were to each other, now. For a while he'd been scared their relationship would be over before it started, until Hollingshead had called Chapel one fine morning and given him one piece of excellent news.

Both of them were negative. There was no trace of the chimera virus in either of their systems. They'd caught a real lucky break there. They wouldn't have to be quarantined. They wouldn't be separated by medical necessity.

They would always be buddies—but now, maybe, they had a chance to be something more.

Not that he could exactly come out and say as much.

"How's your dad?" Chapel asked, to keep his mind off the question.

"They say he'll make a full recovery. The bullet pierced his jugular, but my field dressing held." She shrugged. "I don't know what to make of things, yet. He told me—well. He told me why he did it all. I hope someday I can forgive him. I'm going to try."

Chapel nodded. He hoped she would find some peace there, eventually.

"What about Samuel?" she asked.

His eyes widened. He'd barely thought about the last living chimera. Already they were receding behind him, like a bad dream. "He's going to get new hands, for one thing. I can vouch for what they can do in that line, these days."

"But what is his life going to be like?" Julia asked. "Where will he go?"

Chapel shrugged. "Back to Camp Putnam, if he wants to. Or maybe he can go live with Ellie. Try to find a place for himself in the human world." Ian had realized at the end that was impossible. But maybe Samuel was different. "I don't think his life will ever be what we think of as normal. But it will be what he chooses."

"That's nice," Julia said. "It's nice somebody gets that. After all the people who got hurt. Who didn't get to choose."

"You're thinking of the women. Olivia Nguyen and Marcia Kennedy and Christina Smollett. All the others."

"I think about them a lot," she said.

"Hollingshead told me that he's taking personal responsibility for what happened," Chapel said. "He's setting up trust funds for them. All of them. They'll never need to worry about medical care or rent or anything else as long as they live. And the president's going to give them an apology."

"I guess that's something," Julia replied.

"Hollingshead's trying to do the right thing. I guess that's all we can do now." He looked up. This wasn't the time to dwell on the past. "Are we close?"

"This looks like the place," Julia said.

They were standing outside a little café with an open air seating area. It looked like a nice place—white linen tablecloths, waiters in bow ties. "Do you see her?" Chapel asked.

They were finally going to meet Angel.

Chapel had begged her to let him buy her lunch. He wanted to thank her for saving his life so many times. He wanted to see what she looked like, too. He'd cajoled and pleaded and bargained with her and finally she had relented. She'd sent him—and Julia—an e-mail telling them to be at this restaurant at this time.

There was a woman sitting alone at one of the tables. She had on a floppy hat and sunglasses and she was studying a menu. A waiter poured mineral water from a sparkling decanter into her glass.

Chapel walked across the seating area with a smile on his face. His new arm was still being fitted, so he had pinned up one sleeve of his uniform tunic. He'd put on his best dress blues for this. He walked up to the table and clicked his heels on the pavement. "Ma'am," he said, "may I have the pleasure of introducing myself?"

The woman looked up with one arched eyebrow. She lowered her menu and looked him up and down.

"What are you supposed to be? Some kind of war hero who picks up random women when they're trying to enjoy a drink?" she asked.

Chapel's face fell. Was this some kind of joke?

A waiter tapped him on the shoulder. "Sir," he said, "I think you're mistaken. You're looking for Ms. Angel, yes?"

Chapel blinked in surprise. "Yeah," he said.

"Right this way."

The waiter led him to another table where two glasses had been set on the tablecloth. Another waiter emerged from the restaurant with a pair of beer bottles on a tray. He poured the drinks, then departed. The first waiter held Julia's chair while she sat down. Then he produced a piece of paper from his apron and handed it to Chapel. Without a word he walked away.

"Only two glasses," Julia said.

"Yeah," Chapel replied. He unfolded the piece of paper. It was a letter written in a loopy cursive hand. "'Sweetie,'" he read. "Um—"

"Go on. Read the whole thing," Julia told him, grinning.

Chapel read it aloud:

> *Sweetie:*
>
> *Sorry to disappoint you. I'm afraid that's as close as we're going to get today. If you and I are going to keep working together, we have to keep things a little professional.*
>
> *Enjoy the drinks. They're already paid for. Enjoy each other's company. Get to know Julia a little better. Find out if the two of you still like each other when nobody's trying to kill you. Enjoy this beautiful weather.*
>
> *Maybe someday the three of us will get to-*

gether. One way or another. But for now, just
raise a glass for me. And know I'd be there if I
could.

> *Hugs and kisses,*
> *Angel*

Chapel set the note down on the table. He grinned sheepishly at Julia. "You think she's watching us right now?" he asked.

"I'd count on it," she replied.

They raised their glasses and clinked them together.

The weather that day was, indeed, beautiful.

Author's Note

This is a work of fiction. The prosthetic arm I describe in this book does not currently exist. Although it is based on real technology, I have in many cases exaggerated its abilities. However I do not wish to take away from the incredible strides made in prosthetics in the last fifteen years. Largely as a result of the high and terrible number of amputees coming home from our wars, hundreds of scientists and engineers have done Herculean work creating new and (much) better prosthetic limbs than existed previously, and the results are simply staggering. The DEKA "Luke" arm in particular is a miracle of design and technology, and it has improved immeasurably the lives of many people who deserve it most. I would be remiss if I did not offer my deepest respect to its creators.

Turn the page for
an early look at the next

Jim Chapel mission from

David Wellington,

THE HYDRA PROTOCOL,

out in May 2014!

Dust motes hung in the early light streaming down through the archive's overgrown windows, twisting slowly in the dead air. A card catalog cabinet lay overturned on the cracked linoleum, its contents gutted onto the floor so the fine handwriting on them was bleached to sepia by years of sun exposure. One wall of the main room was lined with stacks of periodicals held together by fraying twine—old party literature from discredited regimes, outdated factbooks and bound analyses from long-dead KGB agents, all marked STATE SECRET, all still forbidden long after the Cold War had ended.

She stooped down in the dust and picked up a photograph of Brezhnev that had been filed in with the rest. It was just a standard portrait, the kind that might have hung in every office building in Russia forty years ago. Still it had been stamped as secret, with a warning indicating the penalties for unauthorized access. Most likely the librarians here had gotten in the habit of stamping everything that came across their desks.

The Soviet Union had never had time to come to trust computers. Right up until the end hard copy had been the rule—all secret information must be printed, bound, and filed, even if by 1991 no one wanted it anymore. What she was looking for had to be here, in this old archive building on an uninhabited island on the wrong side of Russia. For years she had tracked down the information, the last piece she needed to complete her mission. Her life's work, she thought, with a little grim humor.

So much had been lost when the coup failed and Yeltsin took the reins of the country. In the first flush of liberty the country had gone mad, like a dog chewing at its own paw. KGB installations across the country had been ransacked and set aflame, people who knew vital things had been taken away and quietly killed before they could be debriefed, computers had been smashed, archives razed. Of the seven KGB libraries in Russia that had once housed the information she needed, six had been pulled down and their records burnt. This one had survived only because no one remembered it was here. Even the librarians who once worked here had disappeared, some crawling into bottles to drink themselves to death—the traditional suicide method for ex-KGB—some emigrating to breakaway republics or even nearby Japan.

Here was the last repository of the records the KGB had kept on dissidents, on foreign spies, on people who simply could not be trusted. Here was the institutional memory of a police state.

Here—

Here it was.

One of the twine-bound stacks held theater asset reports, dry technical papers listing every rifle, tank, and canteen the army possessed in a given region. Hidden among them was one marked with the sigil of the Strategic Rocket Forces. It was not only marked secret but sealed with a red band and actual wax. One glance at the title and she knew she'd found it:

STROGO SEKRETNO/OSOVAR PAPKA
SYSTEMA PERIMETR PROJEKT 1991

After so long she could hardly believe she held the report in her hands. The last copy on earth, and the only piece of paper that could make the world safe again. She placed it inside her coat, close to her heart, and then pulled up her zipper to keep it in place.

Hurrying to the door she almost missed the sound. A crackling, the sound of someone stepping on broken glass outside. She stopped in the doorway and tried not to breathe. She heard a man speaking, though she could not make out the words. Then someone else laughed in response. It was not a kindly sounding laugh.

She didn't know what to do. She'd known they would follow her, that they would chase her to the ends of the world. She'd accepted the risk. But here, in this lonely place where only seabirds lived now, she'd thought she would be safe.

Evidently not.

"Will you make us come in, little friend?" someone called out, in Russian. "There is no other exit. You must come this way eventually. And we will not wait for long."

She closed her eyes, trying to get an idea of where the voice came from. To the left of the door, she believed. But there were two of them. If they'd been trained by the KGB, one would stand directly before the doorway, the other to the side. If they were Spetznaz—much worse—they would flank both sides, because they would expect her to come out shooting.

She was unarmed. She had not even thought to bring a gun to the island. After all, there were no people on it.

There was no solution except to march forward, into the sunny doorway. Outside the larch trees that covered most of the island fell away to form what looked like a natural clearing, just large enough for them to land their helicopter. She saw it first, a small late Soviet model that could not be hiding too many men. At least there was that.

Next she saw the man who had called out to her. He was in front of her and a little to the left. He wore a turtle neck under a well-tailored blazer and had the dead fish eyes of a man who had killed before. He had a knife in his hand, the kind one might use to pry open an oyster. His much larger partner, who wore a denim jacket, was off to the right a little ways, watching her. His hands were in his pockets. Perhaps he wanted her to think he had a gun, but if he did he would have already shot her.

Just knives, then.

Konyechno, she thought. Okay.

The man in the blazer came toward her, his knife held low by his thigh. He spoke softly, as if he wanted to persuade her to come quietly, though she knew his orders were to make sure she never left the island. "Did you find it?" he asked. "The thing you came to steal? It will not—"

He didn't get to finish his sentence. She moved in fast, sweeping her leg across the back of his calf to bring him off balance. She brought her right arm across her body, protecting her torso while delivering a strong blow to his forearm. It was not enough to knock the knife out of his hand, but it left him unable to strike, his knife arm stretched out to his side. He tried to recover by shifting his footing but her foot was already behind his leg and she kept him balancing on the other foot. With his free hand he tried to grab for her throat but she twisted away, shooting out her left hand to grab his wrist. She dug her thumb deep into the tendons there and his hand released, dropping the knife.

He had been trained in fighting, she could tell. He did not panic or try to break free—he knew she had locked his leg. Instead he brought his hands up to punch at her face and her throat. He had the advantage of mass and arm strength and one good blow to her trachea could put her down, but she was faster and managed to take his strike on the side of her head. Her ear burned with pain but she ignored it. She had too much to do, yet.

She threw her arms around his waist and pushed her head under his armpit. He was already off balance so she threw her own weight backward, letting herself fall onto her posterior. His own weight carried him over her back, head first, and she both heard and felt the moment when his skull struck the ground behind her.

KGB, she thought. He'd been trained by the KGB.

She'd been trained by Spetznaz.

She threw his dead weight off her back and twisted around, her toes digging into the hard ground. One arm pushed up from the dirt and she was half-standing, half-crouching and facing the second man.

He looked surprised.

"When I was a little girl," she told him, "I wanted to be Ecaterina Szabo. You know, the gymnast?"

He seemed to remember then that he'd been sent to kill her. He moved quickly, his hands coming out of his pockets, and both holding knives. As he came closer she saw just how big he was. The moves she'd used on his partner would be useless on such a bear—his inertia would be too great for her to counteract.

So instead she snatched up the fallen knife from the ground and threw it into his stomach.

He grunted in pain but kept coming, his eyes wild.

There was no time to get out of his way, so she didn't. Just before he fell on her she lanced out with her foot. Her heel struck the pommel of the knife she'd lodged in his belly, driving it in deep until she felt it touch his spine. She rolled to the side as he collapsed on where she'd been, and scuttled away as he began to scream.

"I was too tall to be a gymnast."

For a second, no more, she let herself breathe. She let herself feel the panic she had suppressed before. Her breath made a little mist in the cold morning air.

She touched her jacket and felt the paper folder inside it. Made sure it was safe.

Then she got up and dusted herself off. Went over

THE HYDRA PROTOCOL / 587

to their helicopter and found no one else inside. In a few minutes she was airborne, headed for Sakhalin Island. From there she could find her way into Japan, and then on to America. Where the real work would begin.

SOUTH OF MIAMI, FLORIDA: JUNE 10, 18:16 (EDT)

Jim Chapel leaned on the prow of the yacht and peered down into the water that foamed and churned beneath him. Ever since he'd been a kid, growing up not far from here, he'd loved the ocean. He knew no more peaceful feeling than looking out over its incredible blue expanse, watching it roll in from the far horizon. What human problem could mean anything measured against that blue infinity? Whatever was waiting for him back in New York, whatever Julia was going to tell him, for the moment, at least, he could put it in the back of his mind, tuck it neatly away and think about—

Behind him a vast rolling thump of noise shattered the peace, followed quickly by a squeal of feedback and another squeal, less loud but far more human, the sound of a woman screaming. Chapel spun around just as the beat dropped in and the DJ really got the party jumping.

The yacht was rated for fifty people—it had that many life jackets on board, anyway. Nearly two hundred men and women were crowded onto its main deck, leaping and swaying and throwing their fists in the air as the DJ asked if they were ready to tear it up and burn it down. More squeals and screams came as men in surfer shorts grabbed women and hoisted them up in the air, tossed them into the on-deck pool, poured liquor down their bodies to suck it out of their navels. Chapel had to smile and shake his head as he watched the bacchanalia unfold.

"Jimmy! Jimmy, goddamnit!" someone shouted, and a man ten years Chapel's junior came running across the deck. "Jimmy, get away from there, can't you see you're in the wrong place? The party's over heeeere!"

Chapel laughed and braced himself as Donny Melvin came rushing at him like a linebacker. The younger man barreled into him and wrapped his arms around Chapel's torso, and for a second Chapel thought Donny was going to pick him up and bodily carry him over to the party. Donny could have done it, too—Chapel had a couple inches of height on Donny, but Donny had nearly twice his mass, and the vast majority of it was muscle.

Donny had always been a big guy. He and Chapel had gone through Ranger School together, and bonded over the fact they'd both grown up in Florida. Back then, Donny had constantly complained that the life of a soldier interfered with his ability to lift weights and that he was running to flab. That had regularly elicited nothing but groans from the other grunts, who wanted to bitch about how heavy their packs were—some of them suggested Donny could carry their packs for them. When Chapel went off to Afghanistan Donny had gone to Iraq. Flabby or not, after one particularly nasty firefight in Fallujah, Donny had ended up carrying two wounded soldiers off the battlefield, one under each arm. He'd gotten a medal for that.

Since his discharge Donny had clearly returned to working out almost full-time. Nor was he particularly modest about his body. He wore nothing but a pair of white-rimmed sunglasses, some floral print board shorts, and a neon pink pair of flip-flops. One of his massive biceps had been tattooed with a banner reading 75 RANGER RGT, while his other arm had been decorated with a multi-colored banner showing he'd fought in the war on terror. Neither of those tattoos was regulation, though now that Donny was a civilian again he was allowed to do with his skin as he pleased.

"How many times did I invite you down for a cruise, and you always said no? I don't know how you did it, but you picked the perfect time to say yes. There is some serious action over there," Donny told Chapel as he released him from the bear hug. "I'm talking *talent*, Jimmy. Normally, I call one of these boat rides, I'm looking at five or six girls I would do bad things for. Today there's at least a dozen. At least come take a look, huh?"

"Maybe *just* for a look," Chapel told Donny.

"I promise, your redhead girlfriend will not mind if you look," Donny told him, smiling. "And anything else that happens, well, we *are* in international waters."

"That doesn't give me a get-out-of-monogamy-free card. And stop calling me Jimmy. Only my elementary school teachers and my mother ever called me that."

"Sure thing, Jimbo," Donny said, grabbing Chapel's arm and pulling him back toward the deck.

Chapel couldn't help but grin. Donny Melvin deserved a little fun after what he'd done in Iraq. If he was a little raucous about it, where was the harm?

Back on the deck a group of girls in bikinis shouted and squealed as Donny burst into their midst. One of them threw her arms around his neck and kissed him on the cheek. She had a plastic cup of beer in one hand and she spilled half of it down Donny's back by accident, but Donny just whooped at the icy touch and hugged the girl. "This is Sheila," he shouted over the thumping music. "She's a student at—what school was it?"

"Shelly!" she shouted back.

"What?" Donny asked her.

"My name is Shelly!" she shouted. "Shelly!"

"Seriously?" Donny spun her around and squatted to take a look at the tattoo that rode just above the top of her bikini bottom. "Oh, man! King James, meet Shelly," he said. "You can recognize her by the butterfly back here."

Shelly spun around with a mock scowl on her face, which prompted Donny to get a shoulder under her stomach and lift her up into the air. She screamed and giggled and spilled the rest of her beer as he carried her through the crowd toward the open air bar. Dancers and drinkers alike moved out of his way, some of them raising cups in salute as he barged through their midst. This was, after all, Donny's party. And Donny's boat.

Donny had not exactly signed up with the army

for the GI bill. His father owned half the orange trees in Florida. One day Donny was going to have to learn how to take care of orange trees himself. But clearly that day was not today.

"Shots!" Donny shouted, and a hundred people all around him shouted it back. The two bartenders grabbed for bottles with both hands and started lining up waxed paper shot glasses on the marble top of the bar, which was already strewn with empty cups and discarded pieces of swimwear. Donny laid Shelly down on her back across the bar and one of the bartenders poured a good measure of liquor right into her open mouth. Two other girls had already come rushing up to hang on Donny's arms. It didn't seem to be slowing him down any.

"Who's your friend?" one of them asked, a blonde with elaborately plucked eyebrows. She gave Chapel a look that might have melted him on the spot if he was ten years younger. It threatened to melt him anyway, old as he was.

"A fellow soldier, I think," another woman said, from Chapel's right. She had a slight accent he couldn't place, and when he turned to look at her he saw she wasn't like any of the bikini-clad co-eds surrounding Donny. "He has the bearing. And the quiet that hides behind the eyes. Yes?"

The woman was significantly older than the co-eds. Early thirties, Chapel thought. Short dark hair surrounded vaguely Asian features and instead of the orangish tan of the girls, her skin was a rich, warm shade that looked like it actually came from spending time in the sun. Shelly and the blonde and all the others were beautiful, in a sort of mass-produced girl-next-door kind of way, but this new-comer was striking, the kind of woman you would take a second look at wherever you saw her. She wasn't wearing a bikini, either—instead she had on a short sundress that tied at the back of her neck. The dress gave just the subtlest sense of the athletic body underneath and somehow seemed more scan-dalous than a bikini would, since it left so much to the imagination.

"He's got soldier hair," the blonde said, reaching around Donny to run her fingers across the stubble on the back of Chapel's neck. "I love that feeling! It tickles," she laughed.

It did more for Chapel than just tickle. Still, he found himself turning to look at the older woman. He found he wanted to look at her very much. Noth-ing more, of course, not with Julia waiting back in New York. But like Donny had said, there was no harm in looking.

"Quite a lot hidden back there, I think," she said, as if the blonde didn't exist. "Jim here could tell us all a few things, if he let himself."

Chapel's mouth started to curve into a frown. How had she known his name? Nobody had intro-duced them. But it seemed the mystery would have to wait.

"In the pool, now," Donny called out, lifting a pair of plastic cups over his head.

"You go ahead," Chapel told him, smiling at his friend.

But Donny wasn't having it. "My party, my rules. I'm getting hot and I want to cool down. With you," he said to the blonde, "and you," to a brunette who looked up with the wide eyes of someone who had just won the lottery, "and Sheila, of course."

"Shelly!" the girl yelled from the bar, sitting up and knocking over the paper shot cups the bartender had been arranging on her stomach. Nobody seemed to mind. Shelly jumped off the bar onto Donny's back and howled in laughter as he ran with her over to the pool, only a few feet away. He jumped in with Shelly still clinging to his neck, sending up a great wave of chlorinated water that splashed half a dozen dancers nearby. A general roar of excitement went up and the DJ switched to a new track, one with an even faster beat. One by one girls and men jumped in the pool after Donny, until the deck was awash with their splashing.

"Jim-meeee!" Donny shouted. "Where's my Jim Dog? Jim-Jam, you get in here right now or I'll have the captain throw you overboard!"

Raising his hands in protest Chapel tried to laugh off the invitation.

Donny wouldn't hear it. "In. The Pool. Now!" He lunged out of the pool and grabbed Chapel's leg. "Now!"

"Hold on," Chapel said, suddenly alarmed. If Donny pulled him into the pool just then it was going to be a problem. "Let me just—"

"Get that shirt off of him," Donny shouted, and a couple of co-eds came giggling up to do just that. Despite his best efforts they managed to pull Chapel's polo shirt over his head.

Chapel knew exactly what would happen then.

The girls in the pool stopped laughing. One of them wiped hair from her eyes and stared at his left arm, and especially his left shoulder. It took a second for others to notice, but he could tell when they did because their eyes went wide too. Nobody said anything, of course. But it looked as if the water in the pool had suddenly turned twenty degrees cooler.

"Damn it, Donny," Chapel said, under his breath.

Under the polo shirt, Chapel's left arm looked just like his right one. It had the same skin tone and the same amount of hair. The illusion ended at the shoulder, though, where the arm flared out into a wide clamp that held it secured to his torso.

There was no point in trying to hide it anymore. Chapel reached up with his right hand and flipped back the catches to release the arm. It was a prosthesis, an exceptionally clever and well-designed replacement for the arm he'd lost in Afghanistan. When he took it off and laid it down carefully on a deck chair, it looked like something torn off of a mannequin. He worried about just leaving it there, but he doubted anyone would get too close. None of these people would want to touch the thing.

The DJ didn't scratch a record. Most of the party-goers saw nothing and their roaring clamor of excitement didn't drop by so much as a decibel. But around the pool the whole atmosphere of the party had changed, grown more subdued. The party was ruined.

Chapel stepped down into the pool and submerged himself until only his head was above the water. He looked over at Donny with half a grimace on his face. He wanted very much to duck his head under as well, and just disappear.

"Does it hurt?" Shelly asked.

"No," he told her. "Not anymore."

"How did . . . I mean, how—"

Donny swam over to stand next to Chapel. "Shelly," he said, "do you remember 9/11?"

"Of course I do!" she squeaked. "I was in fifth grade when it happened. We got to go home from school for like three whole days."

Donny's face squirmed as he tried to contain a braying laugh, but he couldn't quite manage it. Eventually he just gave in and let the laughter boom all around the pool, until somebody else picked up on it, and then everyone was laughing. Even Chapel. "This man here," Donny said, "is an American hero!" and he grabbed Chapel's right hand under the water and dragged it up into the air, making Chapel stand up and show his ruined left shoulder again.

The pool erupted in one huge roaring cheer, as cups everywhere lifted in the air and pointed in Chapel's direction. The dancers jumped up and down and the bartenders grabbed new bottles and the party lurched back into full-on mode, back to exactly where it had been before Chapel's shirt came off.

Good old Donny, he thought.